After the Hurricane

After the Hurricane

A NOVEL

Leah Franqui

wm

WILLIAM MORROW

An Imprint of HarperCollins*Publishers*

FIRST EDITION

Library of Congress Cataloging-in-Publication Data has been applied for.

ISBN 978-0-06-320459-1

22 23 24 25 26 LSC 10 9 8 7 6 5 4 3 2 1

For, and to, my father

Oh, disappeared one!

How I grafted my soul in the blue to find you!

And thus, crazy, gazing upwards,

Boiling my eyes in the reddest light to attain you

How I followed the fleeing of my most avid emotion

Through the hospitable twilight golds!

Until one morning . . .

One night . . .

One evening . . .

I was left like a curled-up dove,

And I found my eyes through your blood

—*Julia de Burgos, excerpt from* "Poem Detained in a Daybreak"

After the Hurricane

One

"I think you need to get some help." Elena has been practicing these simple words for almost a year when she says them to her father, over lunch, peering through the beer bottles on the table, all his, to look into his eyes. These words are so simple, so stupid, that they feel impossible coming out of her mouth, they feel like something from a television show, in fact, she thinks she might remember them from a "very special episode" of *Saved by the Bell*. And yet they are all she has, all she can offer him, and she hopes they will be enough.

They are not.

All she sees looking back at her on her father's face is confusion, willful and broad. She wants to remember him as he used to be, when she was very small, so present and alert that it hurt her eyes to look at him. But it has been years since she saw him like that. She would like to cry. That hot hard feeling haunts the back of her throat, and her face prickles.

"Help with what?" her father asks her. He is smiling. She never knows how he will react to anything. Sometimes he becomes angry and sometimes the same thing will make him laugh for long minutes until he coughs, a deep dragging smoker's cough. She is pleading with him, begging him to change, to give her the thing she wants, himself, just himself, but sane. Sober. The way he was until a few years ago. She is asking him to stop crumbling away, she is asking him to stay, although the way he is now is less than what he once had been. She wants to halt the decay. *Why does he not see himself disappearing?* And he smiles.

"Help with your problems."

He waves at the air like a cat batting at a moth.

"Problems. What problems? You've been talking to your mother, haven't you? She just worries. She's got that anxiety thing. Now, enough. You tell me about something, tell me about your job," he demands, taking a deep sip of his beer. They are at a Korean restaurant on St. Marks Place in Manhattan, and it is 1:00 P.M. on a Tuesday, and he has been drinking deeply.

"I'm just working at the university library, Papi," she reminds him. He looks confused for a moment, and then nods, vigorously, covering up the evidence of his memory lapse.

"Tell me about classes." Elena is in graduate school at NYU, getting her master's in history. She is writing her thesis about the way cotton production in South America changed the fashion industry in the United States, and the lives of garment workers in New York City. She is working with professors from Stern for the economics, and students from NYU's Costume Studies program for the fashion. She has sent her father article after article about her research. She tells him everything about her life, and he tells her nothing. She comes home to Philadelphia at least once a month and she has listed her classes for that semester at least three times, watching her mother's hand tighten on her wineglass in frustration as she, who knows her daughter's life well, mouths along, watching her father nod and smile, knowing he will remember nothing, hoping she is wrong.

"What are you taking?"

But she is never wrong about him. Heat rises up her throat, and she swallows water, pushing it down where it belongs.

"I think you need some help with your mental health," she tells him, her voice low.

"What is this bullshit term? I read about this in the paper. What is this?" he asks, his voice curious, amused.

"Your mind. Your mental condition," she says. They have never talked about this. Her father does not really talk *with* anyone. He talks at people. He talks at her. He tells her what he thinks of the world, and when, as a little girl and then a teenager, she asked him about his life before she existed in it, he told her he had been poor and now he wasn't. And that she should stop asking. So she did.

"Have you given any thought to what you are going to do after you graduate?" he asks her, finishing his beer. He gestures to the waitress for another one. The only other people in the restaurant are a group of college students filling up on the free kimchi, four kids sharing a single order of bibimbap. Elena's father looks at them.

"Poor kids. I was like that."

"In college?" Elena asks, timidly. He never talks about himself. She knows he won't answer her questions, but something inside of her compels her to ask. Maybe it is the disappointment that her carefully constructed attempt to talk about his mental condition burned down so quickly. Maybe it's the beers, which she can see have loosened him, the way alcohol sometimes does. Other times it tightens him, making him tense and sharp. Even in his drinking, he is inconsistent and impossible to predict.

"I used to live around here. Did you know that?" Elena nods, her body trembling. She did know that, it is one of maybe five pieces of real information she has about her father before her birth. She does not want to speak, does not want to disturb his mood. How awful she is, that she can put aside her planned speech—her plea for him to stop drinking, to get more serious help for his bipolar condition, to stay on his medication instead of going on and off whenever it suits him, to see a therapist, to want to help himself—for a tiny piece of information about his childhood. She is pathetic, she knows.

"At First and First. Center of the universe. Not then, though. Then it was . . . God. What are those rents like now?"

"Expensive." She breathes out. He nods, like she has delivered vital wisdom.

"We should go over there. You want to go over there? I can show you my old neighborhood. We can take a walk. You got time?" Elena has class in an hour. She does not care. She has never missed a class in her life, not in college, not now. She is due a skip. She nods. He smiles at her, and for a moment he is not the man in front of her, his jowls sagging from the weight he has gained, hair thinning, his body sinking under the load of the alcohol and lithium and time. For a moment he is the way he was when she was ten years old, lean and tall and tan and vibrant, and it is enough for her, Elena, that he hug her, that is all she needs to know she is loved.

"Great. That's great. I want to show you this. I can show you where I lived with my mother, all the places, we moved around a lot. And where my grandmother lived, everyone. My whole family was there. Did you know that?" She did not. He has never answered a single question about his family in her twenty-four years of life, never responded to any inquiry, never volunteered more than a morsel of information. Now he is offering her a feast. She feels frozen, unable to move. Her heart is beating and she can hear it, she can feel herself vibrating. She doesn't know what to do with her body. She wants what he is offering her so badly she almost extends her hand, like this information is a tangible thing she can feel, hold.

He leans back in his chair.

"We can walk for a bit, but I have to go around four." His words break the spell. Where is he going? He still has not told her why he is here. She got the call the night before, that he was coming, taking her out to lunch. He has never just come to New York before. This is why she wanted to say something, her planned feeble speech. Because he had come, and she thought that might be a sign of something.

"Your mother and I, we've decided to take some time apart. I'm heading down to San Juan for a while, give her a chance to cool off. You know how your mother is, more now than before, she just flies off the handle. She's hysterical. No logic, turns herself against me. I'm going to wait out the storm down there until it's safe, you know?" Her father is laughing, smiling, as the waitress brings him another beer. Elena remains as still as before, as pain replaces the anticipation in her body. "I'm just gonna be down on the island until she's ready. Don't you worry, though."

She is never wrong about him. But he can still surprise her. He can always be worse than she imagined.

"When?" Elena forces the words past her mouth. Her father looks at her, uncomprehending.

"When are you going?"

"Tonight. From JFK. Cheaper flight." Her parents have never once flown out of New York to go to Puerto Rico, not since Elena was born, at least. They fly from Philadelphia, regardless of the cost. And he said *flight,* singular. One-way.

"I see." She had hoped so deeply that his calling her for lunch was an act of love. An opening of a door. But it was merely a rest stop.

"I'm gonna take a leak, okay, and then we'll go for that walk. Sound good?" Elena nods, her neck stiff with tension. The walk. She will still have that. That is something, more than anything that has come before. That is an act of love, is it not? That is a gesture, he will show her his young life, one of the many parts of him she has never seen. Maybe he will talk to her, maybe they can discuss what he is telling her about her mother, about their marriage, maybe it is not so serious, like he says, just a storm passing over the horizon.

He kisses her on the forehead, and stumbles to the bathroom. She watches him, turning her head to see him as he goes, and then turns back to her meal. The soup she had ordered is a beef bone and leek soup with a milky broth and she usually loves it, leaves the bowl empty. Today it has cooled and it turns her stomach to smell it, to see the fat floating on the tepid broth. She picks up her father's latest beer bottle and drinks it, mostly to prevent him from doing so, but also for courage, and a little numbness. She does not want to feel as deeply as she does, for fear she will not be able to stand it. She trembles. Her hands are shaking, and she doesn't know if that's from anticipation or panic. She clasps them together so hard her nails bite into her flesh, but it's better than the shaking, she decides. He has to give her something real now. If he won't try to fix himself, get better, at the very least he has to give her some part of himself, some history that she can have. She is sick of studying other people's stories and not knowing her own.

Maybe if she knows him better, he will find her more worth loving, more worth changing for. She hates how much she hopes for this, longs for it, cannot cut her need for this out of her no matter how much she tries. She never knows who she is angrier with, him or herself.

This is why, forty-five minutes later, although she knows that he is gone, that he has left her there, and isn't coming back—not for their walk, not to pay, not to be her father at all, to be there, with her—Elena sits at the table still, looking at the soup she will never order again, and the remains of his spicy stir-fried squid, and the many bottles of beer he had to drink to tell her he and her mother were over, and hopes against hope that all of this is a mistake, that any minute he will appear.

He does not. She would like to break the bottles, she would like to burn the restaurant down, she would like to cry because she has less now than she did before she saw him, at least earlier she had hope. But she learned from an early age to cover her father's mistakes, and so she instead pays the bill and walks out of the restaurant.

After she has walked from Manhattan to Brooklyn because the energy inside of her, the anger, is buzzing so brightly she can't sit on a train, she will call her mother and ask just what the hell is going on. During a phone call that feels like someone stabbing her in the gut, she will learn that it is her mother who has asked her father to leave, that she has exorcised him from her life, trimmed him out of photos and taken him off the deed to their Philadelphia home.

In that call, she will learn that her father has been in the grips of a manic spiral for over nine months. That he overdosed on his lithium, accidently or on purpose no one will ever know, and then, after a hospital visit to flush out his liver, declared he would never take it again, that it made him numb and too calm, that he couldn't move fast with it. That in the spirit of moving fast he then crashed his car driving drunk on the New Jersey Turnpike, and somehow walked away from it whole, with nothing more than a black eye. And $15,000 of damage. She will learn that he lost his license to practice law, that he has left his life behind, or been pushed out of it, by her mother, who is finally done. The anger that will fill her veins and clog her throat learning these things will be overwhelming, a murderous rage that makes her tremble, that she tells herself she cannot feel, will not feel. It will seem historic in nature, ancient Greek, and humans can't survive that kind of thing. She will ask why her mother didn't tell her any of this, and neither of them will tell the truth, which is that between them they have formed a habit of silence on the subject of Santiago, and habits are hard to break. She would like to hate her mother for her silence, but she can only hate one parent at a time.

She will begin to edit her father out of her narratives. She will learn how to say she is visiting her mother, not her parents. She will find that no one questions her, or points this out, and this makes her sad and angry in a way she will tell no one about.

Her parents will divide territory, him on the island, her mother taking the mainland, and Elena will not venture to San Juan. It would feel disloyal, and while her mother will never say it, Elena will know she is happy Elena has chosen not to go. Elena has always been an obedient child. She had hoped that would earn her love. It rarely seems to.

She will get a call from him a few months later, which she will answer, despite the sight of his name on her phone inspiring dread in her stomach. He will not remember this lunch, this moment, his offer to give her a piece of his past. He will tell her life is wonderful and perfect and that she must visit him soon, and she will say nothing. He will ask her *what classes are you taking,* and she will end the call before she can start crying. Before she can scream. She will tell herself that she is sad, very sad. She lies.

He will look at the phone, puzzled, these devices never make much sense to him, and wonder if he has hurt her, but only for a moment, before the rum clouds his chaotic brain chemistry, before he can, really truly can, no longer think of anyone but himself. He will return to his life on the island. He will sink into this new way of being and it will be as though all of the things that came before—his marriage, his child, his ambition as a lawyer, his friends, the first and last he ever made, his deceptions, his distant past and childhood all buried deep, his mother most of all—are behind him. He will have escaped them, left them all in the past, where they belong. He wants to be light, he wants to carry as little with him as possible. That has always been his deepest and truest dream.

This day, this lunch he will not remember, as he stumbles out into the fall sunshine, looking at the world through a haze of cheap Japanese beer, will be the last time in his life that Santiago will ever see the East Village, the place where he was born, the place he thought was the whole world for so long until he thought it was a prison.

Six years later, it is September once again. Her brain buzzing from wine, Dutch courage, Elena will find herself alone at night in the neighborhood that her father lived in long ago. She will pass First and First. She will not notice the schools he once attended, the apartments belonging to the family she has never heard of, will never meet. Eventually, she will stop, and stand at Avenue A and Third Street, looking at the first housing project, her bleary eyes reading the sign mounted on the brick wall, and she will take a picture, the historian in her never truly dormant, no matter that she works in real estate now. She will have no idea that she is on the walk, the one he promised her, and that this would have been a place her father would have shown her, now will never show her. Then, she will take the subway home, and sleep, and wake, and go on with her life, and look at other daughters and fathers and think, *Well, that's it for that, then.* She will, she knows, be done with him, her own father, forever. She is never wrong about him.

But sometimes she is wrong about herself.

The next day, the storm comes.

Two

When Elena wakes up four months, two weeks, and five days after
Hurricane Maria landed in San Juan, she feels, for no particular
reason, a sensation of deep dread. Her stomach rolls, and breathing
through her nausea, she stumbles through her tiny apartment, her
studio, single women in New York live in studios. Her head bows
over her small porcelain sink, its white surface split by fine cracks
that resemble the shoulder-length curly hairs on her head, and she
retches. Thin yellow mucus, bitter and foul, floods her mouth,
and then her sink. She leans backward, smiles weakly, grimly congratulating herself. *At least you know you aren't pregnant.* She hasn't
had sex in a long time. Not since she ended things with Daniel.
And besides, she knows, this happens, it means something bad is
coming.

For most of her adolescence, Elena Vega threw up every morning.
Not after breakfast, not to be thinner, though she would have liked
to be thinner, as would everyone. She would throw up after brushing
her teeth, deep racking spasms throughout her body, saliva pooling
in her mouth, and then, a flood of bile. She would brush her teeth
once more, and descend the stairs of her unhappy home. She never

told anyone about it. What would she have said? *My body is trying to eject itself. My stomach is trying to escape. Even my insides want out.*

It would have been another worry, another thing for her mother, Rosalind, named for the famous film actress her own mother had so adored, to worry about. Elena has never wanted anyone to worry about her. There is no room for worrying about her in their family.

She should have known the day her father met her, six years ago now, that it would be a bad day. She had thrown up that morning, too. But that was all before she understood that her nausea is a kind of prescience, that her innards are augury, foretelling the future.

She had thrown up after Daniel had asked her to marry him, and every day afterward until she gave him back his ring. It never fit her well, anyway, and after she did her stomach had left her alone, settling into solitude with more contentment than her mind. Even now she was unsure why she had done that, given it back, she who was so lonely, who had wanted to be with someone badly. Her mother, who she loves deeply, does not understand it. Daniel was so kind to Elena, and her mother has come to value kindness more with every passing year. He was so stable, and her mother has always *always* told her stability is more than passion will ever be. Elena knows her mother speaks from experience, and she would like to follow it, really she would. But Elena knows she would never be happy with Daniel. Daniel loved her the way her mother does, because she is obedient, because she does and says all the right things. Somewhere in Elena something is burning and angry and it wants to explode all over her life. Daniel did not deserve to be there when it does.

It is not, as one friend says, joking but not joking, because Elena is an only child, so no man's love will be enough for her. Some only children are spoiled, or at least, that is the myth Elena knows well, the one she smiles at and pretends to be amused by, donning an invisible mimed princess tiara and making others laugh. But Elena was not spoiled, not in the sense of being given too much and placed

in the center of the universe. *But in other ways I am spoiled, milk allowed to sit too long in the sun, curdled now.* Living with her parents,
with their clouds of unhappiness, with her father and his so very
many things, so very many things she had to account for, understand, avoid, she had never been the center of anything.

The phone rings. A photo pops up, a frozen image of her mother,
Rosalind Goldberg, her full name spelled out in Elena's phone book,
just like everyone else's. Elena likes names, full names, something
about how much time she has spent looking at historic records bled
into her and everyone now must be known in her life, in her devices
and notebooks, the way they would want to be remembered throughout time.

Elena wipes her face, hiding from her mother as she always has;
no matter that she cannot see her, Rosalind will *know,* and Elena
cannot have that. She cannot have her mother worrying about her.
Elena is already too worried about herself. She takes a deep breath
and accepts the call.

"Elena, it's me. It's about your father. He's gone missing."

Whatever Elena's guts were trying to reveal to her, she had not
expected this. She cannot breathe. She can feel her stomach bile rising again, and imagines it choking her. She is silent for a long, long
moment. It is insane to her to hear about her father from her mother.
She has been a locked vault about him since the day he left. Before,
even. Rosalind has never answered any of Elena's questions about
Santiago's past. After they separated Elena thought she would finally
get answers, but Rosalind was loyal to Santiago in this way, and gave
Elena as little as he had. When Elena pressed, Rosalind said that
Santiago's past had dark things in it and he had wanted to protect
Elena from that, and she, Rosalind, had to respect that. Elena does
not feel protected. She feels lost. And so, apparently, is he.

"Elena? Did you hear me?"

"What does that mean, he's gone?" she asks, trying to keep her voice calm, she can feel it rising, feel a keening cry at the back of her throat.

"He is missing, has been missing, actually, but we, I, didn't know." Rosalind's voice sounds stuffy and nasal, as it always does when she has had a cold, or been crying.

"You said he was okay. After Maria. You said you talked to him."

It has been months since the hurricane.

"I talked to his neighbor," Rosalind admits, her voice small. Elena closes her eyes, containing herself.

Elena had been frantic after the hurricane, truly, deeply frantic. It had surprised her. She had thought on the subject of her father she was entirely neutral. Then the storm blew through the island and through her.

She works for a company that manages a group of buildings in Brooklyn Heights, Park Slope, Crown Heights, and Clinton Hill. Most of the time she works from home, or shows prospective renters apartments, but twice a month they have company meetings in their central office space in downtown Brooklyn. She had been in one the morning after the Category 4 storm hit Puerto Rico, on September 20, and while she was waiting for her turn to talk about the recent rentals she had completed, Daniel, who was still her fiancé at the time, sent her an article about the destruction. *Doesn't your father live there?* She was shocked by what she saw. Storms were normal on the island, but the images she was looking at were all flooding and destruction, downed power lines and whole towns under the waves and rain, and deaths, lots of deaths. She stared at the words on her phone screen, wishing they would reconstitute into something else, something good.

She realized she could not remember how words worked, their order, because she had lost all sense of nouns and verbs, how they interact. When she spoke, she sounded like she had taken every word in her head and jumbled them, a child's block set of words, and then tried to arrange them again with no sense of meaning, just an interest in the color of each. She had excused herself and found a corner to curl into, breathing like she'd run up five flights of stairs, her heart burning with pain. A fellow agent, Jeff, found her and sat with her, silent and calm in the face of her panic. It was the closest she had felt to someone in months.

Elena and her father do not speak. Not really. He rarely called or texted her, preferring instead to email her random things he found on the internet, photos of cats in teacups, articles about cheese-making in Nepal and the Singaporean economy and the French legal system. She never knew what they meant, what he wanted to tell her with this information. She never responded, and he didn't seem to care about her reaction. She dutifully sent him messages on his birthday and Father's Day. She received emails twice or three times a month. That was the extent of their communication.

But after Maria, Elena thought he would call. He could not be so far from reality that he would not have noticed the storm, not have understood the way people would be fearful for him. He must have run out of alcohol at some point, sobered up enough to know that this was not business as usual, that the island was in crisis, that people would want to know that he was alive. But she heard nothing.

Her panic flared out at the edges, waking her at night. She went from trying to learn as little as possible about the problems, reading only the good-news articles, the stories of help and care and false positivity, to reading about disaster, starvation, anger, pain, plane-loads of people fleeing to Florida, children turned away from hospitals, food running low, nights in total darkness, the crimes that darkness hides. She consumed everything, devoured everything, hoping to catch a glimpse of her father, but she never did.

Finally, after a week of this, after she realized that she hadn't had a full meal since the storm, that her jeans were looser and she could not even celebrate the fact, Elena called her mother and demanded that she contact her father. Rosalind was reluctant, but understood, and she told Elena that everything was fine, that Santiago had found the only working liquor store on the island and was enjoying the evening sky without light pollution. Elena went home that night and made herself a roast chicken, a steak, a *cacio e pepe,* a salad as big as a cat, and a chocolate mousse. She ate them all by herself. A month later, she gave Daniel back his ring, and that night she slept with Jeff at his going-away party, relieved that the reality of him was a disappointment compared to the fantasy of him she had been building since he had comforted her. She is always relieved when people disappoint her, because she is always waiting for them to do so, anxious until they do, the way she feels deep relief on the way to the airport when she finally remembers whatever it was she had forgotten to pack.

All because she knew that her father was fine. And now Rosalind is telling her that her father is missing. She wants to curl up inside herself all over again. She wants to cry. She wants Daniel to hold her. She wants Jeff inside her again, however disappointing his performance. She wants Rosalind to laugh and tell her it isn't true, that she is playing a horrible joke, that she will never do something like this again. She wants to hear her father laughing in the background, she wants to hear Rosalind shush him because he is spoiling her prank, she wants to be ten again when they were happy in San Juan and she watched her parents smile as the sun set and they sipped their wine.

And she is also angry. His house must be a mess. She doubts that he maintains it well, he never had a sense of maintenance, not like her mother has, not like Elena herself has, she does it for a living. That house is a piece of history, its floors from different centuries. Her father, she is sure, is letting it go to ruin. He never takes care of anything, *anyone,* Elena knows, and it enrages her, hurts her in her very soul.

"I talked to Gloria, you remember her, she has that little West Indian place, takeout lunches, she always puts it in Styrofoam, which I hated, but the food was good."

Rosalind is rambling. She is talking about takeout containers instead of her missing ex-husband. That means that she, too, is nervous. Elena is as sensitive to her mother's moods as a piano tuner is to vibrations. She can see her, a hundred miles away, as she picks at her nailbeds, turning the thin skin into a shredded mess of epidermis, red and swollen, easily infected, Rosalind's long slim fingers ruined by her anxiety. This is why Elena can never worry her mother. She cannot be the reason for Rosalind's hands to hurt.

"I remember Gloria, Mom," Elena assures her, trying to quiet the screaming in her mind, the knowledge that she knows, always, that something is wrong, has known the whole time, somehow.

"She said she saw your father every day, he gets food from her, it's not good for him, I'm sure it's got a lot of oil, you know how Puerto Ricans are, they love their fat, his heart . . . I don't even know the last time he's seen a doctor." Gloria is not Puerto Rican, although she speaks the lazy island Spanish well, far better than Elena, to her shame. Santiago never spoke Spanish with Elena. She learned it in college. Gloria is from Antigua, and her years in San Juan have given her more Spanish than Elena has.

Elena does not correct her mother.

"Why didn't *you* talk to him?" Elena is trying to be calm, trying not to explode at her mother, trying to contain herself. She can feel steam hissing off her words, though, regardless.

"I tried to," Rosalind insists. "He wouldn't answer me. Gloria said his phone was broken by a power surge when the city grid came back on, but I don't know. He might just not have wanted to talk to me. You know that he is difficult. I'm sorry."

The storm hit the island in September, the height of hurricane season.

When Elena was nine, she had visited the island with her parents and gone to see her grandfather, a smiling happy man who made both of her parents very unhappy in very different ways. That year, Hurricane Hortense had blown Abuelo's gardening shed away, and damaged his avocado tree. He teared up when describing the pain the tree felt, and her father had nodded, and said nothing when later her mother, livid, railed against Abuelo's pain at the tree and disregard for the son he had abandoned. Elena, half asleep, her stomach swollen with her step-grandmother's *arroz y habichuelas*, was woken up by her father, who, drunk, pained, stormed from the house and then drove their car off the road to avoid the truck that he had almost run into. They did not return to the island for a year after that, and she had wondered for a long time where the garden shed had landed, if someone else was using it now, if her grandfather had stayed sad about his *aguacates*.

Hortense had been a terrible storm. This one was worse.

"But today Gloria called *me*," Rosalind says. Her nasal voice makes her sound like she is telling a joke, her tone makes Elena want to hold on to something, for safety. "She hasn't seen your father in days, she says. Usually he gets food from her place, like I said, she said sometimes she checks on him because he can be in one of his bad periods. She thinks he might be missing."

It is now mid-February. Months since the storm hit, and the island is creeping, slowly, toward recovery, denied the support it needed, needs, from the country that taxes it without representation, largely out of the headlines, an occasional piece popping up here and there to remind people that it exists, that it is still struggling. But as far as most people Elena knows go, despite their initial social media furor, their Instagram throwback vacation photos underscored with #prayforpuertorico, the hurricane is a thing of the past. Power has been restored, shakily, to parts of the island, to San Juan completely. The damage is very bad, but the storm is long gone. How can her father have disappeared *now?* Where has he gone? How has he left the house? And why doesn't he have better *timing?*

"I hate to ask you this, honey, but would you be willing to go? I just . . . I can't. I'm worried, but I can't go there, Elena. It's a haunted place for me. Would you go and just make sure your father is all right? And the house? The house is yours, anyway, or it's supposed to be, when he's gone."

Rosalind will not say that he might be gone now, but they both know that this is a possibility. That the house might already be Elena's. That Santiago Vega might already be dead. Elena cannot decide how she feels about that, and that fuels her anger, bile forming again in her mouth.

She swallows deeply.

"He was supposed to put it in your name, it might be yours already," Rosalind says. Elena sighs, deeply. *Might be mine?* Of course Rosalind does not know. Of *course.* What a mess all this is, what a mess it always is. If the house is already hers there is so much Elena will need to do, taxes she will need to pay, but also if it is hers, well, she will have something, her own property to restore, a historic home in one of the New World's most historic cities. A piece of the past would be hers. A part of history, a part of the island for her, all her own. The house is a piece of her. But she doesn't want it to be hers this way.

Elena is silent, her heart twisting.

"You can find out when you go, you can see how the house is, look at what might need to be done, and you can also see if, if he is there. Please?"

"Mom. Please."

"I can't go, Elena. I just can't." Elena never wants to feel negatively toward her mother but the bile rises in her throat again at what she is being asked to do. She knows that since their divorce, Rosalind simply cannot deal with her father. She cannot, she will not, she won't. She says that she has done it for too long, but the truth that she knows and Elena knows and neither of them discusses is that Elena's father is still perfectly capable of breaking Rosalind's heart and she is, despite her strength, her capability, her neatly tailored suits and beautifully designed life, a fragile thing. She is shattered bone held together with pins, a dinosaur in the museum, and if she breaks again, she is not sure she will be able to reassemble.

Elena so wants to say no. It is a haunted place for her, too. She barely speaks to her father, he barely speaks to her. She loves him, she barely knows him. She loves him, but she cannot forget the last time they saw each other, won't even walk down that block of St. Marks, passing the restaurant that has changed hands three times since then but remains cheap and Korean. She loves him, yes, but she might hate him, too.

She wants to tell her mother to be the adult, to deal with her missing, mentally ill ex-husband, that this is not fair to Elena, that she is not qualified to do this. Elena wants to say all of that, very badly. But that is not who Elena is. Elena says yes when people ask her to do something. Elena says yes when Rosalind asks her to do something. So before she can let herself say something else, she says:

"I understand, Mom. Of course I'll go."

Three

That day in the fall of 2007 when they bought the house in Puerto Rico was the beginning of the end for Santiago Vega's marriage. He would never know this, never would have believed it if told. By this point in his life, his sense of the world and other people was becoming shadowy, smeared at the edges. His condition included more than a little paranoia, more than a little delusion. There were people who fought that, medicated it, watched for it, and people who didn't. He was in the latter group. He used to be better than this. He used to fight every day, and win, to own his conditions instead of letting them own him. There was a time when he was so careful with his medication, so sure that if he took what his doctor gave him he would be fixed, healed. He used to fear his mother's mind and look for its heir in his own. They might not have shared the same diagnosis, but sometimes, very rarely, he let himself remember that he was her son, that her illness was like a gun he used as a paperweight. Different in his life than hers, but still there. He used to think of himself as recovering, striving, that even at his worst, he could be better. But something had snapped recently and he could feel the fight draining from him, washing away. He looked at his prescriptions now with disgust and longing, missing the days when they seemed to fix things in his mind. They were not magic, and if they could not fix him completely then what was the point of them? And why did he need fixing, anyway? He was becoming content with himself in a way that he used to fear. It was like drowning, but very slowly, and he had begun to find it comfortable underwater.

Another person, even a person with his issues, might have been able to connect the acquisition of a decrepit shell in Old San Juan with the breakdown of their own marriage, but it was Santiago's newly formed ability to miss such connections, to be so blind to things that they might as well not have existed at all. To construct a world in his mind and believe it was the only real thing. *Confabulation* was the term Dr. Moretti would have used, but he had stopped listening in their sessions, waiting patiently until the end when the pills would be prescribed and he could leave. He had stopped listening to most people, to Rosalind, to Elena, so vocal at twenty and sure of the world she knew so little about, only really hearing himself. But he didn't see any of it. His vision, for so long sharp and clear and full of the future, was blurring.

Instead, he decided that the acquisition of land on the island from which his parents had come was a new beginning, a new age of his marriage, by then decades old. It was an achievement that he was proud of in an almost violent way. He had achieved much, most of which felt empty now. There was a time when his only goal was escape, then advancement, then stability. He'd gotten each one. This was his latest vision, letting the others drop away. He, the grandchild of illiterate *jibaritos,* the son of a man who had left him to rot in poverty, could now afford more and better land on that island than anyone else in his family. Not some lot of grass out in Bayamon, some jungle patch in the interior, a condo by the beach. He was buying a house in Old San Juan, a piece of history, a stone chipped off one of the oldest cities in the New World. Signing

the deed, smiling, just under Rosalind's neat signature, his flour-
ishes overlapping her square letters, he could feel sweet blood on his
teeth. He was biting off a piece of the world.

His hand shook slightly in the way it had started doing recently,
making his signature a little off. Rosalind looked at him, concerned,
but he ignored her. Dr. Moretti had told him this was a common
side effect of long-term lithium use and asked him if he had been
drinking. He lied, the way he did when he felt this way, powerful,
energized, high. When he felt this way, the lies came quickly and
easily, he knew them to be true, he willed them into veracity. He
wasn't drinking like the doctor thought, it was just to calm down, it
was to sleep. Dr. Moretti didn't need to know, wouldn't understand.
Besides, hadn't he said it was because of the lithium? Wasn't he
himself the one who had prescribed it all those years ago? Sometimes he didn't even take it, wouldn't that help his hands? He was
medicated. He made money. He was fine.

He remembered the day, two years ago, when he had watched his
only child graduate from high school. An expensive high school, one
he had helped pay for, its campus covered in trees and sweating with
privilege. She was dressed in white, like all her female classmates,
her dark hair falling down her shoulders. She looked so clean, so un-
tainted by anything. Eighteen then, and she had so much more than
he had at her age. She walked up to get her diploma, to collect the
prizes she'd won, his smart and wonderful child, and the audience,
all children of privilege and their rich parents, clapped for her with
manicured hands and white clean smiles. She was one of them. She
had lived her life around people like them and would do so until she
died. She was going off to college, there had never been any question of that. She had a future so secure it might as well have been
a bank vault. If he died that day, he knew, she would still be fine,
she would be supported and whole. He had felt pride but also, like a
knife wound, a jealousy so strong it blinded him. He had loved his

daughter in that moment, oh yes, he clapped like everyone else. But he might have hated her for a moment, too. Certainly resented her. He was jealous of his own child.

He had gotten drunker that night than he had in years. Something had opened up in him, and he couldn't close it. Didn't want to close it.

Now she was twenty, and she came home on vacations with stories about what she was learning, what she was doing. When she called something at the school stupid or pointless he wanted to wring her neck. He wanted to shove her into the gutter and make her crawl with the rats, so she could understand what she was taking for granted, what entitlement she lived in, how lucky she was. He shouldn't want to do that to his child, but he did, and it made it hard to look at her, talk to her, sometimes. He wanted to rub her face in his past, but he also wanted her to never ever know about it, never let it taint her. It would change the way she saw him, she would pity him, the way he had pitied his mother. He couldn't have that happen, not ever. He was no thing to be pitied, he had made himself something else, and the parts of him that were pathetic and poor and weak were parts Elena could never know. He settled for not speaking to her much at all. It was better this way. And of course, the drinking helped. He rarely thought of it as a problem anymore. Why should he? It was helping him. If Rosalind couldn't see that, how was that any of his fault?

"Are you done?" Rosalind asked, bringing him back to the present. The signing. The success.

He looked down at the deed, and the pen he was holding, noting the tremor again. He could feel Rosalind watching his hand as he signed the paperwork on the house, even though he wasn't looking at her, and it made him furious. What was she doing, watching him all the time like this, policing him? She was out to get him, she didn't understand either, she was against him, she wanted to take away the things that helped him. Hadn't he done everything right? Hadn't he made money, sent Elena to school? She was done now, Elena, she was an adult, so what the fuck did Rosalind want of him?

His rage was sudden, electric, and he had to press it down, contain it. It made him laugh with its energy.

"I'm done!" he said, proudly, the anger gone as he chuckled. "It's all done now!"

"Really? We have so much work to do now. It's just beginning," Rosalind said, dourly, in that way of hers, looking at him strangely as he laughed. His anger flared to life again, a salamander twisting inside his gut.

"Why do you have to be so negative?" he shot back, his voice sharp. Couldn't she be happy?

Rosalind looked away, her eyes taking in the shell that they had bought, the mess of it all, the plants growing through the floor, the salt-stained wood and pitted plaster-cement walls.

"This is a ruin," she said, calmly. Their real estate agent, Wilfredo, a little man with impossibly canary-yellow hair, neatly dyed and carefully combed back from his forehead, nodded enthusiastically.

"*Una ruina!*" he said, delighted. Strange creature.

"We're ready for it," Santiago assured him, in Spanish, and they nodded at each other with the confidence of men. Rosalind smiled limply. She had talked to friends in the architecture department at Tyler School of Art and Architecture, who had drawn up plans for them, found contractors on the island, and she communicated in her broken Spanish what they wanted, sourced local materials; looked into the permits they would need, how they could restore water and electricity to the long-empty building; what historic-board standards they would have to meet to pass the stringent rules of the city's codes. But he, who had done nothing for the house, was so confident in their readiness. He felt that flash of gratitude he so often felt for her, that moment when someone else permitted his brain to rest for long enough to help him focus on them, and he kissed her cheek, promising himself, as he did each time, he would be better from now on. A bird cooed and fluttered in the corner of his eye, and he promptly forgot, as he watched Elena, now a college sophomore at the University of Chicago, her limbs pale and softened from long library nights, shoo a pigeon that had flown into the space through the unpaned windows.

His daughter. His daughter, who had achieved time and again, who was smart and sweet and strong, he looked at her and wondered at her existence, that she had come from him. He could see himself in her face, the only reminder sometimes that she was, indeed, his. He bit back that little bile he felt, that jealousy, that rage she made him feel. It was wrong to think that way, even in his deteriorating state he knew that. He had worked hard to give her everything. Why didn't he want her to have it now? Enough, he swallowed it down. All of this was for her. He, they, would fix the house, restore it to the livability it had once had two hundred, three hundred years earlier, for it dated back to the 1700s, and then someday Elena would have it for her own. It would be his legacy to her.

Santiago had inherited nothing from his family but hunger. Want. He used to read the phrase in old-fashioned books when he was a child, *I wanted for nothing.* He had wanted for so much. For everything. Not Elena, though. She had been fed and clothed and loved and nurtured, and she would receive more, above all that. He would give her this, a piece of the island itself. He would stop telling himself she didn't deserve it, stop loathing her just a little for having all he had given her. He wanted to hug her, to strangle her, his trembling hands itched and he didn't know for which action.

His conflicting needs almost felt like voices in his head, and that horrified him more than anything. He was different. He wasn't his mother. God, he needed a drink. He needed a river of them.

"I'll be back." The Realtor was gone now, and Rosalind and Elena were walking around with a notebook, Elena noting Rosalind's murmured thoughts. They looked up at his words, their faces twin reflections of annoyance warring with resignation.

Elena had until lately looked like him far more than she looked like her mother. Her skin was not as dark as his, a fact that would have delighted his own mother, had she lived to see her granddaughter. She had always wanted to be fairer. Elena was paler, yes, but her skin was still olive tinged, making her look pale sickly green without frequent sun exposure. Her hair was dark, and curly, and abundant, and her chin set, firm, her cheeks rounded like his. When she was a toddler, a little girl, she had grasped his face hard with her plump hands and squealed, asking him, *Why is your face my face?* And he had laughed and told her that she had stolen his, chasing her until she promised to give it back.

Now, though, she looked more and more like her mother, not in the architecture of her features, but in the expressions that haunted them. There was such knowledge there, as she looked at him, that he would let her down. Such judgment that he could not stand it. He walked to her, kissing her on her forehead, feeling it knit and furrow under his lips, and had to fight not to explode at her in anger, in shame. How dare she judge him? He paid for her education, he had just bought a house to leave her, and she thought to judge him? Her lack of gratitude made him breathless. He pulled back and looked at her for long moments, daring her to speak. But she didn't. She never did.

"We have dinner at seven," Rosalind said, neutrally.

"We're celebrating. Don't forget," said Elena, looking at him, willing his brain to remember.

"See you back at the hotel at six," he said, walking out the door.

Hours later, lying on the hotel bed alone as Rosalind and Elena left for the meal without him, too drunk to stand on his own, he wondered what it was he couldn't quite remember. It niggled at his brain, tugging at the edge of his inebriated consciousness. He should have made it to the dinner, they were celebrating something. The house? No, oh no, it was more than that, but what?

It was Elena's birthday. And the anniversary of Neil's death, the one he celebrated at least. His daughter, who he was not there for; Neil, who he could never be there for again. *You gave them everything you could, you are giving her a house, that's enough, something has to be enough,* he thought, but he knew nothing would ever really be enough. He had been born so thirsty, he could never quench another's throat when he himself was empty, forever empty. He gave his daughter the life she deserved because he couldn't give her anything else, any part of himself, it was all too ruined for her to have. He lived in fear of her brain being like his brain. He lived in fear of what he had given to her, or he would have, if he had been able to focus. He was shutting down those fears because they were too much to feel and it was easier for him to live without them. He thought about Elena and Neil, coming and leaving. Doors opening and closing at the same time, and him, as unconscious as he could make himself so he wouldn't have to feel a thing about either.

He was asleep long before he could remember all that he was forgetting.

Four

Elena sits in Newark Airport, and considers the concept of purgatory.

She is not Catholic. Her father is a Catholic, or was, or maybe Catholicism is like addiction, maybe you *are* always Catholic regardless of your consumption patterns. Elena has never met a Catholic who has uncomplicated feelings about the religion, including Santiago. He was always more than happy for Rosalind to take their child to synagogue, and Elena was raised Jewish. Perhaps he was always happy for his own history to disappear. Elena is content in her Judaism, it appeals both to the historian in her, which bitterly enjoys the richness and pain of her religious legacy, and the pragmatist, which finds the idea of heaven hard to stomach.

Besides, she has recently wondered if Rosalind would rather the parts of Elena that are Puerto Rican not actually exist.

Nevertheless, the concept of purgatory has always appealed. As she sits, carving out a tiny bit of space for herself, with her small carry-on bag with slick easy-rolling wheels, between expansive travelers on either side, she thinks that purgatory might be the truest thing any religion has ever invented, because it is so deeply reflective of the human experience.

On her right sit a couple, a man and a woman, whose appearances say, but don't scream, *tourists*. They are late thirties, they do something that makes money—the ring on the woman's finger is big, sparkly, definitive, the man's laptop case is well-tooled leather and subtly bears an expensive brand's initials. The woman pages through a slim guidebook with a matte cover and no photograph, always a sign of a more refined recommendation list, while the man plays on his phone. Both are dressed in a New Yorker interpretation of tropical wear, which Elena can see because they've discarded their layers of wool and fleece, laying down their armor against the winter. Elena imagines the man has dug out a linen shirt from his summer clothing box, happy to get to wear it in the off-season, and the woman has traded out her usual all-black everything for the sand-washed gray tunic with white crocheted lacework over slim white pants. Elena wishes that she could wear white pants and not hear her mother's voice in her head, gently reminding her that white isn't very slimming. Elena thinks that in white pants her legs each look like a lamb, fattened before the slaughter, or like pale German sausages, the pork flesh so light it has a pallid gray sheen.

Elena wonders why they are going to the island now, in the wake of all that has happened. Perhaps they want to support the local economy, or perhaps they got an excellent deal, a scavenger's bargain. Tourism after disaster has an element of ambulance chasing, but then, is it not also exactly what people need to recover? Does it matter if the money comes from a hand soaked in pity, just as long as it comes?

On her left side, Elena is buffeted by two women and what looks like all of their worldly possessions. Their carry-on items are like Mary Poppins's carpetbag; when they sat down next to Elena they were contained but as they open up their luggage it seems to multiply in space, infinitely. The women are nut brown, the skin around their eyes wrinkled with laugh lines, the eyes themselves sinking into their faces. Both of them have hair dyed colors not available in nature, one a vivid purple red, one a blue black, both pulled back from their faces into puffy frizzy ponytails. They are as bundled up as the couple to Elena's right are stripped down, still shivering from the cold of the day. At their wrists and necks Elena can see gold and silver and coral bracelets and necklaces, a cross or two, a saint's icon. They chatter, loudly, about the cold, about the airport, about Elena herself, asking each other if she, like them, is Puerto Rican. Elena does not reveal to them that she can understand what they are saying. Her Spanish is not perfect, her mistakes make her self-conscious, and besides, she herself does not know the answer to their question.

She learned her Spanish in the classroom, over a summer in Spain, and lately, on her phone. She rarely speaks it with anyone. She worries what might fall out of her mouth, how quickly she will be judged as not good enough. Not Puerto Rican enough, as she is and isn't supposed to be.

Who is a Puerto Rican? What is a Puerto Rican? Elena will be damned if she knows. Is it a nationality? A cultural identity? A piece of both? Is it defined by skin tone or language or food or religion or how good an oversize T-shirt spray-painted with the Puerto Rican flag looks on her body? Does it mean hoop earrings or cornrows or sleek waves or a taste for mofongo? Elena has been to the island many times in her life, but trips back and forth have not strengthened her assurance or her denial of what she might be. She wonders if her cultural identity is like a video game, if she gets points for this and has points taken away for that, half a player's life's worth of points gone for a non–Puerto Rican mother, ten points for each trip to the island, three for every time she tells people she is Puerto Rican, minus two for every time she doesn't. But the game is not fully realized in her mind. She has so many questions about how it would be played.

If you know a lot about the island, if you have relatives on the island, do you get to be more Puerto Rican than someone else who doesn't have knowledge or humans? If you are only half, but you've been to the island a lot, does that make you as Puerto Rican as someone who is whole, but has never been? If you are dark but can't speak Spanish, if you are light but can speak Spanish, if you are a blonde but you can cook arroz con pollo, if you have a full-on glorious Latino-fro but you can't cook anything, if you have a really Spanish name, if you don't, if you roll your r's correctly, if you can't stand the taste of rum, if you like "Despacito," if you can't dance, which one earns you the highest standing, the best score?

If someone would just explain the rules to Elena, she could tell these women next to her what she is, she could know herself. But no one has given her a set of instructions to herself, to what she is, and what she fears most is declaring herself only to be contradicted, to be proven wrong, to be told she has no right to make any kind of claim to that identity. And so she sits in silence, saying nothing to them at all.

All of them, the chatting women, the quiet couple, Elena, the handful of other people at the gate, are waiting. Flights to the island have been canceled left and right, air travel virtually shut down for months, and while flights are now available, they are cautious, one a day from Newark, a stark contrast to the previous seven options Elena used to see.

The plane is delayed, just an hour, but they all sit on the edges of their seats, tension humming, worried that it will be canceled for good. People who want to go somewhere, either onward, to their destination, a bright little island torn by an angry sea, or back where they came from, their homes, to put away their bathing suits and shorts, their sunscreen and their straw fedoras, sad but settled. It is this in-between, the waiting, that drives men mad. And women. Purgatory.

Elena stretches, trying not to disturb the people around her who have no qualms about doing the same in reverse. The male member of the couple has already spread his legs into her space and commandeered the elbow rest, while the Puerto Rican women have, in Spanish, commented on her body, confirming her decision not to wear white pants, and asked her, in English, to guard their kingdom of objects as they take bathroom breaks and survey the Spanish-language magazine options in the sparse Hudson News. She checks her purse for the hundredth time, noting the position of the spare key to her father's house that her mother had sent her, amazing that Rosalind had it after all this time; her cell phone, her wallet, her computer, her passport, which she does not need but travels with everywhere anyway; the book she has opened and shut over and over again, unable to read a word of it with her brain buzzing and eyes itching as they are. Nothing has moved since she last looked, nothing has gone mysteriously missing. Everything is just as she left it, and this troubles her more than it might if everything had been turned around. Everything she owns is ready for her to go to Puerto Rico. Why won't her body fall in line?

Her work is flexible, her company understanding. They admit that she can do her job from anywhere in the world, really, with the exception of showing apartments, which only impacts her own commission, really. The company has more than enough people eager to step into that role for Elena. She could see the hungry light in their eyes in the meeting she had held to tell them about the open units. They are all, like her, master's degree holders, sure this job will be a temporary one, but their eagerness to take on her work belies their intentions. *It is so easy to get caught up in something in New York, for the things you do to make money to become the only things you do,* Elena thinks to herself. When was the last time she applied for a job at a museum, or a historic site? A year ago, maybe two, after receiving rejection emails for volunteer positions, neatly worded apologies kindly explaining to Elena that she is not qualified to give her labor away for free.

Time away from her work will cost little to anyone except Elena herself. She will have to respond to emails, schedule repairs, run background checks on renters, nothing more. She had gone in to the office fearful, anyway, concerned that they might find her delinquent, that one of the young hungry people would be waiting for her job wholesale. She sat with her boss, Terrance, over coffee, the day after she got the call from Rosalind, after one of their scheduled meetings, unsure how to begin. She planned to lie, to say that her father was ill. People understood illness, when the concern was something in the body, but when it came to the mind, Elena had learned that no matter how well versed they were in the concept of mental health, no matter the things they said, most people she had met in her life, at their core, believed that anything mental was self-indulgence, weakness.

"My father, in Puerto Rico, he needs my help. With the hurricane, his house and all, it's been a mess, and he could really use some help," she said, surprising herself with this odd little lie, but it was the truth in a way, wasn't it? He was missing. He needed help, generally, weren't those some of the last words she had said to him, that he needed help? She wondered if her boss would throw her out of his office, but instead, his eyes brightened. It was like she had said magic words.

"*Puerto Rico,*" he repeated. He understood, completely, everyone would, of course, absolutely, hadn't they read all about it, didn't they think it was a terrible tragedy, and of course he of all people understood about the house her father must live in, all that property damage. They had all been in New York for Sandy, hadn't they? Elena nodded, she had been there, not working for the company then, but still. She had been in graduate school in her second year of the program, and had been stranded in Brooklyn for four days, living on microwave popcorn and boxed wine.

"Take all the time you need," he said, firmly. "We completely understand what a hurricane can do to a building. What a nightmare." Elena nodded again, wondering if there was something wrong with her boss, with her, that they thought of the buildings first, before anything else. Surely a better person would think more about people than buildings? And yet it is this instinct that makes her good at the job she thought would be a temporary measure, the job she has been at for over five years.

Elena is so certain they will be cancelling the flight that she stands, ready to leave the airport, when she is called to board the plane. The women to her left scramble to contain all that they have unleashed from their bags, while the couple to her right are, with New Yorker efficiency and disdain for others, already walking toward the gate, somehow managing to convey their irritation with their very strides. Other travelers fall in line, some of them, like Elena, looking hesitant, disbelieving. Can it be real, that they are leaving purgatory, that they will reach their destination? They look eager, excited, and Elena is jealous.

When she was young going to Puerto Rico was like going to paradise. She could never sleep on the nights before flights to the island, too joyous, too full of anticipation to let her brain stop thinking. She hasn't been to the island in almost a decade, and now, after Maria, all she feels is fear, fear that while the hurricane has come and gone, ahead of her lies more and more destruction. Afraid that her father is gone, afraid that he is waiting for her. Afraid that his home is hers now, afraid that it is not, that he has reneged on this, his promise, his duty, as he has on all other duties, all other promises.

She would turn back, but she is a coward, she cannot turn around when the line has formed behind her, when the press of people are already waiting, when everyone would see her, when this is her task, like it or not. When it is time to move forward, she moves, not because she is brave about her future, but because she is too ashamed to turn away, too frozen, she lets the crowd carry her forward like the tide, onto the plane, off to the island, into whatever will come next.

When Elena arrives in San Juan, the humidity embraces her sweetly, and leaves her gasping for breath. As she walks off the plane, her hair immediately begins to rise out of its controlled ponytail unbidden, forming a fuzzy halo of curled frizz as the air-conditioning inside the terminal freezes the sweat on her back. Her bag takes forever to make its way to the baggage belt, and the late takeoff of the flight means that she has arrived just before sunset. She wishes she had booked a stay at a hotel, what if her father's home does not have power? She arranged all this so quickly, arriving in Puerto Rico a little less than a week after her mother's phone call, and she is suddenly overwhelmed by everything she did not consider. Does the house have potable water, should she have brought a generator, more to eat, more to donate? But it is too late now, and many of the hotels are closed, anyway, recovering from Maria themselves. All she can do is grab her bag and walk on.

Although it has been a decade, the cab stand outside the airport has barely changed at all. They have added a ribboned lane, like airport baggage lines, curving around to contain a queue of waiting taxi passengers, but it is almost empty now, and Elena is already at the front of it, behind the couple she had sat next to in the airport. The Puerto Rican women, along with many of the other passengers, do not look twice at the taxi lane, instead making their ways determinedly to the car-pickup area. Elena smiles, thinking, *Real Puerto Ricans don't take taxis, they have large families to give them rides two hours after their plane has already arrived; they stuff themselves and their luggage into clown cars of distant relatives.*

She has a clear and vivid memory of a childhood trip, an hour spent waiting for her grandfather at the car-pickup area, her mother's red face, swollen with heat and anger. Elena read and reread the same book while her face stared into space, whistling, driving her mother insane. Elena remembers her abuelo finally arriving, his car maroon and battered and without working seat belts, and how he ran the air-conditioning while keeping the windows open for the first ten minutes of the journey, to let the hot air out, he said, chuckling. In the back seat, her mother sat, waiting for her father to say something, to complain, while in the front seat Elena's father said nothing, just laughed nervously at every insult tumbling out of Abuelo's mouth.

The tourists in front of Elena are escorted into their cab, and it is her turn. The only vehicle ready is a large van, but this is also the same as she remembers, there are more large vehicles than regular-size ones. She signals to her bag and murmurs, *"Una maleta,"* watching as the wiry driver hoists her luggage into the trunk, and rushes to open the sliding door for her. She climbs up into the van, now at least two feet off the ground, all alone in a vehicle made for at least eight people, and straps herself into the seat.

"Where you going?" says the driver in English, like she hasn't already told the taxi stand monitor and gotten a receipt for the pre-fixed price for a trip to Puerto Rico's capital.

"Viejo San Juan," she says, softly, hoping to cover her pronunciation, not bad, but never so good as a native speaker's, with low volume.

"Yeah, but where?" whines her driver.

"Just by the corner of Tanca and Sol. Near El Jibarito," Elena says, in English. If her driver prefers it, she's not going to insist on Spanish, even if it makes her feel like she has failed. She gives him the best landmark, a touristy restaurant that has seen better days, but still attracts crowds given its pride of place in every guidebook and top-ten dining spots list she has ever seen.

"What hotel is that?" he asks, turning the ignition. "You sure it's open, or okay to stay at?"

"It's not a hotel. It's a house," Elena replies. She doesn't respond to the second part of his question. In truth, she knows very little about her father's home anymore. Back when both of her parents bought it and owned it together she had visited a handful of times, marveling over the wooden ceiling beams, somehow impervious to insects, over the marble floors they restored, over the windows and thick plaster walls. Watching them renovate the house was the first time Elena saw a historic renovation, and she wrote about it later in her graduate school applications, how watching history reveal itself in that building activated her desire to study the past. How the idea that it would someday be hers has given her a sense that she carries history with her, herself.

In the years since the divorce, since her father's self-imposed exile, Elena has not felt right visiting the house her mother built and abandoned in the wreckage of her marriage, visiting the house where the father who left her had curled up like a rat in his nest. While her father has invited her, the invitations have come as drunken ramblings over the rare phone calls and in the strange emails, never revisited in later, more sober moments. Elena does not think she ever really wanted to come. Now she finally is on her way, and he won't be there to show her what goes where, how anything works, just to be there himself. That gives her a strange feeling, like she is going to stay with someone she is related to but doesn't know very well. Which of course is true. Her father, his house, this island, she does not know them very well at all, though they are all supposed to be a part of her, belong to her.

The driver has lost interest in her, and Elena is free to look out the window. Her phone is working, with limited service, given how Maria knocked out many cell towers, making already spotty island conductivity even more sporadic, and Elena lets her mother know that she has arrived. There is no one else to tell, now, a sad thought. Adult friends don't often let each other know when they've arrived safely anywhere. Boyfriends, fiancés, husbands, families, do that. Elena has friends that want to hear about her experience on the island, but they, like her boss, are more interested in the extent of the physical damage, the island's functionality, than her personal problems. She knows that in the grand scheme of things her father might not matter very much, but he matters to her, and she doesn't want to talk to someone who asks her all the wrong things, making her feel guilty for thinking about what is personal, rather than what is important.

It has been a long time since Elena left New York without knowing exactly when she would return. This trip could take no time at all, or weeks, she doesn't know, but it makes her feel disconnected from her life in the city, all at once. If someone had asked her a week ago, Elena would have said that her life in New York is full, that she has her work, and her friends, like Isabelle, who runs a wine store in Ditmas Park and comes with Elena to museum exhibitions even though she finds them boring, and Sylvia, who is critical and loving and blames Elena's problems on being an only child, and Eli, who works in advertising and always shows up to brunch hungover with the funniest stories from the night before. These people have known her for years, and they care for her, Elena is almost completely sure of it.

But Elena feels so far away from them all in this moment, and she wishes she could have brought one of them with her, even as she knows that would have been impossible, and strange. They know her father is different, difficult, and that Elena and he are distant, but there is no one in her life that Elena has ever told about everything, all the contradictions and pains that make up her feelings toward Santiago, not even Daniel, and she is struck by how isolated she has made herself, how everything that she feels now is her own fault. How much is inside her that she has never said, because saying it would make it too real. As long as she says nothing about her father, she can pretend she is a normal person with a normal parent. But how can you be close to people, really close to them, if you don't tell them who you are? If you don't know who you are, where you come from, what you are made of?

Elena is dislocated from so many things, and she dislocates herself from others. She never knows if people really like her, because she doesn't know if she's enough of a whole person to be liked. She never trusted that Daniel loved her. She hadn't given him enough of her to love.

So much of her world in New York moves without her having to do anything about it. So much of it just fell into place, driven by demand, utility, practicality. Work, gym, home. Sometimes there are drinks or movies with friends, people from high school, from college, people she knows would like her to give more of herself to them, share more with them, ask more of them, give more to them. She would like to do this, like to feel truly close to them, but has never found the trick of it. It is like when she sees them she is talking to them through a thin pane of glass, and she cannot crack it, not even when they hug, when they reach for her, when she wants to reach for them. They feel the glass, she knows. People learn to keep their distance from her, learn to ask for less, until eventually they ask her for nothing at all.

When Daniel was still there they had plans, but his life mirrored hers; his work as a tax accountant was busy, demanding, and he was not the kind of person to invest himself in hobbies, to have large groups of friends, to deviate from the path of most stability. When Elena met him, she wondered if he was boring, for she could not really tell, anymore, what bored and what excited her. There was nothing about Daniel that did not fit neatly into her life. Nothing disruptive. Friends of hers talk about the euphoria of new relationships, how they demand all your time, all your energy, and you are thrilled to give it, so intoxicated are you with this new person, the scent of new skin. Elena has never felt this.

Before Daniel were other men like Daniel, men whose lives ran parallel to hers, men who seemed like they were on the same route that she was, toward good jobs, stable lives, practical existences. She lived in fear that they would leave her, and tried to ask for as little as possible from them so they would have no excuse to do so. When they began to push for more, try to understand her better, she gave them crumbs, whatever she could spare, and watched their interest turn to pity, to sadness for her, watched their shoulders sag under the weight of how very much she needed, how desperately she longed to be loved, to not be left behind. Daniel had lasted longer than any of the others, and it had come as a complete surprise to Elena that *she* had been the one to pull away. She did the leaving.

Elena has always thought, at the back of her brain, in her secret heart of hearts, that she does not do well at forming deep connections because of other people, that the people she has met were not the right people for her. But now, as she stares out the window looking at graffiti and Burger King ads and squat colorful buildings on the road to San Juan in the dying light as the sun sets, she wonders if it is her. If there is something about her that makes people leave her, something she cannot control. If she is simply a person worth leaving. A person incapable of drawing others close, in getting them to change, to stay. After all, this is certainly the case with her father, and she is his child. What chance does she have with anyone else?

Some of the streets are getting dark, but most, the highway she is on, are lit, streetlights shining, their orange tinge dull against the bright ball of fire dipping into the sea. She sees debris, downed palm fronds, but those must be more recent than the hurricane, it's been months. She knows that there are overturned trees and destroyed roofs all over the island, but here, it all looks the way it looked before to her, other than a few new restaurants here and there. She realizes that she was expecting a wasteland, a postapocalyptic vision. She expected to see what she has seen on the news, roads torn asunder, downed buildings and power lines, crying children. The knowledge that they are out there, and that she is completely separate from them, that the road from the airport to San Juan has no evidence of what has occurred, is strange to her, wrong. Chilling.

They pass Condado, and this, at least, looks different. No destruction, but some of the hotels are completely dark, they haven't reopened yet. The curved lagoon with its sleek hotels and resorts is the place many people stay when they come to San Juan, she knows. She has met people whose entire experience of Puerto Rico begins and ends with a hotel in this area of Santurce, be it the historic Vanderbilt or the newer, more modern Marriott. When she was a little girl, her mother would insist that they take her father's family out for dinner during their trips, and it would usually be a place in Condado, which made her mother sigh with relief, at this return to civilization, to prim places with cloth napkins and all-English menus, while her grandfather would scoff at the prices and order too many Heinekens.

The road curves and they zoom past Escambrón beach, where she once saw a family carry a whole sofa out of their car onto the beach, blasting reggaeton the entire time, and then a coal grill, a crib for their squalling baby, and a cooler bigger than Elena was at the time. They pass El Hamburger, another of San Juan's top-rated dining establishments, shuttered now but, Elena is sure, hardly defeated by the storm. She sees the sea on the other side of the car, framed by palms bent like old men, but unbroken. They pass the capitol building, the stone statue of San Juan Bautista, his finger wagging disapprovingly at Elena, who, as she has since she was young, waves in return, and then hang a left after the San Cristóbal fort, a hulking structure that has shaken off this and hundreds of other hurricanes.

The steep hill of Calle Norzagaray opens up to another view of the ocean, churning, a blackening sea as the sun dips and dips. Then, suddenly, Elena blinks and they are there, in front of the house that her mother had been so excited to have, now so eager to give away. It is a bright shade of violet, or at least, it was when Rosalind finished renovating it. Now it has cracked, faded, her father has not maintained it. Violet was Rosalind's choice, which had been strange to Elena, who had never seen her mother in that shade, never heard her remark upon liking it. Perhaps, though, Rosalind had known the whole time that this would never be hers, and painted it something she could walk away from easily. Perhaps she was always planning on giving her part of the house to Santiago, giving him something he can pass on to Elena, the way she used to buy him birthday gifts to give to her, every year. Elena does not know, has never asked. There is so much they have never spoken about in their family, so much Elena has not been able to ask, and now she does not know how to start. Why has her mother, at least, never told her anything? Why have they both left her alone in the dark? She swallows her resentment as she always does, like cough syrup. Like vodka.

She pays her driver and pulls her bag onto the high sidewalk, off the blue street tiles, taken from the rivers of Spain and transported as ballast to the New World to become cobblestones. They make San Juan so pretty, and so dangerous when it rains, which it does for a little bit almost every day. The bright tiles turn slippery as wet glass, twisting more than a few ankles with slick ease.

The day has officially become night, and she is conscious of how alone she is, not just on the street, which is deserted, not even a stray cat to keep her company, but on the island. Apart from her father, who does she know here? Where is the nearest hospital, how would she call the police, if she needed to? Most of her life has been well researched, well planned, neatly ordered, safe. This part of it, though, is a wild garden, made ever more impenetrable by the storm. She has left it untouched, and now she does not know it from Adam.

Her key sticks in the lock for a moment, fighting rust. Elena feels panic, sharp in her side; if she cannot even get into the house, what will she do? Where will she go, sleep, be? She thinks of the empty hotels in Condado, shuttered and worthless to her now. The key turns, her panic lifts. She pushes, hard, at the door, and it opens, creaking at the hinges, the smell of mildew, distinct to the tropics, filling her nose instantly.

"Papi?" she calls. Why? She knows he is missing, somewhere that is not here. But, maybe he is not. Maybe it was all something silly, a broken phone, a bender, maybe he *is* here, sleeping in his bed, maybe he will laugh at this, laugh at the thought of her mother worrying about him, his eyes twinkling as if they are young again, as if she still loves him, and he will hug Elena, and show her that he has signed the house over to her years ago, that he remembers everything, that he is whole and fine, and laugh at her worry, and tomorrow they will go to the beach together, their bodies warm and cradled in the sand, in the ocean, in the world.

Nothing.

"Papi!" Her voice echoes in the house. She has never called him anything but *papi*. It is what he wanted to be called, and even when she realized it was a term of endearment for a lover or a child in other parts of Latin America, she could not think of him otherwise. Although when talking about him she describes him with more distance, as her *father,* when she speaks to him or calls to him, he is always Papi, nothing else. She listens, no response. He is not there. The place is dark, stagnant. Her heart lurches, and she hates herself for being stupid, for having hope.

She drags in her suitcase, sweat forming on her forehead, and looks around in the dying, dead light for a switch. Will the house even have power? Who would she call if it does not? She finds a switch, says a prayer, and flips it. Light fills the foyer with a suddenness that somehow surprises her, startling a small lizard and revealing dead flies and roaches in the corners of the room, and she thanks God for it, for the house having power, for the generators that have helped the city run, for the feeble grid repair that has focused on San Juan first, unfair as that might be to the rest of the island. Tonight, it is there for her, she is grateful, she will take it.

She looks around. When she was here last it had been a graceful space, the foyer; funny to have a foyer here, but this part of the house was constructed in the 1800s, a time when a foyer was as important as ten pounds of petticoats and a good horse. Her mother had restored the white marble floors, had the wooden stairs refinished and polished, painted the walls a calming pale blue, and made sure flowers were placed in a vase there when they visited, *azucenas,* fragrant lilies, brought down from the country and sold in San Juan by a street hawker. Now, the marble is dull, some tiles chipped. The stairs are fading and splintered and the blue paint has bubbled and cracked with humidity, shedding chips around the edges of the room. The vase has no flowers, instead it is filled by a broken umbrella and a bunch of rolled-up newspapers. Objects sit huddled in corners, piles of things, and Elena has no energy to explore them this evening. It is enough that she has made it, that she has opened the door, that some feeble current runs through the wiring. She needs water, and a place to sleep, and she can sort it all out tomorrow. Dust covers every surface, and as Elena inhales she catches it in her lungs, coughing deeply. Her wheeled suitcase makes tracks in it as she walks through the doorway, surveying the bedroom on the first floor.

The house is a two-story two-bedroom, the bedroom and bath on the bottom floor for her, the bedroom and other bath on the top for her parents. Then, all rooms for Santiago. Now, she supposes, all rooms for her.

Her old bedroom is populated with more things, so many more things. She does not recognize most of them. Where did her father get all of this? Light from the foyer shows her old dolls and bottles—green and clear and brown, empty, or at least without caps—and piles of books, and broken furniture, and unbroken furniture, and paintings, hung on the walls and stacked against the floor, a birdcage, more newspapers, more clothing, half of a mannequin, wooden statues with chipped paint of saints, and so much more, so much she cannot see. She turns the switch in this room, but nothing happens. The bulb must be out, she will go to the hardware store tomorrow; she hopes it is in the same place it was ten years ago, something that would have been almost impossible in New York, a bit unlikely in Philadelphia, but here, perhaps, it could be true.

She cannot sleep in this room. She isn't even sure if there is a bed. Can she sleep in her father's room? Is it all like this? How can he be living this way? The house, so far, doesn't seem like one that someone has abandoned a few days ago, instead it seems like something that has been hibernating for years, layers of dust falling on layers of junk.

She climbs the stairs, carrying her bag with her, sweat seeping out of her, rolling down her arms and thighs. Everything is shut, all the windows, and the air feels dead. The second floor has the kitchen, the living room, a bathroom, her parents' room, *why does she still think of it that way when they haven't shared a room, a bed, in years?*, and the stairs up to the roof. The light in the living room also isn't working, but the kitchen light is, and she turns that on, hoping that there isn't any food going bad. How long has Santiago been missing? She has no way of knowing if he walked out on a full larder, or if his cupboards are bare. The fridge is empty, to her relief, even though her stomach growls, except for a beer or two. Half a bottle of rum sits on the counter, and Elena's lip curls, wondering why her father left it

behind, she has never known him to be a man to leave alcohol unfin-
ished. The pantry has a can or two of soup, a small bottle of olive oil,
some dried beans, and some *pique,* vinegar infused with chilies, used
as hot sauce on the island.

Elena fills a glass with water from the sink, relieved that that,
too, is running. She drinks it down in one gulp, then fills her glass
again, walking over to the windows, doors, really, which run from
the floor almost to the ceiling, in the living room. She opens them,
opening the house to the street, to the world, and enjoys the breeze,
leaning against the wooden waist-height bars. Every window becomes like a balcony when it is opened in this house. Elena loves
this about it, loves opening up the door-windows and letting the
city, the night, into the place, loves all that she can see from up here,
loves the wind that comes in two directions, from the bay and from
the open ocean. She thinks about Santiago. Does he love that, too?
Does he close his eyes and feel the breeze and feel happy, even when
his house is like this, this mess?

This floor isn't much better, more piles, more things for Elena
to sort out in the morning. She moves to his room, where, at least,
there is a bed. When were the sheets last changed? She looks—
using her phone for light, for the room's light works but not the
closet's—for more bedding, a towel, anything she needs. She finds
stashed pottery, jumbled shoes, more books, cracked glasses, empty
rum bottles.

There is a couch in the living room. She will sleep on that. She
grabs the rum off the counter, and strips off her pants, which cling
to her. She drapes them over her bag, and walks, in her blouse and
underwear, up to the roof, where her mother had placed potted
plants and her father loved to sit for hours, watching bees buzz and
lizards sun themselves, where Old San Juan spreads out in front of
her, damaged and defiant and smelling like the night. She should go
get something to eat, she should make an effort to do some clean-

ing, she should shower. She has no energy for any of these tasks, no way to imagine herself doing them. She has made it, arrived intact, that is enough for now.

She sits down in her father's chair, weather-beaten wood cracking and dry against her sweaty body, and takes a sip of his rum, and wonders how she got here. She wonders where he is, and if she will really be able to find him. She wonders what it must have been like when the hurricane came, when wind, an invisible force, hit the island like a boxer, pummeling it over and over again, no bell to end the round. She wonders if it felt like death, and rebirth, letting something like that move through your body, tear out the other side.

She drinks more rum, feeling it moving through her veins, sweet numbness, and wonders if her father is still alive. If he is tucked into a doorway somewhere in the city below her, or lost in the jungle, or dissolving under the ocean, his body food for fish. If he is lost and gone forever, or if he will be there when she wakes up the next morning, smiling and ready to take her out for breakfast. She wonders which one of those would make her feel something, anything at all.

When she wakes up, it is to the cooing of pigeons, somehow soothing and grating at once. The sun is small in the east, the day not yet flooded with light, and her body is stiff, her right arm asleep, her head aching. She swings her body forward, unable to move her arm otherwise, and watches it swing, dead weight. It will soon prickle in pain, and then it will be normal, under her control once again.

She blinks, her eyes crusted at the corners, and stands, stretching. She is an idiot for falling asleep on the roof, it was uncomfortable, and besides, it could have rained. It usually does, at least a little bit. San Juan is just a little over half an hour from El Yunque, a small rain forest, and the rain part is no joke. She was lucky, she thinks to herself, grimly smiling. Yes, lucky is exactly what she feels.

The house looks no better in the morning light. Darkness, in fact, had covered many of its sins. The wooden windows are faded and dull, their hinges rusted. The kitchen is sticky and dusty, the original color of the polished granite countertop invisible under a layer of grime and knickknacks.

The couch, she can see now, is the cleanest thing in the room. She lies down on it, her back aching from the chair, and watches the ceiling fan move lazily. The house is a disaster. But is that because it was left to decay weeks ago, or because this is how her father lives? She will not find answers on this couch, she knows, but how she would like more sleep. Since her mother told her Santiago was missing, sleep has not been a frequent visitor in Elena's life. She gets it in fits and starts, ten minutes on a crowded subway, thirty seconds in the middle of a lease signing, an hour on the flight from New York. Sleeping on the roof, as strange as it was, is the most she has slept in days.

Her exhaustion has made it hard to see her friends, not that she sees them much anyway. Relationships have never seemed to stick to Elena. She watches them pass her by, and the people she calls friends today are similar, comfortable meeting once a month, comfortable with long silences in communication, and conversations without profundity or prying. Daniel had been the stickiest thing in her life in a long time, and she could not deny the relief when he unlatched. Easier to let people go than have them wake up and realize they were sticking to someone not worth the effort.

She manages two more hours of sleep before she concedes to the fact that she is awake, now, for the day, and peels herself off the couch, and strips off her clothing. She finds a towel in the bathroom, and tries not to think about when it might have last been washed. There is a dried-out bar of soap in the shower, and nothing else. She washes quickly, scrubbing her scalp with the soap, knowing it, and the humidity, will make her hair a crow's nest as it dries. She dresses quickly, a pair of shorts and a top from her bag, lightweight garments sure to mark her as not from the island, where natives wear jeans and slacks and long-sleeve shirts for these chilly winter days in the low eighties. She brushes her teeth, and struggles with her hair. She thinks of everything she needs to buy just to make this house livable, making a list in her head.

She checks her phone, and sees an email from her boss, Terrance. She responds, giving him the information he needs, and she is surprised when her phone buzzes a minute after she hits *send*. He's calling her.

"Hello?" It's still early, she wouldn't have thought he would have been up.

"How are you doing, babe?" he asks, his tone dripping with sympathy. She hates men who call women *babe*.

"I'm fine, I just emailed you back—"

"Did you get a chance to look at those rental agreements for March yet?" She is technically on vacation. They told her she could have this time. And they barely have anyone checked out and ready for a March move-in yet, everything in New York is down to the wire.

"I haven't, no. I'm sorry." She wishes she hadn't said she was sorry. Why does she always do that? There is silence on the line.

"Can you look at them today?"

"I, I don't know if I will have time, actually," she stammers out. More silence.

"Tomorrow, then." It's no longer a question. She should remind him he told her he could have the time. She should ask him to have someone else do it.

"Absolutely." God, she's a coward. The call ends and she contemplates all of the things she is afraid to do. She can't even stand up to her boss. How the fuck is she going to look at those agreements on her phone? She doesn't have Wi-Fi in the house, perhaps she can find a café, but there is so much else she needs to be doing. She needs to talk to Gloria, ask her what happened. But she does not want to see Gloria, does not want to see what time has done to the woman she knows and still loves, does not want to explain away her absence, does not want to ask her if she knows anything more about Santiago. She knows the answer will be yes, that Gloria will know far more about him than she, Elena, might ever know, and that knowledge of her perpetual ignorance weighs on her. She will not be able to carry anything back from the market if she is carrying that, too.

So she, coward, *doubly coward,* walks first to the Plaza de Armas, taking Calle San Francisco, instead of Calle Sol, to avoid where Gloria lives and works. It is early, and she knows Gloria, a large and placid figure, will be busy cooking, and that on the days her business is open she rarely steps much out beyond the luncheonette, behind which she has her apartment, all on the first floor of the building so she doesn't have to deal with steps. It is Gloria's kingdom, that corner, that block, but for Elena today it is enemy territory, and she skirts it, moving fast. She passes the hardware store, still there, yes, but closed, opening soon. She reaches the plaza, an oft-visited area with a large gazebo in the middle. She can remember being a child, her father posing her in front of the ornate hunter-green structure, a large hat on spindly legs, and crying because the pigeons of the square, accustomed to being fed by passersby, wouldn't leave her alone, flying against her body, their wings brushing her hair. She thinks of how her father wouldn't let her leave until he got the picture he wanted, how he had laughed like it was a great joke as she swatted at the birds, miserable. Where had Rosalind been? Her father had framed the photo, keeping it in his office for years, and Elena wondered whenever she saw it, *How does he not see that my smile is fake?* He always laughed when he told the story. It was one of the scariest moments of Elena's childhood. Elena wonders where that photo is now. She hasn't seen it for years.

She skirts the pigeons today, which, despite the hurricane, despite everything, gather in large numbers, a conference of gray bodies with wild red eyes. She enters the one supermarket in San Juan, and finds, to her relief, that it is not completely without food, *but of course it isn't,* she thinks, *San Juan is pretty, it is where tourists come, it must not be permitted to be a disaster, that's for the places non-natives don't see.* She makes her selections, milk, eggs, fruits, bread, wine, raids the limited home section for light bulbs (the hardware store is on the route she will not take), cleaning agents, trash bags, goes to pay. She smiles feebly at the apathetic clerk, whose crop top reveals soft sections of bronze stomach skin, whose eyebrows reveal her to be a brunette despite the brassy blond of her hair, whose nails are longer than Elena can understand. Elena bags up her things in tote bags, which she has brought from the house, where she found them stashed exactly where Rosalind used to keep them years ago, *has he used them since?* She trudges back, the sun already punishing, the humidity already swelling the air. She avoids Gloria once again, her heart hurting over her own lack of courage, and lets herself back in, that sticky lock groaning.

Where to begin? She cannot stay here, cannot begin to try to find her father, if this house is unlivable, more dust than rooms. Besides, this might be hers, she must find out if it is, maybe there is a hall of records or something, and even if it is not, it will be hers someday, she might as well start maintaining it. She will start with her room, preferring the idea of staying there than staying in what she still thinks of as her parents' space. Or worse, her father's space, soaked in boozy male sweat, marked by his body. She turns on the lights, noting anew which bulbs are out, replacing them. She opens up the windows on the first floor, leaving the door sections of them closed, letting in light but not the whole outside world.

Looking around, her task seems impossible. He has become a hoarder, Santiago, and his home is a rat's nest of objects. *You could just go ask Gloria, ask around,* she tells herself, *you aren't going to find him here in this mess,* but she ignores that thought. She is not ready yet to go into the world looking for her father, despite the fact that this is what she is here to do. She has Gloria she could be asking, she has some family on the island still, two of her aunts live in Bayamon, even if her uncles have moved on, one in Florida, one in the Dominican Republic. She could call them, Rosalind had their last known contact information. She could go to Bayamon, she has addresses, she could ask questions, she could begin.

Instead, she cleans. *Coward.* Three hours later, she is covered in grime and dust, her forehead beaded with sweat, her shirt soaked. She has made it to the back of the closet in the bedroom that was hers once, clearing a path for herself. She has started with the obvious trash, the newspapers, the plastic bags, the broken things, the appliances and pots and plastic plant containers with dead plants shedding in them. Those have gone into garbage bags, sitting in the foyer. In the light of day she can see that her father has put up shelves in this room, or at least, shelving units, and in the closet as well, and they are filled, *filled,* with things. A pair of Coke-bottle glasses, 20 photo albums, books ranging from high school textbooks from the 1960s to political science tomes from the 1970s to law books of the 1980s and 1990s, all the academic periods of her father's life. He was the first member of his family to go to college, he would tell anyone who listened. It was one of the only things she knew about his past. *Why is my father such a mystery?* she thinks, angry.

She looks along the shelves in the closet, revealed when she pulled off the torn sheets that had been covering them. Had her father thought to *protect* these things? This trash, his treasures?

She notes a group of books, histories of the island, of the larger area. She sees a copy of *History Will Absolve Me,* Castro's oft-referenced speech, and a book about CIA involvement in South America, and the gruesomely titled *A Short Account of the Destruction of the Indies.* For all her study of history she has always avoided the world of Spanish and Portuguese conquest. Perhaps she felt that was the realm of her father, who himself had studied it in college. She picks up the book on destruction, telling herself she could use some light reading material.

In between three greenish glass bottles advertising a local pharmacy in 1889, and a mug that has a map of the island printed in cheerful yellow and red paint, she sees a rosary, wooden, with blocky beads, hung on a Santeria candle. She picks it up, examining it, tired from her labors. It is inscribed, she realizes: *Para mi hijo para su primera comunión en la Iglesia San Sebastiánn Mártir.*

For my son. This must have come from her abuelo, or her abuela. Elena didn't know that her father had taken Communion.

She pulls out her phone and looks up the church. It is in a town called San Sebastián, almost a hundred miles from Old San Juan. When her family came to visit the island, they always came to San Juan, and to Bayamon, nearby. She has never been to this town, never heard of it. Her father has never mentioned it to her. Is this some place that is important to him?

Next to the Santeria candle is a map, a driving map of the island. In this age of digital navigation, her father still uses maps, Elena supposes. She opens it, noting routes messily highlighted in red pen, marks along cities like Rincón, Cabo Rojo, Ponce, San Sebastián itself. When did he do this? Is this recent? Is this a *clue*? The map is dated May 2016. Not so long ago, then, but does it mean anything? Does any of this have meaning, this flea market of a home, or is all of it equally worthless? Can it lead her to her father, or is it just a junk shop, an indicator of his brain, filled with cluttered things and broken objects that don't fit together?

There is a big star on Rincón and a name, *Diego.* Who is Diego? Is Diego important? She has never heard her father say this name before. The things she has never heard him say are endless.

She takes out her phone, and before she can stop herself, she calls her mother. Rosalind picks up after the second ring, her voice panicked.

"What happened? Did you find him, is he—"

"Why didn't you ever tell me anything about Papi's past?" Elena blurts out.

Silence.

"Did you—"

"No, Mom, I haven't found him. I barely know where to start. Because I don't actually know anything *about* him."

More silence. *What else does she expect?*

"He didn't want you to know where he came from, Elena. I had to respect that."

"Why?" Elena asks. She has asked this question so many times, but she has never meant it this way. She has always wondered why he didn't want her to know. Now she wants to know why Rosalind agreed. Why both her parents surgically removed her father's past. Why Rosalind assisted, and keeps handing him the scalpel, even though he is no longer there to make the cut.

"He wanted to—"

"Why are you *still* doing this?" *Coward.* What Elena wants to ask, really ask, is why is she even here? Why are either of them still beholden to him? Why do either of them still care? Why doesn't love ever let go of you?

"What would it change?" Rosalind asks, her voice bitter. Elena doesn't know how to answer her. She doesn't know how to tell her mother how lost she feels, knowing so little of her father, of where he, and she, came from. Because telling Rosalind will mean that what Rosalind has given her, with both hands always open, isn't enough. That Elena's worst fear is that she is only half a person. Not enough of anything to be someone.

"Have you ever heard of someone named Diego? Someone he

knew?" she asks instead, closing her eyes and breathing deeply. She doesn't really expect a real response.

"Why are you asking about Diego?" Elena's eyes snap open at her mother's words. Her mother knows this Diego?

"Who is that? Who is he?"

"Diego is someone we both knew once. But we haven't spoken to him in a long time. I didn't know your father . . . well. I don't see how it matters, anyway. Honestly, a lot of Santiago's life, I don't want you knowing about it either."

"*Why?*"

"Someone like your father, he was, is, always trying to get away from where he came from. He didn't want to share it, didn't want to get lost in it. Seems like he did anyway, though." Rosalind's voice is bitter. Elena wants to scream. Even separated for years her parents are united in hiding his life from her.

"You have to tell me something. Anything. I don't know how to do this alone."

"Have you spoken to Gloria?" Elena doesn't know what to say. She doesn't know how to explain her fears. "That should have been the first thing you did!" her mother scolds her.

"She was out. I'll try tomorrow," Elena lies, her voice leaden. "Who is Diego?"

"I am sure that's not important now. I don't see how that would help you, Elena."

"How would you know?" Elena asks. She doesn't want to tell her mother about his name on the map. Rosalind isn't the only person who can keep things from someone.

"I don't like your tone, Elena. If your father wanted you to know about his life, he would have told you. I'm sorry that you feel that you have to lash out at me because I'm the only remaining parent you have, but that's not a very mature reaction and frankly, I'm surprised by it." Elena wants to cry. She wants to apologize. She wants to slap her mother for deflecting like this, for making this about Elena's bad behavior and not Rosalind's own. *Just tell me something, anything, please, I have so little of him.*

"I'm sorry, Mom. I'm just . . . I'm frustrated. I saw the name somewhere, and I thought it might be important. Obviously I was wrong," Elena says. Of course she does. Obedient, calm, defusing the tension, ignoring the problem. "I should go. I'll talk to you later." She almost throws her phone on the ground, but the floor is marble, it will break.

She is sure Diego *is* important. Something in Rosalind's voice . . . there was a longing there. She knows who he is. He means something to her father, maybe even to her mother. But Elena will not find the answers alone. She will not find *him* alone. She is tired, hungry, disgusting with dirt and sweat. She knows, her heart hurting, she needs help. And if Rosalind won't help her, she knows someone else who will.

Five

Santiago Vega looked around the parent-teacher conference for his fourteen-year-old daughter, Elena, surprised to find that he was one of the only men there wearing a suit. For him, the suit was armor. Essential. It insulated him against the world, it showed others what he was, and wasn't. He had never seen his own father in a suit, even at his wedding to Rosalind. Even at his father's own wedding to his second wife. Santiago wore suits, unlike his father. Santiago wore suits to prove he was nothing like his father. He was a professional. He was someone of importance. If he had been a man who wanted to consider himself more deeply, which he certainly was not, he would have thought of his suit as a disguise, just like a superhero's, just like a con man's. But he didn't allow his mind to move in those directions.

After the hour of boring explanations of what the children would be learning this year as the September light faded slowly against the large windows of the cafeteria of the criminally expensive private school Rosalind had insisted on for their only child, Santiago felt like his tie was choking him. It wasn't that he didn't care about this. He did. He was, in fact, deeply invested in his daughter's education. Elena would be everything, have everything, he hadn't. But he couldn't erase the faint whisper of judgment that he felt watching these white teachers with their nice clothing and expensive glasses speak seriously on the support and care they were providing for the children, on the challenges that awaited them in the coming school year. What challenges could a bubble like this offer children? What challenges ever really came to people with money? Each of Elena's classmates, like Elena herself, would study the Silk Route and geometry and read *The Catcher in the Rye* in safety, with full stomachs and clean hands.

And he had given it to her. That was a source of true joy, it was. He just wasn't sure all these other little shits deserved it.

When the talking finally, *finally,* ended, he slipped out at a side door, relieved that no fire alarm exploded as the sign on the glass door warned it would. He wondered if the students of the school knew how many of these signs were lies. They probably didn't question them. The kids at this school might scrape their parents' cars against each other and steal their parents' scotch, but they probably never bothered to see if the fire alarms were real. They'd never have to run out of a building, never been chased. *They would grow up to commit the crimes of the rich, not the petty ones of the poor,* he thought. *God, I hope Elena isn't ruined by the life I've given her.*

Leaning against the side of the building, making sure no one could see him, he fished a flask and a pack of cigarettes out of his inside jacket pocket. Things like this, he hated them. He hated feeling jealous of his daughter. Look at this school, with its maple trees and soccer teams and *meetings about what the children would learn.* Look at his daughter, with parents, real ones. Or one. Most days he thought of himself as a father, but sometimes, when his skin was thinnest, he had to admit to himself that he was an imposter. He had no idea what he was doing. He lived in fear that everyone would know. He craved everyone knowing. He wanted to stand up in front of them, all these *nice people,* and laugh, mock them, tell them he had tricked them all, they had let him in among them, he had won. But it didn't feel like winning.

He took a sip.

"Got another one of those?" A male voice to his left startled him. He turned and saw a man, also in a suit, that was something. He hated these men who came to the school in casual clothing that probably cost more than his best shoes. Hated the way they were so secure in their lives, their place in the world, that they didn't need the armor he needed to belong. He handed over the pack, watching the man, *who was he,* "Something" Anderson, his daughter had been in Elena's class for a few years now.

"It's Paul, right?" he said, inhaling deeply on his cigarette.

"Yeah. Rachel's dad."

How strange, and sometimes a little wonderful, it was to be someone's father, to be identified as someone's father first. Not by his job or his school or his life, but by this child he had helped create, in a way, although really, it had been all Rosalind. It was still all Rosalind. His wife did everything for their daughter. She was the authority on how to be a parent. She read books on the subject, she knew the doctor's appointments they were supposed to have, she met each horrifying new reality of parenthood like it was paradise. She had wanted to have more children, when just the one had overwhelmed him completely, but after several miscarriages it became clear that Elena would be their only one. Santiago hated himself for his relief, but it paled in comparison to other reasons for his self-hatred, and over time he had forgotten he had ever felt it, forgotten Rosalind had wanted more than the one. They both told each other they had one wonderful kid, and that was more than enough.

It was, really, often far more than enough for him. There were so many things, steps in Elena's life, that he couldn't understand. He felt sometimes that he had to study other parents to understand how to react appropriately to a child, even his own. Sometimes small moments filled him with wild outsize despair and sometimes he missed the point of big things completely. Recently, Elena had her first period and Santiago had wanted to die. His daughter, his child, bleeding, her body ready to give birth itself, from a biological perspective. It was insanity. Elena had come out of the bathroom terrified and mortified and he had stared at her, the unreality of her. She was a person, she would grow and grow and grow and someday have her own daughter.

It was horrifying. She was crying and he could feel tears in his own eyes, screams bubbling in his throat. What was he supposed to do about this? But Rosalind had just nodded, and shown her how to use a pad, or so she said. He hadn't really wanted to know, and Elena had said nothing, the both of them pretending it had never happened, that it didn't happen month after month. For years he had been involved in the diaper changing and the potty training but there came a point at which his daughter's body was something beyond him. She was becoming a *person,* a woman, what the fuck was he supposed to do with that? He wished she could stay a child forever. The older she got, the more clearly she would see him. The more she would investigate him, find out all of the things he had hidden about himself from her. He would become small and pathetic to her. He wished he could make her blind.

No, you're fine, you've done everything right, and she'll never see any of that. You're not any of that anymore, and no one will ever see anything you don't want them to. He told himself this. Every day.

"These fucking things," Paul said, distracting Santiago from his thoughts.

"Absolutely." They shared a smile. Inside the expensive cafeteria, where Santiago was sure some of Elena's tuition money had gone, other parents were locked in conversations with teachers, arguing the benefits of this or that, why the kids had to read *Romeo and Juliet* this year not next year, and why they absolutely couldn't learn about the Holy Roman Empire yet and *shouldn't they be doing precalculus by now* and what was the school going to do in biology, dissection was cruel, no, it was necessary, no, it was archaic. So many opinions, like they were experts.

Santiago took another sip from his flask, and then, hesitantly, offered some to Paul. He wasn't sure if the man would have an opinion about him bringing booze to this event, and if he said yes, well, less for Santiago. Paul looked at the flask.

"What the hell." He took it, and sipped, handing it back.

"Glad there is someone like me here," Paul commented. Santiago looked at him. Paul was blond and stocky, his face slightly red. "I was already done with mine." Paul took out a flask from his own pocket and waved it, indicating that it was empty. Santiago smiled.

"Helps," Santiago said.

"Absolutely," Paul said, echoing Santiago's own words. "Denise doesn't get it. She can be a real bitch."

Santiago found himself nodding. Rosalind wasn't a bitch, but she didn't get it either, that sometimes he needed this. This escape. This thing that shut down all the thoughts, that calmed his moods, that helped him be normal. But Paul got it. Santiago wasn't something abnormal. There were other people like him. *Thank god for Paul.* Paul thought he was normal. He must be, then.

"Back to it," Paul said, stamping out his cigarette.

The first time Santiago Vega Jr. had brought his infant daughter, Elena Vega, to Puerto Rico, for the wedding of his youngest brother, Jorge, he felt like he was stepping back in time, to when he could remember visiting the island himself for the first time, at the age of seven. He had been back before then, but seven was the first time he really remembered arriving, and so little had changed that it took the air from his lungs and he had to remind himself he was an adult, a man, a lawyer, someone real, and not just the ghost of his father's former life.

He stood, waiting for their luggage to arrive on the belt, as nearby, Rosalind tried to calm Elena, who at eighteen months old had been an angel on the flight down, sleeping peacefully. However, as soon as the plane landed and the many Puerto Rican passengers clapped enthusiastically, congratulating the pilot, and each other, on not dying, Elena let out a scream to wake the dead and hadn't stopped since. He didn't blame her. His own heart felt like lead and he longed for a drink, a mouthful of rum to quell his dread of what was to come. But he wasn't drinking now, he had promised Rosalind. He faltered, every now and again, hiding a night out with mouthwash and cologne, but for the most part he was good, he was strong, he abstained. He hadn't had one in almost a year now, and while it killed him, he knew it was for the best. He had to be careful with Elena, with his *daughter,* a little doll whose giant brown eyes looked at everything, who grabbed his nose and pulled and made him wish he could give it to her, who he was more in love with than he had ever thought humanly possible, who was screaming so hard he worried her lungs would shatter as he spotted one of their suitcases.

"I'm going to walk her up and down for a bit," Rosalind told him, her face flushed. The people around them were looking at his irate daughter with affection, but Rosalind never wanted her kid to be *that* child, the one annoying everyone with their unhappiness. He nodded, tickling Elena's feet. She stopped screaming for a moment, looking at him with shock and dismay that he had tried to make her laugh when she was so set on crying, looking so much like her mother that it made him smile. Elena did not appreciate his amusement at her distress, and went back to her shrieking.

"Very helpful," Rosalind said, dryly, pointing out another suitcase as she walked away, jiggling their daughter desperately.

An hour later, they were still at the airport, waiting for his father, who was, of course, late. Elena had exhausted herself and was sleeping on Rosalind, who had found a single spot of shade in the waiting area outside the airport, trying to escape the harsh tropical sun. Santiago sat on the curb next to them, feeling his skin baking. He never burned, but sweat coated his whole body. Rosalind looked at him, her gaze accusing, and he shrugged.

"We can take a cab. This is ridiculous, Santiago."

"We can't." She knew the way his father was. He would be furious if they denied his hospitality, his *help,* he would mock his son for the expensive cab ride, goading him about his money, his success, even as he needled his other sons about their lack thereof. Time with his father was like time in a dog racing arena, with him and all his siblings as the dogs, eager for love, spurred by abuse, and all of them panting at the end, spent and sad and alone.

"Where the hell is he?" Rosalind asked, hissing. Elena wiggled in her arms, and settled, her little face as flushed with the heat as Rosalind's. "We have a child with us, Santiago, and your father is an hour late. More! Our flight was delayed, which he had no way of knowing."

"What do you want me to do about it?" he hissed back. "I can't make myself important to him, can I?" He wanted to bite his tongue. Where had that come from? It was a ridiculous thing to say. But Rosalind's expression softened, perhaps it had been useful. She laid a hand on his shoulder.

"Is this hard for you?"

"It's fine, I'm happy to be here. Happy I got the time." He looked away from her. He'd been at the firm for over a decade now, and while it was clear he was never going to make partner, any more than any other Puerto Rican lawyer at a corporate firm in the United States would in 1989, he was doing well, with a strong caseload. It made vacations hard. It made sobriety hard, but he was better, more in control, he was sure of that.

After Elena's birth, and everything that had come with it, Rosalind had finally succeeded in forcing him to see someone. He had done it to make her happy, and he spent the session with the little man with half-moon glasses mostly in silence, answering a few questions as simply as possible and revealing nothing of himself he would not tell his boss, his clients, or a waiter at a restaurant he'd happened to get friendly with. At the end of the session, the doctor referred him to a psychiatrist, who was a man around his own age, Dr. Anthony Moretti. This was much more comfortable for Santiago, the world of illness and cure, not this ephemeral invasive talking, uncovering what was buried for a reason. You didn't go around a cemetery digging up corpses, why do that in your own mind? If he fell backward, if he opened up the past and talked about it all, he would never escape it. He had to go on, he could not turn back now. Dr. Moretti understood, he listened to Santiago talk about his moods and actions and he nodded and gave him a pill, small and white. Santiago took it when he felt like it, and it helped sometimes, numbing him the way a stiff drink would. But sometimes it put him in a fog there was no path out of. Drinking, he could control how he felt. This pill controlled him, and he loathed it. Still, he took them, every day like he was supposed to. Medicine made you better. This made him better. He had to believe that.

"It's okay if it is. It's been a long time," Rosalind said, her nose wrinkling. She liked Puerto Rico, at least, she had in the beginning, when he first brought her here years ago; but she hated its effect on him, hated the way his father was with him, with everyone, hated how even now his father, Santiago Sr., didn't call her by name, referring to her simply as *tu esposa*. Rosalind was a feminist, unhappy with being referred to solely in terms of her position as his wife.

And she knew that it was not just because she was a woman, but because she was not Puerto Rican, not what Santiago Sr. had wanted for his son, no matter how absent he had been in that son's life.

"Everything is so much slower here." She sighed. Santiago nodded. He used to come every summer. Now he only came when someone got married. After Jorge, maybe it would be Beatriz, his youngest sister, who was only ten. It would be a long time before she got married. Could he wait that long again? He loved it here. As soon as the airport doors had opened he had felt back home, although he had never really lived here. The island wrapped him in its humid arms and he wanted to hug it back, to embrace it and apologize for being away for so long, like a lover he was returning to after a long trip. But it was a lover that came with so many strings attached.

"Is that his car? Jesus, how long has he had that thing?" Santiago looked up to see the old Cadillac his father had had as long as he could remember huff and puff its way up to the curb.

"You getting in?" Santiago Sr. chortled out, in Spanish, grinning madly.

"*Hola, Papi,*" Santiago Jr. said, opening up the rusty trunk. Rosalind was looking at the car in horror, clutching Elena in her arms. Santiago watched as his father leaned down, hard, on the horn.

"You coming?" Santiago Sr. asked her, in English this time, his accent thick, his tone derisive. But his face lightened at the sight of Elena, who squirmed, annoyed by the horn. Rosalind, furious, opened her mouth, looked at her husband, and shut it, inhaling deeply. She got into the back of the car, clutching Elena fiercely, as his father made cooing sounds at the baby. Santiago Jr. slid into the front seat, feeling like a teenager again, getting into his father's car on one of his visits home during the summer to the island, as the old man cackled at him.

"You're getting fat," his father told him, laughing again, that nervous laugh which sounded cruel or kind, depending on what else he was saying. Santiago returned it, unconsciously echoing it, and in the back seat, he could see Rosalind wince.

"She's a big baby. She looks like you, poor girl," his father said of the grandchild he had never met. Santiago Jr. had sent him some photos, but received no reply. He rarely did.

"How have you been, Santiago?" Rosalind gritted out, determined to be polite as she always was. His father spoke and understood English, but pretended not to most of the time. He nodded, though, to Rosalind's question.

"Good, good, last son getting married! Jorge is becoming a man. I try to take him to a whorehouse five years ago but he not go. So I pity his wife tonight!" He laughed again, and Santiago Jr., knowing his role as audience member, laughed, too. "That's what we did back in the army."

"Charming," Rosalind said, leaning back against the beaten-up seat, and then straightening again when the pressure forced a cloud of dust out. She held Elena up to the open window, pointing out things, palm trees, flowers, buildings, which Elena repeated back in toddler babble.

The car took the familiar route toward Bayamon, where his father lived now, his islander children surrounding him like chess pieces. They lived nestled together, while Santiago Jr. lived on the mainland, far from them all. But this had always been the way it was, his father putting distance between the two of them, then children between the two of them, a new family, a second, better try.

They arrived quickly in front of the squat cement house; no longer split-level now, it seemed to have grown an addition. His father pointed to the second floor as they got out of the car, excited at his bounty, explaining that he had added it and improved the value of the house. Rosalind snorted behind him, but walked in, mentioning that she needed to change the baby, as Santiago Sr. led his son straight through the living room and kitchen and into the garden, where he threw his body on a chair, inviting his oldest son, who he never called anything but "Junior," to do the same.

"Nice girl, the one he's marrying. She's from Mayagüez." Santiago knew what his father was telling him. It was a rebuke, comparing Jorge to Santiago Jr., who did not marry a nice girl from Mayagüez. He sighed. He had helped pay for this wedding, as he helped with everything, without question or complaint.

"I'm sure she's great," he responded. His father nodded, like he had said something more meaningful than he had, and shouted out for a beer, two beers. Within a minute, Chavela, his wife, emerged from the house. Santiago hadn't seen her on the way in, but rose to greet her, as he always did, with a hug. Chavela was nothing like the evil stepmother of fairy tales. She was soft and tiny and warm, and she had always been kind to him, kinder than his father, or anyone else in his family, really. She could not have been more different from his own mother. For one thing, she was sane.

"So good to see you, Junior. You look wonderful, and your daughter is so pretty!" Chavela was as kind as his father was mean. She handed him a Heineken, and his father the same, frowning.

"We have the rehearsal dinner tonight at eight," she said, gently. Santiago Sr. dismissed her with a wave of his hand. Rosalind hated this most of all, on the island, the way his father treated his stepmother. But Santiago Jr. was helpless in the face of this, as he was with everything regarding his father. He sipped his beer, closing his eyes at the taste of alcohol, the feeling of it. He should have said no, should not have accepted the offer. It had been a year. But here, with his father, the reasons not to drink seemed far away and strange and stupid. He could have one beer, couldn't he?

"I heard about your mother," his father said, frowning slightly. Santiago Jr. did not want to discuss this with his father, so he said nothing. His father had, indeed, been in the army, and still sat with military attention until he had had enough to drink that he could sink into a chair unself-consciously.

"I couldn't go to the funeral," his father said. Santiago Jr. nodded. He knew. He had been there. Surely he would have noticed if his father had come as well. It had been a bizarre affair, much like his mother's life. Rosalind sat beside him, clutching his hand, as Elena, then only three months old, slept peacefully. A motley crew of mourners, people from the old neighborhood, people Santiago Jr. had hoped, prayed, as if he believed in God, to never see again, sat around him crying for his mother. Santiago Jr.'s eyes were bone dry.

In the middle of the sermon, a thing of hellfire and brimstone delivered in formal Spanish in the funeral parlor at First Avenue between Second and First streets in Manhattan, a man had come in, off the streets, homeless, or he looked that way, and started speaking, interrupting the preacher. He had rambled about ancient gods and their demands and *how there must be sacrifices and blood, they needed blood, everyone knew that, and that death was just a mirror and that he needed five dollars right now, why wouldn't someone give him five dollars, it wasn't right, wasn't Christian, wasn't human.* No one had known what to do, what to say to make him stop. The entire funeral party had been frozen in shock, as his mother's body sat, calmer in death than in life, and bore witness to this madness. Eventually, facing an unresponsive audience, the man had departed of his own accord, and the service continued, the priest's words faint in the haunted air.

Elena slept through it completely. He'd been jealous of her, that deep baby sleep. It was like it hadn't happened at all.

"Well. Better this way, I guess," his father said, shrugging. Santiago Jr. looked at him. He had felt many things for his father over the years, but this, this spike of loathing, was entirely new, and he was not prepared for it. *Better this way.* He wanted to strike him, wanted to cry. He drank his beer, to stop himself from doing something else.

Rosalind appeared, then, in a change of clothing, with Elena looking awake in a frilly dress. She looked at him, and the beer in his hand, and her mouth tightened, but she said nothing. She put their child down in the garden, where Elena immediately started stumbling around pulling at things. His father chased her down, careful to guard his precious plants from her fat fumbling fingers, and grabbed her. She struggled, amazed at the land crabs his father kept in a cage at the edge of the roots of his avocado tree. She reached out for them, and they reached back, sharp pincers ready.

"No, *linda,* no, not that, let's find you something better to touch," his father said, tenderly, in the English he rarely offered Rosalind. He led Elena to bright flowers, and plucked them for her baby hands to shred.

Santiago Jr., already affected by the beer, looked at the scene of his father, who had just said his mother was better off dead, cuddling with his own daughter with petals covering them both, and wanted to throw up. He had never felt such rage than at this moment. He turned, downing the rest of the beer, and went to shower, to change, to prepare himself for his brother's wedding, for the onslaught of family who would celebrate him and ask him where he had been and avoid the gaping hole between him and his father, the past that stretched out between them, the way his father had left his mother, and him, behind, to build all this back here.

He would get extremely drunk that night, but subtly, so that Rosalind, exhausted from the trip and caring for their daughter and interacting with the loving, nosy, judgmental hordes of Puerto Rican family members, barely noticed. But it would not help him sleep. Instead, it would keep him up, and he spent that night staring at the ceiling as his wife and daughter slept around him, wondering if Elena would ever feel for him what he felt for his father now: hard rage. In the morning, it would have faded, and he would, over the days and weeks to come, through the wedding and the trip home and the many days after, press it all down until it was over, forgotten, as he did so many things, but for a moment, he mourned what might come, would come. His child would hate him someday, when he failed her, the way he had been failed. He had never been more certain of anything in his life.

But in the morning, he looked at her and was certain he would never, ever let her down.

Six

After finishing the work on the March contracts, because Elena is nothing if not conscientious, she sips her coffee, grimacing at the bitter burnt-bean taste. Puerto Rico has much better coffee than the Starbucks she is drinking, sitting in the air-conditioned café and watching waiters set up outdoor seating in front of the many touristy restaurants that line Calle de Tetuán, the curved street that has an assortment of cruise ship–friendly bars and establishments. From the window she can just see the bay in the distance, where the massive ships dock and spit out lobster-red people daily. Or they used to. Hurricanes are bad for cruise lines.

She is here for the Wi-Fi, and now that her work is done she doesn't really need it, but still she uses it, marking time, delaying the inevitable. She looks at her phone, scrolling through social media apps, looking at people she knows better through their Instagram profiles than in real life. She thinks for a moment, and then searches for her aunt Beatriz, who lives in Florida and is her father's youngest sister and often more than a bit of a train wreck. She posts a lot of photos of her beautiful children and Elena enjoys seeing them, likes to imagine being close to them, having a big family to surround and love her. It is a fantasy Elena loves, even when it cuts her. She passes photo after photo of the kids, a boy and a girl with tan skin and wild curls, and pauses when she sees something different from the usual content on her aunt's feed. Instead of family photos or selfies, this photo shows a view of a beach from the ocean. It looks deserted, wild, with a horse caught mid-canter sprinting across it. Elena realizes it's been reposted, from @vidaboricua12, with the line *so proud of my Jessenia beautiful niece!* written by her aunt as the caption. Who is Jessenia? Elena clicks on the handle.

The original profile says, *Looking for Puerto Rico's lost, or lost to me, history, one day at a time,* in English and in Spanish. Scrolling through the photos, Elena realizes that they are images of things on the island, from historic structures to plants, from aging photographs from the past to images from the present of locals, and each image is described, the viewer urged to check out the full story in the linked blog post. Scrolling back farther Elena sees an image of the poster introducing herself, and she realizes that she knows who this is: her uncle Juanito's wife's daughter, from her first marriage, Jessenia. A cousin who is not really a cousin, a few years younger than Elena. She remembers her, vaguely, from the last full family dinner a decade ago, and her face hasn't changed much. Still pretty, still bright and shining, surrounded by family who look like her. Her photos are as full as Elena's are sparse.

Elena clicks on the blog link. She sees the titles of post after post, poems, stories, pieces of history that her not-cousin has been gathering and publishing. There is so much here, so much to read, so much that Elena could learn. She feels like she has stumbled upon a pot of gold, a secret treasure. She bookmarks the link, and stands. She would like to sit and read the blog, spend the day with all this history and insight, this connection to a not-really-family member whose life is, somehow, linked to hers. To Santiago's. But she must keep it as a treat, the carrot to dangle in front of herself as she does her duty.

She walks outside, and takes a right; now she is on her way to Gloria's place. When she misses the next road that would take her more directly there, well, she is simply taking the long way, she tells herself, seeing more of the city, it has been a long time and she has a right to see things, does she not? But this is all justification of her avoidance, and she knows this as well as she knows the fact that she will continue doing it, walking well out of her way, past the hulking fort El Morro that makes San Cristóbal look meek, down the road with a thousand napping cats, toward the one original gate to the city that still stands.

She looks around, realizing she has walked to one of her favorite parts of Old San Juan, a street called Caleta de San Juan, a little one that only runs for two blocks and slopes down toward the old gate. It has large trees gracefully providing a natural archway over it. Elena remembers being a child and walking down this street with her parents, the papaya ice cream in her hands melting as she looked around with wonder. It has barely changed since then, and she lets herself wander up it, telling herself she will just be a minute, lying even in her own head.

She spots a sign, *Wilfredo Garcias Real Estate,* and a bolt of recognition shoots through her. Of course, this is where the Realtor's office was, the one who sold the house to her parents. They had looked at several homes with several people, overrunning her vacations in her first year of college with sojourns through dusty broken buildings, but Wilfredo, he of the sun-yellow hair, had ended up with the one they wanted. She and her mother had discussed his hair at length over dinner the night her parents signed on the place—a night her father had been too drunk to join them, another time she had pretended it was normal that he hurt them this way—

and they wondered where Wilfredo got it done, and what had led him toward such a shade in the first place, a color no one could ever imagine to be natural. *Blondes have more fun,* she had reminded Rosalind, trying to entertain her, trying to distract from the sight of her father, sleeping, dead to the world, both of them forgotten. Elena wonders what her father remembers now, if she, Elena, exists in his mind or if she has become a ghost to him, the way he is to her. She tries to remember the smell of his aftershave, a kiss on her cheek, but instead all she can remember is stabbing pain, which she pushes down, trying to breathe normally.

Would Wilfredo know about the deed? she thinks, suddenly, her brain kindly distracting her. She should go to Gloria, she should try to find her father, but the insidious part of her that wants, wants, *wants*—a sign of his love, yes, but also the house itself, a piece of the history of the island for her own, the thing she was promised, the thing she is owed for all of his nothing—pushes her to the doorway of the office.

She opens the door and finds the man of her memory sitting at a desk in the cozy office, his face a little more lined, but his hair the same shade as it was a decade ago, ever more impossible in the bright daylight. A tiny flower, almost like a sticker, sits on his hair near his right ear, and Elena looks at it, transfixed.

"Hello, good afternoon, can I help you?" he says in Spanish, then repeats himself in English as Elena looks at him, struck dumb by how much, and little, time has meant on his face.

"I'm not entirely sure," Elena replies in English. She remembers his own English was good, and what she wants to ask about is something legal, something she does not have the words for in Spanish. "I'm sure you don't remember me, or my parents, but you helped us buy our house a bit over ten years ago, a place on Calle Tanca? I'm Rosalind and Santiago Vega's daughter." She omits her mother's last name; it will do her no good here. She winces inside. She almost never says her father's name anymore, it pains her to do so. But needs must.

Wilfredo's eyes light up, and he looks like an elf.

"Of course, of course, your parents wanted a *ruina,* they got that one on Sol, and such a nice job they did, no one puts this kind of money into renovation like they did, wonderful! I sell so much to see it just stay like it is, but they make it really nice."

"They did, yes." Elena has no comment for what it is like now, the way it is falling to ruin all over again.

"Your father is here a lot, no? Living here now? Retirement?" Wilfredo asks, his eyes kind. It's a small city, this, a town, really. Of course he knows her father lives here now. Elena is grateful for his discretion, how he doesn't ask about her mother, the way it allows her to avoid explaining things.

"Yes, yes, he is. He loves it," Elena says. She has no idea if this is true. Wilfredo nods, smiling still. "I actually had a question for you, which I don't know if you would be able to answer, but I thought I might ask?"

Wilfredo nods again, gesturing to the chair in front of his desk, but Elena just hovers. Sitting will give her time to think.

"How would I go about finding information about, um, my parents' house? That is, the history of the property, the records of who might have owned it in the past, the, the current deed, things like that?" She is clouding her purpose with other things, hoping her real interest will slip past him, but once the words are out of her mouth, she realizes she really does want to know more about the house. She has a vague sense of its history, from when her parents bought it, but even that information she has never verified. As a historian, lapsed though she now is, she realizes she should be ashamed of herself, to never investigate the house, its origins, its owners. And if it is to be hers, if it is already hers, shouldn't she know more about it? Was it built on the back of slave labor, or some Spaniard's olive oil money?

What haunts the house, other than her own pain and her father's past?

Wilfredo looks at her, his smile turning vague.

"Why?" he asks her, bluntly. She shrugs, affecting an innocent smile.

"I'm thinking about writing up the history of the place. Just for us. Everything here is a piece of San Juan's history, right? I thought I should document it. Might be nice, for the future."

Wilfredo looks at her suspiciously.

"Are you going to put it on Airbnb?" he asks, his eyes narrow.

"No, no, nothing like that," Elena assures him. She almost feels like lifting her hands up, giving herself up like a bank robber. He smiles, relieved.

"Good. That thing is ruining the city. With the hurricane, people will leave, put their apartments up on that thing, and then what?" Elena nods. She has heard this before, in New York, and is amused, and sad, to know San Juan is having the same problem.

"Well, if you wanted to know about a place in this city, el Instituto de Cultura would be the place to start."

"For the deed, too?" she asks, trying to sound innocent. He shakes his head.

"That, maybe public records? Deeds are different here than in the States. We are under French civil law, not English. So they aren't recorded in the same way." Elena nods. She vaguely remembers something about this from her graduate school thesis, the way the legal system here impacted trade laws.

"Are your parents thinking about buying again? Or you? I have some nice places on Sol."

"Oh, well, I don't think so, but if we do, you will be the first person we go to!" Elena says, smiling. The clock behind his desk tells her that she has missed Gloria's open hours, and she can feel relief singing through her veins. *Coward, idiot, coward.* Still, she has learned something from him. That is useful, isn't it? *Who are you trying to convince?* she mocks herself.

Her expression must show her disdain for herself, for Wilfredo is frowning at her now.

"You okay?"

Elena nods.

"Thank you so much for everything. Nice to see you again."

"Say hello to your father," he says, his eyes kind. He does not mention her mother, and Elena does not know if this is chauvinism, from the man with the tiny flower in his hair, or knowledge that Rosalind won't be coming here any time soon. Elena nods, smiling, and walks out into the fading heat of the afternoon.

Taking out her phone, Elena looks up the Instituto de Cultura, which is close, and closed. Of course it is. It is 4:00 P.M. on a Friday. Elena doubts it is truly open more than an hour or two a day, and likely has different hours each day too. Efficiency is for mainlanders, and those who speak Germanic languages. Tomorrow, then, she will try again.

She walks home, past Gloria's place, because she knows it will be shut, and it is. She had told herself she had to talk to Gloria today, had to. And then she didn't. She thinks about her own pathology as if it is someone else's, the pathetic way she can only muster the courage to walk by a woman who she has known for a long time, a woman who cares for her, cares for her father, when she is sure that woman isn't there. She wishes this were all already over, that someone would come up to her on the street and tell her that her father is gone, or that her father is living happily in Morocco, or that her father never existed at all, so that she can know, and be done. She has been on the island for less than a full day, and it is already exhausting her, painting her with pain.

She is relieved when, entering the house, it is as bad, worse, than she remembered. If she is busy cleaning, she will have no time to think.

Lying on the couch after several hours of cleaning, her arms aching, she lifts her phone up and opens Jessenia's blog. She shouldn't be letting herself read it, she knows, she didn't talk to Gloria, she doesn't deserve her reward. But for all the work she has done, her mind is still buzzing and racing, and reading this might calm her. Anything that distracts her from the empty house would calm her, she hopes. She scrolls down, down, to the very first post, *begin at the beginning,* she thinks, and clicks on it.

> *There is a part of the world which is paradise and hell. To come from the island is to be the inheritor of things as they are somehow sweet, ripe, rotten, all at once, to graft onto the patch of vivid emerald in a world of blinding turquoise even as it tries to wash you away with storms and waves, with earthquakes and with desperation.*
>
> *On many days, as I sit on my boat in the wide bright teal sea and look back at the shore, I think I can see what it must have been, that first sight of land flashing against European retinas, that first moment when the old world met the new. What must they have seen, sweaty, starving, lice infested men with beards and nothing but seagulls, Jesus, and each other, for company, when the island came upon them? What must those grimy, stained men have thought it was, that patch of palm and stone, wet with rainforest droplets? They had come from dry lands of oranges and palaces and pox. These men had boarded hunks of rotting wood and set out for a land, a triangle in the sea, that they knew nothing of, save that it had pepper, that black wrinkled pimple, that jewel worth each of their lives ten times over.*

Before they left Spain, they had filled their floating homes with pigs and guns and bodies, soaking their wool trousers and linen shirts with sweat as their boat made its journey to the land that held everything they craved, everything that would make food worth eating. Was this it, they asked, the place beyond the edge of the world, beyond the Holy Land, halfway to China where God hadn't even made His way yet? A spot of green, pure, vivid green, a color so lush and sweet they opened their mouths to taste it although they were still miles away? Would they know India when they saw it? Or had they died, and was this paradise?

What must the boricuas have seen, the many pairs of eyes watching the gigantic brown ships on the ocean come closer and closer to their world, their island? What did they see coming on the horizon, in such an ugly form, pale ghosts in heavy bags of fabric, great stacks of dead forests charging through the waves? Perhaps they thought it was an illusion, a mirage. The island knew it was one of many, as did its inhabitants, but the sailors who approached it could only see what was right in front of them. Like something from a dream. Beckoning to them, welcoming them to its pristine shores.

This is what history has taught me. Be careful with your invitations. To welcome is to leave your neck vulnerable, your blood available to be sucked dry. Oh, that I could have told this island, do not call. Do not invite these strangers to your doors and shores. You will regret their hands on your lands, their fingers rooting into the streams of your earth for shiny things, their bodies rooting into the caverns of your women, their thoughts and their gods and their needs becoming yours.

But it is too late for that now, far too late. To want is to become, to call is to transform, and I, we now are all what we are and cannot pull apart the threads between them and us, we are them, all of them, too late to warn the island, too late to turn back the tide.

So we must be all the things we are now, the discoverer and the discovery. The oppressor and the oppressed. Enslaver and enslaved. We have the blood of each one buried in us, and there is no turning back that tide.

Elena closes her phone, and her eyes, sure that visions of conquistadors will plague her dreams, but soon she is sleeping, her body buoyant in her dream of the sea.

The Instituto de Cultura is closed when Elena gets there in the morning. Elena had checked the hours carefully online, and arrived at 8:00 A.M., when it opened, but she had forgotten to check the days, and it is closed all weekend. She feels like kicking the door in frustration, but she cannot do that to a historic building, and unfortunately, this policy eliminates most of the city of Old San Juan. She contents herself with kicking the sidewalk, instead, and her foot begins to bleed.

She turns back and limps through the large orange courtyard of the Museum of Art and History of San Juan, which, to Elena's surprise, now houses a weekend farmers market. The museum is one of several very large buildings in San Juan that, once inside, reveal themselves to be at least half courtyard. She stops, her foot throbbing, and looks around at the market. Signs in English and Spanish hanging from the lampposts tell her that this was the traditional market area of the city, and now, with this farmers market, it is that again. Another sign encourages her to buy, support local farmers deeply affected by Maria. Elena sees people with dreadlocks selling vegan empanadas and a red-faced white woman standing behind a stall as a burnished tan man hands her little bags of soft white cheese and beautifully vivid peppers to arrange. A florist shows off ginger blossoms and birds-of-paradise while a wizened woman arranges soaps just so next to a young male duo dusting excess flour off their loaves of bread. It looks like Saturday in Brooklyn, a little bit.

Elena walks out, down Calle Mercado, a street whose name has become a truth again, and onto San Sebastián, where she stops for a coffee, saying nothing but please and thank you to the friendly barista, who clearly wants to know more about her. Elena pretends she doesn't understand, and sips her drink. She is stalling. She cannot fill her time with errands and clouds of dust forever.

Gloria's luncheonette is a small place just south of Elena's father's house, on Calle Tanca. By foot, for there is no other way to get there, it is less than ten minutes from where Elena sits and drinks coffee, to Gloria's, but Elena's feet are leaden, and besides, she takes the long way around, tripling the distance for no reason at all, rehearsing what she will say, how she will apologize for not seeing Gloria in years, how she will cover up the sticky shame of her family, her father, as best as possible.

She walks beyond Tanca. Her brain is aching with her own bitterness, with the anger she keeps pushing down, and she's going to need another round. She stops. If she keeps walking, she will circle the city, over and over again, until Gloria closes for the day, until Elena has avoided her by default for a second day in a row. Insanity, she knows, is doing the same thing over and over again and expecting a different result. She turns back, and sees the luncheonette, its sign proudly telling customers to *Come get fat at Gloria's,* and she walks toward it.

The place is a little greasy spoon, a residential apartment that Gloria has converted, quite illegally, into her kitchen, where she seats one or two customers, but mostly packs them lunch. The menu, hanging on the side of the door, is a lie. Gloria cooks whatever it is she wants to cook that day, two, maybe three options, and you can take them or leave them. They are always excellent, always better than whatever you might have wanted to order, anyway, and the islanders have learned by now to trust her taste.

Elena stands in the doorway, the smell of this grease so well-known to her that she feels tears forming in her eyes. Grease is grease, but this grease is chicken fat and garlic and cilantro and canola oil and onion skins, this grease is one she never smells in New York or Philadelphia or anywhere else but here. It makes her feel like a child again, the way her parents would bring her here and her grandfather's wife would cook dish after dish soaked in these flavors. Elena would eat and eat while her father drank nervously with his father, and her mother counted down the minutes until they could leave. Puerto Rico was like paradise to her, then.

"We not open yet!" a voice, warm, with a West Indian accent undimmed by years in Puerto Rico, calls out from the back—a lie, the doors are wide open, the lights are on. Elena sees a plump shape moving and then Gloria enters her field of vision. Soft, toffee-brown skin stretches over a small full figure, a modern Venus of Villendorf, with slicked-back kinky hair, shining with oil, whose red-rimmed brown eyes squint, then widen, when they see Elena, taking her in. Elena is suddenly self-conscious. Has she changed? Everyone does, of course, but is it bad? Elena doesn't think, tries not to think, thinks constantly, about her appearance and what the world sees when it looks at her, both from an aesthetic perspective, *am I passable, decently sized, hiding it if I'm not, how do my face, hair, stomach, arms, eyebrows, knees look today?* and also from an identity perspective, *do I seem empathetic, reasonable, permeable, professional, knowledgeable, valuable, weak, cool?* These question buzz through Elena's mind when she meets prospective tenants, or talks to contractors, or buys a cup of coffee. Elena once tried to describe just a piece of this to Daniel and he laughed at her, declaring it must be exhausting inside her head. Elena did not know that other people were not exhausted by themselves until that moment.

"Elenita! Can't be you. Girl, it's you?" Gloria breathes, her hand at her heart, and then reaches out for Elena. Elena nods, bashfully, as Gloria pulls her in for a hug, warm, panting from the exertion of moving from the kitchen out into the dining area. Elena, who is short, towers over Gloria, and as she embraces her she bends her head down to dig it into Gloria's shoulder, smelling coconut oil and that *grease* and more onions on top of that and oregano, and *culantro,* which is not cilantro, but something totally different, a long spiky leaf she has never seen anywhere but here. She breathes deep.

"Look at you!" Gloria exclaims. Elena tries to smile.

"How are you, Gloria? Are you well?" Two small frail questions to encompass all that has happened in ten years, all that has happened in the last few terrible months. But Gloria nods, smiling, as kind as ever, as philosophical as can be. Gloria is like the oil she cooks with, everything slides off her. Elena has never seen her truly worried, or upset, or perhaps Gloria just does not express those things the way other people do. As long as Elena has known her she has delivered all information in the same calm rich voice, from the death of a loved one to the weather report.

"A little bit of heart problems, but I'm doing good. My daughter brings me medicine from Louisiana when she comes with my grandbaby. You know about Maria?" Gloria asks, sitting Elena down in a plastic chair and taking a seat herself, her legs sticking out like a doll's. Elena nods, and Gloria proceeds to tell her the saga of the storm as she lived it, the days without power, the whoop that went up when the generators started kicking back in in San Juan; the people she knows who were on other islands, other parts of Puerto Rico; the pain, the deep acts of kindness, the stupid acts of evil. Gloria tells the story without drama, heat, or excitement, and there is something strangely soothing about how even she is, how all things are equal in her eyes.

"It's been real hard. But they came with these boats, I got a free physical. They tell me I gotta lose weight. Now, who gonna trust a skinny chef, you tell me?" Gloria concludes, panting from her monologue, her eyes indignant, her first real spark of emotion coming from the insult. Elena smiles and nods.

"You tell me about you. It's been so long, I almost didn't recognize you. Your father, he come in here, he talks about you all the time but never any good stuff. Just your job, you go to grad school, he say, but he never has the good stuff. Tell me, you got any kids now?" Gloria's hand sweeps across Elena's stomach like she's reaching inside for the children already. Elena blushes, and shakes her head, holding up her ringless hand. "Girl, you don't need a husband to have a baby!" Gloria reminds her. She would know, she had several with different partners over the years, all without a ring on her finger. Elena ducks her head, smiling. Gloria's face sobers. "I was sorry about your parents. Your mom a real good lady. Your father lost without her." Elena winces. *Lost.* That's what she is here to talk about.

"Actually, Gloria, about my father—"

"He been missing!" Gloria said, like a revelation, like Elena hadn't up and left her life in New York for that very reason. "He comes in here regular, twice a week, three times, I give him extra, he don't eat, that man, and then what cushions his stomach against all that rum, I ask?"

Elena has heard the expression *full-body blush* but has never experienced it until now. Her father has always been so careful about people knowing about his drinking, people thinking a certain way about him. Elena has never told anyone much about her father, about his problems, not even Daniel, especially not Daniel, she gave him such an edited version of things. She has never heard someone say this except her mother, both of them keeping this strange covenant with her father even now. To hear it spoken of openly shocks Elena to her core.

"Not like he listen. Sometimes he goes off, but he always tell me, so this time, when I don't see him, two, three weeks I don't see him, I know something is wrong. I laugh, that man survive the hurricane like nothing, sitting on his roof getting soaked, not even a cold, electrical pole could've fall on him, killed him, hit that house of his, nothing. Then he just go off, just like that? Ridiculous. I tell your mom how he is every few weeks, months, anyway, so I call her this time, telling her he gone. Where he gonna go? Everything is a mess here. Crazy man."

Elena couldn't disagree, on any count. She had no idea that Gloria had been updating her mother all this time. Another thing to store inside her anger box, another thing Rosalind has been keeping from her. But she does not have time to focus on that now.

"Actually, Gloria, that's why I came. After you talked to my mom, she wanted me to come down here and maybe see if I could, um . . . find him. My dad." As she tells Gloria, it sounds so stupid. Find him? A grown man? He's not a puppy, an umbrella, a set of keys. If he wants to be lost, he can be lost, can't he? But Gloria is nodding, sagely.

"That's a good idea. Your father. Well, you know, he a good man." Gloria continues to nod as she talks, her face shaking vigorously. Elena cannot honestly say that she does know that. She does not think her father is a *bad* man. He is someone who does not think of others, someone who does not remember his promises, but is that morally wrong, or simply destructive, of himself, most of all? Is he good? Looking around his house here, filled with things she has never seen, things like that rosary with places she has never known were a part of him printed on it, she is surer than ever that she does not know much about her father at all.

"But he's not right. He's not there anymore. I mean, he never all totally, I mean, you know your father! So crazy!" Gloria says, laughing broadly. Elena nods, easier than the truth, *coward again, always a coward*. "He the life of the party, he always have a joke, two, three if you're not lucky! He love life, I know that. But lately. Last couple years I been noticing, he forgetting things, he letting himself go sometimes, he not what he used to be. I don't know, some kinda problem, maybe. Maybe some health issue. He couldn't come down to the boats like I did, too busy, I guess," Gloria says, kindly, glossing over all the things Elena is sure she must have seen, or understood: the years of alcohol consumption; the medication for his manic-depression that he took more and more absentmindedly, in public, despite his previous, lost, iron-clad discretion; the mania, the energy that comes with an upswing, when he talks and talks and barely makes sense.

Maybe some health issue.

"So I worry about him. He's fine, I'm sure he's fine, I'm probably just being crazy, too, but when I tell your mom I not seen him for a while, well, I just feel like someone should know. And I'm glad you come. Of course, he probably gonna come back tomorrow and laugh at us. He just like that. But still, good you're here. Haven't seen you in so long, too, Elenita. What happened, you don't miss me?" Gloria asks, playful, swinging her body up off the chair and gesturing for Elena to follow her, like she used to when Elena was a little girl, when she was shorter than Gloria, even. Elena's heart hurts at the idea, even in jest, that she didn't miss Gloria, didn't miss *this place*.

"Of course I did. Just . . . busy."

"I know! College, graduate school, your father say you study some kind of history, he so proud of you. He show me photos from your graduation, when you move to New York, you travels, everything." Gloria smiled. "You go all over but you don't come here!"

Elena smiled too, unable to deny the truth of this. She went everywhere, but not here. How had her father gotten photos of her?

She herself dutifully sent him a photo or two in emails, sporadically, but nothing substantive, and nothing from her everyday life. Had her mother sent them? But she and her father never spoke, did they? *More things they don't tell me, more things they hide.* The wall of silence between Elena and her parents was thickening by the hour.

"Tell me about the last time you saw him, Gloria," Elena asks, watching the chef work. Gloria rinses the rice, so much rice, which she will cook to accompany all of the meals she will dish out today.

"I'm doing chicken curry today," Gloria announces, instead of responding to Elena. "Pork chops, fried, and a steak with onions. What you want?"

"The chicken, please. Do you have plantains?" Gloria smiles. She serves her customers sweet bananas, fried—*dulces*—but Elena has never liked those. She likes tostones, crisp, a dull marigold color, with salt clinging to them.

"For you I'll make. Sit. Let me remember." Elena sits as Gloria pulls out raw chicken and carefully cuts it up, attacking the joints, then making small cuts in the thighs, drumsticks, breast, just along the surface of the meat. Elena watches her knife slide easily into the dead pink flesh. Each piece, as she finishes it, she throws into a bowl, the sound of flesh hitting metal and more flesh a *thwack thwack* in the empty place. For as long as Elena has known Gloria she has never had any help, never another chef. How long can she do this, Elena wonders, and doesn't it exhaust her, to stand, bent over a dead bird, and slice its surface time and again?

"Makes it more tender. Let's the curry in," Gloria explains. Elena nods. Cutting things open lets the outside in. It makes sense. "I saw him on a Tuesday. No, Monday. That's when this place is closed, so I was sitting outside, resting." Gloria acts as a de facto mayor of the block-cumneighborhood watch. More than once, in the past, she told Elena stories of scaring off young graffiti artists about to deface nearby walls, directing clueless German tourists back to their cruise ships, and chatting with celebrities shooting movies in San Juan's picturesque streets.

"How long ago?" Elena asks, taking out a notebook. She should be recording this, her father's movements, Gloria's curry recipe, everything. She has not been to the island in years, who knows when she will come back again after she finds her father, if she finds her father, if the house is hers or will never be hers. She should record it all. It is living history.

"Three weeks. What's today, Saturday? Three weeks and five days. I call your mama on Monday because I think, I don't see Santiago all this time, that's not normal. Even after the storm I see him every other day, every three days, like that." Gloria reaches up to grab a large plastic container labeled *Jamaican Curry Powder: For Goat and Other Meat*. Elena stands to help her, but Gloria has her own system, hopping gently to grab the yellow spice mix, and landing gently back on the tiled floor, slippery with cooking oil. Gloria doesn't even waver, her balance is kitchen adjusted. Watching her here, Elena sees an artist at work, a jewel in its setting. Gloria fits in her kitchen, moving through it gracefully, perfectly. Rosalind is a ceramic artist, and she is like this in her own studio, assured, aware, unself-conscious. Elena feels that if you can see people in the place they know the best, feel the best, it is like seeing a part of them, the line between person and space blurry. *What in my life is like that,* she wonders, *the office?* She knows this is not true. *My apartment?* This is not true either. If she never finds a place like this, will she be a whole and happy person? *Are you either of those things now?*

Where is my father those things? Has he ever been either? a new, sad voice in her head asks her mournfully.

"That Monday when I seen him, he was not, eh, he had started early." Gloria is coating the chicken in curry powder, shaking her head slightly, delicate in her description.

"He was drunk," Elena says, flatly. Gloria looks up at Elena, and nods, shrugging. This doesn't affect Gloria, she doesn't see the problem, but why should she? It's not her problem.

"He stopped over here. He wanted pork chops, but I closed on Monday, so he told me he was going to Mallorca." Here Gloria snorts, dismissing, with the honk of her nasal passages, Cafetería Mallorca, one of her rival lunch options, near the Plaza de la Barandilla.

"Did he say anything else?" Elena asks, feeling a rising sense of panic. If this was all the information there was, well . . . but she couldn't think like this, she had told herself she couldn't.

"He say he missing his mother," Gloria says, drizzling oil over the chicken and setting it aside. She picks up two large Spanish onions and begins cleaning them, preparing to dice them. "He wants to visit her. He think she lonely. I tell him he should. My mama been dead nineteen years." Here Gloria wipes away a tear as she dices, and Elena does not know, is it the sadness or the onions, should she say she is sorry or pretend she didn't see?

"Damn onions," Gloria says. "Sometimes you get one that attack your face, you know?" Elena laughs, the sound a nervous eruption more than true humor. "He say he might go visit her. I ask him where she be." Gloria soldiers on with the onions, tears running down her face. "He tell me she move back from her hometown. Nice life. I gonna do that someday."

"The neighborhood will revolt," Elena says, lightly, as her mind races. Her father's mother is dead. She died when Elena was a baby. That was what Elena thought, had always heard. Would her father have lied about this, keep his mother a secret somewhere? Or has his mind corroded this much, imagining his mother is still alive, that she had moved back here instead of what Elena has thought was true, that her body was returned to the island after her passing. Could his brain have already degraded that much? He had been at the top of his class at Yale Law School. A prodigy, a brilliant man. If not for the sin of being Puerto Rican in the eighties, he would have gone into politics. As it was, his victories for his clients had been what allowed him to retire early, allowed him to come down here, while still paying Rosalind alimony. Elena has always thought her father is the smartest person she has ever met. Now she wonders, *Is his mind going, or has he lied to me all my life? Which would be better?*

She writes both possibilities down, her hand shaking slightly.

"Then he say he got some friend in Rincón he want to see, too. I say, you make up your mind, man!" Gloria laughs then, at her own wit. She has finished the onions now, and she walks over to the sink to wash her hands, stretching her back with her wet fingers pushing just above her buttocks. "My friend teach me this stretch. You ever try it? Opens up the heart." Gloria puffs up her substantial bust as she leans her head back, her hands imprinting her shirt with water. Elena stands, and tries, but her heart is pounding too hard to be stretched. Where is her grandmother's hometown? Has he gone there, or Rincón? Rincón is famous for its surfing, something her father has never done in his life, at least, not to her knowledge, limited as it is. Would he go there? Or some other place entirely? What friend does he even have in Rincón? Is that Diego? She tries to remember the map.

"He say he will. He just gotta think it through. I tell him fill his stomach, even if it not as good as my cooking, and whatever he do, be safe, the storm make a lotta these roads dangerous. He nods, he tells me he probably won't go anywhere at all, and he goes on down the plaza. And then I don't see him, a few days, even arroz con pollo day, and that strange because he always like that. Fridays I make it. You come back then, I put some aside for you."

Elena nods, absently. Gloria is cutting peppers now, fat red ones and long skinny buttercup-yellow ones, and little crimson ones that look like rose heads.

"But when he don't show up for a week, I think, what happened?

So when I talk to your mama, I tell her I not seen him. Usually I see him pretty often. Still, he gets funny sometimes, he go to Bayamon, see his sister, the good one. Which one is she?"

"Maria," Elena admits. Her other aunt, Beatriz, has been married three times already, most recently to a man half her age who she met in an ex-convict reform program at which she was teaching adult literacy. Beatriz is a warm, kind woman, with a specific ability to attract horrible people no matter where she goes and a terrifying loyalty to them that transcends logic or loyalty to her own family members. Anyone who comes near her ends up the poorer for it, a contributor to Beatriz's husband's empty pockets, no matter the husband. Maria, on the other hand, is easily driven to screaming, laughter, and tears, and has been married to the same man since she was twenty-two years old, Elena's infinitely patient uncle Javier, Javi. Maria sells Belleza Por Siempre, BPS, a Latin American Mary Kay—style product, and uses her twin daughters, Mercedes and Innocenta, as models for the brand. They are far younger than Elena, fourteen, and Elena winces whenever she sees them in full contouring makeup on Maria's Instagram page. Nevertheless, by virtue of Beatriz's track record, Maria is, indeed, the good sister.

"But then after two weeks, Maria came by, asking about him," Gloria says, reaching up, another little hop, for a medium-size heavy pan. She sets it on the stove, swirling oil onto its dark cast-iron bottom, and then throws the chopped onions and a spoonful of something from a jar into the pan. The jar, when she sets it down, says *paté de ajo,* "garlic paste."

"Tía Maria came here?" Elena asks, writing it down, the pencil trembling in her grasp. Gloria had not told her mother about this on the phone, perhaps she didn't want to worry Rosalind. And it would have, deeply.

For most of his life, her father has financially supported his family in one way or another. He has been their protector, their benefactor. The idea that they, now, would be worried about him meant something might be actually, well, wrong. He had sent money to her uncle Juanito to study to be an electrician, and helped Beatriz find a teaching course in Miami. He had supported Maria in her initial steps into BPS; although she had repaid his investment in full, the only one of his siblings to do so, Rosalind had fumed to Elena. Elena doesn't know if that is still true. Like her father, she has not seen her aunts and uncles in a long time, other than digitally. The last she heard about her uncle Jorge, the second youngest of her father's siblings, he was trying to be a bodybuilder in Tampa, something else her father had funded for his family.

"She was looking for your father. He tell her he maybe going to see his friend in Rincón, but she don't know if he did it or not. So I figure, so many people don't know where he be, your mama might. But she don't know either."

"Did Maria tell you their name, this friend? Where they lived? Anything?"

"Sorry, baby. No. Your father, he tell her he'll be back soon. But when she try calling back, the phone is off. And when she come here, Monday maybe, I still not seen him. So that's when I think, I should call your mama. We talk every so often anyway, she probably wanna know if he gone somewhere. And maybe she know where he is."

Elena fights the urge to laugh, bitterly. Her mother does not know where her father is. It causes her mother a great deal of pain that she still *cares* where Santiago is. But love is not something you can turn off just because you don't want it to exist anymore. Rosalind, like Elena, does not get to decide how she feels, only how she will act.

Gloria shrugs. Worry is not something Gloria concerns herself with. Things will be, or they will not be, and she knows she can do little to change anything. Except her food—that she controls like a general. Elena watches her cook for a long moment, thinking.

"Okay," Elena says. She should, she knows, venture to Bayamon tomorrow, or the next day, to ask Maria a bit more about where he might be, and if they know this friend in Rincón, and if that's Diego or not, and who the fuck Diego *is*. And perhaps they will know something more, too, something Gloria doesn't, like where her father's mother's hometown is. Anything to explain his sudden disappearance, anything to explain *him*.

"Thank you, Gloria," Elena says.

"Maybe something happen. You never know," Gloria says, wisely and meaninglessly. Elena nods. "He come back soon. He not gonna miss you visiting!"

"I'm sure," Elena says, not sure at all.

"Good to see you, Elenita. You looking healthy. You come back for the chicken, should be one hour, maybe two." Elena knows this means more like three, or even four. It can be her dinner just as easily as her lunch, she supposes.

Gloria has stirred and stirred the onions and garlic paste, and added more curry powder, more oil, water. She tips the chicken into the pan, curry meeting curry, oil meeting oil. The bubbling pan sends up sprays of liquid, coating Gloria's round, sweet, smiling face. Elena smiles back, her heart heavy. She hugs Gloria, now fragrant with curry and sweat, and leaves her to her cooking.

The sun is high now, at the hottest part of the day. Elena thinks of the house, all she must do, what clues might live in it about this friend in Rincón, or showing her where her grandmother is from, or illuminating a path in some other direction, to another country, maybe, to a new woman in her father's life, to something. The sheer unknowns, the weight of her task, flatten her heart, and she has to pause, to force herself to breathe. Rage fills her so deeply that her stomach hurts. Why does she have to do this? Chase her father down like a fugitive? The unfairness of her task will break her back.

An hour later, she is in the ocean.

Her father had told her once, in a rare lucid moment during a typical, delirious conversation on the phone, in between nonsensical advice on buying fruit and a description of the book he was reading about Cornelius Vanderbilt, that the city of San Juan had recently constructed a set of steps near the large statue of San Juan Bautista across from the capitol building, a twelve-minute walk from their home, that led to a beach. He told her that he only went to this beach now—so close to his home, so quiet because few people knew about the steps, discreetly tucked into the side of the road—rather than walking for thirty minutes, or walking down to the bus station across from the Sheraton Old San Juan to take a bus, to Escambrón, which had been the closest beach they could access for the entire time she had been coming to the island.

She had followed the directions he had given her, still clear in her mind although the conversation had been years ago. She had walked past San Cristóbal fort, flags fluttering in the wind at its parapets, and past the statue of San Juan Bautista, large and bluntly fashioned and stern, *what did it have to be so stern about, it showed the saint before beheading, after all,* and down the steps, thinking, *What if he is on the beach? What if I go down and there he is, like he's been waiting for me, like when I was little and we two would love the water, float in it for hours, stay all day even as Rosalind turned in, even as the sun set?*

He is not there. Of course he is not. He's never anywhere she hopes he might be. She does not know if she wants to see him, or never wants to see him again.

Before she can think much about it, her clothing is gone, the simple dress she had slid over her swimsuit when she had gone to the house to change now on the ground, with her bag, a tote containing keys, her phone, a book, sunscreen, water, nothing else, she will dry off in the sun, and she is walking toward the clear, impossibly blue, teal, turquoise, navy water. Its color depends on its depth and the sun and sometimes it is every shade of blue Elena can think of, but today it is a cool perfect teal and she wants to be in it more than her next breath.

When she reaches the line of the tide it is also impossibly warm, like bathwater. It will cool as she walks out, although she cannot go that far out, this beach, she can see, is shielded by a natural seawall, a line of rock formations some hundred yards from the shore. As the ocean hits her calves, her knees, her thighs, she can feel it leeching the tension from her body, pulling her pain out of her pores. She can never be unhappy in the ocean. Never divided, panicked, sick with fear, angry, tired, defeated. That is for the land. Here, she simply is.

She looks down, and can see straight through to the sand, her skin tinted slightly blue, slightly green, like sea glass. She holds her body under the waves for a long moment, feeling the sea, feeling that she is home in a way that she cannot describe, does not know if she likes, for it breaks her heart that this, here, is home, and she has been lost to it for so long. She breathes out, watching the bubbles trill from her mouth, watches small silver fish dart around her feet, curious and brave, and imagines what it would be like if she could live down here, where it is quiet, where nothing can touch her. She did not want to be a mermaid as a child. She wanted to be a fish, an anemone, a piece of seagrass, swaying with the movement of the water. She wanted to be allowed to *be* here forever. Her lungs begin to burn.

She emerges, sputtering, her hair streaming. If it weren't for oxygen, she would have stayed, she knows. She looks out at the shore, a thin strip, a curve on one side, the side closer to the fort, and on the other, far in the distance, a wrecked building, only skeletal stone remains standing, half in water, half on the shore. She is alone. If she were alone on a street in New York she would be terrified. Here, it is bliss. She knows there is violence on the island, as there is everywhere. But somehow it seems far from her, in this moment. In her solitude, the ocean making her buoyant, she feels free, and safe.

She closes her eyes, letting her body fall back and float, and sees him in her mind, standing on the shore, the way he was when she was young and her family was happy. He reaches out to her, calling for her, telling her it is time to come in, time to come home, her mother has dinner ready for them, enough time in the water, enough time in the sun. But she knows he is lying, she knows they both think there will never be enough time in the water for a lifetime, for two lifetimes, his and hers. She floats, still as a corpse, letting the water lap at her body. In her mind, her father is now in the water with her, coming to get her, to try to take her home, but she slips away from him, a young porpoise, out and out and out into the ocean, away from real things. She focuses on that image, the two of them, lost in the waves, forever, embedding the fantasy in her memory until it becomes a reality, a better one than the real one, where they went in for dinner and then, years later, he left her life in stages, and then all at once he is gone, and she is here and does not know how to find him ever again.

Her body hits something, a rock? But it is warm, and the rocks are cold. She opens her eyes and screams. She is not alone, at all. She straightens, disoriented, and finds that she has floated toward the shore, the water is a foot here, maybe less; when she sits a person, a male person, towers over her. She stands, her body crying out for the weightless feeling of water; it is all back now, all that she feels, all that she hates about herself, and stronger for having been banished.

"*Estás bien?*" he says. He is taller than she is, but not by much, and his skin is warm and tan and olive toned. He is not wearing a shirt, and she can see he has a tattoo of a tree on the left side of his breast, above his heart, a beautiful palm, it is precise and clear, like a botanical illustration. His stomach is soft but not fat, and his swim trunks hang on his hips. Looking in his face, she sees he wears glasses, and has brown eyes with wrinkles around the corners, not many, he is not much older than she is, perhaps. She realizes, with a jolt, that he is attractive, not that she desires him, but just that he is, in fact, a decently handsome person, and she has floated into him, and there is something about that that embarrasses her, even though she knows it should not matter.

"*Sí.* Yes. I'm fine. Sorry about that. *Lo siento,*" Elena says, flustered.

"No problem," he says, his English accented but only slightly, around the vowel sounds. Elena has met people on the island, even in her own family, who do not speak English, but rarely in San Juan, and rarely anyone her own age. She is torn between relief that her faulty Spanish will not betray her, and disappointment; it is nice to practice, nice to try. She is not good with languages, yet Spanish tastes good in her mouth, like chewing meat, it tests her jaw muscles, and she feels that she has gotten stronger when she does it.

"You're all right?" he asks again, in English, and Elena wonders what in her face makes it clear she is not.

"Of course. Just floating."

"You looked dead," he says, bluntly.

"Well. I'm not," she replies, clearly. He looks at her, and she fights the urge to cover her body, to protect herself. He has light brown eyes and they feel like X-rays on her skin. "I'm Elena," she says, holding out her hand, to break his gaze, to break the tension that should not be there and somehow is.

"Fernando Rivera," he says, taking her hand lightly, like it might break, and then giving it back to her. "How long are you visiting? First time?"

"No, I—my father lives here," Elena says. Fernando's expression changes, from tour guide mode, host mode, to normal person.

"He's from here?" Fernando asks. Elena nods. "You live where?"

"New York," Elena admits.

"My cousin lives there. I've been there," Fernando says, without enthusiasm or censure, entirely neutral about what many call the greatest city on earth, although Elena doesn't think it is. She never has. She wonders if her father liked living there, he never said one way or another. *He never said a lot of things,* she thinks, rage flaring again. *Who the fuck is Diego?*

"Do you live in San Juan?" Elena asks, because Fernando now knows where she lives, she wants it to be even. He nods.

"You come here a lot?" he asks, still holding her gaze. She nods.

"But it's been a while."

"Before the storm?" Fernando says.

"Years before."

"This island has two periods now. Before Maria and after Maria," Fernando informs her.

"B.M. and A.M.," Elena says.

"Yes," Fernando responds, gravely. Elena does not know what to say. She decides to ask a question, one she could ask the internet, but he is here, in front of her, a person, what a novelty, to ask a human for information. Besides, so many of the sites about San Juan, about the island, hadn't been updated for months, years. Google is no match for islanders.

"Do you happen to know if the ferry to Bayamon is operational?" There are two ways to get to Bayamon: by car, the long way around, or straight across the bay, the quicker way. Ferry trips, however, at least the ones of her childhood, would often come with an extra hour or two of waiting for Santiago's family to pick them up on the Bayamon side, hours her parents would spend fighting and Elena would spend reading or playing with the sweet sad stray dogs that curl up near the ferry terminal, hoping to be fed by passengers.

"Why do you want to go to Bayamon?" Fernando asks, and Elena considers not responding. She does not have to tell him, after all. He is a complete stranger.

"I have to visit some family," she says, offering no other details. He looks at her with a new look, again, each thing he learns about her changing his opinion of her, she can see, but not why, or what it is.

"I think it is. If not, we have Uber now. You can take a car. They could use the money." Elena stiffens. In other visits, long ago, islanders often made comments like this to her, assuming that as a nonresident she makes, and has, more money, even though the last times she was on the island she was in high school, college, and made no money at all. They are not wrong, perhaps, but she does not like it.

"Thank you. Okay, well, nice to meet you, then. Sorry, again," she says crisply, turning away from him, walking back to her bag, her clothing. She is done with her dip, she knows. She cannot sink back into the ocean with this man here, watching her, assessing her.

"You drink?" he calls out. She turns around.

"Yes," she says, simply, offering nothing else, he has had enough from her.

"I go to El Batey most nights. Maybe I'll see you there."

"Maybe." Elena smiles, to be polite, to help the conversation end, to be safe. She smiles for all the reasons women smile at men they do not know, to keep them calm, and happy, long enough for her to leave. She throws on her dress, feeling her suit soak through it, not caring. Soon she is up the steps, walking not too fast, not too slow, leaving the beach and Fernando and her own thoughts, her desire to hold her body underwater forever, her memories of her father as he once was—her friend, her protector, her home—behind her. There is only so much she can carry, after all.

Although part of her wants to, just to be near other people, she does not go to the bar that night. Instead, she works, and works, and works away at the house, poring over piles of junk, coughing through clouds of dust, and sipping from her glass of water and her glass of rum over ice alternately as she wades her way through her father's messy life. Has she been on the island less than two days? Can that even be possible? She feels a hundred years must have passed, at least, since she felt her plane hit the runway.

Perhaps this is because the objects in her father's home come from all over the world, and span decades in origin. There are resin bangles from the 1950s and copies of Mesoamerican pottery from the 1970s, and a shirt advertising Wharton Business School from the 1980s. There are books, so many books, from *The Count of Monte Cristo* to *What Color Is Your Parachute?*, from a thick hard-bound set of *The Rise and Fall of the Roman Empire* to a slim paperback with a bright magenta cover proudly declaring *History Will Absolve Me.* There are piles of clothing, ripped, stained, missing buttons or with broken zippers, as if their owner had meant to throw them out and then forgot they existed. Which well may have been what happened. Elena sorts these into "fixable," "worth giving away," and "worth cutting up for rags," something she can use to clean the house when she has made her way through it, if that ever happens. Hanging in the closet is more clothing, suits from Santiago's past life, a warm wool coat poked through with moth holes, a wedding gown. Elena fingers the torn lace around the neckline, feels the smooth satin of the bodice and the sweep of the skirt. This was not her mother's. Whose was it?

It is not until it is late, when she is contemplating sleep, for her body is tired and her brain is numb, that she finds the albums. By this point, she has removed five large trash bags from her room alone, filling the bin on the corner of the street from which garbage is collected daily. Other bags sit in the dusty foyer, ready to be taken to the junk shop on the corner or the recycled-goods store a few blocks away, two institutions that Elena fervently hopes have survived the storm.

The albums are tucked behind a large beach umbrella and an ice-cream maker. When had her father made ice cream? As far as Elena knows, he couldn't cook anything, let alone a multistep frozen treat.

She moves the ice-cream maker, planning on putting it into the trash pile, her sixth bag. When she does so, a stack of books leaning against it, ones she has not even noticed, slides down, falling with a dust-cloud *thwap*. The books are large, leather-bound, almost Victorian in their style, ornate, from a time when people thought books were something precious. She reaches for one, and hauls the heavy thing into her lap. Opening it, she realizes, it is not a book, it is an album, and flipping the pages, fast, she sees yellowed photos of a baby, held by a woman with a sweet face and dark wavy hair pinned into the styles of the late 1940s and early 1950s. Next to them stands a small man with a large mustache who reminds Elena of her own father, despite the fact that he looks nothing like him. It is something in the smile, some nervous aspect, some hesitation, like smiling is an act that he isn't sure he is doing right.

Elena looks up, around the mess of the room that she has had to tear apart to start putting together again, the chaos around her. She gathers up the albums, five in all, and hauls them up the stairs, up up up to the roof. She climbs back down again, retrieving the glasses, and giving herself refills. Ice bobs in both glasses, and clinks as she ascends to the roof, the only sound in the house, other than the chirp of coqui, which permeates the city.

She sits down the rum and the water, places her chair directly under the roof light, and opens the album, the first she had found. She opens the next, and the next, searching the outfits and eyeglasses to tell the decade, to order the collection in time. The third album has photos of her mother in it, her hair long, ironed flat like Cher's, looking at a college-age Santiago with stars in her eyes. The fourth is deep in the 1970s, and the fifth, the last one, is in the 1980s. Elena wants to thumb through that one the most, wants to catch sight of herself, to see her parents with her, as she will never see them again. But she has restraint, and besides, she has seen photos from her childhood. She has never seen any from her father's.

As she was growing up, it was like her father had sprung, fully formed, like Athena, from the head of his own father, another person Elena knew little of beyond her childhood memories and her mother's opinions. When asked about his childhood, his life before he met Rosalind, Santiago would change the subject or make a joke, telling her that he *had* no life before Rosalind, that she had invented him, like Pygmalion. Elena, who had been going through her Greek myth phase at the time, had giggled at the thought. He refused to talk about it, referring to it the way prisoners talk about prison, as both a physical place and a time period. What mattered was that he was never going back *there*. The *there* was unclear, and the more she wanted to know, the angrier he would become. By the time Elena was a freshman in college, there was so much that made her father angry, lost as he was in a yearlong manic state and freely drinking, that she made a decision not to ask, not to push. Someday he would tell her, when she was grown-up, and understood it. But he never had, and she did not know where he was, or how to find him, or what she would say to him if she did. Still, she had *this*, these. There could be answers in these albums. Wasn't a picture worth a thousand words?

She opens the first one again, the solemn baby, the man with her father's nervous smile on his face, the pretty woman. She must have moved, perhaps it was a long exposure, for her face has a vagueness, like she is out of focus. But as Elena turns the pages, she realizes, that is just her face. Photo after photo, of the woman standing over faded farmland in a slim skirt, her hair rolled into small victory rolls, of the woman on her wedding day, in the dress Elena had seen downstairs, *had her father kept his mother's wedding dress, how had it survived?* And her face is always the same, a little vague, like there is something missing.

Elena leans in, looking at the woman who must be her grandmother, a woman her father never talked about, ever, furious if she was brought up. A woman her mother once described, quietly, to Elena as insane, but only when Rosalind had been sure Santiago was out of the house. Esperanza Marin Vega. Elena knows her name, at least, that much had been acceptable to mention. Looking at her, Elena sees now what it is, what is off. No matter what, her eyes are somewhere else, seeing something out of frame, not looking at the viewer or her child or anyone around her. Some other place, somewhere only her burning eyes can see. For Esperanza's eyes burn with the fire of angels, enflamed at something only she can see.

Elena pages through the albums, one after another. There are so many strangers in the pages, photos that when she gently removes them to look at them closer, to look at their backs, she sees her father's Catholic schoolboy handwriting, beautiful and barely legible, informing her that this is *Tía Goli, Tío Luis, Rowdy, Abuelo Isadoro, Teofilia la Bruja* (the witch), *Irena, Carmen, Roberto,* and so many more names she has never heard, people that her father knows, is connected to, that she does not. As the photos grow closer, relatively, to the present, she sees her mother, friends of her parents from college, her mother's parents. She sees photos from her father's time in New Haven, Santiago standing next to another tan man, and she flips the photo over. *Me and Diego, 1974.* Diego, again. And if he knew him in law school, Rosalind must have, too. Pain flashes behind Elena's vision, numbed a little by the rum.

Another one is of her parents with the tan man and a white man, someone she has seen in other photos from Santiago's college days. *Neil and Diego, 1976.* There are other people in the photo, but her father has only noted those names. Who are these men? They occur more than almost anyone else, she notices, over and over again, from 1968 onward. And then they stop, in 1987, the year she was born. She can see her chubby baby face, her glowing mother, her proud father, but not these people, not anymore.

Why do I know nothing of the people who matter to my parents? she asks herself. She has never seen most of these photos in her entire life. Her father kept all of this tucked away, all these people in his life, in the back of a closet. She doesn't know who most of them are, what any of this means to him, and if this is a way to find him, by looking through the past he has always, *always* barred to her.

The next morning, Elena is on the ferry to Bayamon as the morning light pours in, strongly, making her eyes smart. In the bag next to her are a large set of heavy books, slapping against each other on the bumping bruising ride, which is somehow rough despite the fact that the water around them is entirely flat, it is a bay, after all, shielded from the waves. The bag slides on the metal floor, and Elena clutches at it, compulsively. It is a new discovery, and heavy as it is, she is bringing it to Bayamon to see if her aunt can shed light on what she has found.

What Elena knows about her father's past is this, and this only: Her grandparents moved from Puerto Rico, town, city, province, hamlet, unknown, not important. They got a divorce when her father was a child. Her grandfather remarried, and created her aunts and uncles. Her father was poor, and he went to college, and met Rosalind. Her grandmother died. Her grandfather and step-grandmother died. Nothing more, nothing less. She knows of no other family members, other than Santiago's siblings, and she has no other stories. She knows nothing about her father personally between his birth and college, where he met Rosalind. She knows little about college or law school, and all from Rosalind's perspective, never from his. She knows nothing about her grandmother at all. She knows what her grandfather told her about himself, that he loved pork and rice and beans, that he loved pool, that he loved the beach like she did. He died when she was fifteen, her step-grandmother soon after him, and her aunts and uncles tell stories of their childhoods, yes, but mostly what they talk about is their adult lives, and needs, the problems and the pains, money, always money, and how little of it there seems to be. She has never known if they, like her father, grow angry at the thought of being asked to excavate their histories. It was always clear to her that she should not ask.

But sitting on the ferry now, those *should's* burn away from her. What does any of it matter now? What do his desires matter to her, now that they have left her with nothing? She has spent her life avoiding the truth of her father because he demanded it. Fuck his demands. He has left her with so little. She will find the rest, find what he has hidden. She owes him nothing now.

She is a historian, she reminds herself. She will not avoid the past because it is *inconvenient*. All pasts are inconvenient, for they contradict the present. But they also explain it. Elena, looking out into the blue bay, thinks about the fact that all her life, she has accepted what she has been given. But now, if she cannot have what she needs from her parents, either of them, it is time to ask someone else for it. What Santiago wanted doesn't matter anymore. It is time for her to have what she wants.

Seven

On a rare clear day in July 1987, Santiago Vega Jr. took the first flight out of San Francisco in the morning, the first ticket he could get, as sober as Diego had hoped he would be, terrified and hollow with grief. By 5:00 P.M. that evening, he was walking into Rosalind's hospital room. She had delivered while he had been in the air, after fourteen hours of labor, and now she was sleeping, exhausted.

Next to his wife, wrapped in a pink blanket, lay their newborn baby, a daughter, he could see, pale pink swaddling her limbs. *A daughter.* It wasn't until that moment he realized how much he had been hoping, praying, that he have a girl and not a boy. How unprepared, horrified, he would have been to have someone who was a reflection of him.

Her tiny fists were squeezed tightly shut, like she was shaking them at someone in her dreams. He was a mess, reeking from sweat and liquor and stale from his flight, bone tired from his own pain, his sadness. But here she was, this new thing that belonged to him, this whole new person in the world. She had come early, desperate to be in the world, to take the place that Neil had left behind. How was this possible, to say goodbye to a piece of himself yesterday and to say hello to a piece of himself today?

She opened her eyes. Most babies' eyes were blue and cloudy, but hers were not. Even then they were large, and brown, and she looked at him, stretching out one of her little fists toward his face. He picked her up. She was so light, he could not believe it. *How do we become people when we start like this?* he wondered. *How do we ever get bigger?* She continued looking at him, her face so solemn. Rosalind had made him read books about babies, one of them had said they didn't know how to smile immediately, that they had to learn. He smiled at her, letting his teeth show. He had no idea how to be a father, but this, he knew, he could teach her. He had always been good at faking smiles.

They had agreed on "Elena," for a girl. It meant "bright one," and he can see that she will be bright, this baby, she will be brilliant, he can tell by the look in her beautiful eyes, bright as his mother's but without that flame, that madness.

"Elena," he said, softly, testing it out. This was who this was, Elena. His daughter.

He thought of all the ways his own life had hurt him, failed him, and all the ways it had been generous, what it had given him. Rosalind. His work. His education. Neil. Diego. And now Elena. The world was a new place for her, and he would make it good, and clean, and perfect. He would do what Neil would have done, he would be a better father, a better man, for her.

He had to. He did not know how, but he had to do it. In that moment, he could not imagine any other reality but that. He would will it into being, like he had willed his life into existence, like he had willed his mind to be sane, like he had willed his past away. Santiago Vega Jr. would not fail, of this he was absolutely sure.

You just have to put them first. That's all it is.
He was so sure he would not fail, this time.

Santiago Vega Jr. was drunk when his wife went into labor with
their only child, drunk and howling with grief in California. Across
the country Rosalind admitted herself, on her own, to the University of Philadelphia hospital, as inside of the birth canal Elena Vega
started moving, reluctantly, from the safety of the womb to the light
of the world. As his daughter prepared her body to experience pain
for the first time, the pain of birth, of being cold, of the long years
to come in which she would not be able to communicate what she
needed, Santiago's own pain, decades deep, was carving its way across
his heart.

When he got the call, he was not alone in his inebriation. He
sat, raising an empty glass to his mouth, uncaring, weeping, while
next to him Diego sat, head in hands. Grief muted both men, men
who talked for a living. They were at the hotel where Santiago was
staying in downtown San Francisco, at the bar, the better part of a
bottle of whiskey long gone, when the concierge interrupted them,
telling Santiago there was a call for him. It was Rosalind, breathing
hard, her contractions eight minutes apart.

Technically Neil had died a week ago, but Diego and Santiago
and everyone else who remembered Neil celebrated the anniversary
of his death on this day, the day they, along with scores and scores
of mourners, had scattered his ashes in Golden Gate Park, watching him blow away in the wind. Over the years, they would forget
Neil's real death date, and only remember this day. Diego, who had
been numb since the machines had beeped their last long beep,
since his love, his life, had gone gentle into that good night, since
that plague-marked body had released whatever the soul might be
and become flesh, ready to rot, did not remember the time between

that moment and the memorial. He must have done things, called people, slept, a little, but if he did it was lost to him, a wash.

Santiago took the call, his eyes on Diego, wondering what had happened to them both. Where had their past selves gone to? Who were these men looking out at him from the mirror behind the bar? He remembered the time they put ties on, for their law school mock trial at Yale, and Diego had laughed that it was choking him, that they were capitalist pigs in the disguise of rebels, that they would be the first ones killed, the betrayers of the revolution. Santiago had laughed, nervously, never as secure as Diego in privilege, never as comfortable putting himself with the bourgeoisie, he who had spent more than one New York winter without heat, sleeping in every item of clothing he owned. Now they both wore suits daily, and Diego had loosened his around his neck. Both of their necks were fatter, how had that happened? They had been skinny boys just the day before, hadn't they? Now they were real adults in suits, their jowls softening, their skin stretching. There were deep deep circles under each of their eyes and scant white hairs in Diego's stubble. Was his own hair thinning? Santiago wondered. But they were still young, weren't they? Ten years ago they both said they would be, should be, everyone should be, dead after thirty-five.

Now Neil was.

"It's happening, oh god, Santiago, where are you?" *Where are you?* He did not know how to answer that. Who was talking to him? He thought the voice was familiar but it was so strained with pain, who was that? "I'm having our baby!" she said, like something from a television show, or a movie. *Our baby.* Rosalind.

"Oh my god," Santiago said, his words slurring with panic and drink. There was an inhalation of breath on the line.

"Santiago." All the pain was gone, now, where had she put it? He could not put his pain away like his wife could, he could not cleanse his tone of emotion, he, the lawyer. She was the artist, she was supposed to be the emotional one, but she could wring her words dry of feeling in a way he had yet to manage. The woman was giving birth a country away from him, but she could still find a way to lecture him. "What are you doing right now? You need to go to the airport, and you need to buy a ticket, and you need to come home. Now."

"The memorial," was all he could think to say.

"Is over. I'm sorry, you know I'm so sorry. I hurt for you. For Diego. I loved Neil," she said. Santiago took a deep swallow, straight from the bottle, finally realizing his glass was empty.

"Fuck you," he said. And then he started crying. That in-drawn breath again, and a muffled scream, as Rosalind tried to contain her rage and let the pain of labor out at the same time.

"You have to come back now, Santiago. You have to have some coffee, and, and come back. Come be a father. Someone needs you now."

"Rosalind, I'm sorry."

"It's not just me now. *We* need you. I'm putting down this phone, and I'm going to give birth to your child, and if you do not come back now, you cannot come back, ever. Do you understand me?" Her last words were another scream, as a contraction pummeled through her body, and she dropped the phone, the connection lost.

Santiago stared at the receiver for a long moment, his vision blurring. Perhaps that was what he wanted. To never go back. To walk away from it all, the responsibility, the work, being a person. Being normal. It drained him. He was not built to be this way. What did he know about families, about people?

"Who was that?" Diego asked, face emerging from the cradle of his palms. It looked like a tragedy mask, something Santiago had seen an image of in one of Rosalind's art history books, a cartoonish face pulled into a pained sob forever.

"Rosalind. The baby is coming," Santiago said, softly. He did not want to make the words loud for fear that they would engulf Diego in more pain, shoving joy into the face of a mourning man. Besides, the idea of it was too much for him, Santiago, to bear, really. *Come be a father.* He had never wanted to be a father, never wanted to have children. He was terrified of this, of what waited for him. She had offered him an out, had she not? His brain was fogged and whirling and pained but she had said *if you do not come back now, you cannot come back, ever,* and that meant he *could* not go back, could he not?

Is that what you want? To be like him? a voice asked in his mind, breaking through the haze. He knew the *him* his brain meant, thought of his father's face. He reared back, violently, almost falling off the stool, but Diego caught him, a hand warm and congratulatory on his back, joy on the face of his friend, overlaying the tragedy mask with happiness.

"My friend. That is the most wonderful thing," Diego said, careful, formal, in Spanish. He spoke like a Puerto Rican aristocrat, which was almost what he was, the son of wealthy plantation owners from the island, as far from Santiago's own illiterate *jibarito* forebearers as one could be. In another age Santiago would have been Diego's servant, not his friend. But no one here knew that, everyone saw them as just the same. And now he was the richer one, Santiago, the one whose life was filling as Diego's was emptying.

"I'm sorry," Santiago said, wishing the words could mean more and bigger things. Wishing they could encapsulate the world. Diego looked surprised, his drooping eyelids opening wide.

"Why?"

"Because, because of Neil. Because this is something happy and we shouldn't feel this right now. Because I have to go, I can't stay, and I—"

"Neil would have loved this," Diego said, tears in his eyes. "Your child born on the day of his big gay memorial? He would have pretended to be offended, being upstaged like this, and said your kid was already a bitchy little queen, a diva, and that he never would forgive it, and in reality he would have been completely fucking delighted." Diego coughed, once, then twice, and it took a moment for Santiago to realize he was laughing, hard and into the bottom of his lungs. He smiled, weakly. "Don't tell me I have to comfort you," Diego said, flatly. "I'm the person who lost the love of his life. This works one way right now, okay?"

"Okay," Santiago said. Diego was right, of course he was. The blood was rushing in his ears and all he could think of was the panic, the panic, and the fact that Neil would never know Santiago's child, that his child would never know Neil, and what a fucked-up cosmic prank that was. What a joke all this was, this plague killing his friends, these people who thought it was for the best, this president who didn't care, this death robbing Neil of the future, this child who was right now pushing its way out of his wife's body into that future without Neil in it.

"Sometimes I think it should have been me," Diego said.

"How often is *sometimes*?" Santiago asked.

"Every fucking day," Diego said. He drank deeply. "You know, he laughed at me, the way I've always been so careful. In sex. Teased me that I couldn't get him pregnant, so why did I bother with rubbers? Told me it was all that Catholic education, the way I saw sex as unclean. Always needing it to be sterile, so the sin couldn't touch me as hard. And you know what? I wish I hadn't. I wish I was dying like he was."

Santiago couldn't breathe.

"Fuck you," he said. Diego looked at him. "Fuck you for wanting that. Fuck you for wanting to rob me of *two* friends instead of one."

"So I have to live without the love of my life so *you* can be fucking happy?"

"Yes, you fucking do," Santiago said, so angry. So scared. "You don't get to leave me, you asshole."

"You're the one leaving. You need to get on a plane. You're having a baby, idiot."

"I can't go," Santiago said. "I, I can't face it."

"You're telling me you are going to leave your pregnant wife, not meet your baby? That's what you're saying to me right now?"

Santiago nodded, and burst into tears. Diego watched him for a long moment, then handed him a napkin. He grabbed for the bottle and poured out the rest of it into two glasses, nudging one into Santiago's hand.

"Shut up and listen to me," he said, although lovingly. "You are being terrible right now and I will only forgive you because we won't remember this. This is to Neil, the world is lesser for his loss. This is to your baby, the world is better for her birth. You're going to drink that, and get on a plane, and hopefully by the time you get to Philadelphia you are going to be sober enough to take care of your wife, better than you've done for me. I'm going to drink this, and go to sleep, and tomorrow the world will be a terrible place, like it is today, and the next day, and the next, but maybe your baby will make it better, I don't know. Okay?"

"What if I can't do this?" Santiago asked, so quietly he could barely hear it himself.

"Then you'll give the drink to me."

"Be a father," Santiago muttered, sipping before Diego could take his whiskey. Diego shrugged.

"You'll figure it out."

"How?" Santiago asked, plaintively. How did someone be a good father? He had no idea.

"You just have to put them first. That's all it is. Putting your child first," Diego said. Santiago had watched him with his family earlier that day at the memorial. Unlike Neil's family, who had not spoken to Neil since college, Diego's family had come in droves to support Neil in his illness, and Diego. They sat with Diego, his father tall and broad, his mother small and soft, Diego's many sisters and brothers and nieces and nephews fluttering around them, translating the English into Spanish, holding him up as he faltered. How easy it was for Diego, to know that he was loved, to know how to love others, to care as he had been cared for.

In another life, Diego would have made an excellent father. Not like Santiago at all.

"That's all?" Santiago tried to smile. He had no idea how to do it. Rosalind did all the work with them. The only way he had survived his life so far was by putting himself at the center of everything. Diego held him close, kissing him gently on the forehead.

"That's all. And if you fuck it up, well, Neil's watching." Santiago laughed, surprised by the joke. Diego grinned, then wiped away the tears that had begun to flow again. He raised his glass, more tears pouring down his cheeks.

"If I have to keep living, then so do you. If that's our curse, if that's what he left behind, then I'm not doing it alone. You want to know something so stupid? He used to make me read him Neruda. In Spanish."

"He didn't speak Spanish."

"Like I don't fucking know that? Like we didn't talk about him to his face like it was some kind of stupid code? He made me read it to him. Poems. Said it was romantic. So fucking cliché, but I loved it. I never told him that. I complained every time. I pretended it was idiotic. But I loved it." Diego closed his eyes. "'When I die I want your hands on my eyes: / I want the light and the wheat of your be-loved hands / to pass their freshness over me one more time / to feel the smoothness that changed my destiny.' You remember that one?"

He did. He'd studied Neruda in college, he'd had to. He'd read the poems to Rosalind, who didn't even like poetry, but she'd loved Neruda's sonnets.

"Do you remember how it ends?" Diego asked.

Santiago shook his head. "How does it end?" He didn't think
Diego was asking about the poem. He was asking about love, really,
what happens when that ends? *Can it end? When the people who feel
it die, where does the feeling go?* God, he was drunk. Diego closed his
eyes again, his glass up in salute.

"'I want for what I love to go on living / and as for you I loved you
and sang you above everything, / for that, go on flowering, flowery
one, / so that you reach all that my love orders for you, / so that my
shadow passes through your hair, / so that they know by this the
reason for my song.'" He paused, and laughed. "Slick Chilean fucker.
You know he was also a senator? These South Americans really make
us look bad, eh, Santi?" He looked at Santiago. "Neil is gone. But if
we aren't allowed to follow him, then we have to go on."

"I don't know how," Santiago said.

"You will. If I have to, you have to. Right? One way or another.
We just have to. That's all it is."

Santiago put his arm around his friend, blessing the uncaring
bartender, and each man sipped his whiskey, tears ruining the vin-
tage. But inside, Santiago was crumbling away.

Rosalind had been pregnant once before, almost two years ago, back
in 1985. They had met young and been together for a long time, almost two decades, and he had hoped that it would continue, just the
two of them, for the rest of time, but she wanted a child, she was desperate for one. There had been so many compromises she had made
in that time, so many ways that Santiago had not been the man they
both thought he would be, that he did not know how to deny her
this, no matter how much it terrified him. And besides, perhaps they
would be one of those couples unable to have children. He agreed
to start trying, this hope in his mind, and she was pregnant within
three months. Terrified out of his mind, Santiago had dipped into

his emergency stash of whiskey, which he had promised, then, never to have again, never ever, he had promised Rosalind and Dr. Moretti and everyone, but it was medicinal, surely they would understand that. And then, drunker than he had been in a long time, his system no longer as used to alcohol as it had been, he had called Neil to tell him the "good news." But before he could say anything, Neil told him that he was dying.

"This is a terrible joke, Neil," Santiago said. But he didn't hear laughter, Neil breaking the moment, just silence.

"It really is, isn't it?" Neil said, sounding thoughtful, and exhausted. "Who knew fucking would have consequences? Fuck that free love. Now I've got the bill. I thought I could avoid complications with men, no messy pregnancies. Turns out this AIDS thing is real, no matter what Reagan says. Doesn't say. Can you believe it?"

"No. I can't. I don't. What . . . how did . . . I don't understand," Santiago stammered, his heart lead. "How long do you have?" *How could you not tell me this before?*

"I knew you would want to come out here." Neil answered the question Santiago hadn't asked. "You have Rosalind, work. I didn't want to fill your life with my tragedy." *You are my life,* Santiago thought. *You and Diego and Rosalind, that's it, you're my family.*

"How long?"

"They don't know. They tell me medicine isn't an exact science. But, Santi, if you were planning on coming out here, well. Better make it soon."

He was on a plane to Los Angeles the next day. Neil was a skeleton, and Diego was barely speaking to him, furious.

"What's happening?" Santiago asked, as they sat in Neil's garden, passing a joint back and forth.

"He's mad at me."

"Obviously. Why?"

"I wanted him to kill me. He said no. I don't know why he's got to make such a big deal out of it but that's him, I guess," Neil said, his voice weak but still him, as irritated by other people's idiocy as ever.

"Why are you always trying to kill yourself?" Santiago joked, and Neil smiled at the gallows humor.

"I wanted *him* to kill *me*. Totally different."

"How?"

"Poison. Like Socrates. Anything else is too messy. And I want an open casket, so all my queens can mourn the loss of my beauty."

"One of those queens gave you this thing," Santiago observed. Neil nodded, his face peaceful.

"I forgive them. It will take them, too, in time. I'm so glad I didn't give it to Diego. At least I didn't do that. That's the best thing I did, I think, not doing that. The best thing I did is the thing I didn't do. I wouldn't wish this on my worst enemy. I wouldn't wish this on *Nixon*."

"That's big of you." Santiago smiled. "Do you want me to do it? Kill you?" Neil looked at him, and shook his head.

"No. Diego would never forgive you. And he will need you when I'm gone. You might need him, too. I couldn't do that to you."

Santiago took Neil's hand in his own, and kissed it, tears blurring his eyes.

"I called my father," Neil said. Santiago reared back.

"Why?"

"I wanted to forgive him," Neil said, simply. "So I did."

"What did he—"

"Nothing," Neil said. "It wasn't for him. It was for me." Santiago shook his head.

"I could never do that."

Neil shrugged.

"You never know what you can do."

"Do you regret anything?" Santiago asked.

"I wish I had been a parent," Neil said. "Not that I would have wanted to undergo the process that entails, that sounds disgusting. Don't know how you straights do that shit. But I wish I could have had a kid. If only to be better than he was, my dad. To show him that I could. And to leave something behind. Something that says I was here. Now there will be nothing left of me when I go. I don't think I will care much, when I'm dead, but for now, it's a sad thought. If I had a kid, it would be a happy one. I could use that now."

They watched as the sun set, in silence, each thinking about their future, however much of it there would be.

He came home to the news that Rosalind had miscarried, and hated himself for the relief he felt. But by December 1986, she was pregnant again. She swelled with life as Neil withered. Santiago traveled to California as much as possible. He followed Dr. Moretti's medical regime, he stopped drinking. He was, unconsciously, bargaining, hoping that if he was good, and did the right things, Neil would live, he would be spared the plague.

But he wasn't. And Santiago knew that nothing he had done, would do, really mattered.

There was a freedom in that curse.

Eight

Elena's aunt Maria's home is one her cosmetics sales built, and it looks like a tropical Barbie Dreamhouse. It is pale mint, trimmed with pink, and its inside is full of gloss and chrome and marble and furniture, all violent teal and lavender dyed leather, heavy and strange. Nothing like what anyone should have in the Caribbean, but Maria compensates for the climate with constant air-conditioning, and Elena, sweaty from the walk from the car, a pink Cadillac that Maria won years ago for her strong sales, shivers.

Her aunt only kept her waiting for twenty-six minutes at the ferry terminal, so practically on time. She talks nonstop on the way back to her house, bright and bubbly, and Elena nods and smiles and supplies the words that Maria, despite her excellent English, sometimes loses in her enthusiasm for talking. Maria's new dog, Charo, a ratlike thing Elena has seen in a thousand Facebook photos since Maria got him after the storm from an animal rescue center, now runs around them both as Maria deposits Elena in the living room and turns to summon her daughters.

"Mercedes! Innocenta! *Tu prima,* your cousin, she's here!" Maria screams up the stairs, turning her already loud voice up several decibel levels. Elena winces but Charo doesn't react, clearly the little dog is used to it. Elena hears footsteps and then there they are, two burgeoning teenagers with more cosmetics on their faces right now than Elena may ever wear in her life. Their curls are gelled and pulled sharply back from their faces, their eyebrows neat perfect lines, their tan skins powdered and buffed and shined so that they are somehow both glowing and matte. They don't look like children, but like dolls, and Elena hugs them, gingerly, not wanting to smudge anything. They kiss her cheek, and she brushes her face afterward, but nothing has rubbed off on her. They smile uncertainly. They do not know each other well, she is a stranger they are related to, and it is Sunday, they probably have better things to do than talk to their weird grown-up cousin.

"Would you like something to drink?" one of them—Elena does not always know which name goes with which face, the two similar yet distinct, both through makeup and through nature—asks.

"Water?" Elena says, and they both nod, and disappear into what must be the kitchen.

This is a new house. When Elena was young, Maria and her family lived with her father, Elena's abuelo, on the top floor of his two-story house, cooking for him and caring for his home after Maria's mother died. Rosalind found this baffling, and made it clear that as far as she was concerned, her father-in-law could take care of *himself*, and she felt it was a waste of Maria's life to wait on the man. Maria, though, always protested that she was happy to look after him, and when he died she was inconsolable. Still, no one could argue that his passing was without benefit to her, it had freed her, and the house she had built on the land she had inherited from him was clear proof of her prosperous new life. His old house still stood nearby; they hadn't knocked it down. It turned out when he died that Elena's abuelo, Santiago Sr., a cheap old man, had been very careful with his pensions, both the one from his years as a mailman and his army funds, and he had bought the land next to his house in some strange plan to extend his garden, building himself a little suburban farm. He had never gotten around to it, and now that land was Maria's Technicolor mini-mansion, while his own home lingered, grubby and squat, next door.

So much of the island is like this, Elena thinks, *new and shiny next to decrepit and old.*

"What are you looking at, Charo?" Maria squeals to the dog, which is growling at the albums Elena placed on the coffee table.

"I brought something. I wanted your help, actually," Elena explains.

"*Mi ayuda?* Of course, *carina,* anything I can. You want some concealer for that?" Maria points to Elena's entire face. Elena smile-grimaces and shakes her head. "I got a good one. It blend right in, cover those dark circles."

"I haven't been sleeping well." This is a lie, she slept like the dead, her body lulled into unconsciousness by physical exhaustion, anxiety, and a glass from her father's bottle of rum. Charo noses the albums again, reminding Elena of the task at hand.

"My father is, um, missing." Elena admits the thing they already both know. Maria's face, which usually resembles that of an overly made-up Ewok, falls, becoming drawn and gray. She nods vigorously, relieved, Elena thinks, that she can drop the pretense that this is a normal trip.

"I talk to Gloria, she tell me she no see him!" When she is emotional, Maria's English verbs and tenses are the first thing to go. When her grandfather passed away, over a decade ago, in the days before her father's exile, Elena had come to the island for the funeral. Her father had spent it silently, rum soaked, unsteady, and dry-eyed. Maria, tearstained and wrecked, had repeated the same thing over and over again to Elena, her husband, everyone they knew, *he gone, he gone, what I do now he gone?* No one had had answers for her, least of all Elena's own father.

"I know. My mom is worried. That's why I came, actually." Maria's eyes widen comically large at Elena's words. The truth of her parents' divorce must be more visible than her father had thought, for Maria clearly knows what a big thing it is that her mother, a woman who has cut her husband out of her life as cleanly as an expert kidney surgery, is trying to find said husband. "I've been staying at the house, it's a mess, I don't know how long he's been gone. But I was trying to clean, because it's, well—"

"*Yo sé, yo sé!* I try to help him but he so stubborn, Junior. He not let anyone do anything. He say it all where he want it." Elena sighs internally at these words. Her father will be very angry at her when he finds out what she has done, how much she has thrown away. This thought spurs some anger of her own. *Don't fucking go missing if you don't want people to clean your house.*

"I found these, though. And I just, I thought maybe . . . he never talks about anything and I thought these might have some clues," Elena finishes weakly, realizing she sounds like an idiot. "I also found this." Elena pulls out the rosary, the one she found dedicated to Saint Sebastian, canonized because he survived a hail of arrows, a sagittation, a word Elena loves and would love to use someday, only to be clubbed to death. Elena knows a lot about the lives of saints for a Jewish girl, but who can resist such drama? Jewish prophets die in their sleep. Catholic saints die *everywhere.*

Maria takes the rosary and reads the words printed on it, smiling.

"How did he keep this? I got rid of mine when I joined our church." Now that she's calmer, Maria's verbs have returned. She and Javi joined a Pentecostal church before Elena was born, despite the disapproval of Maria's mother, Chavela, who died, as she lived, a Catholic. Elena's *abuelo* never said anything about it, but then, he rarely commented on religion, and he was buried in a military cemetery, anyway, picking the U.S. Army over any other god.

"This is from his First Communion," Maria explains, and Elena nods, not mentioning that she knows that part. "Back home." That part is less understandable to Elena. Aren't they home? Isn't Bayamon home, at least for Maria? Does Maria mean New York?

"What do you mean, home? Is this church around here, somewhere?"

"No, no, El Pepino," Maria says, almost absently. She is smiling at the rosary, and Elena wonders what it cost Maria to give up her own, what piece of herself she let go of when she changed from her own faith to the practice of her husband, Javi. Or maybe Maria herself instigated the change, Elena has never been sure. Trading one kind of Christianity for another baffles her, but she knows it is more complicated and difficult from the inside. Most things are.

"'The cucumber'?" Elena says, after a minute. She likes to cook, and she just went to the grocery story, so food words in Spanish are close to the top of her memory. Her father, who never cooks, rarely knows food words for anything, despite his perfect Spanish. One thing Elena does know, because a waiter at a Mexican restaurant asked her father about it once, is that her father ironed out his Spanish in college, like a starched shirt. He sounds now like someone from Spain, or Venezuela, or anywhere, really, his accent is without region, hiding his origins as neatly as a mask. He's like a newscaster, scrubbed clean of any markers of where he is from. His whole self is like that. Elena wonders how much of her father he has killed to be who he is now.

"That's another name for San Sebastián. It in the mountains." Maria looks a little off, her normally wide-open expression closing up. "It's where Papa and Mama were from."

This is news to Elena. There is a place, specifically, more than the island itself, that she is *from*? For if he is from this place then she, too, by extension, is from this place. A piece of her past, her unknown history, reaching out into the present. A place to be from.

"My grandmother, too?" Elena asks. Maria winces.

"I guess so." Maria, close as she was to her father, was never comfortable that her mother, Chavela, had not been his first love, his first choice.

"I thought everyone was from here," Elena says, looking around helplessly. Maria is already shaking her head.

"No. Little place. We live there when I was little, when *bisabuelo* was still alive." Her great-grandfather, a man Elena knows nothing about. "Then, when he pass, we moved here. Papa got a new route for the mails, and the schools were better. Mama liked this better; up there, it's like another century."

"Why did they get a divorce?" Elena asks. She has always wanted to know. Maria looks at her, her eyes hardening.

"Sometimes things don't work out," Maria says, and Elena wants to shake her.

"There must have been a reason. Abuelo just left my dad behind, why? Why didn't he have him move to the island?"

"He didn't leave him! He send money, he send the ticket for him to come every year. Papa no do that, he would never. He was such a good papa. It was his mother. *She* didn't want him around," Maria says, and Elena looks at her. Maria never wants to hear anything negative about Santiago Sr.

"Was there something wrong with her?" Elena asks. She thinks about the photo she found, the way the woman's eyes blazed.

"I don't know," Maria says, and Elena can tell that she is lying, she's bad at it.

"Well then, Abuelo just abandoned her and my father for no reason?" Elena knows this will incite a reaction. She just hopes it is one she can use.

"He didn't! He . . . he had to go. She wasn't good."

"Well, if she wasn't good, then why did Abuelo leave my father with her?" Elena asks, trapping Maria in her logic.

"No, she was. I mean, I never met her," Maria says, cagily. "But Papa wouldn't do something bad. She wanted to keep Junior, that's all I know. It wasn't Papa's fault."

Loyal to the end, Elena thinks. *The man's been dead for years, was drunk for most of the decades before, but his perfection shines forever.* Whatever Elena feels for her father, she has nothing but disdain for her grandfather. *Just like your mother,* she thinks to herself. Is she too influenced by the way Rosalind sees this world, these people? But they are all a blur to her, really, this lost generation she will never know because no one will *tell her anything.*

"Please, *tía,* just tell me something. I feel so stupid, I don't know enough, I don't know how to find him, I don't know anything *about him.* Tell me anything. Please?" Maria looks at her, biting her lip. "If you don't, I'll always think Abuelo just left my father," Elena says, a gentle threat. Maria sighs.

"She have problems. Lots of mental problems."

"But she looks so normal," Elena says. It's a stupid thing to say, she knows. What does the woman's face have to do with what is in her mind? Mental issues don't advertise themselves. But what does that mean, mental problems? Like what her father has?

"You see her?" Maria seems confused. Elena slides a photo out of the album sleeve, handing it to Maria. Maria looks at the woman, her burning eyes.

"She saw demons," Maria says, moving to cross herself and then thinking better of it. "Your father tell me once, we were very little. She saw demons all around her. She want to kill them, make them bleed."

"She was . . . what, did she have a disorder?"

"I think she spend some time in a facility. Papa help pay for it for a while, until your father could afford to do it. But I don't know what she have, why she like that. It was different, too, we don't talk about things the same way when I little. I don't really know what she had. Junior never want to talk about it. He just want to get away."

"I never knew her," Elena says. A facility. That was serious.

"I guess she was also from there," Maria says, softly. "That's San Sebastián." In the background of the photo is a house, a field, a horse. Gloria's words echo in Elena's head, *he was going to see his mama.* But she's been dead for a long time. Was she buried there? Was that where he had gone?

"So it's more rural?" Elena asks, but Maria wrinkles her forehead. "Farmland, I mean?"

"Oh yeah. All farming. That's why we go, too. All you can do there is farm, what would we have done later? Of course, Papa, he no think I gonna work, but still. For the boys. Our family, Papa and Mama's side, all *jíbaritos.*" Elena's confusion at the last term must show on her face. "How you say this. 'Sugar people.' They cut the cane, so you can make sugar, rum, whatever. Very poor, usually. That's why Papa joined the army. He figure, he don't wanna work the field, you know? And he could read. So he could do more. He was a very good father," Maria says, firmly.

"Was he the same way to you as he was to my father?" Elena asks, just as firm. It sounds like he was good to some of his children. And completely absent for the life of another one. Maria looks away.

"He try his best," Maria says. "He send him a ticket every year to come visit, like I say. Every year," she adds. "Here, this was his First Communion." Maria found the photo, one Elena had missed, between a photo of *Rowdy, Irena, y Hermando, 1961,* a trio of cute kids between the ages of fourteen and one, and a photo of Esperanza holding a young boy, his smile wide, missing a tooth in the front. The boy, Elena realizes, is her father, for it is the same face she sees, this time solemn, holding the rosary, between Chavela, young and smiling, holding a baby with a giant bow around her head to tell the world *this is a girl* despite her baldness, and Elena's grandfather, looking stern, his hand on her father's shoulder.

This is her father. She has never seen him as a child before. Not as a baby, or a teen. The oldest photo she had ever seen of her father, before these in the albums, comes from his graduation from college. He told her once that when he came to Stanford for college, a school that he knew nothing about, he realized that he was the only person in his class missing a front tooth. While he was able to get a gold one within his first year, scraping together savings from his scholarship as well as the jobs he worked on campus, he overheard a classmate, a rosy-cheeked farm girl from out in Wyoming who would end up serving on the California Supreme Court, joking with another girl that he looked like a pimp with it. So he had perfected his closed-mouth smile, never smiling another way, even when he was able to get a natural-looking tooth-colored implant years later. The stories about his past are so rare and precious to Elena that she committed it to memory, reciting it to herself like a myth or a prayer so that she would not forget it.

"He came once a year, every summer. Then he come when he was in law school, the summer he brought your mama." Here Maria's face darkens. "He didn't come for a while after that. He and Papa, well, Junior has a temper." From what Elena can remember, her abuelo had quite a temper, too, and a complete disinterest in being sober after 5:00 P.M., which only made it worse, but of course Maria wouldn't deal with that.

"After you born, he come back. We all want to meet you, of course. He come for our wedding, everybody's wedding. You so cute at Jorge's wedding, I got a photo." Maria pulls a framed photo off a shelf, and Elena can see herself as a baby, her head swathed in a bow bigger than her face. Maria seems flustered, and Elena wonders if she is avoiding something.

"Did they have a fight?" Elena asks, and Maria sighs.

"It's like I said. Your father has a temper. I think, your father, he have a lot to deal with. With his mama. Her family. All those people in New York. I think they fight about his mama. She was sick then. What to do about her. Why Papa didn't give more for her care. Maybe they fought about that. I was planning my wedding, I wasn't listening too much. I never liked fighting. And Papa didn't owe her anything." *But what did he owe his own son?* Elena cannot ask her aunt this question.

"He never take you out there? To El Pepino?" Maria has changed the subject to a safer place. Elena shakes her head. "We still have family there, you know. I go once a year, maybe. So boring. Pretty, though. I wonder if your grandmother buried over there. Since she from there?"

Elena does not know what to do, how to tell her aunt she does *not* know, had no idea that her family is more than the people she knows, that she has been asking herself the same questions about his mother's grave.

"Do you think he would have gone there?" Elena asks. Maria knows who she means. She shrugs.

"I call Tía Goli last week. He not there, then." Of course, it wouldn't be that easy. "But maybe he going there soon. I don't know. He's been . . . off. That's why I ask Gloria about him. Normally, I don't hear from him, I don't worry. But he never gone off like this before. And the island, after Maria, it's different now. Roads are destroyed. People are desperate, they've lost a lot. They could take advantage of him being, well . . ." Elena wishes Maria would just say it. Maria bites her lip, her teeth digging into the rich pink color on her lips.

"Drunk." Elena isn't sure whose mouth it comes out of until Maria looks at her, surprised. Her aunt nods, once.

"Yeah. Like Papa," Maria says, sadly. Elena wonders now if her father has inherited all of the bad things from his own parents, his mother's mental illness—not the same as what she must have had but something—and his father's love of the bottle. Painful gifts from damaged people.

"When I see him, he seem . . . different. He seem like something is wrong. He more . . . he not as here as before. Is he different when you talk to him?" Maria asks, and the question stings, although Elena knows it wasn't meant to.

"We don't really, um, talk. Sometimes I get a call, he emails. But we don't talk much." Elena looks away, knowing she will see pity in her aunt's gaze.

"He's all alone," Maria says, and Elena says nothing.

Daniel had told her once that she was very angry at her father. It had come as a surprise to her, when he said it. *You seem really angry at him.* She had been telling him a story about Puerto Rico, because he had only been on some spring break trip in college with his AEPi frat brothers, and his understanding of the island was very different from Elena's. She had been telling him about her birthday there one year, the way her father hadn't made it to dinner because he was drunk, how it had made her feel. She was talking about being sad, and he had told her she wasn't sad, she was mad, like he knew what was inside her. She had gone hot and cold all over her body and told him, *I'm not angry at him, I'm angry at you,* sparking a fight, setting a fire to distract from a flood. She told herself it wasn't true, like a mantra, over and over again. What was there to be angry about, really? *The fact that a grown man has gone missing. The fact that you are here, alone, trying to find him. The fact that he has been missing, in some way or another, for most of your life. It's not true, it's not true.*

"Do you know anyone else in these?" Elena asks, changing the subject, unable to keep a thread of hope out of her voice. There might be clues, more clues, to where he went, to where she comes from. Maria takes the first album in her lap, and begins turning the pages. Her head shakes until she sees the first color photographs, marking the shift from the fifties and sixties into the seventies. She smiles.

"That's Tía Goli and Luis, her husband. Papa's sisters. They stayed in Bayamon. Luis is gone, but Goli is still here. This is Mariche, she marry some *mean* man, Eduardo, he died. Next she marry a nice one, Ronaldo. She died. He still here, too. This, oh, I know who this is." Maria points to a woman who looks like she might be in her early twenties at the oldest in the photo, standing next to a younger man who shares her nose and looks stoned, in front of a house that looks like Elena's grandfather's house. "That is your papa's aunt Irena and his uncle Hermando. They stayed with us for a while, in Papa's house."

"But, they look younger than he was then." The back of the photo says *1978*. Her father was twenty-eight in 1978, and the woman in the photo can't be more than twenty-five. Maria looks at her oddly.

"They younger than him, *sí*. They move here, that's how I know them. They live in Ponce now, she's a witch." Maria says this matter-of-factly, like *she's a plumber, she's a chef. She's a witch*. Of course she is. "They mother is your father's grandmother. She marry three, four times, I not remember. But she have lots of children for a long time, so your papa have aunts and uncles older, younger, same age."

"He never told me that." Elena breathes, taking the photo. More relatives, live ones. In Ponce. Would her father have gone there, gone to see them?

"Do you think . . ." She looks up and sees it again: pity.

"I not know why he not tell you this." Maria's English is slipping again, and Elena can see tears in her eyes. She sighs. Her aunt can be very emotional. All of her family in Puerto Rico can. So can Elena, for all she tries to hide it. She can feel tears gathering in her own eyes, and blinks, fast.

"Me neither."

"It's like he ashamed," Maria says, shaking her head.

"I don't think—" But then Elena stops herself. She doesn't know, really. And it could be shame. All this, all the ways he has buried the past, this could be shame.

"He do a lot, your papa. He accomplish a lot in his life. They have nothing, my papa and . . . her. He come here, he do better, but she stay there. That family, I don't know them much, just Irena and Mando—he come here, get off the drugs, he got a bar now. But their mother, your papa's grandfather, they say she was bad. And they got *nothing* there. Just living on nothing. Not your papa, though. He got out. Maybe it too hard for him, remembering all that, telling you about it."

"Maybe," Elena says. "Would he have gone there?"

"Ponce? Maybe, I don't have Irena's number. We don't talk much." Maria looks faintly disapproving. It could be because Irena is a distant connection, through a woman Maria prefers to forget. Or it could be because her church probably isn't big on witchcraft.

"And of course, this Diego," Maria says, smiling. Elena looks at her, and the photograph in her hands, it's the one that says *Me and Diego, 1974.* Maria knows who Diego is. *Maria knows who Diego is.*

"Diego. Do you . . . do you know much about him?" Elena asks, her heart hammering hard, hoping Maria will take this as an invitation to tell her more. She is lucky that her aunt takes most things as an invitation to say more.

"I always like him. Papa thought he too fancy. Once he have us all over his father's hotel for dinner and they turn Papa away! They thought he was some kind of homeless, maybe. He didn't dress up."

Elena has no idea how to respond to this, and it must show on her face, because Maria looks at her, and sighs again.

"Your father no tell you about Diego," Maria says, disappointment in her eyes. She shakes her head again. "I never thought he would no say about Diego. They meet in law school. Diego also Puerto Rican, but, how do I say, fancy. Probably directly from Spain. His family own two big hotels, and a coffee plantation, all kinds of things. They still wealthy. He was one of your father's best friends."

"Was?" is all Elena can manage.

"Is. He move back, actually. He on the island. He retire in Rincón. I call him, too, sometimes your father go see him, but last time I call his phone was off, I not know. They might have more problems there, it's on the sea." Elena knows her aunt is speaking English but it might as well be Greek for all she understands what Maria is saying. How, why, would he keep this from her? Her father has never mentioned this man, one of his *best friends*. He has never told her anything about him, and she had no idea he, too, had returned to the island. Frankly, beyond anything else, she was shocked Yale Law School in the 1970s had admitted more than one Puerto Rican. Although it sounded like Diego was more aristocratic than her father, just the kind of Latino people liked, like Ricardo Montalbán, someone only slightly foreign.

"He's in Rincón," Elena repeats, trying to make herself understand. The name on the map. That was his location. Somewhere in Rincón. How big could Rincón be? Could she find him? And was her father there, or in San Sebastián, or somewhere else entirely? *Or at the bottom of the sea?*

"Sí. You want his number? I got an email, too, but I no use email. Takes too much time to type everything I gotta say!" Maria says, laughing. Elena nods vigorously. She wants his number, his email, any trace of this person. Diego is someone who knows her father, knows his past, a guarantee of some kind of information. Maria writes the email address down and Elena takes the paper, slipping it into her purse carefully, reverently.

Maria looks up, and Elena smells something, food. Her stomach rumbles. The only thing she has put in it today is coffee. The twins are carrying a tray with something that looks slightly burnt on a floral plate, and a glass of soda.

"Come, you eat, I look through these, see what else I can see. I write it down for you. The girls make them for you. So sweet they are. *Mis muñecas!*" Maria coos, and her dolls, as she calls them, blush with happiness. Maria, who was married so young, at twenty-two, had always wanted to be a mother, and she had the girls after almost fifteen years of trying, praying, worrying, talking about it, *not* talking about it, everything under the sun. She still treats them with a kind of wonder, living miracles in her home, as does their father, Javi.

They've brought her *croquetas,* no doubt courtesy of Goya, little fried packets of potato and meat that they have reheated—unevenly, Elena finds as she bites into one, and has a mixture of hot and frozen food in her mouth immediately. She is hungry, and they look at her, shy, waiting for words of praise.

"Wonderful," Elena says, lying. "Thank you so much." They glow. They are sweet girls; for all the adoration they receive from both of their parents, they are not spoiled or entitled. Instead they are kind, quiet in the face of their mother's noise, tranquil.

"Ay, your mama!" Maria exclaims. She has gotten to the albums that are more familiar to Elena, but still full of things she barely knows. If this is her father's life, most of it is a mystery. She has had so little of it, knows so little about it. She sips her soda, and eats the terrible food, and asks her young cousins questions, in Spanish and English. They speak in slang, which they explain to her, and ask her if she has seen several movies based on Nicholas Sparks novels, and does she listen to this or that Colombian or Korean singer, and can they visit her in New York? She nods, smiling. One of them, Mercedes—Elena has gotten better at telling them apart—looks at their mother, lost in the photos, and leans into Elena.

"You wanna get something with me in *la cocina?*" Elena agrees to go to the kitchen with Mercedes, as Innocenta stays behind, a distraction, Elena realizes. Does Mercedes want something, some contraband? These teenagers are probably much cooler already than

Elena has ever been. When it comes to illicit substances, the most she's ever tried is marijuana, which will soon be as legal as chocolate. She hopes she is not about to disappoint her cousin.

"Maybe you should go to Ponce," Mercedes says. "I think your papa gonna go there, eventually." Elena stumbles, hitting the marble island, hard. She will have a bruise on her side. She doesn't feel it now, though.

"What, why do you think that?" Elena sputters. Mercedes must have overheard her talking to Maria, but how—

"Instagram," Mercedes says, like it is the answer to all things. Well, she's fourteen. Perhaps it is. She takes out her phone and starts tapping away, motioning at Elena with the other hand to come closer. "I follow Mando. He's cool. He's younger than a normal *tío,* nicer, too. He messages me about bands to follow, he listen to everything. He have a bar in Ponce with a performance space. We wanna go, maybe when we are older." She is so sensible and knowledgeable, her young cousin. Elena thinks of her other cousin, Jessenia, and her blog, and all the things she could learn from that. She wishes she could be friends with Jessenia, wishes she was a part of Mercedes and Innocenta's lives. She has so much family and she knows so little about them, and they don't really know her. How can she have so much family and still be so alone in the world?

"Do you follow cousin Jessenia?" Elena asks, curious. Mercedes nods, smirking.

"Yeah. She's good. She mostly lives in Florida but she comes here sometimes to visit. She brought me stuff from Madewell. We don't have that here. Her posts have, like, too many words. But she's cool."

"I don't think I've seen her for years," Elena says, softly. Mercedes shrugs.

"You never come here. If you come more, you'll see her. She comes more," Mercedes says, matter-of-factly, piercing Elena's heart. She hasn't realized how much she's missed this place until she returned to it. "Your posts also have too many words," Mercedes informs her, with the casual cruelty of the young. Elena nods, promising to work on that.

"Sorry, you were saying something about Mando."

"Look." Mercedes points out a recent photo, dated three days earlier. The location tag says *Mando's Place.* A man in his fifties, dressing like he's far younger than he is and half pulling it off, sits with his arm around a woman in a flowy dress, her gray hair wild, charms and crystals slung around her neck.

"I don't see—"

"Mando is your papa's uncle," Mercedes says, and Elena blinks, startled, at the authority in her voice. This child knows so much more than she does. "And that his aunt Irena." Looking closer, Elena sees it, remembers younger faces from the albums and sees how time has lain on top of them.

"Your papa like to have a good time. He have two beers every time my papa have one. Maybe he go there? Mando always throwing parties." How strange, Elena thinks, that people talk about shielding children from things, when they always, *always,* already know. *Maybe he go there.*

"Thank you," Elena says, hugging Mercedes, who squeaks.

"I hope you find your papa," Mercedes whispers. Elena wants to say *me too,* but in that moment she feels another spike of rage, pure fire in her body. Although she came here for information, for a way forward, she does not know if what she really wants at the end of this is to find her father or not. Part of her hopes he is already gone. It would be so much easier than this, chasing his undead ghost.

So she does not say anything at all.

Her aunt insists on driving her back, rather than letting her take the ferry. Elena protests, but Maria is adamant.

"I need get gas anyway, I forget after church. Besides, there is a place near Viejo San Juan which is a nickel cheaper a gallon."

Today is Sunday, Elena realizes with a start, of course Maria went to church this morning. Time has quickly begun to lose meaning for Elena in Puerto Rico, where the days are lazy and hot and tourists pour in, treating Tuesdays like Fridays. That means tomorrow is Monday, and the Instituto de Cultura will be open, Elena can visit and find out more about the house, see if there is anything to indicate that her father kept his promise. But more than that, she is eager to learn about the structure. She is aching to know more, where the building comes from, who might have built it, how long it has been standing.

It is sunset as Maria drops her off, smacking both of her cheeks with kisses and asking her to keep her updated. Elena promises to do her best, and Maria seems relieved. The tension between them about Elena's grandfather seems to have dissipated, but Elena cannot help but feel a little resentful that everyone who is supposed to love her, Maria included, is so eager to hide the past. Elena is sure her aunt knows more about her father's mother than she is saying. More pieces of her history Elena will never get to see.

"It's good you come," Maria tells her. Elena smiles, bitterly. *Good for who?* "You take care. You sure you no want the concealer? It would really help with this." Maria gestures to Elena's whole face, and Elena smiles, again, accepts the concealer, and says goodbye.

That evening she sits on the roof again, her Instagram page open on her phone as she sips water, the ice melting and the glass sweating into her palm. She checks on her friends in New York, but they are doing things without her, and while she does not begrudge them this, she does notice that no one she knows has checked in yet, asked how she is doing. *Of course, no one knows that this is hard for you. You've never told them.* She reminds herself this, but it doesn't make her feel any better. She thinks about telling Daniel. He would understand a little piece of how this is for her, she knows. She let him in more than most other people in her life. She's never really wanted to tell anyone much about her father, never wanted to burden them with her baggage. *Just like him, just like he didn't tell you anything,* she thinks, and then shakes her head. Why are they all just carrying all their things with them, why can't they ever lay anything down? Why is history so heavy on her heart, on his?

She looks up Daniel's profile, and sees that he's posted something new, an image with friends, male and female, one woman tucked up in his side comfortably, her smile wide. Elena knows she should feel angry at the possibility that he's moved on so quickly, but instead she feels relief. He looks happy. Her biggest fear in life is causing damage, leaving a permanent mark. Her own life has been battered by her father, who does not seem to care about damaging others at all. She doesn't want to leave footprints on someone else's life the way he has on hers.

She thinks for a moment about her conversation with Mercedes, and then opens up the profile for @vidaboricua12 once more, and clicks on the links back to Jessenia's blog. She scrolls back and back, as the steady chirping of the coqui bleats on and on into the night, until she finds an early post that looks interesting titled *What's in a Name,* and she opens it up and reads.

Although now we are pretty short here, this is the land of giants. Boriken, Boriquen, names for this island from people who knew it before Columbus. Does it matter what we call things now? Should we remember the old name, should we tear "Puerto Rico" out of our mouths and call it what it was? Do places care what they are named, and re-named, by the people who think it matters, and will matter, in a hundred years? Words have power, we know that they do, but what's in a name, anyway? If I call this place the land of giants, will any of us grow?

*Of course, we are allowed to be irritated by the name Puerto Rico.
It was clearly a complete afterthought, a total fail. Puerto Rico.
"Rich Port." Not even a saint's moniker, not a soupçon of flair. That's
like calling New York or London or Paris or Tokyo "big city." The
lack of effort, the sheer failure of imagination, well sometimes it
makes one weep. Being a conquistador must have been exhausting,
all that pillaging and raping and enslaving and such, but would
it have been too much to ask that these great men who exterminated
millions took a little time from their busy schedules to be creative in
their monikers?*

*Speaking of names, Christopher, Christopher, why should we
call Columbus that? No one he knew would have done so. In his
hometown, Genoa, he would have been Cristoffa Corombo, "son of
a weaver." His name would be bastardized by his fellow Italians
to Cristoforo Colombo. When he moved to Lisbon, he was Cristóvão
Colombo, when he begged for ships in Spain he was Cristóbal Colón.
And who knows what the people he destroyed called him, some with
direct slaughter, some with diseases none of them, himself included,
would have understood.*

*Christopher is, of course, the "carrier of Christ," a man whose orig-
inal name is long erased, supplanted by his choice to bear Jesus over a
river, cementing his identity forever as a beast of burden. Our many-
named man, too, carried all he needed with him, both crucifixes and
aedes aegypti, a mosquito carrying yellow fever, a hat on a hat. This
man called the island that is now Puerto Rico "San Juan Bautista."
Its port-city was rich, and so they named the place they docked their
ships Puerto Rico. But at some point in time, somewhere between the
extermination of the Taino people and the swinging hips of Richie
Valens, the city and the island switched names behind everyone's back
just to see who was paying attention. No one was.*

*Do you know the story of John the Baptist? He lived off locusts and
honey in the wilderness, he baptized Jesus in the river Jordan, then*

a pretty girl danced for a king and asked for John's head instead of singles tucked into her underwear and he died. To think, we read this book to children.

Maybe it doesn't matter what we call this place. This island wears names lightly, it must, it is older than the names it bears. Who knows what they may be called tomorrow, or when the world is very old? Who knows if there will even be names, then, or people to say them?

Elena thinks for a long time about all of the names she has just learned, all of the names of people connected to her who she will never know, and then, when her brain is so tired it aches, she sleeps a dreamless sleep, for which she is grateful.

The next morning she wakes early, her numb limbs once again nudging her to consciousness. *Everything here is dirty,* she thinks, looking around at the slightly cleaner, but still messy and filthy, place. She wants to rescue this house from her father, she realizes. It hurts her that it is falling apart under his ownership, hurts her because it is a piece of history, not just of the island's, but of her family, her parents' marriage. It hurts her because it shows her how little her father cares for anything, the way he has let this place down.

She arrives at the Instituto de Cultura just as it opens, which amuses her, because she arrives at 9:00 A.M., and the institute is supposed to open at eight, but it is Puerto Rico, what does she expect? Punctuality is for mainlanders and cold places. It is a large yellow building, and above the iron gates, the story of its creation is written out in Spanish, and Elena reads the dizzying long names of the Spaniards who brought the building into being, starting in 1841. One, Manuel Egozcue y Cintron, particularly interests her, and she tries to figure out how to pronounce the name. When she asks the man at the entrance desk how it's said, he looks at her like she is insane, and shrugs, pointing to the paper sign-in sheet. She signs and asks him where the archives are, but she just gets another shrug, more apathetic than the last. He vaguely gestures around and goes back to reading his newspaper, leaving her with no new information.

Elena looks around, but of course there are no directional signs. She does see a sign telling her more about the building, and learns it was built to be a charity house, for the old, the abandoned, and the insane. Elena wonders where all those people go, now. She wanders up the tiled steps to the second floor, only to see a series of closed doors and no people. But from the second floor, at least, she can spot a sign back on the first floor saying *Archivos Públicos,* on a door tucked into the side of one of the courtyards. Heading back down, she is confused by several doors marked *Entrada* that also have a sign saying not to enter them.

"La próxima," says a voice behind her, and Elena sees a smiling woman pushing a cleaning cart.

"Gracias," Elena says, heartfelt. Of course the only truly helpful person in the place is the cleaner. Walking through the next door down, into an office, she is immediately assaulted by a blast of air-conditioning, and she sees that the man in front of her, sitting at a desk, has a jacket on. Everyone on the island insists on making the air colder so they can then bundle up against it.

"Hello, I wanted to ask if it is possible to see the file on 300 Calle Sol?" Elena asks, politely, in Spanish. She practiced on her way over, trying to fix any mistakes, but now she is nervous, and of course she trips over her syllables, giving herself away. "I'm the daughter of the owner," she explains. She has her license and even pulled up photos of her with her father, on her phone, that hurt to look at in case they need proof, but the clerk just nods, once, and walks into another room, coming back mere seconds later with a thick file.

"Oh, wow, that was fast," she says, in English this time, startled. The clerk shrugs. Elena is amazed at the apathy that clearly runs through the building. She sits in the seat indicated by the clerk, who has turned back to his computer, utterly unconcerned with her, and opens the file.

It is, she quickly realizes, the recent history of all changes made to the house, each one denoted by requests to the Institute. Because it, like most of the city, is a historic home, in the interests of preservation each change must be evaluated by the Institute before it can be approved or denied. Changes without petitioning for approval mean legal action, Elena can see, because there are documents informing the owner of the place back in the 1980s about a lawsuit in response to his decision to paint the house gray. Elena flips the pages back to the present day, and sees documented the back-and-forth between her parents and the historic committee about the violet her mother had picked, and how she had had to prove that the house had been repainted by several owners and therefore the original color was unknown. To keep the city pretty, Elena reads, the Institute makes sure there is a balance of colors on each block, and once they had done a survey of the area and confirmed that there were no houses in the immediate vicinity that were close in color, her parents had finally gotten the approval. It had taken two years.

The owners of the building are listed on each document, and Elena can see her father's name on the most recent document, a request to put up a satellite dish that was denied from six years ago. Elena is surprised her father was cognizant of things enough back then to make an official request. Her mother's name is listed on previous requests, ones from when they were still together, and as Elena flips back in time, she sees requests from other owners, photos of the house as yellow, then gray, then powder blue, watching as windows come and go, turning from the wood they are now to rusted wrought iron. A document catches her attention, from the 1960s, a request to rezone the bottom floor of the building from a *Juan Cintron,* and in the document, Elena is fairly sure, despite the formal legal Spanish she can barely understand, that Juan was declaring the property to be his because of the recent passing of his father, *Agosto Cintron,* citing Agosto's will. The response was affirmative about the new ownership, but negative regarding the commercial zoning request, denying Juan a chance to build the *cafeteria* of his dreams. The first floor of the building is even older than the second, the document informs Juan, and therefore Elena. It was built sometime in the seventeenth century, and cannot be rezoned.

"Excuse me?" Elena has switched to English. What she wants to ask is too complicated for her Spanish. The clerk looks up. "Can you tell me, when someone has a property here, how does it change hands legally? I mean, do you have to register a new deed? Do you happen to know?" The clerk nods, slowly.

"You supposed to file a change of hands for property in the Puerto Rico Property Registry, but because you don't *have* to, some people don't." The clerk rolls his eyes, he clearly has a healthy distaste for people who don't respect historic records. Elena nods.

"What about inheritance?"

"As long as the owner has left a will, that's fine. It transfers the ownership, as long as it's a will made in Puerto Rico according to local laws."

So that was how it was done in Puerto Rico. Not changing the name on the deed, but willing the place. Does her father even *have* a will? A will in Puerto Rico, made by a Puerto Rican lawyer, who would understand the legal system here? And if her father doesn't, could he make one now? Is he of sound mind, anymore?

She thanks the clerk, her mind buzzing. She looks down at the file. The documents she is skimming through have a few indicators of the history of the house beyond the requests for changes, but not much.

"Sorry, may I ask you something else?" The clerk looks at her, clearly annoyed. She smiles, trying to appease him, but it doesn't seem to be working.

"Are you going to ask?" he wonders, rolling his eyes. Clearly not working.

"How would I find more information about the history of the house itself? Beyond this?"

"You can go to the Biblioteca Nacional, maybe. If you want to. It might have something more." He shrugs.

"For a historian, you don't seem that passionate about this stuff," Elena comments, unable to stop herself. The clerk just shrugs again.

"Let me know when you're finished," he says, turning back to the computer. "We close at noon."

"The hours on the building say four-thirty," Elena says, confused.

"Yeah. But I gotta do something." Of course he does. These are the people who get these jobs instead of her? This is why she has worked in property management for years, instead of doing the thing she really wants to do? She wonders if she should be applying for jobs on the island, since it seems the competition isn't very tough. *That would mean staying here,* she reminds herself, which she has no interest in doing.

This is a lie, she knows. She has always wanted more time on the island. But imagining the look on her mother's face if she told her that, imagining being in the same place as her father—both are equally devastating in wildly different ways.

The National Library, or *Biblioteca Nacional,* isn't far from the little pocket of San Juan that is the *viejo* part, and Elena can walk there. She sets off, hoping that this place is open less erratically than the institute, but when she gets to the large pale-yellow building, she finds that while the library is open, the archives department is closed because the archivist is on vacation. Of course they are. It will be open next week, they tell her, and she hopes that this is actually true.

Walking back, along the ocean on Avenida Luis Muñoz Rivera, Elena consoles herself with the knowledge that while it would be nice to know the history of the house, it isn't as vital as the information she got at the Institute, that her father needs to will her the house for her to have it. Perhaps he already has. She would like to believe that he has. But it is impossible for her not to doubt him, not to wonder if he has, as always, failed her. Left her behind. Forgotten his promises. Forgotten her.

She stops walking, and looks out to the sea, to the ruined piece of the old battlements that now corrodes, picturesquely, as the sea crashes into it. She reaches into her purse to take a photo, and her fingers brush the paper her aunt Maria gave her the day before, the information about Diego. She should have contacted him immediately but she didn't. She is afraid to talk to him, just like she is afraid to talk to everyone else. She rages against them in her mind, and hides from them, too. She has to be stronger than this, she tells herself. If she wants something she has to ask for it. If someone was going to give it to her, they already would have.

Instead of the photo she planned to take, Elena uses her phone to compose an email. Perhaps she should call this man instead, but she is too timid for that, too afraid he might actually pick up the phone. So she writes, as she is always more comfortable doing, introducing herself and asking him if she could possibly meet him, lying that she is just passing through the island. She does not mention that her father is lost. She does not want to alarm this man, or make him think that she, too, is crazy. He might think that anyway. He knows, better than her, where she came from.

She has more emails from her work, more leases to look at, and now they want her to run credit and background checks on new renters. She is still on vacation. The emails are no longer worded kindly or apologetically, but rather brusquely, *check this by Monday, thanks.* She has been gone for less than a week.

I hate this, she thinks. The air around her feels tight. She doesn't have the time or energy to contact previous landlords and review leases. Her brain is too full. She's not even supposed to be working, she's supposed to be on vacation. What a wonderful vacation she is having . . .

She ignores the emails, she cannot think of them now, can barely read them, and instead she returns to the house, and cleans, and cleans, until her arms ache and her throat is thick with dust. She sits, afterward, showered and aching, and looks around. Her efforts are helping, to be sure, but it still looks like a hurricane swept through the place. She supposes one had, really.

She does not know what to do now. Rent a car and drive some-where, one of the places her father might be? Which one, even? Wait for Diego's response, wait for her father to come home, wait for the archives to reopen, wait for a will giving her the house to flutter down from the sky and find her?

She wishes she could talk to someone, but not someone who knows her well, who will ask her uncomfortable questions and point out the ways in which she is foolish, cowardly, and weak. She wishes she could talk to someone she doesn't have to explain anything to, but there is no one in her life like that, not even her mother. She has texts from her mother that she has answered with one- or two-word responses, so Rosalind will know she is alive. She does not trust herself on a call with her mother right now, a fact that she loathes but knows to be true. Her feelings about her father are leaking into her love for her mother and staining it. She wanted it to stay clean. Nothing around her now is clean. All the work she is doing to set things right is making mess, the kind of mess you need before things can really become orderly, but it's so big it looks like it will never be sorted.

Elena remembers the man on the beach, his palm tattoo. Talking to him had been anonymous. Talking to strangers always was easier than talking to someone she knew. And he understood the island. He wouldn't ask about Hurricane Maria, about *how are things there* with equal parts pity and fascination. He was a blank canvas she could paint and discard. He was perfect. She should have gotten his information.

I go to El Batey most nights.

In a way, maybe she did.

The bar, El Batey, is smoky, and Elena wonders, walking in, when was the last time she was inside a bar where people could smoke. Has she ever been to a place like this? She moved to New York long after it was the trash-strewn town of smoky bars and junkies and party girls and kidnappings, when the subway was a dangerous place. Now New York is filled with hipster parents and Russian mobsters, who are polite and do not disturb the peace, other than to ruin real estate prices, and everyone rides the subway, no matter the delays. She coughs, softly, and looks around. She hopes Fernando is there, behind all the smoke.

She sits down on a stool, which sighs under her. Everything in this bar is scratched and worn and battered, and it makes her comfortable. She can't hurt or break anything here, it's all already damaged.

She looks up, and sees that there is a mirror behind all the bottles in the bar, and she catches a glimpse of her own face, between bottlenecks, and obscured by the dim light and the smoke. She takes a photo of the image, not sure why, but perhaps she will show her father, if she sees him again, *look, I went to your favorite place, I was there.*

"What you want?" The bartender, who, despite the apathy of her expression, is luminously beautiful: wide eyes lined in black, an angled bob perfectly maintained, delicate vines tattooed up the side of her right arm and blooming over her heart in a rose, dripping with blood, all visible under her slightly sheer white T-shirt. She puts down her book, and Elena catches sight of the title, *The Aleph and Other Stories*. She herself has struggled through this book in college, eager to understand Borges, the Argentine genius, and worried all the time that she didn't, and never would. She worries about this still, and is afraid to ask for what she wants from this beautiful bartender who does not seem worried about anything at all.

"Rum and Coke, please," Elena says, in English. She tends to speak to people the way they have spoken to her, here, letting them lead on the language. The bartender reaches for a bottle of Bacardí, her expression blank. "Um, do you have *Barrilito*?" Elena asks, timidly. The bartender looks up and flashes her a smile. Elena's breath stops in her lungs. She is uncomfortable with deeply beautiful people, they make her nervous, they make her long for their approval. She wonders what they see when they look at her, wonders if they find the world to be an ugly place when they compare it to themselves.

"Of course. Most tourists don't care, don't know to ask." The bartender reaches for another bottle.

"I'm only a sort of tourist," Elena says, softly, watching the generous pour of rum over ice, then the dollop of Coke. "My father lives here." A sliver of lime, and it's done and in front of her. She takes a sip.

"Barrilito is the best," the bartender says, shrugging. "Bacardí is whatever. But people want it. They go do that tour and everything. I got a friend whose cousins come from New York every year and that's what they want to do. Every time. It's a factory! It's not like it's changing. It's always the same, you don't gotta go see it more than once. Stupid." Not so taciturn after all, this woman, Elena sees. She nods, though. It *is* stupid.

"It's not even really Puerto Rican," the bartender says, snorting.

"I know," Elena says.

"Everyone knows it's from Cuba, Rita. They just don't care," a male voice behind Elena says, and it is a little familiar. She turns, and there he is, Fernando. She is aware of a feeling of relief and does not bother to lie to herself and pretend it is not there. It is nice to not be totally alone. "They did a new packaging shift, back to the original 1920s label, and people ate it up. Everything is about packaging."

The bartender, Rita, rolls her eyes and reaches for the Barrilito bottle again, pouring out a shot.

"We are slaves to pretty packaging. Magpies, or trained monkeys, reaching for glossy things. Would you buy half of what you do if it all came in a brown paper bag? Think about it." Rita shakes her head; she has obviously heard Fernando's thoughts on capitalism before. She grabs a beer, a Medalla, the Puerto Rican standard, and places both drinks on the corner of the bar as Fernando sits down. He nods at Elena.

"You came. I didn't see you here the other nights, figured you weren't going to show up."

"I was free tonight, so." Elena sips her drink. She wanted him to be here but now she doesn't know what to say, what she wanted, exactly, in the first place. But he just nods, comfortably, and lights up a cigarette. They sit in silence for a moment, and it feels strangely nice to Elena. Like they planned this, like they are friends who decided to meet and spend some time together. She hasn't done that much lately. Her fear for her father, her engagement ending, the feeling that her life is more and more not what she wants it to be, it has all isolated her. She has isolated herself. She knows this. There are people in her life who would have shown up, been there, but she has not let them, has not alerted them that they needed to. Needing things is weak, pathetic. She does not want people to feel bad for her. She does not want to feel bad for herself. *What do you want to feel?*

She takes another sip of her drink, closing her eyes at the familiar taste, the familiar sensation. The last time she came to this bar she was twenty-one years old. She sat beside her father and watched him drink himself into unconsciousness, watched him go from expansive, charming, everyone's best friend, calling every eighty-year-old in the bar *joven,* "young man," flirting with everyone, to diminished, softened, sweetly sentimental, until he became nothing, a blank slate, the rum rendering him a man erased. This was why he drank, she decided then, to erase himself, to forget all of the people he was and get to be nothing. She, who knew then and knows now very few things about her father, very few of the people he was, remembering this moment, cannot help but feel rage. It floods her, overwhelms her, she has to grip the side of the bar. How dare he do that? How dare he carve away the people he is, was, like that, leaving her with nothing? How dare he not be better, leave something of himself for *her*?

She remembers walking him home that night, putting him to bed. It was a graduation trip, his gift to her for finishing college, a trip for the two of them. She spent the days alone, in the ocean, and the nights watching him disappear. She should have realized then that Rosalind wouldn't stay in this for much longer, and she didn't, three years later her father left a Korean restaurant in the East Village and came back here, disappearing all over again, over and over again.

Her nails are making marks in the soft wood of the bar. Elena watches this like it is happening to someone else, like her fingers do not hurt.

"You're all right?" Fernando's voice is rumbly with smoke. Elena nods. This is what he said to her when she was in the ocean, when she was floating, happy, but she is drowning now. He slides over a seat, and now he sits closer, diagonally across from her, they are at the corner of the bar, the only area of a bar where two people can actually talk to each other and look at each other.

"Where's your dad? The one you are here visiting?" he asks, like there might be more than one. This is an excellent question, and it makes Elena laugh, hard, the sound bitter to her ears.

"I have no idea," she says, giggling madly. He looks at her, curious. But she can tell this stranger whatever she likes. "He's lost. That's why I'm here." The rum, little as it is, has hit her mind, and it has already given her that glorious half inch from reality she so badly needs right now. "He's gone missing."

Fernando nods, once, as though this is a normal thing to say, and shoots his rum. He chases it with a swig of beer.

"What does he look like?" Fernando asks, his voice quiet. Elena describes her father, realizing she is really describing a picture of him, one he sent her digitally a year ago. She has not seen him in person in a while. She closes her eyes, remembering the photo and how it swirls around with all the other images of her father she has, how tall and strong he seemed when she was a child, how he looked in his suits getting ready for court, how he looked at her bat mitzvah, how he looked when she was graduating high school, how he looked sitting here in this same bar, life leaching out of him with every drink. How he looked in the photos she now has, at his First Communion, a tiny figure dwarfed by his suit, by his own father, by the shadow of the church. She tells Fernando his height, how his stomach has rounded and pushed out beyond his belt line, how his legs have remained skinny, like a frog's. She describes his hair, still curly and barely gray, somehow, and his big face, his hooked nose, his bright *guayaberas,* the shirts he wears every day now, he told her, in an email, and she thinks, *I could be describing my abuelo.* She wonders how her father feels now that he has become his own father.

"Have you ever noticed how Disney villains all have big hooked noses?" the bartender, Rita, asks, and Elena opens her eyes. Fernando is looking at her, something strange living in his face, but her glass is empty, and the bartender has made an excellent point.

"Maybe Disney is anti-Semitic," Elena says. "Actually, Walt Disney was anti-Semitic. And racist. And anti-communist. Triple threat. Can I have another, please?" The bartender nods.

"Are you Jewish?" Rita sounds excited. Elena nods. Rita mixes the drink, talking about a Jewish friend she has who lives in New Jersey.

"I guess my father looks like a Disney villain, then. Have you seen anyone like that?" Elena smiles, but Fernando's strange expression is bigger now; it's taken up all the space on his face. He pulls out his phone, and he shows Elena a photo. It is him, Fernando, his arm around her father, here, in this bar, some other night, both of them smiling, both of their faces red with liquor.

"Oh," Elena says, flatly. *Of course.* This is a bar for drinking. This is not a bar like the ones on Calle Fortaleza or Calle Recinto Sur, bars built for cruise people, waiting just a few steps from their massive ships so they don't have to wander far to dose their faces in buckets of piña coladas and margaritas. This is not a bar like the many places on Calle San Sebastián, filled with regulars who bury their irritation at the more *authentic* traveler who spends all of four days here, but takes pride in how they bravely chose Old San Juan instead of Condado for a more *real* trip, under layers of wine and beer. This is a bar for people who want to drink because they want to drink. Some come and go quickly, some stay until sunrise, for the bar does not close until six in the morning. This is a bar with a sign printed, quite clearly, above the register, stating: *We do not make mojitos.* Of course her father comes to this bar. It is probably the only bar he would go to in the entire city. He is a man who likes to talk, who loves people, loves an audience. He loves to pay little and get a lot. He loves pool and strangers. Drinking alone in his home would only appeal for so long. He comes to this bar for the same reason she did, this evening. So he does not have to be alone.

"I guess you are a regular," Elena says, neutrally. She does not mean anything by this. Plenty of people go to the same bar a lot. She has learned over the years, through books, and dropping in on her mother's Al Anon group, one Rosalind attends religiously—

well, perhaps it is a religion, in a way, it promises hope, after all—
that to enjoy drinking, to do it with frequency, has nothing to do
with being an alcoholic. This came as a pleasant surprise to her,
because she herself had been terrified that she, too, would become
an alcoholic, and had spent the year before she learned this completely sober. She celebrated her new knowledge over a bottle of
wine with her mother, became drunk on half a glass, and suffered
through a headache the next day that had left her limp. Slowly,
since then, she has rebuilt her tolerance, and now she could sit
here with a stranger who drank with her father and down her rum
and Coke with steely-eyed determination, letting it give her courage and release.

"I am," Fernando says, carefully. "I've known your dad for a while.
He moved here, what, a decade ago?" Elena nods. "I met him four
years ago. I had just moved back myself, from the States. I got a job
at the University of Puerto Rico."

"You teach?" Elena says, tonelessly. Does she really care? They are
both avoiding the point, her father, but it is comforting, in a way,
the formalities, the banalities, the things they can discuss before
discussing the real thing. And in a way, she likes that he is an academic. She has often thought about pursuing her Ph.D.

"Environmental sciences. And biology. I'm a botanist," he says,
curls of an American accent slipping in between his Puerto Rican
drawl.

"Hence the tree," Elena says. She wonders, vaguely, where he went
to college, graduate school, how old he is, if he likes his work, if he
masturbates in the shower, if he reads fiction, if he cooks, if he prefers cats or dogs, if he is a cruel person or a kind one. She wonders
who he is, really, the stranger next to her. She wonders if they will
become friends, if she will sleep with him, if he likes her. She wonders if he will tell her something important about her father. She
wonders if she wants him to or not.

"What?"

"Your tattoo," Elena says. Rita, the bartender, her tattoo has fantasy roses, fantasy vines. His was precise, like a print in an old-fashioned folio, a botanical illustration. She wonders if there is a Latin name printed next to the palm. Fernando nods.

"It's a ceiba. That's the official tree of the island."

"Cool," Elena says, caring not at all.

"I met your father here," Fernando repeats. Elena smiles, bitterly.

"Of course you did," she says, as Rita hands her the drink she ordered.

"Actually, lately, I've been wondering if something was wrong. I haven't seen him for at least three weeks. I usually see him three, four times a week. I like to come, have a beer or two, grade papers here. I live nearby." Elena nods at this. "Your father, he's really smart. He has so much to talk about. I've learned a lot from him. He told me he had a daughter, but I thought you were, like, young. He talked about you like you were still in school or something."

"I don't think he's great at keeping track. And he hasn't seen me since graduate school," Elena says, dryly. He has grown more and more confused as the years have gone by. Living down here, away from everything, soaked in rum, his life a hoarder's nest of objects, maybe his mind has become a medieval painting, with everything happening at once. Maybe to him, she can be both six years old and twenty-three and thirty and none of it is a contradiction.

"What did you study?"

"History. Did he tell you where he might be going?" Elena asks, with little hope.

"He told me about all these places he wanted to visit on the island. But I didn't know he was just going to go."

Elena turns to Fernando, her eyes wide.

"He told you about places he wanted to visit? Can you remember them, any of them?"

Fernando leans back, perhaps the force of her words is so great it has formed a tangible thing, pushing him.

"He's really missing, isn't he?" Fernando says, shaking his head and pulling out another cigarette. He would seem unaffected if Elena didn't see his hands, trembling. She takes the lighter away from him and lights it, cupping a hand around it, until his cigarette is lit. "Thank you."

"You're all right?" She repeats his words back at him. Why does he seem so affected by this? She does not know, of course, but it had sounded to her, from what he said, that Fernando and her father were drinking buddies, nothing more.

"My power went out, during Maria. Well, everyone's did, of course. But, I'm alone here. My family is all back in the U.S. They left the island when I was a kid. But I came back because, I don't know. It felt right. Not being here felt wrong. Disloyal. They don't feel that way, it's okay. But I do. So I'm here. Hence the ceiba. Something about here has always been a part of me."

Elena nods, wondering what this is about, but knowing she shouldn't interrupt. He seems to be building to something.

"Your dad came over to my place. I pointed it out to him once, I don't know how he remembered, he was pretty . . . Well. But he came over one day. I was scared shitless, the nights were so dark and you didn't know if something bad could happen, if someone could take advantage. He knocks on my door and he tells me to come with him, the moon is full, we can make it back to his place, and I can stay with him until the power is back. So I do. He had water, beer, some food. We would sit up on the roof during the night and look out on the island, all dark, but you could see the stars like you never could before. My family asked me if I was okay, when I could charge my phone, all that, they didn't want me to be alone. But I wasn't. I would have been. I never would have asked anyone for anything. But he came to me, and led me to his place, and made sure I was okay. There is no one else here who would do that for me. Not my colleagues, not my students, nobody. Now he's lost. It's just . . . Seems strange, you know?"

Elena nodded. She does know. Something touches her hand, and it is his hand, and it is strange, to touch a stranger, but warm, a pulse of comfort. Fernando is odd, Elena decides. But he is also kind, and he knows her father. He is a friend, now. It is good to have one here.

"He told me he wanted to go to Ponce, and that he has some friend in Rincón he wants to see. And he said he wants to go to his hometown."

"San Sebastián," Elena says, with authority, recently come by. She wanted to try it out in her mouth, anyway. *San Sebastián. My family is from San Sebastián.* It is new, she could use the practice. Fernando nods.

She has three choices, three places to go. Three points on the island in different directions. Which one should she choose? He could be in any of them, or none of them. Her phone lights up with a message. It's a reply from Diego.

"Excuse me a moment." She stumbles out of the bar, thinking about how many people before her have done just that, and opens the email. The response is short. *Dear Elena, I would love to meet you. Any chance you could come to Rincón? I'm always free, joy of retirement. Best, Diego Perez Acevedo.*

And just like that, her choice is made for her.

"Tomorrow I'm going to Rincón," Elena declares to Fernando, walking back in the bar. Of course she is, because whatever Diego offers her, it will be more, more information than she had before. She is going because he might know about the house, how Elena can find out about the deed, anything. She is going because this, somehow, is easier than meeting family members she has never seen before. She is going because she is a coward.

"Okay." Fernando finishes his beer. He lays some money on the bar, and stands. Elena is aware of a strange disappointment. He is no longer holding her hand, and she feels like he has taken something important from her. She is clingy with drink and need, and she pulls herself back, telling herself he has a life and he can go where he has to, of course; obviously, he owes her nothing, he has already given her a story about her father, a sense that he is still kind, despite everything, and confirmation that Rincón might hold something.

"It's not that far, and I got a car. I was going to go to Aguadilla tomorrow anyway for lunch. Do you need a ride?"

Elena smiles at him. A ride is something she absolutely does need, indeed.

Nine

"Can we talk about this?" Rosalind asked him, her eyes large behind the owlish glasses they were all wearing in those days. When Santiago had been a child, he had worn black Coke bottle–style glasses, which he constantly protected from breakage, not in the schoolyard, which was a fairly calm place, especially because he was in the gifted students program, but on the walk home, where gang members would chase him blocks and blocks through the Lower East Side. In college, it had been wire-rim glasses to look like Gandhi or John Lennon, but now it was big plastic frames, for everyone. By the eighties, everything was bigger and bigger.

"Talk? What is there to talk about? You want this. You said you wouldn't want this, and you want this. So, what's the conversation? What's the fucking conversation, then? Fuck you," Santiago said, softly and succinctly. Rosalind drew back, shocked, and the thick lenses magnified the sudden tears in her eyes. He never cursed, *ever,* not in English or Spanish. He thought it made people sound uneducated, poor, and he was terrified of that, of being mistaken, or accurately identified, in his own mind, as less than others.

"Santiago, this is important," she mumbled, her voice choked.

He wanted to fall on his knees before her, beg her forgiveness, this woman he loved more than anything, his lifeboat. She was steady, calm, always moving toward the light, and he knew he needed her if he was to have anything approaching a decent life, if he was going to stop himself from sinking into the dangers that surrounded him, always surrounded him.

He was a little drunk.

He shook his head to clear it, but Rosalind saw this as a no, and she turned away, shoulders shaking.

"Rosie—"

"I want to be a mother," she said, flatly. She had contained her tears. She usually did. She was not a woman who cried easily, or for long. She was strong, his wife, so strong that he marveled at her, even now. She was the pampered daughter of Philadelphia Jews, she'd grown up with more than he could have ever imagined a kid could have, and she was so much stronger than anyone else he knew, himself included, he could barely believe she was real sometimes. But that was why she didn't understand, couldn't see why he couldn't do this. He wasn't strong like her, and he couldn't have a child. He wouldn't know how.

"We said we wouldn't do that," he reminded her, pleading with her. She had said she understood. She of anyone said she understood. How could she change her mind like this, how could she betray him? "We promised each other we wouldn't."

"I've, I've changed. Please, Santiago, let's just discuss it, let's allow for the possibility of it. You aren't him. Or her. You're you. I'm me. We can do this. Why can't we do this?"

"I'm scared," he offered her. It wasn't half, even a quarter of what he felt, of the miles-deep fear, terror really, at the prospect of a child, someone who would inherit the things he carried, someone who would be the next in his line, the next inheritor of . . . what? He had no legacy. He came from illiterate *jibaritos,* from poverty, from madness. He had crawled out of that, but still it clung to him, and he was weak, weak where Rosalind was strong. All that polluted him would seep into his child's blood. Every part of his past, everything in his mind, how could he risk a child who would bear even half of it? Even if Rosalind gave their child half of herself, the other half would be from him, and what he had was not worth giving anyone.

He was *more* than a little drunk. His thoughts, sober, were never fanciful like this. He never let himself think these things, sober. The alcohol was supposed to bury things, not bring them up. It wasn't working like it should.

Rosalind's expression had softened, and she put her hand on his arm.

"I know you're scared, Santi." When she used his nickname, he knew she had forgiven him, but the words still rang through his head, *fuck you, fuck you.*

He was in his thirties now, how had that happened? Wasn't he supposed to stay twenty forever, and then it had been twenty-five, but either way he was going to stay real and never sell out, and now he had cut his hair and he wore a tie every day to his job as a lawyer in a corporate firm, where he helped the people he had once deemed fascist capitalist pigs, rotund white men who mangled his name and patted him on the shoulder like a pet monkey.

And he liked it. He was good at it. The salary they gave him allowed him to finally get a fake tooth implanted in his mouth to fill the hole in his smile, the tooth he had lost as a young kid when his mother's boyfriend slammed his face into a wall, though he would never really smile with his teeth even after this, the habit of hiding too hard to break. The salary they gave him allowed Rosalind to work as an artist, it kept his mother comfortable, paying off her many doctors, softening the world around her with comfort and cleanliness. It gave him status, prominence, importance. He was

Mr. Vega. Had anyone in his family ever been called *mister* before, by white people? By anyone?

He had more now than he had ever had before in his life. They had an apartment at Twenty-first and Spruce Street in Philadelphia. It was a relief to be out of California, where they had always had to pretend to be happy, and a relief to be out of New Haven, where the winters were so bitter birds fell, dead, from the sky, and the food was terrible, except for the pizza. But more than anything, it was a relief not to be in New York, which felt, always, like something Santiago was escaping, could be sucked back into at any moment.

Their apartment was large and comfortable, bigger than any they had had before. Their friends joked that this was because no one wanted to live in Philadelphia, but he didn't care. They had a color television and an outdoor area where Rosalind grew basil and flowers in the summer and he grilled steaks, real large steaks they bought at Sunny's Butcher Shop in the Italian market. Santiago had a car, and seven suits that all fit him well, and a camera, and a record player with all their records filed neatly, from Cream to Led Zeppelin, and space for all his books, and money to buy more books. He had comfort, and safety, and time, and Rosalind. There was nothing more worth adding to life, he knew. This life was perfect. They had so much, so much more than he had ever had, more than he could have dreamed of. And weren't they happy?

A child would change this. A child would break his records and scribble in his books and stain his suits but more than that, a child would look up at him with large eyes and ask him things, need him to be a father. How could he be a father? He did not know what a father even *was.* He had never had one.

"I'm scared, too." Rosalind's voice, bringing him to the present. He almost swayed, gin running through his veins, but he stopped himself. Rosalind's face wrinkled. "Did you have a drink before you came home?"

"I went out with some of the guys from work." Santiago tried to make it sound fun, casual, rather than what it had been, what it always was, a group of lawyers vaguely certain that they were making the world a worse place, not a better one, drinking as much as possible in one sitting to forget that they had just done that.

He had never been much of a drinker before, not even in law school. Yale had been competitive, focused, intent, and besides, everyone preferred getting high, himself included. It made the world easier to understand, gentler, in a way, and it calmed his nervous energy, which had bubbled up more and more during college and afterward, long periods of intense feeling, boundless highs of productivity and emotion. Then would come a low, a dip, and that other feeling, that energy, felt like a dream. When he was up, he felt fearless, bulletproof, a man against the world, like he had a superpower. When he was down, he could not remember ever having felt another way. Weed helped. Rosalind liked wine, but Rosalind didn't like anything in excess, and weed was something he could do and do over and over again and still be, still function, often better than before.

But a few months after joining the firm, after a settlement that had worked out exactly as Santiago, and the firm, had hoped, his colleagues, who had kept their distance up until this point, invited him out for drinks with them. He had been the least senior member of the group working on the case, and he was gratified to be asked, so he said yes. The endorphins from the win, his first big one, even as part of a team, mixed with the energy he was experiencing already, his superpower returned, left him buzzing, and open, so when Mark, a second-year associate, suggested a second round, Santiago said yes, despite his usual distaste for alcohol. Two turned into three, into four, and five. This was how these men unwound, how they enjoyed the end of the day, and they had been doing it for years. The buzz in Santiago's head dulled, but pleasantly. He felt like he could actually sleep, like he was truly relaxing for the first time in years. He had not realized how exhausting both his states of emotional being were, the draining down, the active up. He finally felt just right, like Goldilocks.

That night, months ago now, he fell into bed beside a sleeping Rosalind, and had the best sleep of his life. He had thought that his world was made up of two feelings, the high and the low, but now there was this third way to be, a way he could control. It was astonishing, and he couldn't believe he hadn't found it sooner. He felt like all of the pieces of his world were falling into place. When he woke up in the morning, he was sure everything would be perfect from here on out. He had his miracle, his energy, and now he had a way to make it tame, to control it. With these two things, there was nothing he couldn't do. He had never been happier in his life.

But the problem now, he was finding, was that the effect of drinking became less potent over time, meaning that he needed more and more of it to achieve the same result. Lately, too, it was bringing up the thoughts he had hoped it would repress, meaning he had to consume more to drown those out, too. And he knew Rosalind wouldn't like it, of course. She didn't like things that put distance between them, things that clouded him. She wanted him to go to a doctor, a shrink. She was about to suggest it again, he could see it in her face.

"I've been talking to my therapist. About us," she said. Santiago bit back another curse. The idea that someone knew about him, that she was sharing things about him, things he couldn't modify or control, made his skin crawl. He had tried to get her to promise never to talk about him in her sessions when she first started going a year ago, when they moved to Philadelphia, but she had just looked at him, blankly, and told him he didn't really understand how therapy worked.

"She wants you to come in for a session. I think it might help." Santiago stared at her. "We can talk about some of the things we're both afraid of. What do you think?"

He thought that sounded like walking over broken glass toward the doors of hell. But this was Rosalind. His wife. The woman he loved, the person who saw him and steadied him and led him into this wonderful life they had. He had to give her something.

"I'll think about it," he said. Rosalind's eyes brightened, her face wreathed in happiness. Santiago smiled back, happy his lie could give her joy. He would never talk to a therapist, hers or anyone else's. He would rather throw himself off a bridge. He would rather enlist in the army, he would rather be back in the apartment he'd lived in with his mother and grandmother and his uncles, some of whom had beat him, relentlessly, until some of them ended up in prison. He would rather be back there, again, than see a therapist, talk to a stranger who wanted to pick his brain apart, disrupt all of the hard-won accomplishments and doors he had closed, someone who would see him for what he was, weak, a liar, a piece of trash, who would show Rosalind the truth of him. She would leave him, and without her he would not survive. He had known since the day he met her that if he didn't hold on to her with both hands, tight, he would drown. That's why she was his lifeboat.

That's why, the next morning, his head pounding with his hangover, his eyes heavy from his night without sleep, his brain thinking fast as Rosalind slept, calm, trusting, beside him, he turned to his wife and smiled.

"I think we should try," he said, forcing the words from his mouth, swallowing his deep panic. She couldn't leave him. If this was what it took, this was what it took. He would give her this, and then she would stop trying to open up his brain and let all the corruption and rot within it spill onto her, polluting her and their life together. He would give her a baby, and he would never tell that baby where he came from, what he was. He would keep all of the past, all these things people wanted to pry out of him, hidden from their baby. It was the only way to give his child anything good of the world.

Anything good of himself. Their child could know him for what he was now, a success, a man loved by Rosalind, a man respected by his friends and peers. And nothing else. If he could separate his child from his past, then maybe, just maybe, it could work. This could work. He owed it to her to try. He owed her everything.

"Try?" she said, still half asleep.

"For a baby."

"You want to be a father?" she said, hope etched in every feature on her face. He nodded, once, not trusting his mouth. It was a lie, a horrible lie, but for the right reason. He didn't want to be a father. But he wanted Rosalind. Her arms were around him, his face buried in her neck, then he didn't have to smile, didn't have to conceal his terror, his revulsion. But it would be worth it, he thought. They could both get what they needed. He would have Rosalind, and she would have a child.

It barely occurred to him, and when it did he pushed the thought down with will and whiskey, that *he* would have a child, too.

Ten

Fernando is late, and Elena is sure he is not coming. His offer to give her a ride was so fantastical, so coincidental, so perfect, that she cannot help but feel it was manufactured, that she made it up, dreamed it. Or maybe that he was lying, for what reason she does not know. But with every minute that passes, she is more and more sure that he will not show up, and anger starts to pool in her gut.

She looks at her phone, looking at more emails, *more emails* demanding work from her. Earlier that morning she had quickly looked through leases and run a few credit checks at a café with internet, and now there are already more emails, more work. She is on vacation. They had been so sympathetic. How quickly that had disappeared. The latest from her boss implies that she would have properties removed from her care if she didn't improve her efficiency. She wants to throw her phone in the ocean.

She sits on the front steps of the house, where as a young woman she used to sit and watch Gloria cooking. Back then Gloria had lived, and worked, across from their home, and she could see straight from her front steps to Gloria's kitchen, watch the *habichuelas* soften, watch the tostones crack under Gloria's wooden mallet. Although there are tostone makers, two pieces of wood on a hinge, shaping them into perfect circles, Gloria told her those things were for tourists, making Elena feel sad about the fact that they had one back in their house in Philadelphia, one her mother said Elena's aunt Maria had given her years before.

She hasn't seen that thing for a long time. She wonders if her mother burned it. She wishes Rosalind had just given it to her, instead of throwing it away or wherever it's gone. Just because her mother needs nothing of her father doesn't mean she, Elena, is the same way. *But doesn't Rosalind want that to be the case?* Elena wonders now if her mother's choice to continue to tell Elena nothing about Santiago's past is less a way to honor his wishes and more a way to erase him from Elena's existence. Erasing something that was never really there.

These days Gloria works around the corner, and all Elena can see on the apartment that used to be hers is a sign, *Se Vende,* "for sale." Who will buy here now? Who has ever bought here? When her parents brought her to the island for the first time all she saw was Bayamon. It wasn't until Elena was ten or eleven that she saw San Juan for the first time. She can barely remember it, but there had been some kind of fight, and Rosalind had won, and they had taken a car, which must have been her grandfather's, and driven to San Juan despite his protests. Thinking on that first trip, she remembers that every third building looked like a ruin, trees growing through the roofs, cats bounding through the nailed-up boards colored brightly with graffiti. It hasn't changed all that much over the years, a building renovated here, another there, but slowly. On her last visit, years ago, Elena had seen a few more ruins turning to livable buildings, in various states of progress. There were still houses with trees peeping out the windows and rooftops, but there were also some beautiful, finished places. Places that looked the way this house used to, before her father let it rot. But would any of those nice places last, now, after the storm? Who had brought that money to the island, and would they take it away?

A horn beeps, startling her. Elena looks up, and sees a beat-up red compact car, she doesn't know what type, she never notices things like that, idling on the road next to her father's house. Fernando sticks his head out, looking at her in a concentrated way. This is the way he looks, she has decided, he is an examiner, his focus firm, pinning her down like a lepidopterist with a butterfly. He looks at things as though his glasses were microscopes. Perhaps he wishes they were.

"You coming?" he asks, and Elena frowns at him. He was the late one. But then, he is also giving her a ride, she supposes she can't complain.

"Yes, of course. Thank you."

She stands and shoulders her bag, a dusty tote with *PBS give drive 1998* printed on it, which she found this morning between a pile of torn lace curtains and two stacks of *Life* magazines in her father's room. She slides her body into Fernando's car, a dusty thing. Cups, bric-a-brac, books, litter the interior. She smiles at him, grateful he is here, then a sudden thought gives her pause. She is doing what all children are taught not to do, she is taking a ride from a stranger. *He knows your father, that's not a stranger, is it?* But her father knows so many people she does not know, all of whom are strangers to her. In his piles of papers she found letters from people, people she has never heard of. A letter from 1975 from a Corporal Ortiz asking to come stay with her parents; letters dating from 1972 onward in which Pearl Schultz asks her father how his constitutional law class is going and if he is eating enough and if the elites were slowly destroying him; letters from her grandmother that don't have real words, just scrawling images. Elena is not sure, but they looked like monsters. There are reports on her grandmother's health, all of them bad, all of them describing her condition in terms Elena does not really understand, listing medications and dry descriptions of "incidents," "episodes," full of euphemisms, *why do we hide in words?* But the reports are from Bellevue. The mental hospital. Rosalind had been right in this, at least. Her grandmother had not been sane. As far as Elena can tell, Esperanza had had some kind of mental issue involving voices or multiple personalities. She looked up what she could understand of the symptoms and though she cannot be sure, it sounds the most like paranoid schizophrenia. She doesn't know much about it, although it's different from her father's own diagnosis, bipolar. Elena wonders if one mental illness flows into the other, like Russian nesting dolls, so the baby of bipolar would be what, exactly? What should she be worried about happening in her brain?

Perhaps it doesn't matter if she takes a ride from a stranger. She is a stranger to herself as much as he is one to her.

The car starts, and Elena considers throwing herself out of it. It will hurt, yes, but perhaps something else will hurt her later, more. Perhaps this man will tie her up in a basement and perform experiments on her body, perhaps he will leave her dead in a ditch somewhere. She looks at him out of the corner of her eye, but his eyes are on the road.

"You want to stop for coffee before we get on the highway? I know a good place. They could use the business. Everyone could," he says, blunt, his accent stronger than it was the night before. Elena wonders if he puts it on and takes it off like mascara.

"Sure." A serial killer probably wouldn't offer to get coffee first, would he? That would give her a chance to run. He is probably exactly what he is, a nice man on his way to Aguadilla, a drinking buddy her father knows in passing, a human helping another human. How wonderful it would be to be a man, Elena thinks, to not worry so much about what people offer you, to take it with open hands as your right, instead of inspecting it for poison. But what are women to do, when every story teaches them that nice old ladies with apples are trying to kill them, that wolves sit at every corner ready to eat them, that their stepmothers will abuse them, that simple home crafts will send them to sleep for a hundred years?

The car turns. It is early, nine in the morning, early for San Juan, which is a city of late nights and sleepy mornings, and the streets are empty. Fernando parks on Calle San Justo, explaining to Elena that the coffee shop is on Calle Recinto Sur, but that it goes the wrong way for their purposes, so they will just walk there and come back. This is another good sign, she knows, that he is giving her useful information, not trying to deceive her, and Elena makes a decision to hope for the best with Fernando. She has Mace on her key chain, anyway, and despite what a personal trainer she once did a trial session with implied, she knows full well how to run.

He leads her to a little café, its outside a muted taupe color, a rare neutral among bright exteriors, a handwritten sign saying *Just re-opened, come in,* on the door. Inside it is somehow welcoming, if a building can be welcoming, and the barista, a big man with a big mustache, smiles at them.

"Fernando! How are you?" he says in Spanish, and Fernando responds in kind, he has been well, he is going to Aguadilla this morning, this is his friend, he's giving her a ride to Rincón.

"My friend, Elena," he repeats in English, gesturing to her. She smiles and tells the barista, Mario, it is a pleasure.

"Rincón? What, you like to surf?" Mario asks, courteously, in English, as he starts to make their drinks, an iced latte for Elena, a red-eye for Fernando.

"Visiting family," Elena says, smiling weakly. It isn't a complete lie.

"You better be careful. It's been hit up pretty bad. All that coastal land is wrecked. Lots of detours. Just go slow, you should make it," Mario says, and Elena nods, wondering how he knows. Well, it's a small island, of course, but who is doing much joyriding these days? Parts of the island still have no power. She thinks about the insanity, the thoughtlessness of her father himself, that he has gone wandering at this time, in this world still bleeding and broken from this storm. Anger lashes her, the anger she was so unprepared to feel, anger she does not know what to do with, and she has to clench her fists to tamp it down, to contain it, to find a place for it to hide so she doesn't have to look at it, feel it, so deeply.

She fears she is running out of places to put it.

"How's it been?" Fernando asks, pinning Mario with his stare. Mario shrugs, and Elena notices that he has a few silver hairs scattered in his black curls, and a dried food stain on his shoulder.

"Slow. But people come, little by little. It's been a few days, not too many customers, but it's just important to be open, you know?" Mario slips back into Spanish halfway through, but Elena understands him, in words and sentiment. "We had a lot of people come when we were putting together packages for people stuck in the interior and along the coasts, new faces; since then, they've come to say hello, buy some beans. But we will have to buy beans this year ourselves, the crop was hit too hard for us to just use our own this year. I want to try to get them from the island, but . . ." Mario's voice trails away, sadly. If his crop of coffee was hurt by the storm, then so was everyone's.

"Maybe you make a collective blend, 'Maria edition.' See if any other farms will join in," Fernando says, stirring sugar into the paper cup Mario has lovingly handed him. Here is a man who loves coffee. He dips a spoon into Elena's own drink to taste it before handing it over to her, nodding once.

"You have something on your shirt," Elena whispers to him in Spanish. Mario smiles.

"The cost of having a three-year-old." He points to a large painting on the wall, and Elena sees a rendering of Mario, the mustache marking him, with a smiling woman, who seems to be in mid-laugh, and a baby.

"How's Marissa?" Fernando asks, sipping his coffee and adding more sugar. Elena winces, and Fernando shrugs.

"She's good. She took her old job back, teaching at the elementary school, just for the year. Another teacher left after, so. That was lucky."

"Sure. Lucky," Fernando says, his voice hard. Mario shrugs.

"Lucky for someone. Lucky for us. You going for long?"

Elena shakes her head, and then looks at Fernando. She has no idea what his plans are, what is even taking him to Aguadilla in the first place. He mentioned something about lunch. He is shaking his head, too.

"See you soon. Nice to meet you, Elena. Enjoy your family," Mario says, lightly, meaning nothing of it. It's just the way the phrase is built. But Elena has to keep her head down, focused on her coffee, as she waves her way out, so he cannot see her eyes, how his simple wish for her has hit her in the stomach.

Outside, composed, Elena follows Fernando to the car, watching him down his coffee like water. They climb in and he is energized, driving quickly on the empty streets, and they are soon out of Old San Juan, zipping by the turn that would take them to Condado, to darkened restaurants and empty hotels, passing the Sizzler sign, for the first time in Elena's life experience on the island unlit, as they hurtle onto the highway, the long route that will take them through Dorado and Manatí and Arecibo, and spit them out on the other side of the island, the western coast. Of course it was damaged by Maria, that makes perfect sense, it's coastal land. Elena has looked up the route, because this is the kind of person she is, and because she wants to know how long it will take, but still, she turns to Fernando and asks:

"How long do you think it will take?" Fernando nods as though she has asked something very important.

"Usually, maybe an hour and a half, maybe two. But now? I

don't know. San Juan looks good, but in other places they are still clearing trees and electrical poles and, well, whatever else they have to clear. Fewer resources, fewer people, more looting, more violence. It's been much harder there than here. Some of the roads were wrecked, not just blocked with fallen things, but destroyed. I honestly don't know how it will be, how long it will take us. We might have to get off the highway, if the road is bad, and drive through some towns, but then those roads might be bad, too. Leaving early was a good idea."

"It was your idea," Elena says, amused. Fernando nods.

"Yes. I have good ideas."

"I bet your students just *love* you," Elena says, rolling her eyes. Fernando nods, apparently oblivious to sarcasm.

"So, how has it been for you? Since Maria?" Elena asks, curious. She isn't sure if there is a better way to put it. How do you ask someone about their reaction to a natural disaster? Fernando looks at her, taking his intent gaze off the road for a split second before looking back out the window.

"It's been okay. So much came to San Juan, and we had more generators, got power first. The U.S. sent boats with medical supplies, food, it all came to us in San Juan Harbor, but getting it to the rest of the island, well, that's hard. This is why I go to that coffee shop, I went after the storm to help. I saw on Facebook that Mario was doing these packages. His shop was shut, but he opened it, used his generator, called out on social media and asked friends to come put together packages, then used the trucks he uses to transport coffee from his farm to take them to distribution centers in different parts of the island."

"That's amazing," Elena says, sipping her coffee. She wishes she would have paid double for it.

"This will be a hard year for them. I didn't know them before but we've become friendly. Marissa had quit her job to help Mario with the café."

"They have their own farm?" Fernando nods.

"People are more and more interested in buying local, you know? Helping the island go back to a more sustainable place, in terms of agriculture. Sugar displaced everything. People are trying to put things back into a better place. Of course, we still grow sugar."

"That's good for you," Elena points out, remembering all the sugar he poured into his coffee. Fernando blinks, and smiles, eyes still on the road.

"I'm an addict," he says, solemn, and then smiles again. "Oh shit, sorry." Elena looks at him, his face contrite. "I didn't mean that."

"I didn't think you were really addicted to sugar, Fernando," Elena says, smiling.

"No, I meant, I shouldn't have used that language so lightly. Because of your dad, I mean. He . . . he drinks too much, I think. Not that I can judge. But I guess I'm just assuming, from what I've seen? I'm sorry. I overstepped."

Elena's face grows hot, then cold. She opens her mouth, then closes it. She wants to be offended for her father, for this is what she thinks he would want, that she should defend his honor as he always taught her to do, that she should deny, deny, then attack, punishing Fernando until he must rescind his comment, must apologize, must unthink what he knows to be true.

This man next to her likes her father. He feels strongly toward him, he told her a story of his kindness. He has woken early and is giving her a ride, taking her to find him, a trip that might be painful, or at least irritating, passing through storm-wrecked land. He likes her father, and he sees her father for what he is. He can contain those two things together in his head. Elena does not know if she herself can do that. How can she like her father, how can she love him, when he is a mystery to her? When he is a mess of things, when he is the house he has left behind in San Juan for her to find, a rat's nest of memories and pieces of the past and accomplishments and shames and damage and being damaged himself?

"I didn't mean anything by it," Fernando says, softly. He has interpreted her silence as anger, but it is pain. It is grief. Elena feels exposed, naked before him, even though he has no idea what she is really feeling or thinking. She does not want to show so much to a stranger, no matter that he doesn't seem interested in her rape or death any time soon.

"It's okay. You're right. Do we say *addict* for *alcoholic*?" Elena wonders.

"I think it's allowed," Fernando tells her.

"I wasn't offended," Elena says, trying to reassure him, trying to keep her voice even, calm. "Just thinking."

"What about?"

Elena sighs. It is a dangerous question. She says the first thing that comes to mind.

"I hope Mario manages to help the other coffee makers make an island blend. I like Puerto Rican coffee, and it will help buyers know the industry can survive this bad year." Fernando nods in agreement.

"If anyone can do it, it's Mario. He was a pretty successful banker before he bought the plantation. He used to live in New York, but he wanted to raise his family here."

"Is that why you came back?" Elena doesn't see a ring on Fernando's finger, but that doesn't mean he doesn't have children.

"I came back because I want this to be a better place. I left because I felt, my parents felt, that there weren't good schools here." Fernando laughs, a little bitter. "Well, good enough for *me*. Fine for other people, I guess. But not for their kid. I guess I felt the same way. I don't think you think as much about other people as a kid, you just want what you want for yourself. But when I was doing my master's, in forestry, my research is in tropical tree species—"

"Ceiba," Elena interrupts. She remembers. She'd looked it up. "That's why you put one on your chest." Fernando nods.

"We came down here on a research trip. I wanted to use local kids, from the university, to help. My advisor said it was a bad idea. I did it anyway, I thought he was being a dick. He is a dick. But he was right, it was a disaster, they had no idea what to do, they contaminated samples, they didn't know how to observe, what to look for. I was so angry, angry at them, angry at myself, angry at him—he had been right, the dick. But later, I thought, why don't they know what to do? This was basic science student stuff, stuff I knew back in college. Why didn't they know?"

"No one to teach them," Elena said, softly.

"Exactly. So after I got my Ph.D., I applied for jobs here. It was easy to get one—I mean, all my friends were desperate for anything and I had, like, three offers. I picked the one closest to San Juan, I always wanted to live there. My family is all over the U.S. now, they think I'm crazy. Especially after Maria, they've been sending me job postings for mainland universities. But I'm happy here." The car slows, stops, traffic is being diverted ahead for roadwork. They inch along, the few cars on the road quickly forming *un tapon,* a traffic jam. As they pass the work, Elena gasps. Whole chunks of the road are missing on the left side, all the gravel and asphalt and other road materials stripped away, the rusted metal supports left bare. It looks like someone, some giant bird, ripped through the highway with iron-hard talons, clawing away at it.

"Mario said it was bad. I haven't been out of San Juan much since Maria, I haven't seen this," Fernando says. Elena can do nothing but nod. It takes them ten minutes, maybe fifteen, but then they are past the work, back on the open road. They are silent now, sleepy, perhaps, or maybe both a little shocked, embarrassed to be shocked, but shocked all the same.

The world around them is deceptive. The island is beautiful, in-herently, it holds great beauty. There are lush rich green trees, even some of the ceibas Fernando is so fond of, and bright dancing flowers along the sides of the highway. There are hills and mountains, and if she does not look very hard, that would be all Elena would have to see. The lush vegetation covers up many sins. Downed trees could be from the storm, or a heavy wind. Things grow fast in the Carib-bean, and the landscape has already absorbed the shock of the hur-ricane and started to recover. But the man-made parts visible to her are a wasteland, cracked, bruised, destroyed. She sees cement-block houses whose roofs have caved in under the weight of telephone poles, and downed trees on little streets, their roots still reaching out for what the air cannot give them. She looks over at Fernando, and his eyes are nailed to the road. She wonders if this focus, now, is more to not have to see what is around them than to see the highway itself.

Elena leans her head against the window, and feels her body want to give into sleep. She tries to keep her eyes open, to keep seeing, bearing witness, but she loses the battle, and before she can try to wake herself, she is lost in sleep.

She wakes up somewhere around Quebradillas. She does not know where that is, and the sign does not tell her how near or far it might be, it only has the name of the town, no other information. She checks the time; it has been over an hour since she dozed off, and she is being a terrible road trip companion.

"Good morning," Fernando says. "We're making good time, ac-tually. I wonder, do you want to stop in Isabela? I've heard it's a pretty beach, haven't ever been."

"Oh. Sure, of course." Elena would rather not stop, actually, but it's his car. Fernando's eyes are still glued to the road, blinking slowly behind his glasses.

"They're going to get stuck that way," she jokes. He glances at her, confused, then he gets it, and smiles.

"Old wives' tale."

"What's a new wives' tale?" Elena asks, feeling whimsical.

"You'll know soon enough, right?" Fernando says, offhandedly, but Elena straightens.

"I beg your pardon?"

"Aren't you getting married?" Fernando asks, sounding puzzled. Elena stares at him. She told her father she had broken off her engagement. How had he forgotten? *How did he even remember in the first place?* But then, why is she surprised? Her father rarely retains information, little things, about her. The big things, the achievements, things that reflect his own accomplishments in life, big names and big events, they stick in his brain. The rest, as far as she knows, swirl away in the stream. He has always been this way. More than once, when he was still a daily part of her life, he asked her how old she was. He never knew the names of her teachers or her doctors, all her friends bled together, and Elena does not know if he ever registered a boyfriend, few and far between as those had been. Her mother has detailed folders, labeled by year, that contain Elena's whole life: blood test reports, macaroni art, letters she sent from summer camp, pay stubs from her first summer job, a playbill from a play she was in in college, photos of her on her high school soccer team, postcards she sent from her year abroad in Buenos Aires, a copy of her graduate school diploma, a copy of the lease on her New York apartment. Anything important in her life, Elena brings it dutifully home to Philadelphia, where it is filed, kept safe, contained. Her father never met Daniel. Rosalind was his Facebook friend, still is, in fact. They trade recipes. Elena knows she should consider this a betrayal, but why? She ended things with him. Why begrudge her mother the chance to bake a new type of biscotti?

"Not anymore," Elena says. "No new wives' tales for me."

"Should I be sorry?" Fernando asks, and Elena appreciates him for this. Most people just apologize, a knee-jerk reaction that she understands but dislikes. What concerned Elena most when she ended the relationship was not how much she felt, but how little.

"No," Elena says. "I ended things."

"Why?" Fernando asks, bluntly. Elena realizes that he must in fact be a rather blunt person.

"I realized that I liked what he represented, but not him."

"What does that mean?" Fernando sounds confused. Elena doesn't know what it means, it just came out of her. She thinks.

"He was stable. I like stability. I crave it. But he wasn't anything *more* to me. And the person you marry should be someone you just all around adore, I think. He deserved better than someone who was using him like that." Elena feels freer admitting this. She had been using Daniel, making him a safety blanket. Better that she had realized this before it was too late.

"How'd you meet?" Fernando asks. Elena smiles wryly.

"The university I went to does the nerdiest mixer events. There is a lecture, and then drinks. It's for alumni but other people can come, too. I went to one about this history of Jewish food—my mom's Jewish, I'm Jewish, too, that's how it works . . . well not for everyone, if they choose not to be, but, anyway, I'm Jewish. I thought this food lecture would be interesting. Daniel, that's him, he had tagged along with a friend who'd also gone to my university. Daniel went to Brandeis, he's, like, *very* Jewish." Elena pauses. "Sometimes I wonder if I was, like, leaning into that part of myself with him. Because I've never felt totally really Latina. Maybe I just don't know what it really means to me. Because of my, well . . . Sometimes it's easier, for me, to embrace the part of myself that's easier for me to understand, or that's more welcoming or something. Not that Puerto Rico isn't, I just don't have such a difficult relationship with . . . with the person in my life who is . . . well. Maybe it was just easier to focus on that one part. With Daniel. Anyway, we ended up getting a drink, and he asked me out. He's kind. Moderate in all things. Rarely angry, rarely, never, too much of anything. A totally appropriate amount of person."

"Do you regret it? Breaking it off?"

Elena looks at Fernando, whose eyes are still on the road.

"No. I haven't heard from him since, not much. So I guess he doesn't either. I think, I *think* I liked him, loved him, for all the things he wasn't. And that's not right. I should have loved the things he was."

Elena looks out the window. She has surprised herself with her own candor. But there is a freedom to talking to Fernando, who knows if she will ever see him again after this car ride? This moment? He is like talking to the wind.

"I'm surprised that my father told you," Elena admits. She didn't know he had even registered the engagement.

"He wanted to celebrate. He bought the bar a round," Fernando admitted. Elena winced. "It was six P.M. on a Tuesday, so the only person he actually bought a drink for was me. And himself. Of course." *Of course.*

"I wasn't sure if I was going to invite him to the wedding, actually," Elena confessed.

"Your fiancé? That's a bold choice." Fernando is attempting a joke, and Elena laughs, more out of respect for the effort than because it is actually all that funny.

"My father," Elena explains. Fernando's eyes, already owlish under his glasses, widen larger.

"I didn't know it was so bad."

"It isn't bad. It isn't anything," Elena says, and gets the feeling she always gets in her stomach when she is lying. But she isn't, right? *Do you always get so angry over people for who you feel nothing?* "We don't have a bad relationship. We don't have one at all. But he can be a bit . . . unpredictable. Mercurial. When I was a kid he was so good for years, I mean, he was always up and down but he didn't drink much, and he was more stable. But by the time I was eighteen it was, like, he was done trying. Sometimes he can be great, and then, when he's going through a dark period, or a really manic period, he's just hard to explain. Hard to contain. No matter what is going on, he's going to do what he's going to do. There is no best behavior. No special occasion so he does what he's supposed to do. And that's really hard. How do you explain that to people?"

"You're ashamed of him," Fernando states, flatly.

"No! No, I just . . . I just saw this whole thing, me having to explain it all to him over and over again, to Daniel's family, and them not getting it, and judging him, and how much that would hurt. And I thought, if this is what I'm thinking about, then is this worth it? Having a wedding at all. Being with this person who, I know, I just *know*, will never really get this. Because—"

"Then he'll never get *you*," Fernando finishes for her.

"Yeah," Elena says, breathing deeply. They sit in silence, watching the damaged landscape slide by. This place is a paradise, broken and rotting and lush and gorgeous all at once. *Of course people like to come and go,* Elena thinks. That way they can just see the color and the sun and the sea and ignore all the crumbling things in between.

"Well. Yours wouldn't be the first wedding to fall apart over a guest list. My sister Rosa almost threw her mother-in-law out a window over their rehearsal dinner. Only two stories up, but still."

Elena doesn't respond. She is unsettled by how comfortable she feels with Fernando. Being close to people has never been an easy task for her. There is so much she hides from them, so much she does not say. It's not easy for her to talk about her father, about the mess he has made of her life. She has never told a friend everything about her father, not the real truth, not about his drinking, his mental illness, his self-imposed banishment to this island like a Puerto Rican Prospero. They would have asked questions and she had so little to tell them, she knew so little herself. Even with Daniel she was tentative, careful, spinning the story. She has never had a conversation like this with anyone other than her mother. Never been with someone who knew so much, and was so open about what he knew. It is a new sensation for her, and it makes her feel on alert, waiting for something to go wrong, waiting for him to use what he knows in some way.

Elena looks at her phone, trying to disconnect from Fernando, to distance herself from him even though they are in the same car. She needs space, even just in her head. She pulls up her distant cousin's blog again, and on a whim, searches the posts for her destination, Rincón. Her cousin has written about this place, it seems, and she starts to read.

Rincon is a place where people think it is named for one thing but it is really named for another and they just happen to be the same name. It is this kind of coincidence that makes the island a very confusing place for outsiders, and a perfectly logical place for residents.

Rincon means corner, or nook, and the area is technically sort of a corner of the island, although given that the island is a rather irregular oblong it hardly has corners at all. Many people think that is why Rincon is called Rincon, but many people are wrong. It is in fact named after Don Gonzalo Rincon, a wealthy sugar planter from the 1770's.

It's funny to think of sugar making men rich. That's not what anyone came to the New World for, after all. They came for minerals, metals, and instead they got sweetness and human sweat. By the time the Spanish came to the New World, the Canary Islands, Portugal's

first colonies, were already rich in cane, already desperately process-
ing juice to crystal to sweeten life on the Iberian Peninsula. And yet
Columbus packs his bags with cane plants, no matter that the Indies
he intends to find already have sugar, are the originators of the sugar
plant centuries and centuries ago. Was that a sign, do you think, that
he was not as sure about finding India as he claimed? Or was it like
those people who pack their suitcases with food from home, fearing the
options in foreign lands?

Come to think of it, Spain in the New World looks the way so
many vacations look, especially those taken by college freshmen. They
came for adventure and riches, but the mines ran dry fast, the natives
died even faster, pesky things, and what started as a wonderful Spring
Break vacation fueled by rum and party energy ends up as a century-
long slog where half your landing party are dead with malaria. Who
among us hasn't had a vacation like that?

As Spain moved on to green pastures, untapped veins of gold and
silver, swallowing up Mexico and jabbing its blunt fingers into what
would soon be Colombia, Venezuela, Panama and Guyana, it left its
first loves far behind, the islands clutching yearbooks full of promises
and the hands of the thousands of forgotten dead. Puerto Rico, its
natives gone, its gold gone, its purpose gone, gave itself up to the hearty
pigs and skittish horses that now roam its virgin hillsides. But as the
other islands in the Caribbean are converted into sugar factories, so
too, eventually, is Puerto Rico, and Rincon, this little corner of the
world, is an excellent place for that, its climate agreeable, its crop
yields dense. And soon it is all sugar, from here to there, supplanting
all local agriculture and making men servants to the painful crop.

And so a century passes, like grains of sugar through the hourglass.
Spain, the creator of the conquistador, the terrorizer of the New World,
the bringer of pox and taker of silver, the hungry wolf at the door, has
softened, weakened, it is an old dog now, its teeth rotted away in its
mouth, fat and flatulent, grey at the muzzle and weak at the joints.

It barks like a champion, still, and refuses to admit that times have changed, refuses to see that the 20th century fast approaches, refuses to accept that four centuries is more than enough, it won't just let it go.

But of course it must. And Rincon, its position making it easily attacked over and over again, by English ships and in pirate battles, eventually finds itself invaded by something else entirely, groovy gringos eager to hang ten. A less violent invasion, to be sure, and a more lasting one. Now this area, so vulnerable to hurricane rains and the punishments of the sea, is also a prime tourist spot. Once missing on many maps, it is the only place some tourists to the island have really seen. A corner of the world where you can see the sea rushing up to pull you under, a place where people look at that every day and somehow imagine that they will be safe, on the crumbling land weakened by the sweetener in their coffee.

Question, what kind of person lives in a place like this, knowing what it is? Answer, the kind who is waiting for the sea to swallow him whole.

They have passed Quebradillas, and Fernando takes the exit for Isabela. Instantly the highway drops away, and they are on a much smaller road, twisting through the countryside. The empty countryside. There is no one around, few other cars, and several roadside shacks they pass advertising *aguacates frescas y maduras* and pinchos and *bacalaitos* are empty. It all seems abandoned. Elena's heart aches at all the emptiness, for the coffee plants, the people living in towns that never see a cent of tourist money, ugly little places that will stay in darkness long after most of the island is electrified again, people who will suffer for the sin of not being born somewhere else. For the way this paradise is also a prison, a pretty place with no jobs and no escape, beaten down by the rain and the sea.

"Should be twenty minutes, maybe less," Fernando says.

"I thought you hadn't been?" Elena asks. Fernando points to his phone, which is attached to the dashboard and navigating for him. Of course. And he is right, for twenty minutes later they are driving through the town of Isabela, right through a square with a large church on one side.

It looks like most other Puerto Rican towns she's been to, with one striking exception. It's completely empty. Fernando slows the car down, then stops, and there are no cars behind him to beep at him in anger. He turns off the car suddenly and gets out, and Elena follows him.

"Jesus," he says. Elena nods, looking up at the church, which has a sign declaring that it is the parish of San Antonio de Padua, and another, paper sign declaring that it is *closed*. It's eerie how quiet it is, with only the coos of pigeons audible. A cat wanders through the square, displacing the birds, and stops, looking at the two of them and meowing, plaintively. Elena wishes she had something to give it, but doubts that it wants anything from their car.

"You wanted to see the beach, right?" Elena says, softly, unsure what else to say. Fernando nods, looking dazed, and gets back in the car. Elena follows, and watches him warily. She feels like perhaps he shouldn't be driving but she doesn't want to offend him by offering, and she can't just make him let her, it's his car. The engine starts and Fernando follows the road down a hill and past a large apartment building that is clearly devoid of inhabitants, and past a group of little huts, shut up, and a basketball court, and parks under a tree. Elena smiles, that's something her father would do, to keep the car cool. She looks out and it is true, the beach is beautiful.

"This all flooded." Fernando breathes out, still sitting in the car. He points to a hut, and Elena can just make out watermarks, half-way up the side of the wall. "I saw it on the news. They evacuated the town. I guess a lot of people just never came back."

"Fuck," Elena says. She has no more eloquent thought to offer. There is a shrine on the beach, with an image of a woman holding a child. Her face is blank, as is the face of the child, and the lettering around the woman identifies her as La Virgen de los Pescadores. It looks like a cartoon person. Elena shakes her head, wondering who this woman is, who her child is. She isn't Mary, and that isn't Jesus. There are icons of women with children in their arms in bright robes all over Latin America, and Elena, whenever she sees them, wonders what local goddess has tried on Christianity so she doesn't have to die out. "I will never understand the Catholic Church's obsession with virgins."

"Original sin," Fernando says. "But it is a funny thing. When the Europeans came here, the Spanish, they folded all these local goddesses into the church so they could convert the natives, who wouldn't let go of their gods. And all these poor women had to become virgins again."

"Apparently there is a surgery you can do to *restore* your hymen," Elena tells him, then blushes. This is a strange conversation to have, and it calls sex to mind but it is also entirely unsexy. The look on Fernando's face confirms it, and he laughs.

"If you are trying to distract me from how insane this is, it's working," he tells her. She smiles. Perhaps she was. She gets out of the car, and Fernando follows her. She takes off her shoes, and walks out onto the sand. The beach makes a natural curve, and at one end there are rock formations, probably a part of a fort or defensive wall, long abandoned and decaying prettily. *So much of the decay on the island is mistaken for beauty,* Elena thinks, *and not what it really is, death.* Fernando is beside her, and they make a silent mutual decision to walk along the beach, their feet cooled by the tide. It is a large crescent of yellow sand, which is probably not geometrically perfect, but it looks that way to Elena. The sea is deep teal and, farther out, clear navy today. A few houses peek through the palm trees and plants and vines, but most of the curving shoreline looks empty of human life. A palm tree has grown almost horizontally, and Elena imagines sitting on it and gazing out at the pristine ocean waves. Looking at it, Elena cannot picture hurricane waves and flooding. It looks like every cartoon of a perfect tropical paradise, like a place nothing bad can ever touch. She can almost hear the "Kokomo" lyrics as the sun turns the water ever bluer, and a breeze ripples through the palms. How does such a beautiful place turn so deadly year after year? Maria was not the only storm to ever hit the Caribbean, nor will it be the last. How does the island continue to look so deceptively placid and calm when it has just been lashed by the angry sea and vicious rains? The beauty of the Caribbean is a lie, a lure, an act of lunacy.

"It is very pretty," Elena says, when they reach the rocks and look back. It is desolate and beautiful. Without anyone on the beach, if Elena keeps her eyes on the shoreline, she can pretend they are back in time, before the Spanish entered the New World, that the island is unblemished and whole. Elena can almost see them walking back in time, imagining them centuries ago. Would they be the natives or the conquistadors? What do you do when you are probably a mix of both? She takes a picture of the empty perfect beach before she can think about it. The image is so beautiful she wants to keep it, although she's not sure what for. She just knows she wants to document things, like any good historian would, even if it's just for her.

"Can I tell you something?" Fernando asks her, and she nods. "I don't have anyone to meet in Aguadilla." Elena looks at him, not understanding. "I just said that because I thought maybe you would be freaked out if I offered you a ride out of the blue, so I said I had somewhere to be because I thought that might make it more likely that you would say yes."

"Please don't murder me," she says, pretending it is a joke when it is very much not. This would be a wonderful place to murder her, and throw her body into the sea. There are no witnesses, he would absolutely get away with it.

"Okay," he says, calmly. "Since you said please." He smiles at her, and Elena releases a breath she didn't know she was holding. Her hand is on the Mace in her purse, though.

"Why did you want to give me a ride, then?" she asks. He sighs, deeply.

"Your house. It was my family's, a few generations ago." A feeling like falling, like when you are in a dream and start falling, envelops Elena whole. The house. It comes back to the house. *Of fucking course it does.* "I realized it after I talked to your father a few times at the bar. And then, when I saw it after Maria, well. He's not keeping it up. I was hoping, um, to buy it, actually. I brought it up to him once but he didn't want to talk about it. But you're here now, and I thought maybe *you* might be willing to, well, consider it."

Her body jerks, and the air stops in her throat.

"You want to buy the house," Elena says, flatly. She is proud of that flatness. She worked hard for it.

"I didn't, really, until I saw the way it's been, well, treated. It was a beautiful place when my great-grandparents owned it, and I want it to be beautiful again. They had to sell it to pay for my father to go to college in the U.S."

"I see." Elena's heart is beating fast in her chest. She had hoped, she had thought . . . well, it doesn't much matter now. *Don't get in the car with a strange man,* it's good advice. Too bad she didn't take it. What is it about her that makes it clear to the world she is a damaged animal? Someone there to be hit? "Well. I'll certainly think about it. I guess we really have to find my father now, right?" Fernando looks horribly guilty. *Good.*

"I didn't mean . . . I do want to find him. And I was happy to give you a ride, I'm not trying to, like—"

"Curry favor with the new potential owner?" Elena spits out, bitter. "I guess it's not me you want to murder."

"What?"

"Well, I'm only the owner if my father is *dead,* right?" Fernando stares at her, stricken. But really, the thought must have occurred to him. And if it hasn't, Elena's not so sure he should be teaching anyone anything.

"Elena, I didn't mean that. I'm sorry."

"I guess that explains why you've been so nice to me. Offering me memories of my father, driving me here. Buttering me up."

"That isn't . . ." But it is. They both know it is.

"We should get on the road," she says, walking away from him, back to the car. She had been so comfortable with him, so fast. She liked him, even felt attraction toward him. And he was using her. Well, why not? He owes her nothing. He is a stranger. His little story about Maria and her father, a manipulation. His warm understanding? The same. And what does she care? She doesn't know him. She's using him, too, she needs a ride, he wants a house.

By the time she reaches the car, the sea wind had dried the angry tears in her eyes, and she is ready to move on, on to Rincón, where she can leave Fernando and his greed, and a feeling of betrayal that is so strangely disproportionate to how well she knows him, far behind.

"Elena, please." He sounds out of breath, and when she turns to him, she sees sand splattered up the sides of his legs, evidence that he has run after her. "Can't I just explain? I really do want to help you, I thought—"

"I said I would think about it. Can we go to Rincón now?" she asks, her voice short and biting. He nods once, and silently gets into the car. Elena keeps her gaze out the window, refusing to look at him as they roll out of Isabela. As they leave the ghost town, Elena catches movement in the corner of her eye, and watches a wizened woman with a face like a snapping turtle divvy out handfuls of dry cat food to an eager colony of felines. So there is someone here after all, someone to feed the cats. The thought warms Elena, and she turns to share it with Fernando, then thinks again. Why would he care? He doesn't care about her. She is a means to an end. How stupid she was, telling him things about herself, Daniel, her father, her life, when he just wants to get something from her. How weak she is, always turning to the wrong people over and over again, no matter how they treat her. Her own history repeating itself, into infinity.

Elena does not say anything for the rest of the car trip, and Fernando rushes to fill the silence she has left. He tells her about trees and flowers they pass. He tells her about his own field of study. He tells her how bad it is that they haven't hit more traffic. She lets the words flow over her, but they do not soothe her anger. Her pain.

"This is prime surfing time in Rincón. It's popular for the swells, surfers love it. The fact that there is no one on the road, no one heading there, isn't a good thing. It means the tourists are scared, and the island will suffer without the money."

Elena doesn't respond, merely looks out to the ocean. The waves *are* massive, bigger than Elena has ever seen on the island, bigger than they ever are in San Juan and its surrounding beaches. They are also empty. The mountains of water rise and fall devoid of sun-bleached surfers sliding along them, the movement looking so easy, so free.

Fernando's jaw is set.

"Where should I be driving?" he asks her, and Elena realizes she will have to talk to him, direct him. She opens the email she received the night before from Diego, who gave her his address.

"I think it's off Calle Cambija. Let me map it," she says, her tone sharp, and does so. She directs Fernando with as few words as possible, and they are soon in front of a little beach shack, a salt-faded pitted sign proclaiming that the place is called Tito's. And behind it, twenty feet away, is a bright green house built close to the beach, sitting on cement stilts, raised off the ground, and accessible by a set of cement steps. It is so close to the sea that, no doubt when the tide is high or the storms are bad, the sea will surround the house, leaving it stranded from land.

"Okay. I'm here. Thanks for the ride," she says, refusing to make eye contact, and reaches for the door.

"Wait! I can't just let you go alone, this man is a stranger, something could happen to you," Fernando says.

"I got in a car with a stranger this morning, obviously I'm okay with strangers," Elena says, bitterly. She's an idiot, she knows, all of this nonsense of her own making. She should have known he was too good to be true. Most people are.

"Elena, I'm sorry. I should have done this differently. I'm not, like, scheming to steal your father's house. I just wanted to make an offer."

"I don't have time to think about this right now," Elena says. "I just don't. Okay? So thanks for the ride, and rest assured, if I find out my father is dead in a ditch somewhere I will certainly let you know so you can buy the house and I can get the fuck out of here. Sound good?"

"Look, I'm going to call you, check in on you. I don't feel right about this."

"Of course you're going to call me. You have to check in on your potential investment, don't you?"

She slams the door shut before she can hear his response, and looks at the house, watching as the front door opens and a man emerges. He is tall with graying hair and a leathery face, his long limbs covered in a faded button-down shirt and a pair of board shorts. He walks toward the beach shack as Elena reaches it, and it feels like something out of a movie, some destined thing. Elena looks behind him, a surge of hope as strong as the hard waves crashing to the shore, rider-less, but no one else emerges, this man is alone. *Maybe my father is there, maybe he's sleeping, maybe the door will open—*

"Elena?" the man says, with a hint of disbelief.

"Are you Diego?" Elena asks, like this is natural, normal, what else can she do? He smiles, the wrinkles in his face deep and calming. Before she knows what to say next or do he is hugging her, and it feels so strange, more kindness from a stranger, another thing she cannot, should not, trust.

"Where is my father?" she asks, knowing she sounds like the lost little girl he left at a Home Depot, trying not to care. "Is he here?" The sudden stiffness of his body tells her the truth before his mouth can.

"He's not here, Elena."

Of course not. He's never where he's supposed to be.

"Okay, then. So. Tell me. Who the fuck are you?" Elena asks, rage and pain making her bold. Diego smiles.

"You look like him, but my god, you sound just like Rosie. Is your friend coming in?"

"He's not my friend," Elena says, following Diego into the house, refusing to look back. Only the insane do the same thing over and over again and expect a new result, and Elena is not insane. At least, she doesn't think so. More and more, she isn't entirely sure. After all, apparently she comes from a long line of madness.

Eleven

The winter in New Haven was every bit as terrible as Santiago thought it would be, and he fantasized about California every day. He should have put the application back in the trash. Coming to Yale was a mistake he would regret for the rest of his life. He wondered if anyone had ever thought that before, and smiled grimly.

The truth was, though, that he loved it. He loved the work, even if he hated the place. Law school was hard, of course, but he was ready for how hard things could be this time. And he was confident, this time, not arrogant and ignorant as he had been before, but confident. They wanted him here. No one was going to talk him out of knowing he belonged on this campus, no matter how hard they tried. And they did. The Yale law students were a whole new breed compared with the Stanford undergraduates. Competitive, self-assured, the children of Important People, the capitals clear. But also smart, so smart, and idealistic, and they had such vision for the future. These would not be corporate lawyers, small-claims people, or real estate attorneys. These would be people who would change the American legal system.

Yes, it was hard. But he was not alone, not as he had been. He had Rosalind, who called him every week on Sunday evenings and listened to him talk and talk and talk about laws and precedents and things she didn't care at all about, dizzy from the sound of his voice. He had his professors, who liked him, enjoyed his liberal dissent, enjoyed his defenses of socialism, enjoyed his determination. He also had a new energy that coursed through his veins, bright and electric. He could stay up for hours reading, studying, thinking, without food. He had had moments like this in college, but in his first year of law school he was shot through with a vivid bright energy that made him feel powerful, limitless. It was like a superpower, like the comic books he had loved as a child. He wondered if he had been bit by a radioactive spider, or something, but without the downside. He could not imagine living without this energy now, this wild never-ending jolt. He thought it would never go away, that this was who he was now. But all superheroes forget that power asks a price, and Santiago was no different. He had a new power and that was all he knew.

And he had Diego, who he met in his first-year constitutional law class.

"You must be the other wetback," he heard a cultured voice say, snidely, as he took out his notebook. He was early, he usually was, he liked to be early for class, get settled in. He turned, his lip curling in disgust, and saw a pale-skinned man with the features of a Spanish aristocrat beaming at him, broadly.

"My family took a flight here. Like most Puerto Ricans," he said.

"Doesn't it ever make you mad we don't have a good sob story? People eat that up, talking about how you clung to the side of a boat from Cuba, or swam the Rio Grande." The man had no accent, but he said *Rio Grande* perfectly.

"Maybe you don't have a sob story. I'm poor." Santiago wasn't sure how to take this man, who had moved to sit next to him.

"That's good. I bet that does well with this crowd. Gets you all kinds of ass."

"I have a girlfriend."

"Then it clearly did *very* well. Me, I've got nothing. *And* I like men. You can imagine how that plays out with the WASP setup here in *Connecticut.*" Santiago drew back. He had gay friends in San Francisco but none of them had declared it as quickly as this man.

"What's the matter? You worried I'm gonna jump you?" the man said, with an exaggerated leer.

"Of course not. If you wanted that you would have stayed in Puerto Rico. I'm sure you came here for some variety," Santiago said, grinning. He could fight back. Neil had taught him how. The man smiled at him, a genuine smile.

"Absolutely. You're safe from me. Diego Perez Acevedo."

"Santiago Vega Junior." The *Junior* had been automatic, and he regretted it.

Diego winced.

"I bet everyone calls you Junior, don't they? Fucking Puerto Ricans."

"I hate it," Santiago said. Diego was the first person he had ever told that.

"I promise, on my honor as a gentleman and a scholar, to never fucking call you Junior." They shook on it, and the class began.

Diego was the first Puerto Rican he had ever met who was *truly* proud of being so. He knew more about the island than Junior, he knew about the crimes the American government had perpetuated against the Puerto Rican people and he was vocal in his criticism, especially of the military.

Santiago couldn't wait to introduce him to Neil, who had begrudgingly forgiven him for his defection to the East Coast, and sent him long letters detailing his classes at Berkeley, and the work he was doing as a volunteer for a young politician, Harvey Milk, an openly gay man who he was starting to believe was going to change everything. For all of Neil's social liberalism, his one sticking point in any argument was the army, an institution he stayed staunchly loyal to no matter the numbers pouring in from Vietnam, no matter the protests. Santiago was sure that they were going to *hate* each other.

He couldn't wait.

New Haven might be terrible, the proximity to New York might be hellish, but his life had never felt more complete than at this moment. He had someone who loved him, someone he loved. He had friends, and a direction in life. He was as free from his past as he had ever been. Nothing could touch him, now, not when everything was so settled, so clear.

Later, when he got the call from the hospital that his grandmother had died suddenly, and that he was now completely responsible for his mother, for her care, for her life, he would realize that moment alone in the night was the happiest, calmest moment of his life. He knew that when he compared it to the sheer blinding terror he suddenly felt, the recognition that now everything would slip back into the filth from which he had come, and there was nothing, nothing at all that he could do about it.

He knew, as he began to make the arrangements, to funnel money into her care, to make his mother, once again, the center of his life, that he had been right to fear coming east. His past was always waiting here, to burden him. He should have stayed in California.

Santiago went to visit his father for the first time in years in the summer between his senior year of college and his first year of law school. He could no longer claim he was too far away to make the trip, as he was spending the summer in Philadelphia with Rosalind, working in the accounting department of her family department store while she took classes at the Pennsylvania Academy of the Fine Arts. On the weekends they borrowed one of her parents' cars and drove out to Valley Forge. She took him to the Brandywine River Museum of Art, which had opened just the year before. They went out to Amish country, where she taught him about the Pennsylvania Dutch, and he tried fresh cider and the best cinnamon buns he had ever had. They bought cucumbers and eggplants as big as his calf and Rosalind's mother made a salad with dill and vinegar and onions, and charred the eggplant, preparing a recipe she had learned from a Turkish employee at the store.

Her parents were always so kind to him, not the careful kindness of people around someone they fear to offend, but real bone-deep kindness, consideration. He wondered, if he had grown up in a place like this, with all this love and warmth, would he be as good as Rosalind was, as giving? *Surely it was easy to be giving when you had so much,* he thought, not without bitterness. But he had more, now, than ever before, and he was still selfish, still the same.

He had not seen his mother in months. He couldn't see her. It took too much away from him and he had so little to begin with. He was selfish, he knew it. He remembered a line from a Chekhov play Rosalind had dragged him to in college, incredibly boring but for these two lines: *When you only get your happiness in bits and pieces and then lose it anyway, like me, you begin to get bitter about it. You don't care what you say anymore.* They lived in him, those lines, and he knew his problem was less about what he said and more about what he did. He didn't care what he did or didn't do anymore for his mother. He couldn't, not if he wanted to survive. *And yet you send money and call and worry and think and—* He had to shake his head to clear it, banish those demons. *Like the ones she sees.*

He would have liked to stay in Philadelphia with Rosalind forever, but he had booked his ticket in advance, and so in August he left from Philadelphia International Airport on a plane bound for Puerto Rico. He did not bring Rosalind. He could not. He had not seen his father in years, and he did not know what would happen.

He was not sure what would happen *anyway* when he brought a white woman home. Better to leave it for later, better to make sure Rosalind wasn't going to leave him, whatever happened, whatever she learned there, saw there.

When he arrived, his father picked him up at the airport. Santiago wore a light blue peasant-style shirt over a pair of wide bell-bottoms. He had grown out his hair, and his beard and mustache. He looked like most of the students at Stanford had looked when he graduated, that intersection of hippie culture and California cool. His father looked him up and down, but said nothing. On the drive, though, instead of heading toward his new house in Bayamon, where he told his son over the phone that he had moved two years ago, he headed into San Juan.

"Where are we going?" Santiago asked. They were the first words he had spoken since he arrived. His father said nothing, but stopped the car in front of a barbershop, and motioned for him to get out.

"There is no parking. I will circle until you are done. Tell him to fix this," his father said, and then he drove off, cars impatiently honking behind him. The barber removed the mustache, the beard, and cut Junior's hair high and tight, smoothing it with wax, into a military-style haircut, exactly what his father had. He looked in the mirror grimly, and realized for the first time how much of his father's face was in his own. The beard had covered that. He wanted it back.

When they got to his father's new house, his father directed him toward the shower.

"Clean up. Then we will go see everyone, for dinner." When Santiago emerged from the shower, all of his clothing was gone. He came out with a towel wrapped around his waist, furious, to find his father drinking a beer with the same steady determination he had always shown toward alcohol.

"Where are my things?" he asked.

"I burned them," his father said, dryly. Santiago gaped at him. He had left his new suits and shoes in Philadelphia, but brought with him most of his other warm-weather clothing. That was all he had.

"I will take you to get new things. You can't wear that clothing. You look like a clown. Put this on for now." His father gestured to a pair of trousers and a guayabera, his own, Santiago assumed. The pants were too short and too loose on him, but he cinched them with a belt, and the shirt billowed against his skinny chest. His father looked at him, grunted, and drove him to San Sebastián, where the rest of the family were waiting for him to eat dinner. They spent the ride in complete silence, and for the rest of the trip he only spoke to Chavela and his siblings, who had all grown by leaps and bounds, though they would never be tall, and who listened to his stories about America with awe and disbelief. He did not speak to his father again until he said goodbye, at the airport.

When he got back to Philadelphia, Rosalind laughed at his haircut. He grew his beard out as soon as he possibly could. He would not be clean-shaven for years, not until his father died, and he *wanted* to see his face in his own.

He had had no intention of going to law school in New Haven. He got the call from Yale when he was eating lunch in the cafeteria, something he only did on Tuesdays because he had a full day of classes on campus. They had called the office of student affairs at Stanford because he had no number listed—well, he didn't have a phone. He had received the letter the day before and hadn't known what to do about it. He had already gotten into Berkeley, was already planning on going. Santiago could see his future in California perfectly, and how good it would be. He would stay here, marry Rosalind in Golden Gate Park, or they would live together, whatever she wanted. She would paint, and he would work at a small firm defending immigrants, Spanish speakers like his mother, helping them settle, making sure they knew their rights. It would be a beautiful life, bathed in California sunshine, coated in the fog off the bay.

"I'm looking forward to seeing you in New Haven in the fall, son," the law school dean said to him, his voice warm and rich.

"Sir, I think there must have been some kind of mistake," Santiago said, his voice thin. He heard laughter.

"Not at all. We are happy to welcome you to the Yale Law Class of 1975."

"But, I thought, I mean, Yale doesn't usually admit people like me. I don't know if I will be comfortable there." He was desperate, flailing, maybe he could offend the man, get the scholarship taken away, he couldn't afford to go without it.

"I understand. We've had a very, well, *specific* kind of student in the past, but we want to change that. And you won't be the only Puerto Rican kid here, I promise."

"Really?" When he was growing up, he had frequently seen signs on restaurants saying *No dogs or Puerto Ricans allowed.* And now they were getting into Yale Law School. He wanted so badly to stay in California, to live a golden happy life here. He worried that going back east would eat away at him, corrode this happiness. But he knew he could not say no to this. He thought of the words of Mrs. Schultz, his English teacher, all those years ago at the celebration lunch after his high school graduation: *You are going to go do something amazing with your life. Stanford will open doors for you, open up the world for you.* He had not come this far not to keep going. Yale was better than Berkeley. Yale was better than just about anywhere else for law. He hadn't come this far not to take the best thing he could.

"I'll see you in the fall," he said, a pit in his stomach he wondered if he would just fall right into, and never climb out again.

"I just don't see the point of living anywhere other than California," Santiago declared to Rosalind over breakfast in their tiny San Francisco apartment, throwing the application to Yale Law School into the trash with an easy toss. His New York accent, like his Puerto Rican accent, had all but disappeared through conscious labor, but some words, like *California,* remained sharp and overly enunciated, especially when he wasn't thinking hard, and now the word came out like *Cal-eee-fown-ya,* his mouth tripping over itself.

They had moved in together that year, Rosalind's second year of college and his fourth. It was a longer trip back to Stanford's campus, but it was worth it to be in the city, and not in Palo Alto. At least, it was worth it for Rosalind, he had actually liked being out there. The bucolic suburban setting had been a stark contrast to the rest of Santiago's early life and he loved it, the lawns and the quiet and the way it all felt *normal,* like a television show, a *Leave It to Beaver* life. Rosalind said it made her want to scream.

"I do," Rosalind said, firmly. "California is a nightmare." He smiled at her. He loved it out here, loved how far it was from New York, from Puerto Rico, how distance had cut him off from everything that tied him and bound him and dragged him under. How far it was from his mother, and his father.

She walked over to the trash can and pulled out the application.

"I'll never get in there."

"So there is no harm in applying, is there?" she said, smoothing it out. It was the best law school in the country, everyone had told him that. It admitted people who became presidents, Supreme Court justices, congressmen. They weren't going to let some skinny Puerto Rican kid with no money and a missing front tooth in, he was sure.

"Why sign myself up for rejection?"

"Why not take a chance?"

"I suppose," he said, taking the form from her.

"Besides. You're brilliant. You're a striver. Why wouldn't they want you?" The look in her eyes took his breath away, it always did. There was such admiration, such belief in him. No one in his life had ever encouraged him, loved him, with such devotion and care as she did. If he applied, he could say he tried. And he wouldn't be the one to disappoint her, that would be Yale's action, not his. She wouldn't lose this look on her face, the one she had now that he would do anything to maintain.

"Pass me a pen," he said, smiling. He'd never get in, and even if he did, he'd never leave the West Coast. The farther he was from New York, the better, the freer, the happier, he would be. He was never going back there, not ever. That place, that coast, was poison for him. He'd escaped it once, but if he went back, he knew he would never escape again.

Twelve

"You went to Yale with him," Elena says, for the second time, repeating the fact like a mantra, trying to place Diego, someone she has never heard of before, in space and time. Diego nods, smiling.

This man is her father's best friend. This man she has never met, never heard of, who knows both her parents intimately. This man has been living on this island with her father, has known him longer than she, Elena, has been alive, and no one has ever told her about him. *Rosalind* has never told her about him. He knows her father, he knows her mother, and Elena knows *nothing*. Why has Elena allowed the past to be a distant country for her parents, the place they fled and never spoke of again? Because it's not just her father, it's Rosalind, too. Oh, Elena knows about her great-grandparents fleeing pogroms in Russia, and her mother's high school friends and her Tyler colleagues, but Rosalind has blacked out the windows of so much of her life with Santiago that no light can get through. There is some loyalty that Rosalind has to Elena's father that even now, all these years into their separation, is more important than telling Elena about her past. Her history. The places she comes from.

No wonder Elena has always felt so alone. She was raised by people more tied to each other than to her. Even now as they untie, fray, and disintegrate, neither is tethering her anew.

Elena's phone is buzzing with work calls and texts from her mother and Fernando and she is seriously considering taking a hammer to it because *fuck all of this, who the fuck is Diego and why don't I know him?* Why does everyone want to hide her father from her? The very island, the world, is against her, and she doesn't know why she hasn't started screaming yet.

Because even if you did, no one you know would hear you, or care.

She is sitting outside his house, a drink in each of their hands, as he cooks up steaks on a grill. It is an idyllic sight, barbecue and booze and the ocean's soothing crash, or it would be, if she knew this man, knew why her father had never mentioned him, knew where her father was, knew anything.

"He never mentioned me," Diego says. It's not a question. He knows. Everyone knows. A giant conspiracy.

"Neither of my parents did," Elena says, and her tone could season cocktails, it is so bitter. Diego turns to her, his smile rueful and sad.

"I'm sorry. I think I might understand why but I can see how that must be very hard for you."

"It's nice that you can understand why because I sure as hell can't," Elena says, taking a deep sip of her drink. Diego looks at her, pensively, like he's wondering what to tell her, and something in Elena snaps.

"Please do not excuse his, their, behavior. You knew both my parents. You've been in touch with my father. I've been asked to come down here and find him and I know nothing about him anymore, if I ever did, and everyone is *lying* to me and hiding things from me, so you know what, no reasons are ever going to be enough for me, okay? I don't have to understand him. I don't have to forgive him. I'm just trying to fucking make sure he's alive. And if he's not, I need to plan a funeral."

Diego keeps looking at her, and she knows she has exploded on a total stranger who is not a stranger to anyone but her but she doesn't care. Elena knows life isn't fair, but at least her father, her family, could have tried to be fair themselves. Parents are supposed to be better than their children. *Even when they are just people in the end?* She hates the voices in her head that ask her to understand, to forgive, when all she wants to do is rage.

"Your father has always been a very secretive person. As long as I've known him. I used to think that was about trust. It took me a long time to realize it was about shame," Diego says, his tone kind. Elena looks down. Her father was always the smartest person she knew. What did he have to be ashamed of, before his failures toward her? Where is his shame *now,* when Elena needs it most?

"Neither of us could believe there was another Puerto Rican in the program. It's a small school, and, well, I don't know how many Puerto Ricans had even been on Yale's campus before, unless it was to clean something." Diego smiles ruefully, "They even told me, when I got in, that there would be another Puerto Rican, so I was on the lookout for him. He hid it well, but I knew his background, it's hard to not know where people come from when you know the signs. I knew what it was like to grow up with money, and I knew what it looked like when you hadn't. He didn't like people to know how poor he was, but I did know. I could tell. Money can sniff out no money like a bloodhound."

"I know they didn't have much but—"

"He had nothing. Wasn't hard to see. The way he ate. The way he was about money. About his clothing, always so clean. Rich people don't fear dirt like the poor do. It doesn't give us away. We don't fear being called dirty because we can always get clean," Diego says. Elena nods, slowly.

"My parents, they taught me a lot of shit I unlearned as soon as possible. Sent me away from here to boarding school in the snow, god help my freezing ass, so I wouldn't be tainted by the *natives*. Pure conquistador blood and proud of it, if you can believe that. Like being proud of being related to Stalin. When I met your dad, I used to joke he was my first 'real Puerto Rican' friend. We both joined Despierta Boricua, this Puerto Rican student group that was a few years old then, and there were maybe one hundred Puerto Ricans on the whole campus, mostly undergraduates. So I got to meet some more 'real Puerto Ricans,' although most of them were more like me, rich kids. We would buy them beer. That's when your father started going by his real name, not just trying to make white people more comfortable by letting them call him whatever they wanted."

"His real name?"

"He always went by Junior. Hated it, but it was easier than Santiago. Less foreign. I guess he could just pretend to be really tan before. No pretending with 'Santiago.'" Diego smiles, ruefully.

"That must have been hard for him. All of it," Elena says, reluctantly. Diego is giving her a window into something she isn't sure she wants to see, no matter how much she's been asking for it.

"He would never admit that. But of course it was." Diego is looking at her again and she wants to hide her face. "You look so much like him. I've seen pictures of you, but it's different in the flesh. You have his face."

Elena has heard this so many times. When she was a child, her mother said it to her with happiness, and now, as an adult, Rosalind says it with something else. Pain? Probably. Elena wonders how many times she has apologized in one way or another to her mother for having her father's face.

"He never . . . I didn't know he had a friend here. We used to visit, but we never saw you here," Elena says.

"I wasn't here." Diego smiles. "I moved to California after law school, never left the West Coast. I've only been here a few years. I moved back here after I retired from the bench."

"You became a judge?"

"I was a lawyer for twenty years, then I became a judge. First civil, then family court, out in Washington State. Family court was absolutely brutal. Worst years of my life. That's what motivated my retirement, I couldn't take it anymore," Diego says, frankly, sipping his drink, a beer. Elena nervously takes a sip of her rum and it burns her down the back of her throat. She coughs.

"Why did you move to Washington?" Elena asks, not sure why she cares. Diego's eyes flicker.

"I wanted to get out of California. I needed, well, a fresh start."

"Bad breakup?" Elena quips.

"Something like that," Diego says, staring out at the sea.

"Why wouldn't he have told me about you? It sounds like you were close." Elena struggles to keep her voice something outside of pathetic. Diego looks at her again, smiling sadly.

"Your father is very good at leaving things behind that hurt him," he says. "That's something he learned early, and never un-learned. He wasn't one for unlearning, not like me."

"Do you . . . are you in touch now?"

"When I moved back here, I went to San Juan to meet him. Made him see me. Had some drinks, told him I wasn't going anywhere and he had to get used to it. He's stubborn, as I'm sure you know, but so am I. Now I see him whenever I go to San Juan. Whether he wants to or not."

Elena does not know what to say.

"How does he seem? When you see him, how is he? And when did you last see him and how was he then and have you seen him lately and, and, I don't know what else to ask. He's missing, I've never met anyone from his past before who isn't family. I wish . . . I don't know." The questions tumble out of Elena. Diego looks at her, as if he is deciding what to say. "Please, tell me the truth. Tell me *any-*

thing," Elena begs. "I know so little. It doesn't seem right to know so little about a person who is . . . who is still alive. Still connected to me. Related to me. Half of me. Someone with my face."

Diego looks at her with love and pity and it makes her skin crawl.

"Look, I haven't seen him in a while. Maybe two months ago, after the storm, just wanted to make sure everyone I know in San Juan was okay. I've noticed the past few times that he might be forgetting things. We all do, as we age, of course. But your father, it's like he's letting things go. He's always been one of the sharpest people I've ever spoken to. In his manic periods he is sharp and frantic, but in his depressive periods he's, well . . . faded. And his memory is going, faster than mine, at least. It seems like he is dulling, his intellect, his brain, it's dulling," Diego says, his voice apologetic.

Elena feels nothing but relief to hear a truth spoken, known. To hear what she knows to be true. *This is real,* she tells herself, *this is what is happening. A dulling. He goes up and down and around and around but every looping cycle chips a little something off of him, like old paint, like cloth fading in the sun.*

"But surely you've seen him? I figured he would have come with you. I'm looking for him." Elena quickly lays it out for Diego, the confusion after the storm, the confirmation that her father was fine, and this more recent panic. She had not planned to include the questions about the house, a will. She does not want to seem grasping, even if that is what she is. She tells him about Gloria, and her aunt Maria, and the albums. Once she starts all that, though, it is difficult for her to stop and it all pours out of her, the house, his promises, her confusion, Fernando, the drive here. Diego leans back, looking at her with assessing eyes, when she is done. He does not seem surprised, really, which makes her sad, but who is really surprised at this, honestly? No one she has met so far, so why start now?

"I'm sorry. That was a lot." Elena is self-conscious, her throat dry.

"Let me get you another drink." She hands him her glass.

"I must sound insane," Elena says, half to herself, then winces. "Not insane. But . . . unhinged, I guess."

"Ah. Well, that's the island for you. Islands dislocate people from their sense of reality. It's all the water. We're all alone on an island, and our brains start to imagine other realities, because our eyes can't see any habitable ones anymore. You go on the mainland, you want to be somewhere else, you can just go there. Get in the car and drive. But here, there is a limit to how far your body can go. At some point, your mind just has to take over." He pours her a large rum, and drops ice cubes into it, and turns off the grill. She had completely forgotten about the food, which now smells burnt. "You aren't driving anywhere tonight, are you?" he asks, hesitating before handing her the glass.

She has not thought this through. How is she going to get back to San Juan? It is afternoon now, and she had made a plan for Fernando to pick her up on his way back from Aguadilla, but there is no lunch in Aguadilla, and she has sent Fernando away. She takes the drink.

"Maybe you could recommend a hotel or something nearby? I was going to go back to San Juan today, but I think now that won't be possible. Unless I can get a cab to take me." Diego shakes his head.

"You could, but it's terribly expensive, all that way, and people aren't really back up and running on Uber yet. You're welcome to stay here, and I can give you a ride back to San Juan in the morning. It seems that we have a lot to talk about, anyway." Elena thinks about it. Her most recent attempt to trust in the kindness of strangers had not worked out well, although she couldn't say Fernando had intended to hurt her, or been cruel to her, just that he had wanted something other than what she wanted to give. On the other hand, Diego was a friend of her father's, for whatever that was worth, and the more time she spent with him, the more she might learn.

"You're very kind," she said.

"I'm not, really. It's just that you seem very tired. Like you are under a lot of stress. It can't be easy for you to have come here and be looking for him, like this. Drink. Stay. I promise I don't mind. I invited you here, didn't I?" Elena smiles at him, suddenly so very tired. "I've always wanted to meet you," Diego confesses. "I've always wondered what you might be like."

"If I had known you existed, I would have wondered, too," Elena offers, and Diego smiles.

"I have plenty of room, and the generators give out at night, since the storm, which means the stars are magnificent. No light pollution. No light," Diego says.

Elena thinks of all the things she was told as a child, is told as a woman, knows to be true. Being alone with strange men is the worst thing she can do, the worst situation she can put herself in.

She does not have to do this. She could leave with him right now, she could wait in San Juan, she could give all this up and go home, and tell her mother that her father is an adult and if he gets lost, he gets lost, she could sink back into her life and forget this ever happened, she could stuff all of the things she feels and wants and needs back down again and pretend she does not know that they exist. She could jump up and down on her anger and pain until they are bite-size, compressed and easier to carry, lodged in the pit of her stomach, safe like joeys in a kangaroo pouch.

And yet she knows she will say yes to this offer, that she will stay here, because her sense of danger is not as great as her craving, her need, to find her father, either in real life or through his past, from someone who knows him, to find the pieces of his life that he has kept from her, to find out if he has kept his promises.

"That would be wonderful," Elena says. "Thank you." She sips her rum, as he drinks half his beer in one swallow. Is he nervous? Or a drunk like her father? But he doesn't seem that way, not all vague and numb like her father is when he's drinking.

"What did you think of him? When you met him, back at Yale?" She doesn't really want to know about this, at least not first. She wants to know the more recent things, the immediate things. But they have all night now. And the other things can wait.

"I thought . . . I thought your father had real chutzpah. Am I saying that right? Could never get the hang of Yiddish, all those *chhhhhuh* sounds, like clearing your throat all the time. Well, you have to have it. Cojones. Something."

"Did he talk much about himself? Where he came from?" She wants to change the subject, go back to the things she wants to know.

"He didn't. But I could tell, the way he talked about his life, the very little he said, I knew his family actually were *jibaritos*. No plantation parties and Spanish lace for them. There is a Cuban film I saw at a film festival maybe ten years ago, from the 1980s, *Cecilia*. Have you heard of it?"

Elena shakes her head.

"It's set in the nineteenth century in Cuba, it's what I imagine my family's lives to have been like. Of course, it ends in disaster because it's about passing for white. And no one in my family ever had to *pass*. Your father never said his family were *jibaritos* but I knew enough about the island to be able to tell. He's from San Sebastián, a farm area, and my family has good records, I would have known if he was from landowners. By the time I met him, he'd cleaned up his Spanish so much it barely held a trace of the island, but sometimes, when he was tired or, um—"

"Drunk."

"I was going to say high. We didn't drink much then. That came later." Diego sighs, finishing his beer. "And stayed long for him. Then a little of that rural accent would come out. I know he grew up in New York, but all his family were from El Pepino, so that's the accent people around him had.

"But largely, your father didn't talk much about his past, and I understood that. Unlike my family, with our proud *legacy*," he almost spits the word out, "I think for him, the only way out was to block out his past. Leave it behind. Never talk about it, never discuss it. See, today everyone is obsessed with 'owning themselves,' right, 'check your privilege,' whatever the kids say. But then, to be anything, you had to be the right thing, the right kind of minority, keep your head down, stay in line. I never heard him talk about his family, beyond your mother and her parents. We talked about everything, your father and I, we were friends, study partners, for years, but we talked about outside things, music, art, law, history. When it came to his life, most of it was closed chapters."

Elena knows exactly what he means.

The inside of Diego's house is clean and tasteful, and far better designed than his beach bum appearance had implied. Art hangs on his walls, signs of a well-traveled life. Black-and-white photographs of carved frescos, Hindu gods and goddesses standing out in sharp relief against a jungle scene. A beautiful piece of Turkish kilim, rusty reds and olive greens in the weave. A mask that looks like it is from a Noh theater production, a print that looks like a Matisse copy. Sleek bookcases in bleached wood that looks like driftwood, and shines in the excellent natural light.

In the center of a large wall in what is clearly the living room is a beautiful painting of a man with light brown hair, looking away from the viewer out to open ocean. His gaze is more toward the water than anything else, but he is rendered with delicacy and care. Elena wonders who the man is to Diego.

"Your home is beautiful," Elena says, honestly.

"Thank you," Diego replies. "I burned our dinner, but I would love to take you out to make up for it."

"You don't have to, I should take *you* out."

"We can fight it out when we get there," he says, smiling.

"Do you have children?" Elena asks. She knows the answer is no. This is not the home of a man who has had that in his life. There is no trace of progeny, no photo of a young person to be found.

"No," Diego says, with an odd smile. "He really never told you anything, did he." But it's not a question. And it makes Elena so angry.

"Not a fucking thing."

"I'm gay," Diego says, calmly. "So kids weren't really in the cards. I mean, I know couples that have adopted, more now, and that's wonderful, but back when I was thinking about family, it wasn't as much of an option. Or at least I didn't think it was for a gay man. So no. No kids."

Gay. Oh. Elena looks at him again, and then around at his home. Her father's law school best friend was gay. That is unexpected, somehow. Not that she thinks her father is a bigot but he's of a generation that wasn't exactly always accepting. She has so many questions she wants to ask her father, what was it like when Diego came out to him, how did he feel, what was he taught about homosexuality growing up, how did it impact his sense of masculinity, so so many things she wants to know that she will *never* know, because even if she finds him, what will he offer her? She feels sick.

"Excuse me, where is your bathroom?"

By the time she reaches it her mouth is already filled with bile, her eyes already clouded with tears. She spits and sobs, silently cursing herself.

"Are you all right?" comes Diego's voice outside the bathroom. How long has she been in there?

"Of course. Sorry. I realize I should check in with my mother, can you give me a moment?" she shouts.

"Absolutely. Take your time."

She rinses her mouth out with water and then takes out her phone. There are more emails from work, *how are there more emails from work?*

One just says *Call me, now,* and it's from Terrance. She checks the time; the email was sent at 7:00 P.M. and it's seven-thirty now. She dials.

"Where are the Hoyt Street property documents?" Terrance barks out, no hello, no how are you.

"Terrance, I'm on . . . not a vacation but this is my vacation time, I really can't—"

"When are you back?" Elena closes her eyes. "I need you back and productive by Monday, Elena." It is Tuesday. Jesus Christ. What happened to *take all the time you need?*

"I can't do that, Terrance, I'm sorry. I have vacation days available so technically—"

"If you can't do your job, Elena, I'm happy to find someone else for your position."

"Terrance, I asked you for this time and you said—"

"If I don't see you Monday, I'll consider that your two weeks' notice. The season's revving up here, Elena, and I can't work with unreliable people. Understand me?" The call ends.

Elena has worked for this company for three years. Her pulse pounds and spit wells in her mouth again. She swallows it down, her face hot.

She can't talk to her mother like this. She doesn't know if she can talk to *Diego* like this and he's a stranger.

"You all right in there?" he calls again, like he can read her thoughts.

"Never better," she says, looking at her eyes in the mirror. *Look at you, a liar like everyone else.*

Diego's favorite restaurant is a place called Cowboy's Cantina, which is rather funny to Elena.

"They didn't even want to put the name in Spanish?" she says, amused, surveying the meat-forward menu.

"'La Cantina del Vaquero' was probably taken. And it doesn't have that same alliteration for the tourists," Diego explains, gesturing to a waiter. They place their orders, *chuletas* for Diego, *churrasco con tostones* for Elena, who suddenly feels that she could eat her own hand, and drinks. Diego tells Elena about his childhood on the island, the culture shock of college at William and Mary, where he conned his parents into sending him after boarding school because he was able to fool them into thinking it was a Catholic university celebrating the Virgin.

"And William?" Elena asks, laughing. Diego shrugs. He tells her about law school, and gives her stories about her father, how Santiago once drove all night to Providence to visit her mother at Rhode Island School of Design on her birthday to give her a kiss and then drove back to New Haven; how he convinced friends of theirs pursing their master's in chemistry to make them LSD; how he crafted an argument for one of their mock trials that surprised and impressed their professors so much that years later, at a reunion, Diego learned it was still taught as an example of innovative thinking. Every story he tells is light, funny, every one shows her father in the best possible light. Elena knows what Diego is doing, but she does not stop him, does not push. It's more than she's ever had, even if most of it isn't what she's looking for. He tells her how supportive her father always was and it floors her, because she has forgotten the part of him that really thought about others and that makes her very sad. But happy, too, because it wasn't a figment of her imagination. It was real, even if it isn't anymore.

"Did he tell you when he was buying a house down here?" Elena asks.

"Oh yes. Told me he was getting a *ruina*. I told him he was insane. He said that's what your mother told him."

"I always thought they both wanted it."

Diego looks away.

"I don't know how much Rosalind really liked it here."

"I always loved it," Elena says, surprising herself. But she has, she has always loved the island. Puerto Rico has become a four-letter word in her life and for her mother because of her father, but Elena cannot erase her love so quickly. She loves it here. She lets herself think that, believe it, and smiles.

"I never would have taken on that work. Restoration," Diego says. "I wanted to build something new. Something my own. I've never liked old houses. Too many ghosts. I've been haunted in every old house I've ever stayed in. Now, I only want to be some place where the ghosts haven't died yet."

"Maybe you'll become a ghost. Haunt the new occupants," Elena offers.

"I hope not," he says, seriously. "I hope when I'm gone there will be nothing left of me, and that my house will be swallowed by the sea. I'm unlucky, you see. I've been left behind by love. I've got my own ghosts that follow me place to place. I hope I don't haunt anyone like I've been haunted."

"I like the idea of ghosts," Elena says, and realizes it is true. She enjoys the idea of history lingering behind for her. She likes places that feel overlayed with stories, with the past. She would welcome a ghost in her home, as long as it would tell her about itself. And then she wouldn't be so alone; with her ghost, she would be with someone. "But I'm sorry you've been haunted."

"That's all right. Makes life a little less lonely, I suppose," Diego says, his eyes sad.

"It's falling apart now. The house. It's a ruin again," Elena spits out quickly, trying to change the subject from Diego's ghosts, the ones that haunt him still.

"So why do you want it?" Diego asks. Elena looks away.

"Well, it has value," she hedges.

"Of course." He is waiting, with a cat's patience.

"It's not like he has someone else to leave it to," Elena points out. Diego just looks at her.

"It's a piece of history," she finally says. "Not just the island's history, but mine. Ours. And maybe my mom didn't want it. Okay. But I'm allowed to. He said it was for me. He promised me it would be mine, my piece of history, I guess. I want him to keep his promise. Even if it's just this once." She is making a habit of these confessions to strangers, strangers who could well hurt her with the soft underbelly she is exposing. It is freeing, the way she imagines jumping off a tall building is freeing, just before the ground breaks your fall.

"I see," Diego says, those assessing eyes taking her in again.

"Do you happen to know if he made a will down here?" It's an intimate thing to ask, although perhaps less so to a lawyer, she isn't sure. Diego nods, slowly.

"Your father asked me about this a few years ago. Apparently your mother contacted him, I think she wanted to make sure her name had been struck from the deed; your father got the house in the divorce, I believe?" Elena nods. "Your father asked me about Puerto Rican law for inheritance, but I didn't know much either. We both practiced in the States, and the laws here are different."

"French civil, yes?"

"Indeed. Well done. I gave him the information for a local estate lawyer, a friend of my family. Victor Padua. I believe your father did contact him."

"How do you know?" Elena asks. Her father says he will do a lot of things he never does.

"I saw him at a lecture a few months later, and he mentioned it. I don't know what happened, if he ended up using him and making a will, but it's likely. Your father was more lucid then. If I'm being honest, every time I see him, there is more gone. I don't know if it's neurological, or what, but . . . I can give you his information,

Victor. I don't know what he can tell you, of course, but you could try." It isn't much. But it's more than she had before. Everything is. She nods, thanking him, and reaching for the check before he can. He reaches out and she thinks it is to grab it back, but instead he takes her hand.

"It's a pleasure to meet you, Elena Vega." And he kisses it, like a courtly knight. She wonders why he is so alone, why he wants to die before he can become a ghost, who haunts him. But just because she is spilling her secrets everywhere doesn't mean he wants to, she reminds herself.

"He really does love you, your father," Diego says. "But not, I think, more than he hates himself."

It has never occurred to Elena that her father might hate himself. Surely everything he has done for years has been for himself, to satisfy himself, to make himself happy. Does that kind of person hate themselves?

Of course they do.

What does she do now? Does she forgive him? Does she pity him? She shivers, although it is warm and sultry like it usually is on the island, and the thick air embraces her. *He hates himself.* Can someone who hates themself ever really love someone else? Was he incapable all this time, and every choice she thought he made was just an inevitability? The idea of this sits in her stomach like a stone and she has to breathe deeply not to throw up, not to succumb to the pounding thud of her blood rushing to her temples.

"I think I'm pretty tired," she says, in a voice she barely recognizes as her own. Diego nods.

It is dark as they drive home, and Elena hears the whir of the generators the moment they stop, and the town goes dark. It is like nothing she has ever experienced before. One minute she is in a normal place, and then it is all darkness, in every direction, except for their headlights, and the stars. The moon is a sliver.

"Strange, isn't it?"

"Were you worried during Maria?" Elena asks. Her voice still sounds strange to her, but she will say anything to distract herself from her thoughts.

"I went inland, actually. I knew the coast would be hurt badly. I wasn't worried, not for myself. I worried for other people. I worried my house might fall down, before I was ready for it to."

"What would you have done if it did?" Elena wonders.

"Rebuilt. I want to die here. With any luck, the sea can take us both," Diego says. "Here we are."

Inside, Diego has candles ready, and he lights a few.

"Do you want to sit on the beach a bit, before we turn in?" he asks, and Elena says yes, she does want that. It is not late, really, but it feels like the middle of the night. The sky is devastating, and reflected by the waves like two paintings, one made by a realist, one made by an abstract artist. Elena gasps at the beauty of it, and can't stop gasping, her breath shallow.

"How could anyone ever get tired of this?" she asks. The stars reflect off the sand, and Diego has brought candles with them, and she can see his face, dimly, see his smile. "What?" she asks.

"That's what your father asked me, too," Diego tells her. Elena is glad the night coats their vision, so he cannot see the liquid in her eyes.

"There are places around here to rent a car, you know."

Elena looks at Diego. What does he want her to do with this information?

"If you want to go somewhere, that is."

"I don't know where to go," Elena says.

"How'd you get here today?"

"I got a ride from, well, I would say a friend but I don't think he's that."

"A fling, then?" Diego smirks at her and she realizes he was probably very popular with men when he was on the market. He's still a handsome man, and very charming.

"Someone who wanted the house," she says, because that's how she has to think of Fernando now.

"Ah. Well. I think you'll be needing to rent a car, then. To go . . . somewhere?"

Elena does not know what to say. Part of her wants to go to San Juan and just be done. Stop looking. Go back to the archives, clean out the house, stay put. Then it would be her father's fault, for not coming to find her. But she knows that's not what she is going to do.

"If you had to guess, where would you say he is?" Elena asks. Diego looks out at the dark sea.

"He's a hard man to predict. But if I were him, well, I'm not, but just for the sake of argument, I suppose I would go to the place that felt the most like home."

"I can't imagine which place that is."

"Well, is home people or a place?" It is a good question. To Elena home is people. And her father has people left in Ponce, family there. More than in San Sebastián. The question is, what is home to Santiago Vega Jr.? If it is indeed home he is looking for?

"I guess I'll find out," Elena says. Because she was never going to just leave. And she won't be back in New York on Monday morning. She should be terrified. She hasn't been unemployed since she left graduate school. She lives in the most expensive city in the United States. But she doesn't feel a damn thing.

She takes out her phone and responds to Terrance, *consider this my two weeks then.* Hitting *send,* she can hear the ocean, a wailing *whoosh* of nothingness, like her future holds. Her mother is going to kill her.

Good. She might just kill Rosalind, all things considered, anyway. Sitting here with this man who both, *both,* her parents knew, maybe loved, she cannot let her mother off the hook anymore. There is so much her mother hasn't told her and so much Elena has been apologizing for, for years, to make up for her father. Both of her parents have been leaving her in the dark alone. The only difference between them was that Rosalind *knew* she was doing it, and for the first time, Elena thinks this might be much worse. She has always thought her father hurt her because he could, and her mother tried to protect her. Now she thinks her father hurt her because he couldn't help it, and her mother, well, she tried to protect them both, and helped neither of them.

The call of the coqui, the little brown frog native to the island, trills out into the night. She listens to it sing. She can hear it in San Juan, and here. Is there anywhere on the island where you can't hear the coqui? And wouldn't that be a very lonely place?

"I hope you find him," Diego says.

"Do you find it hard? To stay friends with him, now that he's like this?" No matter that it is dark, Diego's smile, sad and sweet and calm, is visible.

"Not particularly. You see, your father introduced me to the love of my life. And then, when he died, he broke with me. I never really fixed myself. So I know what your father is. I am what your father is. I'm just a lot better at hiding it."

"Who was that?" Elena asks. There is a hitch in Diego's breathing.

"Neil," he says, simply. And Elena wants to weep, because she does not know who that is, either.

Thirteen

Having Neil as an ally, rather than as an annoyance, changed everything about Stanford for Santiago. He had never had such a close friendship with anyone. California still seemed empty compared to New York, the college campus a huge space barely populated by students. But his life was suddenly filled to the brim with things, with classes, with events, with a friend.

Neil, it turned out, had the best of all strategies for dealing with the many hurdles Santiago did not know how to face. He *refused* to feel inferior to anyone. The only person who Neil was truly affected by, in their opinion of him, was his father, and after that first college break, Neil realized quickly that his father would do his duty by his son financially, but that they would have no other contact, and they never did again. Neil spent every break after that first year on campus with Santiago, or with his mother in Cape Cod, where he watched her drown her own sorrows about his sexuality, and the affair his father had had years ago, in gin. Eventually his mother reconciled herself to Neil's "lifestyle," as she called it. His father didn't even attend Neil's funeral, years later, and Santiago knew he was right not to expect anything from parents.

Neil resisted both intimidation and condescension by simply not
being interested in them as concepts. No one could awe him, not
professors, not fellow students, not visiting lecturers whose accomplishments had won Pulitzer and Nobel prizes. He was not disre-
spectful in any way, but neither was he servile. He shook everyone's
hand, men and women, looked everyone in the eye. He listened to
other people patiently, carefully, and never let his response waver
with insecurity. For such a nervous person, Neil was a steady talker,
and Santiago observed him carefully, watching how he never ex-
pressed a shred of doubt that he did not deserve to be wherever he
happened to be at the time, from dives in the Mission where they
were surrounded by Mexican immigrants cursing so inventively even
Santiago sometimes didn't know what they were saying, to seminars
where they were surrounded by the children of some of the richest
people in America. If Neil didn't know the reference he asked about
it, in a tone that made it clear he was not less than anyone else for not
knowing it. He wrote it down carefully, and just like Santiago did,
sought it out later, to understand at least a piece of it. But he didn't,
as Santiago did, duck his head, ashamed, when he had to ask.

He gave Santiago a crash course in literary theory and brief intro-
ductions to many of the political figures and philosophies Santiago
was trying desperately to grasp. Unlike his textbooks, which had
assumed a certain background knowledge in the subject, Neil found
out what Santiago knew and didn't before explaining anything, over
disgusting lunches in the cafeteria or walking around the campus.
He could spot holes in his friend's knowledge and help Santiago fill
them, rather than making them feel insurmountable. Because of
Neil, and his own hard work, Santiago managed to scrape by his
second semester of college with a few C's and mostly B's, not quite
the triumph he had imagined, but far and away better than he could
have hoped for, and it was just good enough to keep his scholarship
intact.

After a summer working in New York, he returned to Stanford, eager to shake New York off his skin. It had begun to feel claustrophobic to him; he was learning to love open spaces. Neil had had sex with another man for the first time that summer, a fact that he had told Santiago over the phone but recounted in greater detail when they were physically back in the same place and didn't have to waste dimes on the conversation. Emboldened by his sexual summer, Neil decided they should join more clubs, perhaps make friends other than each other, while acknowledging, of course, that they would remain each other's best friend in the most masculine way possible.

Santiago had no problem with this. School had become, not easier, exactly, but he knew how to do it, knew how to study, knew how to rise to the college standard. And he was enjoying it, as the classes became more complex, more focused, more specific. He loved learning about Latin America. It was like when he had been a kid and he had heard Puerto Rico mentioned in *West Side Story*. There was a thrill of being recognized, of being seen. And besides, it was fascinating, the way Spain had torn through the New World, the way European wars and later American intrigues had found theaters to play out their conflicts, in Bolivia, Venezuela, Brazil, Cuba. His classes were very pro–United States, of course, but he didn't know that then, when for the first time he was reading about people with names like the ones he'd grown up with, people like him, in some small way. The first time the history of his own world seemed significant.

He took Spanish classes to change his accent, make it purer, less specific to the lazy drawl of the island. He and Neil joined the debate team, attended parties, met girls and boys. Santiago became popular, in a way he had never anticipated, couldn't have known. His skinny body had started to develop more muscles, more bulk, and his skin had cleared in the California sun, and suddenly what had

made him different, other, now made him *cool*. Stanford was filled
with newly liberal girls looking to liberate their bodies and upset
their parents through flings with men of color, and Santiago was
more than happy to oblige. He lost his own virginity not six months
after Neil did, to the twanging thwacking chords of Jimi Hendrix's
"I Don't Live Today" on the radio. He developed confidence in his
classes, participating actively, challenging his fellow students, dropping his own references and recognizing the looks on their faces, the
confusion they covered quickly to hide their ignorance.

He began having *fun*. Education had always been about survival,
improving his existence, a platform to good jobs, a better future.
This was joy, this was argument for the sake of itself, this was academic rabbit holes he could fall into and climb out of. He and his
fellow students smoked pot and talked about Russian intelligence
and Greek philosophy, they talked about the war, they talked about
the very concept of peace.

Santiago's confidence didn't just get him noticed by women. In
the second semester of his second year of college, he met the second
teacher he would have who would change his life forever. His Spanish teacher, Javier Rojas, a man in his late sixties from La Paz who
wore half-moon spectacles and was forever mocking Santiago's sloppy
noun endings, pulled him aside after class one day and handed him
a novel whose cover was in Spanish.

"One Hundred Years of Solitude?" Santiago translated. "What is this?"

"I went home this winter for Christmas. First time I've been back
for five years." Professor Rojas had a roundabout way of addressing
things, and he liked to wax eloquently before getting to any real
point. His Spanish was flawless—every other Spanish professor, all
natives to the language, commented on it—his accent impeccable
and cleansed of all Bolivian lilt, so Santiago didn't mind waiting.

"That sounds nice," Santiago said, patiently.

"This book is everywhere. I picked up a copy, it's the first by a new author."

"I thought you only read things from the Golden Age?" Santiago said, pushing his luck with a joke. Professor Rojas was a humorless man, who didn't respond well to teasing. He looked Santiago up and down, his mustache twitching like the whiskers on an irritated cat.

"Normally I do. But I was curious. My niece liked it, and she hates everything."

"I guess you didn't enjoy it much, if you are giving it to me," Santiago said, carefully enunciating each noun and adjective ending.

"It is because I loved it so much that I am giving it to you." Santiago looked up, stunned. He had not thought Professor Rojas liked him at all, let alone enough to give him a present. "You are the only student in this class who is Hispanic. Have you noticed that?" Santiago nodded. Of course he had. "I would imagine, growing up in this country, that you have never read anything by a Latin American author, much less a current one." Santiago nodded again, thinking. It was true. He had read the words of French and English and American writers, mostly men. He had read Russians and Canadians, and endless parades of Greeks. He had read more work from before the twentieth century than during it.

"This is worth reading. And there is a lot more worth reading, as well. And not just from Spain. There are writers from every Spanish-speaking country and they are good, great, even. Writing about real things, things that matter to us today. Not chivalric ideas from five hundred years ago," Professor Rojas said, sternly. Then he leaned in, and touched Santiago on the shoulder. "When I was growing up, they gave us Dickens, and Shakespeare, and Balzac, all translated into Spanish, and they told us this was what was great. Well, it is great. But the mistake is thinking, believing, that it is *all* that is great. That greatness only lives in one place. That we have not also achieved some greatness. They will make you as small as they can. They will use books and history to do so. They will make you feel like you do not belong here, that you come from people who have done nothing of note. You must remember, son, that you come from people who have done great things, with their hands tied behind their backs, and their eyes burned out of their skulls. We have done great things *despite* the harm done to us, then and now. And we will keep doing them, keep writing great stories. But how can we expect anyone else to read them, to respect them, if we ourselves do not?"

"Professor?" Santiago was stunned. The man looked like he was about to cry. Professor Rojas wiped his eyes, looking self-conscious. Santiago looked away, giving him all the privacy he could.

"Read the book. If you like it, I will bring you more. You won't know all the terms he uses, even I didn't know them. But you will learn. He's something else, this Márquez. Mark my words."

Santiago devoured the novel. It made complete sense to him, even though the professor had been right, he did not know all the vocabulary, but he *understood* it. It showed life the way Santiago had lived it, as absurd, but also as honest; it was the truest thing he had ever read in his life. And Professor Rojas did bring him more: he brought him Borges and Neruda, Alejo Carpentier and Carlos Fuentes. These novels set his brain on fire, they electrified him. He saw the way economic and social injustice rolled through Latin American life like it had haunted his own. He read Castro's speeches and shook at the brutalities of Trujillo, he traced the path of Bolívar's armies on a map with his index finger and studied the writings of José de San Martín. He decided that the world changed under the leadership of two kinds of men, soldiers and lawyers. He had no interest in the army. It would have to be law.

By the fall of his third year of college, Santiago felt that he had become the person he would be for the rest of his life. He did not go home the summer before, but instead he worked in San Francisco. His mother had had another incident in the spring of 1970. Esperanza had stopped taking her pills, hiding them in her cheek, and once she shook off the lingering sedative effects, she escaped her mother's housing project, had gotten lost for four days, and was found in Battery Park screaming at the river for its betrayal of its mother, the sea. No one in his family had a way to contact Santiago, and so he only found out that she had been admitted to Bellevue once again when he'd called, several weeks later, to wish her a happy birthday. She had been put on a treatment program of electroshock therapy and heavy antipsychotics, and he had been informed by his grandmother that the doctor was doubtful Esperanza would ever be able to live outside of the asylum again, she simply could not function in the real world. Esperanza had told her own mother that the medicine made her blind to everything she wanted to see, and it had to be forced down her throat in order for her to swallow it. She was thirty-nine years old. He knew then that he would not be returning to New York, not ever. He would not admit it until years later, would tell people he planned to go back, but he knew in his heart that the city had died for him, that it was over. New York would be the place of his childhood, the place where his mother lived. There was nothing left for him there. He could leave it behind, and had, he thought. It did not need to touch him, to pull at him, anymore.

On a cool day in early November, on one of his usual walks stretching his legs after a particularly challenging seminar on contemporary American policies in Central America, Santiago tripped over a pair of legs. The person attached to these legs had been invisible to him, so lost was he in his anger. The seminar had broken down into a debate about the moral implications of American imperialism, and a fellow student in a sweater vest had smugly lectured Santiago about the Monroe Doctrine for five full minutes, talking to him like a child, while the professor did nothing. Santiago had restrained himself from retaliating, and was planning his response for the next class, when his head crashed into the ground beneath him. As was his habit from childhood, he checked his glasses first, his precious glasses, then the rest of his body, which seemed to be on top of another body, a female one.

"I'm so sorry," said the owner of that female body, and looking up he saw a blurry shape. He slid his glasses on his face and a small brunette with wavy hair and a rust-colored sweater came into focus. She was peering at him over a book, and he saw the words *One Hundred Years of Solitude* on the cover.

"I didn't know that book had been translated," he said, breathlessly. She looked down at it.

"It's recent," she explained.

"Do you like it?" he asked.

"I've just started it. It seems different. The first line is good," she said, shrugging. "'Many years later, as he faced the firing squad, Colonel Aureliano Buendía was to remember that distant afternoon when his father took him to discover ice.'" As she read the first line of the book, Santiago closed his eyes, trying to remember the exact words of the original. This was close enough, he thought. He looked at the girl. The longer he looked at her, the prettier she became. She had big serious eyes, hazel, and her hair, which at first looked brown to him, had reddish tints in the sunlight shining down between the leaves of the tree she leaned against. Years later, he would tell people that he fell for her right away, and she would laugh, explaining that it was literal.

"I don't think you'll finish it in time," he said, pointing to the book.

"In time for what?" she asked, confused.

"Our first date," he said, confidently. "Maybe by our fourth, or tenth, depending on how fast you read."

"Who dates anymore?" she asked, but she didn't say no, he noticed. "I don't even know your name."

"You tell me yours first." He smiled with his whole mouth. It was a mistake, he never did that, never liked people to see the missing tooth, but looking at her he could not stop his lips from parting. She didn't frown at him, though, her expression stayed just the same as before she had seen his teeth, and he closed his mouth, quickly, a lucky escape.

"Rosalind Goldberg," she said, reaching out her hand.

"Santiago Vega." He left off the Junior. He didn't need it. He shook her hand.

"I read fast," she told him. She really did. By the time he actually convinced her to go out with him, two weeks later, she had finished the novel. He took her to a movie, a Western, and she fell asleep after the opening credits, because she had been up reading the night before, trying to finish it so they could talk about it. They shut down a coffee shop in Palo Alto because they had too much to say, each of them. He learned that she came from Philadelphia, that her family owned a department store, that she loved animals, that she wanted to study art and architecture and that she believed buildings had souls, that she hated her sister, that she loved French theater and good coffee, that she had eaten more kinds of foods than he had ever heard of.

She kissed him good night and told him he was strange when he didn't accept her offer to sleep with her, and he told her that he was going to marry her someday.

"Great, you'll be married. What will I be, then?" Neil asked him, annoyed, when he came home, lighter than air.

"I'm sure you'll find someone," Santiago said, placating him.

"*You* better find me someone, then, if you're all sorted out with this Rosalind. Now you've got time to help me," Neil said, firmly.

"I'll do my best," Santiago promised him.

After he arrived in San Francisco a week before school started his first year of college, it took Santiago three separate train rides to get from the San Francisco airport to Stanford University. It was his first time anywhere other than New York and Puerto Rico, and everything about California seemed strange to him, like entering an alien land. He could see the city through the train windows because a lot of it was *above ground,* which only happened outside the borough of Manhattan in New York City, and confused him. But what was even more confusing was when he changed trains again and boarded the final train to Stanford, which passed through greenery, nothing but greenery. Then, neighborhoods, pristine and well tended, like he had seen on television. Perfect little box houses, one after the other, and trees so tall they looked like they would never end, and palm trees, and strange spiky plants like something from *Lost in Space.* Later he would learn the differences between cacti and succulents, would learn about the plants and animals of Northern California, would learn to find them beautiful. But on first glance they were strange, another sign that he was far from home.

The campus itself was beautiful, and so very big. The buildings looked a little bit like some of the buildings in San Juan, but instead of being brightly painted they were all golden brown with terra-cotta red roofs. And there was so much space between them! How could so much empty space exist, anywhere? How could anything be so very open?

He walked from the train station into the campus area, looking for the admissions office, where his letter had informed him he should report immediately once arriving. All around him he saw lanky coeds, boys and girls, some with the wide-legged pants and vests he had seen in photos of members of bands he liked, some in jackets and ties, dresses with full skirts that had been popular throughout the last decade. Most of the students were surrounded by people, families. He straightened his shoulders and kept walking, stopping to ask one or two people if they knew where the admissions office was. One, another freshman like himself, looked terrified when

Santiago talked to him, and it was then that he realized everyone around him in this moment was completely and totally white. Santiago, whose fair skin was his mother's pride and joy in her more lucid moments, was the darkest person there.

Someone tapped him on the shoulder. He turned around and almost sighed with relief to see a Black male student in front of him, his hair teased into a modest Afro, his expression friendly.

"Are you looking for the admissions office? I can show you the way." Santiago nodded and let Julian Lee, as he would introduce himself on the way, guide him. Once they were past the green where Santiago had only seen whiteness, Julian grinned at him.

"That kid looked ready to shit himself," Julian said.

"Probably thought I was going to stab him. Seen *West Side Story* too many times," Santiago replied, smiling back while carefully concealing his missing tooth.

"Oh shit, you're Puerto Rican? Then you are most certainly the first Puerto Rican kid he's ever met. But round here, you might be the first Puerto Rican most people have met. This is Chicano country. Where are you from?"

"New York," Santiago said.

"Chicago," Julian said, pointing to himself. "This might be California, but this campus is pretty snowy." Santiago looked at him, confused. "White."

"Oh," Santiago said.

"Here you go, you're going to go through those doors and meet your scholarship liaison. Mine was a nice girl named Shirley from Michigan who flinched every time I reached inside my pockets. She absolutely was sure I was going to knife her, but she did her best. We still exchange holiday cards," Julian said, calmly. "You're gonna get some rich white kid who is going to settle you in and make sure you know how things work. They might ask questions that make no sense, but think of them like people at the zoo trying to understand animal behavior, because that's how they are going to look at you. Smile and don't make any sudden movements. The more the university values you, the higher up the food chain the liaison is. Shirley's family owned a steel mill." Julian smiled, confident, a little arrogant, and Santiago saw the shark behind the friendly face. This was a competitive place, he realized. He'd never been in one of those before.

"Good luck." And he was gone. Santiago walked into the building, another golden-brown Spanish edifice, where a smiling woman asked his name and for his identification. Santiago gave her everything, and watched her mouth his name to herself, obviously trying to figure out how to pronounce it.

"You can just call me Junior," he said. "Everyone does." She looked at him, smiling gratefully this time, and pointed him over to a stiff-looking boy his age, sitting on a nearby chair, who jumped up as Santiago approached him.

"I'm Thomas. You must be—"

"Junior," he said, and watched that same look of gratitude flash on this boy's face. It would be a look he would become very accustomed to within his first few weeks at Stanford, the relief people felt at not having to learn to pronounce a name they were not familiar with. The relief they felt that he would accommodate them, their clumsy tongues, their complete lack of understanding of anything outside their own experience. It was a look that would haunt the rest of his life, that would, years later, fill him with rage and shame, hatred at himself, that he allowed this, supported it, made it possible. That he did not on that day and every day after patiently let them stumble and mumble and fail, and teach them how to say his name, perfectly, naturally, as he already knew how to say theirs.

Thomas was the son of an oil family from Texas, and he had numbers after his name, so Santiago privately concluded that he was, indeed, important to the university, a worthy competitor for

Julian and anyone else who came along. Thomas showed him the
campus, pointing out the libraries, cafeterias, schools of law and
business, the dorms, the class buildings, the fraternities, the gym.
He showed him his room in Lucie Stern Hall, where Santiago would
be living with a boy named Neil Stevens, who looked askance at
him over thick glasses. Thomas told him he was there for Santiago
if he had any questions, or needed anything. Then, his eyes alight
and curious, he leaned in close and asked Santiago if he had been a
member of a gang back in New York and how he learned to speak
English so well and was it true that Puerto Ricans were closer to
apes than any other race, at which point Santiago bid him a polite
farewell and started to unpack.

He didn't have much. All of the things he had thought were
worth bringing had fit into a duffel bag and a small shopping bag
he had taken home on his last day bagging at Gristedes. He had fifty
dollars in his wallet, which was supposed to last him for any addi-
tional expenses until the end of October. It took him less than an
hour to find a place for his clothing, his copies of *The Count of Monte
Cristo* and *The Grapes of Wrath*; the rosary from his First Communion; a Santeria candle Irena had given him when she had hugged
him goodbye, crying into his collar like a baby; a toy car courtesy
of Hermando, who had tucked it into his pocket when he wasn't
looking; an extra pair of glasses he had used his precious summer
job money to buy; a Bible from his grandmother; and a photograph
of his mother. The rest of the room went to Neil, who quickly filled
it with posters and knickknacks and books and a globe and items of
clothing and snacks and a piggy bank and all kinds of things Santiago couldn't imagine having enough money to own.

Santiago didn't mind sharing a room, in fact, he was rather happy
not to be alone after his years of solitude. But Neil did. Neil was
pale, vampire pale, his eyes adorned with deep dark blue circles
every day no matter how much sleep he got. Neil was twitchy, and

a little odd, and he looked shocked when anyone spoke to him, at all. At first Santiago thought that Neil was terrified of him because he was Puerto Rican, but after their first meal together in the cafeteria, which had so much food, more than Santiago could have ever imagined, Santiago realized that Neil was terrified of *everyone*. Neil's father was a military man, a general, in fact, and he had grown up near Quantico. Neil didn't talk much about him, but it was clear from the comments Neil made that his father wasn't particularly proud of his timid little son. Santiago wasn't tall, but Neil was shorter than he was, slight, soft-spoken.

Neil was anxious about everything, but Junior learned quickly how to adapt to him. He announced himself before entering the room, calming Neil's shaky nerves; he told Neil whenever he was turning the light on, or off; he made sure never to touch Neil's things or leave the room differently than he'd found it. Neil was appreciative, and apologetic, and deeply neurotic, and Santiago began to long for the horrible apartment he'd lived in alone in the East Village, where he hadn't had to tell anyone anything.

Santiago hadn't known exactly what it was he wanted to study in college, but he met with his advisor and described what interested him, what he wanted to know more about in the world, what he was curious about, what he had done well in in high school, which was everything, and therefore no help at all, and what he might like to do with his life. Santiago didn't know about that many professions, but he liked the idea of the law. Lawyers were the ones who defended people. Most of the great figures he had learned about in his high school history classes, John Adams, Monhandas Gandhi, Abraham Lincoln, Thomas Jefferson, Thomas Cromwell, were all lawyers. Lawyers had changed the world, made it a better, more just place. It seemed as good a job as any.

His advisor told him to try political science. He had thought it sounded interesting, and it was interesting, in fact. It was also a lot of reading, writing papers, learning about politics, history, law. It was hard, harder than he had ever known school could be.

Understanding things had always come easily to Santiago. Learning made sense to him. It was the only reason he had been able to be at the top of his class, year after year, despite his family, his poverty, the violence that lived in his world, his mother's illness. No matter what, school had been easy. Santiago had always been one of the smartest people he knew. Of course, he met people who knew more about things than he did, people like Mrs. Schultz, but he had always been confident that this was a matter of time, and exposure; that if he had some more years, and more money, more hours to read, less exhaustion from work, he, too, would know as much as she did, if not more.

However, Stanford was, quickly, and with astounding force, challenging this assumption. It was challenging *him*. Everyone was like him, but more so: smart, very smart, and all confident, ready to talk, to question, to answer, to debate. They had done the reading, yes, but also knew about secret readings, things that hadn't been assigned but for some reason they all *knew* about, had read, and they connected those things to these things to other things, making a mosaic of information and thoughts that Santiago did not understand. They spoke their ideas and thoughts with such definitive tones that Santiago was tempted to write them down as facts. Their teeth gleamed and their hands moved and they *knew* what they were saying. He did not dare speak, most of the time, did not dare raise his hand to answer any question. He worried that they would see his missing tooth, see the mended lines on his clothing, hear the touch of Spanish at the back of his English, and know him as a fraud. He began to have nightmares that it had all been a mistake, his admission, that he was in class, his hand raised, finally ready to answer a question, and just as his mouth opened, a group of goons in suits entered the classroom and announced that he was a fake, a phony, that he never should have been admitted in the first place, and they dragged him out of the room as the other students laughed, relieved that their suspicions had been true. The goons carried him off the beautiful campus, so pristine and clean, and threw him out of the gates, where his uncles were waiting to beat him and take him back to New York. He usually woke up just as Roberto was aiming the first punch, and Neil woke up with him, terrified by Santiago's moaning and harsh breathing.

When he got his first paper back in his English class, he was astounded to see that he had earned himself a C on it. He had never gotten a C in his life. He hadn't gotten a B since the seventh grade, and that was because he had fallen asleep during the test, having been up all night with his mother, assuring her that she was not, in fact, a tropical bird, but was his mother, and that they could not fly to Brazil, but had to stay in New York and sleep.

His other classes were no better, some were worse. He did not know what to do. He had no way to understand this, no way to deal with being challenged academically for the first time in his life. Physically he had never been better: he slept and ate well, he even played basketball with a small group of Black and Mexican students sometimes on the weekends. He went for walks around the beautiful campus and the weather, while very strange to him, being neither good nor bad, rarely promised rain. But he was struggling. The work was so intense, so much more than ever before, trying to keep up with the reading, trying to understand his fellow students, his professors. It was in his first year at Stanford that Santiago realized just how much he had missed, just how much these other students had learned in their high schools. He was behind, so very behind, and he did not know how he would ever catch up.

It wasn't just the classes. He was behind on everything. They had lives he had never had, they had families, sane mothers, all the things they needed. They had traveled, they had been to museums outside of a school trip, they played instruments, they knew about foods and what it was like in Rome and how to pronounce all the words Junior had only read, never heard spoken aloud. They had money, all of them. Some of them had a lot, some of them had less, but they all had it, money for clothing, money for the train into San Francisco, money for beer. They drank, they smoked cigarettes and marijuana, they had money for all that, too.

Some of them, the type who wore sweater vests and pearls, and had names like Alison and Clint and Grant, asked Santiago about his missing tooth and why didn't he fix it and when he said the obvious, that he couldn't afford it, they did not know where to direct their gazes, they turned red and found a way to exit the conversation. They were embarrassed for him, they pitied him. Some of them, the type that wore peasant skirts and plaid shirts and grew their hair out long, boys and girls, called themselves social activists, organizers, and asked him what he thought about Castro. He told them what he had been taught in school, that communism was dangerous to American values, and they looked at him, shocked, they pitied him, too, for how he thought so conventionally, how he didn't feel more for his fellow Caribbean islanders. Some of them, the type who wore nothing of note and answered every question first in Santiago's classes, didn't ask him anything at all. He did not merit their notice, he was not competing at their level.

Getting into college had been the battle of his life. It was a dream he had not thought he could have, let alone achieve, and now he had, with money to support him, with all his needs met, and he had thought that once he got here, the rest of his life would unfold before him, a road of endless possibility. He saw himself happy, with all the time and space to learn that he wanted, with the chance to meet people who might like him, people he might grow close to. A woman he might love, a friend he might trust. He assumed he would thrive. Instead, he was drowning.

He finished his first semester with grades that just barely met his scholarship requirements, how, he had no idea. Perhaps the Santeria candle worked. He finished it with no friends, as well. He did not know how to relate to the people around him, he was terrified of them, sure they would reject him. Alone on an empty campus, he celebrated Thanksgiving with a cup of noodles, trying to wrap his mind around Locke and Hobbes, reading and rereading the same sentences over and over again. He spent the winter break on campus, too, trying to read all of the books he had taken out of the school library, the references his fellow students had made that he had noted down, all the people he hadn't heard of, didn't understand. He had no place to go, no money to get there, anyway. The idea of going back to New York called to him, and he longed to return, to smell the garbage of the city instead of this fresh clean air that made him feel like he was never clean enough. To see Mrs. Schultz, to tell her how hard this was. He called her once a month, sent her letters full of lies about fascinating conversations, academic triumphs, new friends. In person he could tell her the truth, confess his shame, that he was not enough. That this was wasted on him, that he would never be anything more than what he had been born.

He took long walks, living alone once again, as Neil was home in Virginia. He looked at his result sheet over and over, willing the grades to change before his eyes, but they didn't, unless he took off his glasses, turning them to fuzz. He sat through meetings with his advisor, who told him the same thing, gently but insistently: he had to do better or he would lose his scholarship, lose his chance here. He nodded, smiled, promised, shattering on the inside. He did not know *how* to get better. He had always done everything on his own, understood everything with his own brain. His brain was failing him, now, and he had no way to change this reality.

As the year changed at midnight on December 31, 1968, becoming 1969, after a long walk around the entire campus, which had taken him hours, Santiago made a decision. He would quit. He would leave Stanford, leave this place where he knew nothing, mattered to no one. He would go back to New York before they threw him out, as he had suspected for so many weeks that they would. He would enroll in SUNY. He would stop pretending that he could escape his old life, his old self. He would return to his obligations, his mother, his family, and let them swallow him up. Anything would be better than staying here and knowing every day that he was beneath these people, beneath this place.

He let himself into his dorm room, relieved that he would not have to announce his presence, for Neil was not there, only to find his roommate suspended from the top bunk, Santiago's bunk, trying to hang himself with a bedsheet.

"NEIL!" Santiago screamed so loud it tore his throat. He scrambled up to his bed, his hands moving quickly on the knot Neil had made. Neil was so small that his legs didn't touch the ground, and his face was turning a deep purple, his eyes frantic. Santiago struggled with the knot, trying to loosen it, thinking about pulling on the sheet, but that would only quicken Neil's death, wouldn't it? It seemed like hours, trying to work the twisted cloth, but it was only a matter of seconds until he felt a loosening, and Neil's body slithered to the ground. Santiago threw himself off the bed, not sure what to do next, untrained in CPR, but to his immense relief he heard a cough, and then another, and Neil was inhaling deeply, gasping, coughing, pulling at the sheet around his neck, *alive*.

"What the *fuck* was that?" Santiago asked. He never cursed, ever. His uncles cursed, loudly, colorfully, in English and Spanish. Santiago didn't. He believed that it made them sound what they were, uneducated, like thugs. He never wanted to sound like that, like them.

"I didn't know you were here. I came back early, and the room was empty. I thought it would be okay," Neil said, his voice hoarse.

"To *kill* yourself?" Santiago asked him, incredulous. Neil was nervous, yes, and more than a little off, but as far as Santiago knew, he had performed well in school, he had no reason to want to die. Not like he himself had. Neil looked down at the sheet in his hands.

"There is no point in living, anyway," Neil said. Santiago looked at him in disbelief and then, so quickly he wasn't sure how it was possible, hit him in the face. He didn't know how it happened. He didn't have any thought or desire to do it, it wasn't until his fist connected with Neil's jaw that he realized it was happening.

"What was that for?" Neil asked, clutching his face.

"What does that even mean, no point? You're *rich,* you're doing well in school, what the fuck do you not have to live for? What could possibly be your reason for saying that? Self-indulgent little prick, what the hell do you—"

"I'm a homosexual," Neil said, flatly, his voice a dead thing. Santiago looked at him, not understanding.

"So?" Santiago said. He knew lots of men like Neil. He'd met friends of his uncles, of his father, men who preferred other men. There were slurs about men like that, *maricón,* but they were usually said affectionately, at least in his family. His grandmother didn't exactly approve, calling it against God, but then, she didn't approve of anything. People didn't always talk about it openly, but everyone knew about men like that, and as long as they didn't make it too public, especially around the police, all the Puerto Ricans he knew at home and on the island just shrugged, and accepted it. Who cared who other people slept with? The only problem was when you slept with two people at once, although according to a lot of the conversations that Santiago overheard in the cafeteria, that was becoming more and more popular among the students, who talked about *free love* and "*rejecting conventions that restricted human connection in all forms.*"

"So, it's illegal. It's a perversion, a mental defect," Neil said, his voice bitter, and Santiago wondered if he was quoting someone else. "People like me should be shot on sight."

"I don't think that," Santiago said, simply. He wasn't sure what else to say. He had his own problems, so many of them. It had never occurred to him that Neil had any, as well.

"My father does," Neil said, squeezing the sheet tightly. "He sent me back here early. Says I can't come home until I fix it. Fix myself. I've tried not to, to want anyone. I've punished myself, I've prayed. I cut myself when I think about men, look." Here Neil rolled up his pant leg and his sleeve, showing Santiago lines of cuts, some healed scars, some scabs. "But I can't stop. I thought maybe this would be the next best thing. To fix it. To make him proud."

Santiago stared at Neil. He had trained himself to want, to expect, nothing from his parents. What would it be like, he wondered, to crave something from a parent so much that you were willing to kill yourself to get it?

"Fuck him," Santiago said, breaking a personal record, cursing twice in one day. "You want to smoke?" He rummaged around in his desk, pulling out a joint. Julian had left it for him before he went back to Chicago for break. He hadn't seen Julian much after that first day, but whenever Santiago did he felt the only sense of comfort he had experienced since he came to Stanford. The last time he saw Julian he was on his way to the airport and realized he still had a joint on him, and hastily passed it to Santiago, saying something about how his mother would kill him if she smelled it, and Merry Christmas.

Neil stared at him, clearly shaken from Santiago's lack of reaction to his confession.

"Pot is for degenerates," Neil said, doubtfully.

"You're already homosexual. What do you have to lose?" Santiago said, feeling unexpectedly light. If this was his last night at Stanford, he might as well make it a good one. He lit a match, and inhaled, coughing as he exhaled. He had only done this once or twice before. He passed the joint to Neil, who took it, his hands shaking.

"You really don't think it's bad?" Neil said, and Santiago recognized the thing in his voice for what it was. Hope.

"I really don't."

Neil smiled, the bruises on his throat from his suicide attempt already forming, moving over his bobbing Adam's apple, and took a hit.

In the morning, when Santiago told Neil about his plan to leave school over breakfast in the cafeteria, Neil grabbed his arm and forbade him from this, absolutely.

"I'm failing. I'm alone here. I have nothing," Santiago said, frankly, shame pinching at his temples. Neil smiled.

"Not anymore. Now you have me." He took his hand off Santiago's arm and held it out. "If you keep me alive, I'll help you learn better. Deal?"

Santiago looked at Neil's hand, pale and soft, the hand of someone who had never had to bag groceries or shoot pool or cut cane. Could he put his future in a useless hand like that? And then he thought of Neil, ready to end his own life in their dorm room.

He took Neil's useless hand, and shook.

The flight he took from New York to San Francisco before his first year of college was the longest flight Santiago had ever been on. He had never imagined it could take five and a half hours, that there could be so much country between California and his home. It was a good thing, he thought. Every minute gave him more time to hate himself, for everything he had done, for everything he was leaving behind.

He had spent the spring and summer after his admission to Stanford in a daze. He kept thinking it was a mistake, it had to be a mistake, but several calls to the admissions office assured him that they would not, in fact, be rescinding his admission or his scholarship, and his leg went blue with pinch bruises before he had to give up. This was real. It was happening. He was going to college, he was the first person in the history of his *family* to go to college.

For the first time since his father had moved back to the island, Santiago declined his offer of visiting Puerto Rico. He claimed he needed to make money for school, but really, he just didn't want to see his father. He worried he might try to talk him out of going, even as he knew that was insane. His father, hearing the news over the telephone, belittled him, *what do you need money for now that they are giving you so much?* But behind his insults was resignation. Years later, Santiago would think back to that moment and realize how much his father resented him, and was awed by him. How dare his son, his namesake, surpass him? And so fast? His father would never forgive him for his successes, never fail to mention them, brag about them, and diminish them in equal measures.

No member of his family had attended his high school graduation. He walked across the stage and accepted his diploma, graduating with honors, the applause apathetic from a sea of parents who had never seen his face before. The only person who had cheered for him with Mrs. Schultz, was, much to his surprise, Eileen Krause, his social worker. He had mentioned his graduation to her offhandedly, but there she was, her soft form rising to cheer him, her arms jiggling slightly as she clapped. Tears stung his eyes as he accepted the diploma, and later, when she hugged him. Afterward, Mrs. Schultz had taken him out to lunch at the most expensive restaurant he had ever been to, white tablecloths so pristine that he worried his hands might mark them, even though he had scrubbed them clean in the bathroom, twice. She had ordered a bottle of wine, a far cry from the beer he had tried with his grandfather and his uncles, or the sweet painful rum his father had made him sip the year he turned fifteen, and toasted him. The taste was rich and strange, and the food was like nothing he had had before. It was French, Mrs. Schultz said, *they really know how to eat,* and Santiago didn't disagree.

"Is France further away than California?" he had asked her, despite the fact that he had looked at maps of the world many times.

"Almost the same distance. One over land, one over sea," Mrs. Schultz had said, and smiled. "Like Paul Revere said."

"One *if* by land, two *if* by sea," Santiago corrected her, his mind a little light from the wine, remembering Longfellow's poem from their poetry unit the year before.

"Of course," Mrs. Schultz said, leaning back in her chair. "May I ask you something, Junior?"

"Yes, Mrs. Schultz," Santiago said, puzzled. She had never asked permission to ask him anything before.

"You can call me Pearl, now, Junior, I'm not your teacher anymore." He nodded, knowing privately that to think of her as anything other than Mrs. Schultz would be impossible. "Your family, how do they feel about what you are doing, going away to college?"

"I don't think they care much," Santiago said, frankly. "My mother doesn't really understand that I am leaving. I keep explaining it to her. Sometimes she is very angry at me, and sometimes she is sad, and sometimes she doesn't remember who I am."

"Is she ever happy for you?" Mrs. Schultz asked, leaning forward.

"Why would she be happy for me?" Santiago asked, genuinely confused. "I'm leaving her."

The last visit he had had with his mother had been the day before he left. She had looked at him with dead eyes, and he had thought that this was one of those days when she didn't know who he was. He was sad, but relieved, in a way, because if she didn't know him, she could not be upset with him. He sat with her for an hour, telling her things about the weather, the world news, reading to her from the newspaper. He was about to go when she had grabbed his hand, rubbing it on her cheek.

"*Mi niño, mi cariño, mi precioso,*" she said. *My son, my dear, my precious.* Now recognition and gratitude, pathetic gratitude, shone out of her eyes, and he stared at her, horrified. She clutched him and kissed his hand, loving and kind, until the nurse came to separate them. *See you soon,* she said, before they wheeled her off. *Soon.* But he wouldn't. He was only happy she didn't realize that, then.

"Stanford will open doors for you, open up the world for you. You will know how far away France is because you will *go* to France."

"I don't want to go to France," Santiago said. Mrs. Schultz's words were hurting him, making him feel something about his mother that he didn't want to feel, deep sadness, that she could never be happy for him, never know the future he might have, that she would only see it one way.

"Somewhere else, then. Spain. England. Morocco. Siam! You will go on and be astounding, Junior. I'm happy for you. And I'm very proud." Mrs. Schultz took a sip of her wine. "I want to tell you something, something I can say because you are no longer my student, because you are very special to me, and because I hope, in some small way, I have helped you in your path toward your future."

Santiago wanted to tell her she had helped in *every* way, because she had, but his words choked up in his throat.

"Loving someone is being happy for their happiness. When you fall in love, when you have children, you will know that you truly love them because you will do whatever it takes to make them happy, even if it means putting yourself last. If that is the right thing for them, you will do it. Your mother may not know how to tell you this, but you know that she loves you. And that means in some part of her mind, she knows that your future is somewhere else, and she wants it for you." Mrs. Schultz put her hand over Santiago's and squeezed it tight, and he wanted to believe her. He wanted to believe that both of his parents had left him behind, one for the island, one for her madness, because they loved him, not because they didn't.

But he knew that wasn't true.

Fourteen

Elena wakes up in the morning and realizes that this is the first time in days she has slept in an actual bed. Diego has two bedrooms, one for visitors, he said, and she wonders who visits him here. He seems so alone. She had not wanted to ask him, the evening before, after he explained who Neil was, why he never tried to be with someone after Neil's death. Perhaps he had. It seemed too private a thing to intrude upon.

She checks her phone and sees a response from Terrance, which she immediately deletes. What is done is done. Panic swamps her, but it is soon numbed with rage, and she remembers the call to her mother she didn't have a chance to make the night before. She looks at the photo she took last night, Diego standing next to the painting of the man Elena now knows is Neil. Neil, who lived with her father in college. Neil, who mattered to him. Neil, who died just before she was born.

It is seven, and Rosalind wakes early. Elena dials before she can tell herself not to, and waits for the sound of her mother's voice.

"You never told me about Diego. Or Neil. You never told me anything," Elena says, trying to keep her voice emotionless, and failing. There is silence, and she can hear Rosalind clearing her throat, something her mother does when she is trying to think. Trying to figure out how to get out of this.

"Your, your father didn't—"

"You knew Neil. Not just him. You knew Diego, too. You were friends with them both. They were a part of your life. Your past. Not just his," Elena says.

"How did you even—"

"I'm here. With Diego. I found him."

"Is, is he there, too?" Rosalind breathes. Elena doesn't respond, and she hears a sigh on the line.

"Your father wanted . . . when Neil died, it was too hard for him. He wanted to leave it behind, in the past."

"Maybe you shouldn't have let him," Elena spits out. How they had enabled him, how they had allowed him to be what he was? Rosalind, and her, too, because Elena has always learned by example.

"When has anyone ever *let* your father do a fucking thing?" Rosalind asks, bitterly. "If I could have dictated his behavior, if I could have controlled any part of him, do you really think I wouldn't have tried?"

"Maybe you should have shared what was yours to share. Maybe we shouldn't have let him be the only person who got to decide what I would know and not know about him. About both of you," Elena says, her face growing hot, her throat tight.

"That's not fair, I've told you about my life, my past, my family—"

"You've been with him since college. Your past is his past," Elena points out, her temples pounding. "You told me so much about your family, our past in Russia, our religion, you saturated me in where you come from but it doesn't make up for everything I don't know. Don't have."

"I, I wanted to make up for him," Rosalind says. Elena knows this, knows how much her mother loves her, hears the regret in her voice. But Elena cannot forgive her, cannot absolve her yet. Perhaps not ever. She loves her mother, she will always love her mother, but for so long she has made Rosalind all that is good, the good parent. Rosalind is a good parent. But that does not mean she is never a bad one.

"I hoped, I hoped I would be enough," Rosalind says. Elena feels that like a knife in the thin skin of her wrist.

"You are enough, Mom. You are enough of *you*. You are enough of a mother for me, for anyone. But you aren't my only parent. And more from you doesn't make up for nothing from him. Or the fact that there are pieces of him that you could have given me. Pieces that belong to both of you, like, like Diego. And you didn't." Elena has tried to keep her voice steady but she can hear the tremble at the end. She breathes deeply. Rosalind is silent.

"I'm sorry," Rosalind says. Elena says nothing. "I'm glad you met him," Rosalind offers her, almost timidly.

"I'm sorry it took this long," Elena says. There is another long pause. Elena has nothing more to say. She has never indicated that her mother wasn't enough for her. Those insecurities aren't from Elena, they are Rosalind's to bear. Elena is carrying enough right now. She hears her mother's intake of breath, and knows that she will change the subject, that this is all too heavy for this moment in time.

"What are you going to do now? Are you—"

"He might be in Ponce. Apparently he, I, have family there." Silence. Does Rosalind know this already?

"Good luck," Rosalind says, tentative. Elena's immediate instinct is to reassure her, and she has to bite her tongue, actually bite it, to stop herself. "Thank you." Elena hangs up before she can slip into old patterns, before she can displace her anger with obedience.

Outside the bedroom, Diego has coffee ready for her, and his clean, clean house makes Elena want to burn her father's house to the ground and start all over again, but just for a moment. She accepts the coffee, gratefully.

"How is Rosalind?"

"How did you—"

"The walls aren't very thick here, I'm sorry." Diego smiles at her.

"Your mother went into labor on the same day as Neil's memorial service. Did your father ever tell you that?"

Elena almost spits out the excellent coffee.

"I suppose not. He'd been gone for a week at that point, but year after year, I always celebrate his life on your birthday."

"You can't think that I'm somehow . . . Well."

"His reincarnation? I'm a lapsed Catholic, not a Hindu. I just think that if he had lived, well, maybe we would have seen Santiago more. Neil's death, it hit your father almost as hard as it hit me, and I was in love with Neil. He was the love of my life. But they were so close. They were each other's first real friend, I think. And Rosalind, she loved them both so much. But when you were born, she could put all that into you. She grieved, she did, but she had made life. I always imagined your father was more split in half, between mourning and, well, you. And I was so jealous of him, in those first years. He had something to wake up for. What did I have? I was the one who . . . for years it was too hard for me to see him, your father, he just reminded me of everything that was lost. And by the time I was ready, so much time had passed. There was a country between us. I understand your parents, they are the ones you feel have let you down. But I let them down, too. I let you down. You just didn't know I was doing it."

Elena looks at him for a long moment, and then she leans over, and kisses him gently on the cheek. He smiles at her, a little sadly.

"So. Where to?"

Elena takes a moment, but she already knows the answer. She

should go to San Sebastián, to the place her family is from. A strong person, a brave person, would do that.

"Ponce," she tells him. She is a coward. Why change now?

The route to Ponce from Rincón takes her around the western and southern rims of the island. It's a coastal road, and these are areas hit hard by the hurricane, the flood zones, fallen trees and evacuations. But now, as she barrels along the empty road in the car Diego drove her to rent, searching the landscape around her for signs of trauma, all she can see is the same beauty she remembers from her childhood trips to the island: rolling hills and little mountains dense with lush vegetation; sweeping vistas of the sea; farmland with cows chewing grass and the occasional horse; flowers that bloom year-round; small black birds with long tail feathers; and the occasional iguana, alive and running with their funny furious run, and a few, sadly, dead, roadkill. This is the season the iguanas mate, she remembers, recalling a trip around this same time as a teenager when she watched them chase each other down the beach, their bearded heads bristling in the sun.

She takes photos as she drives, stopping to frame different views, to try to get images of the birds and the lizards and the rich greenery and the normalcy of it all, the strange aching normalcy of this storm-tossed place that looks just as it ever did. How is it possible that this land is not marked more deeply by all that has happened to it? How is it so very forgiving? It's like a beaten body that doesn't show the bruises, inviting more pain with its apparent indifference.

Every once in a while, she sees the tree that Fernando has inked on his body and thinks of him. Can she really blame him for wanting the house? He wants it for the same reason she does, because it is a part of his history. His family. She wonders if she should contact him, but dismisses the thought. She barely knows him. *But you wanted to, didn't you?*

It takes her three hours to get there, but she doesn't mind. She has deliberately taken the longest route possible, driving along the western coast to Cabo Rojo, then continues following the sea until she finally arrives in Ponce, a city she has never visited before, named for the grandson of the conquistador. She knows this because she looked it up, another stall tactic. She knows where she is going, at least, the bar that her young cousin had found for her on Instagram, but somehow that makes it worse. Having a destination means she has to go there.

She drives around for a while, telling herself she should see the city, of course she should, she's never been, and the bar is not even open yet. She wonders what has closed because of Hurricane Maria, and what has survived, and what will continue to survive, because the storm's impact will ripple on and on over the island as the electrical grid stays broken and frayed and the tourists remain absent. She looks up the hurricane in Jessenia's blog, wondering what she'd said about the storm, and saw a post dated two weeks after it hit.

Huracan, from Hurakan, the Taino god of storms. Even now, we all speak a little Taino, even though we don't know it. Gone forever, and yet the Tainos live, somehow, in disaster, in grilled meats, barbacoa, in uncomfortable beds, hamaca, and in one of the plants that changed the new world, tabaco. Columbus wrote of them that "our highness may believe that in all the world there can be no better people," before he slaughtered them by the thousands. But that's genocide for you. Everyone knows, it couldn't have happened to a nicer group of people.

The Tainos, like many people, worshiped storms. Why worship the thing that can destroy you? Because it is the thing that will destroy you. Volcanos need virgins, rain in dry lands needs a dance, and when you live your life clinging onto a speck of rock and sand and lizard guano surrounded by a hungry sea, the time when it tries to swallow you whole is the time you ask it for mercy.

In the days when people still knew the true names of things, the zemi Atabey, goddess of storms, was, like all women, complex enough to be a goddess in her own right. Guabancex, Atabey on a bad hair day, controlled natural disasters, and her busy schedule meant she hired, delegated, managed, a team of two, Guataubá, who created hurricane winds, and Coatrisquie, who created floods. You need a diverse multi-skilled team to be successful in the hurricane business, everyone knows that.

Now we are in darkness, another thing we used to respect, to worship, and now we ignore. We have so many ways to banish darkness, but we forget how fragile our tools can be. We forget how powerful the elements are, how inescapable, how vengeful. How angry. We sit in angry darkness, and mourn all that we've lost, the people and things and the very idea that we were safe, that the storm could not touch us, that the old gods are dead.

The hurricane is a goddess. Despite the layers of new gods lacquering themselves onto the world, there are places where the old powers crack the veneer, coming when called, taking their believers home with them, back to the place where storms are another kind of magic.

Our mistake is always thinking we are the magical ones, that we can control the storm. There is no controlling this. There is only hope, in the darkness, that the waters will recede and that tomorrow we will find light.

Her phone buzzes, startling her. She was so absorbed in the post, she didn't even notice the wetness in her eyes. Swiping at a tear, she sees a text from Rosalind, *I'm sorry,* which she ignores. She is about to put her phone back in her purse when it buzzes again, and she sees Fernando's name.

Just tell me he didn't end up killing and eating you. She smiles.

If he had, how could I tell you anything? she texts.

Still there? Need a ride? She looks at his response.

I've made my own way to Ponce, she types.

My offer was genuine, even if I didn't make it the right way, he sends back. She looks at the text, frowning.

I'll think about it, she responds. But will she, really? She cannot imagine selling the house. She doesn't even know if she owns it. *Thanks for making sure I'm alive.* She puts her phone away.

She gets some lunch, looks at the historic buildings, which are much like Old San Juan's, like the house Fernando wants to buy, like the house she was told would be hers. She calls the lawyer Diego had referred her father to, Victor Padua, but no one answers, and she leaves an answer in halting Spanish, and then again in English, her hopes slim. She remembers the way her mother talked during the renovation, how no one would ever call them back, give them information, show up at the construction site on time. Caribbean time is not a myth, it's a curse. She will call this lawyer again, and again, but who knows if he is even here anymore, on the island? So many people are leaving now. All her excuses and ways to pass time run out at five in the evening, when her great-uncle's place, *she has a great uncle,* officially opens, according to the internet, and she follows the map to Mando's Bar, her heart heavy.

For a moment, after parking, Elena just sits and looks at the bar, snapping a photo. She keeps taking photos and she still doesn't know why, but she has stopped questioning herself; if she wants to record this trip it is hers to record. The bar is a decent-enough-looking place, nothing fancy, like so many bars she has passed by here: drinks served in disposable cups, outdoor seating, large signs celebrating Gasolina, a premade mixed drink named after the Daddy Yankee song and guaranteed to make one throw up everything they've ever ingested, others imploring partiers to enjoy

Bacardí, Medalla, and Palo Viejo, a horrific rum sold in any bar on the island in which people want to drink for cheap, that is, everywhere on the island. Elena remembers her college graduation trip, her last time here, when she tried a sip of Gasolina and had the taste in her mouth for the rest of the day, cloying and horrible.

When she opens the door of the bar, "La Cucaracha" plays. She had to listen to the song over and over again in a college Spanish class, all of the many verses and their interpretations, in a unit on Mexican revolutions, and she had almost lost her mind in annoyance over the tune. Elena can only think that this must be the most annoying thing possible for anyone who works here, but instead of wincing bartenders and waiters, all she sees is a man in his early fifties, or maybe late forties if he is a stranger to moisturizer, dancing to the song, celebrating the cockroach and her lost back legs.

"Come in, come in, we've just opened," he says in Spanish, turning around. "What will you have?"

"Are you Hermando?" she says, her voice strangely breathless. He looks at her, his smile, the broad bright one of a proprietor, of a bartender, fading.

"I am."

"I'm Elena. I think you know my father." She hands him a photo, now creased from her hand and the humidity, one of him and her father and "Irena la Bruja," according to the lightly written pencil marks on the back of the image, as the door opens behind her. And this time, as the song plays, signaling that there are more customers, Hermando does not dance. Instead, he looks at Elena as if he has seen a ghost, leaving the cockroach with no one dancing to her pain.

The first thing Hermando does is pour himself, and Elena, a shot.

"Have you ever had a *chichaito*?" he asks, in English now, and Elena is amused and surprised to hear that he speaks with a rather strong New York accent, but old New York, *Newh Yoowrk*, the way no one really speaks anymore. She shakes her head. The combination of rum and anise-flavored liquor was described to her, when she was on the island as a college student, as deadly, and she has never wanted to find out if this is true or not. Hermando nods and pulls out a bottle without a label on it, dipping its clear contents into two shot glasses.

"Salut." He downs it easily, while Elena coughs and sputters around a single sip of the concoction, leaving most of it still in the glass, the vile mixture acidic and hard on her throat and stomach. "You sure we are related?" he asks, noting her response to the drink, but his eyes are warm, kind. Elena smiles at him.

"Sure as I can be."

"Shit. Junior's daughter. I heard you never came down here."

"I don't. But actually, I'm looking for my dad. And I didn't even know we had family here anymore, other than my father's sisters."

"Oh yeah, my sister and me, we been down here a few years. Fifteen." Elena coughs again, but this time it has nothing to do with the drink. *Fifteen years.* She could have met them half her lifetime ago, long before her father's exile. How is it that he has the ability to hurt and surprise her, even now? Shouldn't she be done with the disappointment by now? Perhaps the pain parents inflict is infinite.

"Actually, you know what?"

Hermando takes out his phone, and dials. He speaks quietly, but Elena overhears him, he is calling Irena, asking her to come, to meet her. He looks up, ending the call with a smile.

"Your *tía*, well, your *great-tía*, will be thrilled to meet you."

"She's coming?" Elena says, excited. Hermando nods. "That's really nice, I'm happy to get to meet her. But, listen, as I said, I'm looking for my father. Have you, um, heard from him?" Hermando's expression closes, and Elena's heart drops to her stomach, which is still protesting the *chichaito*.

"Your father."

"I thought maybe he was here," Elena says. "He's missing."

Hermando nods, once, as if that is all the information he needs, and Elena thinks, *This is a man who has gone missing himself, isn't he?*

"I'm trying to find him." Maybe he doesn't understand her? She is trying to explain it but he doesn't seem to be responding.

"Let me get us something a little easier to drink."

Within minutes Elena is sitting down with a glass of water in her hand. Hermando bustles around, grabbing things, wine, a beer, giving orders to the kitchen despite the fact that Elena has made it clear she has just eaten. He checks his phone.

"She will be here in twenty. We can all talk then," he tells Elena, and then continues setting the restaurant up for service as he tends to her. It might open at five, but it is clear that people do not really come at that time. They sit in silence for a moment, and Elena marvels at the way blood ties people who have nothing else between them. This man is so different from her, from anyone she knows. Different, too, from her father; he looks utterly unlike Santiago Vega Jr., who took after his own father. He has the same nervous energy, though, that her father has when he's manic, he's tapping his feet, scratching his arm, patting the table to the rhythm of the music.

"So."

"Have you seen him?" Elena says at the same time. Hermando just looks at her again, and sighs.

"Can I see?" He is pointing at the albums in her hands, the two she brought with her that she took out when she wanted to show Hermando the photo, and hasn't put away since. Elena nods and passes one over, the oldest one. He pages through it slowly, taking in the yellowed photographs, the solemn faces staring out at him. His family. Hers, too.

"I haven't seen some of these. God, like a fucking time machine."

"That's Papi." Elena points at him as an infant, the photo she first saw what feels like weeks ago now, but was just three days ago.

"With his parents. It says 'New York, 1951' on the back," she says. Hermando nods.

"That was before I was born," he tells her. Then:

"Holy shit! Look at her, man, looking like a live wire." He is grinning like a little boy.

"Who is that?" Elena asks. He's pointing at a woman in a flouncy dress, mischief in her eyes. She looks all of twenty, her hair falling in soft perfect brushed-out late-1950s waves, and her eyeliner is bold. The photo is black-and-white, but it is clear she is wearing lipstick, too.

"Carmen," says a female voice, that same New York accent that Hermando has, brushed with more Puerto Rican vowel tones, sounding bittersweet. "Our sister."

Elena looks up and sees a woman, the woman from the Instagram image, the same face that she has seen in these photos, the chin strong, the brows, like Hermando's, stern, and she realizes that these eyebrows, these eyes, must have come from Teofila, her great-grandmother, for everyone has them. They skipped her father, but they are on Elena's own face. She has the family's . . . what was Teofila's last name, anyway?

"What was your mother's last name? Her first one?" she asks, suddenly. Shouldn't this be something she should know? Shoudn't she know the names of her ancestors, the track of who has come before her?

"Marin," the woman says, smiling, as if it isn't a bizarre question. "But she wore many. She married over and over again, our mother. We're the last of her children."

"Save the best for last!" Hermando says, crowing it out.

"You must be Tía Irena," Elena says, standing, but before she can hold out her hand to shake Irena's, she is enveloped in a hug that smells like sandalwood and coconut oil and orange-flower water.

"She was a real piece of work, that one."

Elena leans back and sees Irena studying the photo in the album.

"Always running around with some gang member or something," Hermando says, standing next to Irena, who has sat with the dignity of a queen waiting to be served. Hermando pours her a beer with great ceremony, and Irena takes a sip, then nods her head, *this will do.*

"You were some gang member or something, idiot," Irena says, without heat. Hermando ducks his head, and for a moment Elena can see their childhood relationship written on top of their adult one. "That is why we came back here."

"When did you come back?" Elena asks. Maybe if she can get them talking about something they will be more open. It feels like they are hiding something from her, and she wants to know what it is, but if she can't get through the front door, maybe there is a side door she can use.

"We left New York, when Mando . . . what has it been?"

"My chip says sixteen years in July." Hermando takes out a chip proclaiming that he has spent the better part of three decades without narcotics. Elena eyes the beer in his hand, and he shrugs. "This is nothing. With liquor, I'm fine. I run this place, I get a little drunk, I sleep. With heroin . . ." He trails off as Irena's lips thin.

"He was in with a bad crowd. I could see his future. No need to sacrifice anything to *la Madre, los santos,* not for that. You don't need magic to see where that life leads. We came here, fresh start. Your grandfather gave us some help, in the beginning, and we landed here, in Ponce. Of course, I travel around the island quite a bit. People require my services. But Hermando is here, running this place.

"Here." Irena removes the oldest album from Elena's limp grasp, and searches it for something. "This is all of us." Irena shows Elena a photo of a group, a kind-looking man—Isadoro, Elena thinks, one of Teofila's husbands—with a fierce-looking woman, Teofila.

They are surrounded by children, and by a woman whose face is blurry, but those eyes, it is Esperanza, the eyes give it away.

"That's our father, Isadoro, he wanted a photo of everyone. This was a little before Rodrigo, our oldest brother, went to jail. Last time all of us were in one place, I think. See, this is our mother, your father's grandmother, and Isadoro, her last husband. That's Rodrigo, and Roberto, they come from the second husband, a Lopez. That's Carmen, she was a Rodriguez, see, same look, like she's going to set something on fire." Irena sighs, mournfully. She is explaining the photos to Elena, like she understands that Elena doesn't know any of this. Well, she's a witch, after all, isn't she? Elena wonders.

"Where is—"

"Dead. She survived a lot of bad men, but not cancer. Here, though, doesn't she look like she is going to live forever? She thought she would. Sometimes, I feel her spirit, she's come back here with us, back to the island. Then my older brother, Rowdy. He's also gone now, and Roberto. And this is me, of course, and little Mando." She points to the baby in another boy's arms. "And that's your father, holding him. He used to change his diapers." Irena shoots Hermando an evil grin, and Elena sees it again, the way these two are like children still, no matter his sobriety or her magical powers. "And Esperanza, the oldest, next to your father. There we are, all of Teofila's many children and first grandchild. You know, people call me a witch, well they should. But she was a witch, too. The bad kind. I think she cursed us. She was a black witch, and I'm a white one."

"Brown," Hermando says, cackling. Irena shoots him a look. "No, she did, I agree. The men, at least."

"Your father escaped, though," Irena says, crossing her arms. "All that work I did, trying to free his mother, trying to help Esperanza, I believe it all went to him. Maybe she gave it to him."

"Work?" Elena asks, curious.

"I knew my calling early. I knew I was called to be a *santera*. A priestess. Our grandmother, Teofila's mother, she was a *santera* of some power. Teofila brought her over, and our neighbors knew what she could do, made sure she always had food to eat, money for things she needed, brought her flowers and feathers for her altar, helped her find the little shops Cuban immigrants had set up for supplies. But Teofila didn't like this, didn't follow her ways. She believed in the Church, wanted to scrub our power out of our family. Really, I think she wanted to keep everything for herself. She must have used something, some magic to keep attracting these men, these husbands, one after another. She would have liked the magic to die with her, I think. But it's in the blood. And much as she wanted to have it all, she had children, all of us were touched by the magic. Some of us, it was just a violent urge, an impulse. That's the men."

Irena glances balefully at Hermando, who has moved to pour rum and Cokes for two customers who have wandered in, and beers for what look like a trio of regulars, older men setting up the pool table.

"But the women, we got more. My older sister, well . . ." Here Irena falters, her finger tracing Esperanza's form in the photograph, then Elena's father's. "It was too much for her, I believe. The power made her mad." Elena wants to deny this, to say that Esperanza's madness was mental illness, not magic. But she does not. Irena already knows the truth, and has remade it into this narrative. She does not need Elena's correction.

"Carmen used it superficially. To gain a little power over a man she liked, to draw the eye. Useless. But that was her, impulsive, and burning for love. She thought that would bring her power, real power. Doesn't last, especially not when it comes from a spell. No man Carmen turned the gaze on ever looked at her for long, ever wanted to look at her more than he wanted to look at his gun, his money, his gang. But me, I started young, I knew what called me. The orishas beckoned me before I heard their names. I did it on my own, I hung out at Santeria stores; there were more and more immigrants from Cuba, more *padrinos,* to bless, to teach. When it was time to come back here, I performed a healing ritual on Hermando, and we left New York, so he could leave those dark forces behind him, and I could bring my skills here. I travel the island, people in need call me, sometimes I can help."

"How do they reach you?" Elena asks, fascinated despite herself.

"Facebook," Irena says. *Of course.* "Family doesn't need that, though, really. We can feel each other. Did you find me on Facebook?"

"No," Elena says, truthfully. Irena looks triumphant, and Elena doesn't mention Instagram. It doesn't seem worth it. She does not know if her aunt is detached from reality or truly magical or . . . what third thing could she be? Everything she says is bizarre to Elena, but she says it with conviction, with total confidence. Her gaze is clear, her eyes certain. It is obvious that Irena, at least, believes in herself. All the best and most convincing con artists and maniacs do.

Elena doesn't know the real contents of Irena's head, doesn't know if she has a mental health issue like her father and his mother, and probably more relatives Elena will never know about stretching back through time. So far, Elena herself has escaped those bequests, as far as she knows. But will the gifts of her father's mind, her grandmother's mind, emerge later in her life? Will whatever balanced brain chemistry Rosalind has given her be enough to contradict her father's contribution? Elena knows it doesn't work this way, genes are not a cocktail, but she cannot help but fear for her future, for her mind. Is everyone in her family a little mad, more than a little? Is Irena away with the fairies or completely right about everything? Is she, Elena, going to be okay? She has no idea.

"Your cousin Jessenia, you know her? She's not really related but she belongs with us, that girl is one the spirits love. She found me, too, the last time she was visiting. She lives in Florida part of the year, but she comes down here. Sweet girl. I told her about Santeria for that blog of hers."

"I've seen it," Elena says, her smile bittersweet. She wishes she could be like Jessenia, coming back and forth, being a part of this family like this. She wonders if the spirits love her, Elena, but she knows they don't, they can't, can they? Wouldn't they have given her a better life if they did? And now here she is, wishing spirits she doesn't believe in had thrown her a better bone. She shakes her head internally.

"And my father? Did he find you, too, with magic?" Elena asks. Hermando has returned with fresh drinks, more water for Elena and a bottle of Barrilito. Elena takes a glass and observes Irena and Hermando, who are looking anywhere but at her.

"He was here," Elena states. Of course he was. She feels a stab of victory; it is never a bad feeling to be right, even if combined with panic—*but where is he now?*—and anger, the anger that has begun to boil in her, *what is he doing, where is he going, why has he gone, why didn't they make him stay? No one can make him do anything.* The thought rolls through her brain with such deadly precision she feels it jabbing at her eyelids.

"He comes and goes," Hermando says, pouring Elena more rum, although she hasn't finished her first drink yet, doesn't know if she wants it at all. Her mind is already so dizzy, she doesn't really need anything making her more confused. A pinch of despair courses through her: of course he wasn't here recently. "But, Elena, I don't know that he wants to be found."

"What does that mean?" Elena asks, her voice rising. Happy families and magic and rum are all well and good but she *needs* something from these people, why are they hiding it from her? Dangling memories in front of her, family stories like lures, distracting her from the real prize?

"I know he is well," Irena says, firmly. "I can feel him."

"Have you *seen* him?" Elena asks. She doesn't want to challenge Irena's gift, mostly because she doesn't want to be cursed, even if she doesn't believe in any of this, but she has to know if they know something real or are relying on the spirit world.

"I would feel it if he was gone," Irena says, simply. Elena sips her drink to cover her expression. "You don't believe me."

"I just . . . I need a little more evidence, I think. I have to be able to tell my mom something a little more concrete," Elena says, diplomatically, making it her mother's fault, as Rosalind isn't there to mind. "She asked me to come down, to look for him. To make sure he was okay. Look, I understand if maybe he doesn't want to see me or whatever, but I have to know if he's been here recently. I have to know if he's . . ." *Alive.*

"Rosalind asked you to come here?" Irena says, her eyes widening.

"You know my mother? Did you ever meet her?" Elena asks, curious. Irena and Hermando exchange puzzled glances.

"Of course we did. She came up to New York with your father when his mother was still alive. She cleaned up the place, cooked, not that Esperanza ever thanked her, she just told her her food was inedible. I always liked your mother."

Elena does not have room for all the rage she feels toward her parents, *both* her parents, at this moment. Rosalind sent her down here fucking *blind.* She could have told her about Diego, about Irena and Hermando, about anything, and instead Elena is just wandering around looking for one Puerto Rican man on an island full of them.

"When was the last time he was here? Please, please don't lie to me. Everyone is lying to me, or not, not telling me what I need. Please."

The siblings look at each other again, silent communication clear between them. Elena wonders what it would be like to have someone else who shared her parents, who talked to her with their eyes like these two talked to each other. But she wouldn't wish her family on a sibling, no matter how lonely she was sometimes as an only child.

"He called, offered us some money after the storm, but we didn't need it. He wanted to make sure we were okay," Hermando says. "He comes here sometimes. He came a few weeks ago, maybe?"

"Two weeks," Irena says. *Two weeks ago.* That means he was alive two weeks ago.

"What, what was he like?" Elena asks, her voice mortifyingly shaky. Hermando looks at her with pity, and it makes her shrink like a slug sprinkled with salt.

"He's haunted," Irena says, succinctly. "I think it's his mother. I tried to fix it but her spirit is strong. He came for two days and left. Said he was going home."

What does home mean for him?

"That was it? That was everything? He didn't say anything else, what his plans were, anything?" Elena begs, reaching out, holding onto Irena's wrist, desperate for more, for something.

"Yes." But Elena sees her eyes flicker to the side, like she is lying.

"I gotta serve some customers," Hermando says, standing, and moving to the bar. Irena has not let go of Elena's hand, and she pulls her in, her mouth at Elena's ear.

"He is haunted, and he is becoming a ghost himself. He is crossing into other worlds, and you must let him go." Irena's eyes burn, like her mother's and sister's in the photos, like Elena's own; she can feel them in her skull, burning. Irena releases her, and it is like her aunt has returned from some other place.

"Drink your drink," Irena says to her, like it's milk for a child. Elena takes a sip in silence. *Going home,* what does that mean? Philadelphia? New York? California—did he think of that as home? San Sebastián, even? What could home mean to him, a place, a person? Which one?

"I don't think you should give up the house," Irena says, almost absently.

"I'm sorry?" Elena says. Irena pins her with those fire eyes again, smiling.

"It will be yours, won't it?"

Elena exhales at the words. For a moment she wondered if there was something, well, *real* in Irena's magic.

"I don't know if it will be mine," Elena says.

"It will," Irena says, and Elena longs for that certainty, the confidence that has come with Irena's own escape from reality. She thinks of myths she has read, how the gods demand sacrifice for their gifts. Elena is doomed to live in a world of doubt, for she is not willing to pay the price Irena has.

As quickly as she came, Irena leaves, telling her long-lost great-niece that she is needed elsewhere, suddenly, although her phone has not rung, no new message has reached her by digital means. Elena does not think that she really believes this woman has magic, but gun to her head, she does not know what would come out of her mouth. She hugs her goodbye, hoping for a last word, some other prophecy to spill out, but Irena just wishes her luck, her eyes vague, and then she is gone.

Hermando abandons her, too, in service to entertaining new groups of customers who have come, in droves, it is 6:00 P.M. now, the long night of drinking will begin for many. He has offered her a place on his couch, but she will probably get a hotel room. She needs time to herself, and he will be at the bar until it closes, and afterward, she imagines. She does not want to ruin his night with her avalanche of emotions.

Elena takes a sip of water, and lets it hit the back of her throat, trickling down into her stomach. She has to keep going, to find a hotel and make a plan for the next day, for the trip to San Sebastián.

It is the last place for her to look, the last option. If he isn't there, well, he isn't anywhere. If he isn't there she will fly back to New York, beg for her job, won't she? *No, I won't.* If he isn't there she doesn't have a clue what she is going to do. She is exhausted, over- whelmed by her task, sodden with anger and sadness and gratitude, because she is here, with people she never knew existed, people who are a part of her, who together have given her a piece of herself, her legacy. She wants to feel that there is something at the end of this, someone, her father, and something will happen that will fix it, heal it, that he will see her and smile and love her the way she needs him to. That he will give her a piece of himself to carry into the future, that he will get better because he wants to, so she can know him, so he can know her. She wants him to show her the way home. She would like to go home. Wherever that is.

Hours later, Elena lies on a bed, its sheets crisp and clean, the joy of hotel rooms, linen you don't have to wash, and stares at the creamy ivory expanse of ceiling above her. It did not take her long to find a room, and she was checked into the Meliá Century Hotel by eight in the evening. Having avoided the rum, she treated herself to a drink in the hotel bar, wincing at the price, smiling at what her fa- ther would think of paying that much for a glass of wine in Puerto Rico. They had given her a pamphlet describing the history of the hotel, which has been in operation since the late 1890s, and as she looks around at the mix of architectural styles from the described renovations, early deco in 1915, midcentury modern in 1960, she thinks of the people who have passed through these rooms, drunk at this bar, stumbled into bed or climbed gracefully between the cov- ers. Hotels are a strange thing, she thinks, always projecting the im- age of new, impersonal, a room just for you, but they are the village bikes of buildings, used and reused, filled with ghosts. Everyone is haunted, it seems, even her.

Hermando hadn't seemed to mind her turning down his offer to stay with him, as long as she promised to keep in touch. She accepted his request to follow her on Instagram as he watched, like a hawk, and she has already received four messages from him, all in the form of emojis. She writes back, *It was so nice to meet you,* and gets another one, a cat with hearts for eyes. She smiles, happy that he likes cats, happy that he likes emojis, happy to know more about him.

Since she found out about his disappearance, Elena has been calling her father at least once a day. Santiago is old-fashioned, and he still has a voicemail box. When she calls, his phone is off, she knows, because it again goes straight to voicemail, and for a few moments she can hear his voice, telling her that he is not available. He still sounds like a lawyer on his voicemail, carefully enunciating his first and last names, asking that the caller provide the date and time that they have called, as well as the contact number at which he can reach them. Never mind that all cell phones have Caller ID, that he can see who has called, that the number will be saved in his missed calls.

Now, cradled in sheets that someone else will have to wash, the greatest of luxuries to Elena, who lives in a walk-up and carries her laundry to a laundromat a block away once a week, refusing to indulge in drop-off service, she again takes out her phone, ignoring further emojis from Hermando, and calls her father. She knows that nothing will come of it, as nothing has come of the last ten calls.

Then, someone picks up, and her heart stops. "Papi? Papi?"

She hears a fumble, and a click, and the call has ended. She sits up in bed. Was that him? Was that anyone? She didn't even hear breathing or anything. Could that have been him? Or someone who stole his phone, or found it on his dead body, or, or—

She is breathing deeply, too deeply, she is dizzy. She tries to calm herself, to breathe normally. She does not want to pass out.

She calls him back, over and over again, but no one answers. And eventually the calls go right to voicemail, the message she was eager to hear sounding so stupid, so painful in her ears.

When Elena was younger, back in high school, and her father started drinking, heavily, again, a state she had never witnessed but something her mother tightly confirmed later had marked the early years of their marriage until he had promised, *promised,* that he would live life sober, she came home from play practice one Saturday afternoon to a trail of blood spotting the polished wide-plank pine floors of their entryway, kitchen, and dining room. It led up the stairs, marring the carpet, which her mother would replace the following spring, and across the second floor of their home into her parents' bedroom. Elena followed it, in a gruesome parody of Hansel and Gretel, and found her father sprawled out on the bed, his forearm covered in congealed blood, dirt, and gravel. He had fallen off his bicycle on his weekly bike ride from their house around the East and West River Drives, wide beautiful routes framing the Schuylkill River, and hurt himself. After the long ride, he had stopped at a bar on Spring Garden Street and rewarded his labor with liquor, then veered off the road near a small park in their neighborhood and crashed. He had left the bike behind, Elena and her mother would later learn, and had walked home, made his way to bed, and fallen asleep, his blood painting the house. Elena had gone to the park the next day, when he had woken from his stupor and was able to piece together some of his actions, but the bike was gone.

This wasn't the first, or the last, bad thing that would happen to her father. Rosalind tried, Elena knows that she did, to save her father from himself, but no one can do a thing like that, not really, and Elena also knows that her mother's choice to leave him was a painful one because of the pain Rosalind knew her husband would end up causing himself. The fact that he has made it ten years now without her there to clean his cuts, to pick him up at the hospital, to make sure he survives the life he chooses to live, makes Elena feel that he is somehow blessed, touched by grace. But this can't last forever.

Stabbing pain, under her left eye, comes and goes like a large needle. She looks up, rubbing at the spot, but it's internal, her fingers don't do any good. She lies awake for a long time that night, thinking of her father as a dead body, but no matter how long she thinks about the image, she does not cry. She does not feel sad. She just feels panic, and emptiness.

Elena wakes from blissful dreams of drowning to a call from her mother. She doesn't answer it. She can't. She can't talk to her right now. If she does, everything will come out, the bitterness she feels, and she knows Rosalind will not say she's sorry, not say she regrets it, and Elena isn't ready to hear that lack of remorse. She doesn't have the energy to think about Rosalind right now.

She is on the road by nine in the morning. Outside the car the island blows by. According to the Wikipedia page for Puerto Rico, which Elena looked up during the night, unable to sleep, the island is the smallest of the Greater Antilles, and just around 311 miles in circumference. Before Maria, it would be easy to drive around the whole of the island in a day; now, with the ripped roads and cracked bridges, it takes more time. Perhaps the next time Elena comes, it will be healed, or on the way, and she can try that, driving the entirety of the island. *When will you be back here?* she wonders to herself.

No matter what this is to him, she thinks to herself, *this is yours, too. This belongs to you. You shouldn't let anyone keep you away from here if here is where you want to be.* She only wishes she knew where she wants to be most.

Fifteen

The envelope came in the mail for Santiago so long after that lunch with Mrs. Schultz that when he saw it, that thick packet with the words *Stanford University* printed on it in clear deep red letters next to his address, the return address describing an admissions office in Palo Alto, California, he was uncertain exactly what it was, uncertain up until the moment that he saw the words *congratulations* and *full scholarship,* and then his eyes began to blur, even with his glasses on.

It came late, so late he didn't know it was coming at all. He had already received his admissions letters to Marymount Manhattan, Hunter College, and City University of New York. By that point, he almost thought he had imagined applying out of state, wondering what kind of dream that was. He had to stay here, anyway, to take care of his mother. To be in the place where he knew what the world was. Painful as his life in New York was, it was *his,* how could he leave it, really? Santiago felt he should stay put, stay where he had been born, where he had been placed, and know that was the life for him. To go so far, how would he find the way back again?

And now what? he asked himself, sitting in the tiny kitchen, in the empty apartment, his fingers stiff, page after page of information swimming before his eyes. Words like *room and board, stipend for expenses, impressed with your performance* floated in front of him, and he knew that this would change his life, if he let it. *Don't you want to change your life?* But to change his life would mean changing everyone else's as well. He might be alone, but his mother haunted the apartment like poverty haunted his life, ever present, inescapable, as much a part of him as his skin. Could he leave her behind? Could he cut his life into two pieces, and know they might never knit themselves back together again?

Outside one window hung the fire escape ladder. Junior opened the windows and reached out, pulling himself out and up, climbing onto the roof. He had discovered this years before, during one of his mother's bad spells, when she had begged him to let her out, let her meet the great Earth Mother, when she had screamed and moaned and he had stuffed her hands in her winter mittens, so she could not turn the door locks, could not leave, could not physically disappear into the world as her mind had disappeared from reality. She was still a beautiful woman, despite her madness, and he did not know what people, men, might do to her, did not trust her to make her way home. He should have known she needed to be put away, then, but how could he do that? She had protected him, he had to do the same for her. But her keening cry, muffled by her attempts to bite the mittens off her hands, made staying in the same room with her impossible. He knew she would exhaust herself soon, she was rocking on the bed as she muttered and bit at the wool, but he could not stay, could not listen to it, and so he climbed out the window and realized he could keep going up, up, to the roof. Away from her, alone, the city laid out in front of him.

Since that day, it had become his sanctuary. Below him taxis beeped and pedestrians chattered, but he felt like he was on another planet, something from the Twilight Zone, some place quiet like nowhere in the city had ever been quiet.

Now, he sat, his knees curled into his skinny chest, on the edge of the building. It wasn't tall, but sudden death lay below him should he fall. He was alone. Truly alone. He had carved out space for himself in this city, away from the suffocating rooms into which he had been born, away from the choking grasp that held his family, his uncles. Away, even, from the sweet stultifying world of the island, drowsy and dated, a life from another time. Both a trap. And now he had another open window, another place to escape to. He had sought it out, dreamed it for himself, but never thought it would become real. Could he bear to reach out and take it?

Junior's grandfather, a *jibarito,* had cut cane until the day he died. All around San Sebastián, the sugar fields the man had worked and never owned a piece of stretched in every direction. When Santiago first visited the island, he would bring him lunch out in the fields, watching as the lines in his grandfather's face deepened with every bite. His skin was deeply tanned, his back in a permanent bent curve from years and years of swinging a machete, making his body a capital *C.* He was a quiet man, and Junior had wondered where his own father's words had come from, the way his father could talk and talk to other people. When his abuelo was finished, he would wipe his face with the napkin Chavela had packed for her father-in-law, a useless endeavor, Santiago had never seen his abuelo's face dry. Then, he would straighten, as best he could, and return to the work, work he did not need to do for money, work he did because his hands had moved in that motion for too long to stop. He died before he turned fifty. How long would Santiago's father live? And his mother? And all of the people he knew, each one consumed with what was just in front of them, like his abuelo, unable to see beyond the cane?

Santiago looked out at the city. It was so big. And beyond that, what? The things he had read about, the Japanese palace, castles in France, churches in Spain, a wall in China. He did not know if he truly believed that any of it was real. Could anything outside of

New York, and the island, be real? Was California real? This life, here, wanted to take him, and hold him, and never let him go.

He looked out at the next building over. It was barely a foot between the two roofs. Something surged through his body as he realized that, and then looked up, ahead, to the next building, and the next, all the same level, stretching out up the avenue, beckoning him, demanding that he move forward, to the next step, and the next. To leave New York, to walk on and on and on until he was somewhere completely new, somewhere perhaps that was not even real, but would become so, to him. If he could keep his eyes open, if he could see *beyond,* it would be possible. If he cut out the noise, the things that would grasp at him and try to pull him back—the cruelties and jealousies, the hands of his uncles, his grandmother, the pull of the island, the cries of his mother, yes, even those, he could go forward. He could move, he could *rise.*

Before he could think about it, stop himself, he was running, jumping, and over onto the next rooftop. His blood was on fire, his legs were weightless, and he kept running, jumping, roof to roof. He made it all the way to Third Street before he knew what had happened, his heart beating furiously, laughing at how easy it had been, how quickly he could move.

If he didn't carry anything with him, let nothing, no one, stop him, how far could he get?

"Have you thought any more about where you might like to apply?" Mrs. Schultz said, looking up at him, her eyes big behind her Coke bottle–thick glasses. Santiago, looking back at her, wondered if people thought that they were both part of some kind of glasses club, both of them bespectacled, peering out at the world with large magnified eyes.

Mrs. Schultz was shorter than most of her students, a quality that, when she had been transferred to Santiago's public school, had given the principal pause. It was a diverse school, with students from many backgrounds, most of them less than privileged, and the children had a tendency toward disobedience, anarchy, rebellion. They needed a firm hand, and he was concerned that Mrs. Pearl Schultz, with her neatly teased bouffant, her seed-pearl necklace, her twinsets, and her big eyes topping a sharp little nose, would be the tortured mouse to her catty unruly students. In short, he wondered how a woman who looked more like a suburban Jewish housewife would contain, let alone instruct, forty rambunctious teenagers from Lower Manhattan.

However, within her first week, Mrs. Schultz proved the principal egregiously wrong. Her outer appearance may have been that of a rather startled mouse, but on the inside, Pearl Schultz was a warrior. She had been ten years old when the Nazis had taken her city, Jihlava, a benign little city at the border of Bohemia and Moravia, places that would disappear from history, becoming other countries entirely after the war. Back then, her name was Jitka.

As a child, she watched her brother shot in front of her, his body going limp and strange like a marionette's. She watched her sister separated from her children, screaming like nothing Pearl had ever heard before, watched her father be beaten and lynched in the town square. It was Pearl, little Pearl, the spoiled baby, who melted snow for her mother to drink and hid a few precious things stitched up into the soles of their shoes and the hems of their dresses, and held on, tighter and tighter, so that when she and her mother and her sister were being sorted into groups, the three of them were together; Pearl, who pulled her sister Darja on and on, who made sure they always had something, anything, to eat as the three women labored in Majdanek; Pearl, who flirted with the guards to keep her family from the gas chambers, no matter how it turned her stomach, what could disgust her anymore?

Pearl made it through the war by force of will, refusing to die, refusing to let her mother and sister die. When the war ended, she led what was left of her family into America, hollow wraiths that they were. Just before the ship docked, Pearl took a knife she had made in the camp and split open the old shoes, the hems of filthy dresses, things she had not allowed anyone to take from her, and pulled out rings, bracelets, a pearl necklace. She washed her mother and sister's faces, and fastened earrings in their ears and bracelets around their gaunt wrists.

When asked her name at Immigration, she christened herself Pearl, her hand at her throat, touching the things she had kept safe for years and years from men who wanted her and everyone like her dead. The jewelry would begin her family's life in the New World. It would pay for an apartment, it would help them eat. They settled in Brooklyn, where Pearl's mother worked as a cook and Pearl cleaned houses and took classes at Brooklyn College. Darja never recovered, never stopped screaming for her children, and by 1950, just after Pearl's twenty-first birthday, she came home from school, where she was studying to be a teacher, and found that Darja had hung herself with a bedsheet. Pearl's mother wept as Pearl untied the sheet and laid her sister down, setting the bedding to soak in bleach and calling for the rabbi.

Pearl met her husband, a third-generation German Jew who had spent the war in a training camp in Macon, Georgia, through a fellow teacher, his sister, Goldie. Goldie had invited her to Shabbat dinner, and while Pearl wasn't sure how she felt about God anymore, she went, and there, over roast chicken and dry challah, she met Joseph. They were married within six months. When they discovered, after a few years, that they couldn't have children, Pearl did not let this knowledge kill her love for her work, for children. Instead, it made her even better, for if she could not be one child's mother, she was determined to be the best teacher she could be for as many children as possible. She had helped countless students over the years, a recommendation here, extra attention there; sometimes all it took was talking to them, or better, listening to them.

By the time Santiago had come into her classroom, she had been teaching at the same school for four years. The principal's doubts might have been dispelled that first day, but every year was the same with the students. They looked at her and saw someone they could easily dismiss, someone who understood nothing of their lives. What did she have to offer them? It took time, each time, for them to understand what she was giving them, for them to care. Some of them never did, and it hurt her heart. But the ones who learned to trust her, who looked to her for more, more information, more knowledge, whose minds opened to her like flowers at dawn, they were precious to her. They became *hers*. And he, Santiago, was hers most of all.

He sat in the first row, in the corner. He had large glasses, like her own, and his hair was a mass of wild curls that had been smoothed down with something, but were rebelling, springing up, trying to break free. His clothing was old and worn but perfectly clean, his shirt neatly pressed, his threadbare trousers creased. He did not say a word for that first week, did not answer a question, but he drank in everything she said about the book they had been asked to read that summer, *Macbeth,* his pencil moving along his paper like a flowing stream. Then, as they were closing their discussion of the novel, he raised his hand.

"Please, Mrs. Schultz, I have a question. Did the witches *make* Macbeth do those things, or did he choose them? What I mean to say is, does evil live inside of people, or does it come from the outside? And if it comes from the outside, then what are we responsible for, as human beings? How can our actions have meaning if we aren't the ones who choose them?"

Pearl stared at him. It was clear from the look on his face that the answer mattered to him, that he truly wanted to know. She responded quickly, with something vague, disappointing him, and asked him to stay after class. She apologized to him, then, telling him the truth, that she did not *know* where evil came from, only that it was real, she had known it, seen it, and it was as human as anything else. Santiago nodded, slowly, and thanked her, his voice solemn, calm. When she asked him why he had asked that question, he had told her, *My mother needs to know.*

Over the last two years, Pearl had learned bits and pieces of Santiago's life, putting together a mosaic image of his existence. She doubted anyone but she at the school knew that his mother was in and out of an institution, that he was living alone. He came from a poor and violent family, like many of her students, and his brain was eager for worlds beyond his own, he was eager to talk about justice and truth and humanity through Shakespeare and Dickens and Faulkner and Melville.

She had given him what she gave any talented motivated student who came across her path—her time, her guidance, more books to read, more conversations after class—but now she was giving him more. It was September, and school had begun a few weeks ago. Santiago had worked all summer and read every book on the list that she had given him, and told her yes, he wanted to go to school, he *would* go to school, but he needed her help. So they were sitting together in a little place in Chinatown that served hot tea and hotter pork dumplings, may God forgive her, may she forgive God, with five college applications in front of them, and they were not leaving until they were done.

"I was thinking maybe somewhere far away. Maybe somewhere in Chicago or, or California," he said, responding to her question. He didn't list schools, just areas, and she wondered if he even knew what colleges were out there, or if he just wanted to go as far away from his life as possible.

"California," Pearl repeated. "Why do you want to go to California?" Junior reached into his bag and pulled out a library book, one off the list she had given him, *The Grapes of Wrath.* Pearl smiled, wryly. "I would think that book would be an argument against going to California, not an incentive."

"It's not the Great Depression anymore," Junior said, earnestly. "I hear it's a lot better there now."

"From whom?" Pearl asked, amused. Junior shrugged.

"It sounds nice there. Sunny. They make movies out there, and it's always warm, and people seem happy, don't you think?"

Pearl sighed. He was a brilliant kid, but he was a *kid,* who had seen very little of the world outside of New York, who barely seemed to understand that there *was* a world outside of New York. What was he going to do in California?

"Do any of those schools give people any money? Ones in California?" he asked, his eyes intent. Pearl studied him. He smiled his normal smile, the one that hid the missing front tooth he told her had been knocked out of his mouth, but didn't tell her how. He'd grown over the summer, and he was a little too tall for his pants, his ankles poked out of them, knobby and bare. He had such hope in his eyes.

Pearl reached into her bag. She had some other applications, things she had picked up for other students, schools she wanted him to consider. He had never heard of any of them, so asking him to choose was telling him to pick something at random. She thumbed through the papers, looking for one place in particular, one she thought might fund him. It was a long shot, but weren't all of them? Santiago was smart, and hardworking, but the other students who would apply would come from money, from pedigrees that would guild them into these schools, into these lives. All he had was her.

"'Stanford,'" Santiago said, reading the top of the application, testing the word out in his mouth.

"It's near San Francisco," Pearl said. She had studied maps of the United States when she first moved to the country, wanting to know everything about this new place, wanting to erase the old names of old towns and villages and streets that lingered in her, haunting her, wanting to become new in the New World.

"San Francisco is in the north, right?" he said. "Is that far from Hollywood?"

"Yes," Pearl said, smiling.

"How far? As far as from here to Yonkers?" Pearl smiled again at Junior's question.

"A bit farther than that, I believe." Junior looked sad at her words, then brightened.

"Maybe if I do well and get a good job I can have a car sometime, that will make it easier. Do they have a subway between them?" Pearl shook her head. Santiago nodded. "That's all right. I'll be too busy with school, anyway. If I get in. Is this one really hard?" Pearl did not know how to answer him.

"Only one way to find out," she said, smiling, feeling the weight of his future on her chest.

She spread out the pages of the application.

"Let's begin."

The summer before his senior year of high school Santiago did not return to the island. It was the first summer he could remember not visiting since his father had moved back. The ticket came in the mail, just like it always did, and he looked at it for a full day, sitting on the kitchen table, a rectangle of thin cardboard, an invitation to paradise.

He wanted to go to the island. Wanted it more than he had ever wanted it before. He wanted to escape all this, to spend a little time in a world where his life was not made up of visits to his mother, and dinners with his family here, and lying to everyone he knew about having parents, having care in his life. He wanted to *be* cared for, to let go of caring for his mother, himself. To eat the food Goli had prepared for him, to sit with Luis as the sun rose, to know that all he had to do each day was work and eat and sleep.

But he could not have it. He could not go and have that taste of goodness, and return here. He could not leave his mother behind, not as he had been left. He could not go and pretend that his father was a good man, watch him be a good husband and a good father to other people, while back here, his mother slowly faded beneath the onslaught of her insanity. His father had seen the madness lurking in her mind, and found a way out, leaving Santiago behind. He could see that, now, and he could never accept anything again from his father. Not this plane ticket, not anything. The next time he went to the island it would be because he himself had made it possible. And he *would* make it possible.

Mrs. Schultz had told him about scholarships, how he could apply to places that would give him money to go to them. He would apply to college, something no one else in his family cared about, and go wherever they paid for him to go and get a job and make something of himself. He would make enough that he could help his mother, keep her comfortable, keep her safe. He would make enough that he could buy his own plane tickets.

He tore up the ticket, and told his father his mother needed him here. The truth was, he didn't know if it was better for him not to visit his mother at all, but he did, every other week, regular as clockwork.

The worst visits were when she did not recognize him at all. After those, he wondered if she was gone, completely gone from him. She came back, time and again, her face lighting up the next time she saw him, *cariño* on her lips. But what if she did not, someday? What if she went away and never came back, her body there, her mind gone? Then they both would have left him, both parents, each of them abandoning him, leaving him completely alone.

Although he could never tell anyone this, the two years Santiago spent living alone while his mother lived in Bellevue Hospital, lost to herself, from August 1966 to August 1968, were the two happiest years he experienced in his early life.

Happiness would be a fickle visitor in the house of his mind, unfortunately, as the years wore on and he reached adulthood. It would approach as fast as a summer storm, and be gone just as quickly, a torrent of happiness that rapidly dissipated, leaving him drained and empty. He would never understand its comings and goings, never learn to read the signs that rain was on its way. But then, before all that, a skinny sixteen-year-old found happiness, much to his guilt, living alone in New York.

For as long as he could remember, his world had been filled with noise. New York *was* noise. When he and his mother had lived with his family, the noise had been constant, all-pervading. He had never been alone in the apartment, rarely alone in a single room for more than five minutes. He had not minded always; when it was him and his mother he was happy, for despite all the demons that plagued her mind, all the people crowding in her trying to emerge, he knew that she loved him. The violence of Esperanza Marin Vega's life was confined to her mind, to herself, to scratching her own skin so hard it tore, to pulling out her own hair, chewing the flaking skin around her own fingernails until it bled.

The other people he knew were saner, but less kind. The hum of conversation, punctuated with yelling, screaming, shrieking, chattering, crying, haunted his life. Even when he and his mother finally moved into their own place, they were sandwiched between scores of other people, yelling, hitting, laughing, singing, crying, imploring, needing, living, around them. In their trim apartment at First Avenue and Second Street, for which they payed $35 a month, with its yellowed walls and rusted pipes and death-trap stairs between units, he choked on sound. At least, until his mother was gone.

Then, the apartment, which had always felt permeable to every-thing, made of paper walls, like the screens he had seen in a picture in his history book of a Japanese palace, was suddenly immune to sound. In the hallway it was the same rattle of tongues: Spanish and Greek and Ukrainian and Yiddish rang out with abandon. But in the apartment, it was silent, like a spell had been cast. The silence made it easier, easier to think, easier to read, to work hard, to count his limited money, to move through every day.

Yes, he was a sixteen-year-old Puerto Rican boy with limited re-sources living two doors down from a pool hall where he had once watched a heavyset Ukrainian man take out a gun and shoot his pool opponent in the face for allegedly "weighing" the balls, while the rest of the bar sipped their drinks, apathetic and unsurprised, but at least he was *sane*. Junior still saw that man in the hall sometimes, and while he had learned to be excellent at pool early, both as a geomet-rical exercise and a way to make extra money, he never challenged the Ukrainian. This was further proof of his sanity, and comforted Junior on cold and lonely nights through the winter of 1966 and into the winter of 1967, nights in which he lay awake, swaddled in every sweater he owned, layered under all of the blankets in the apartment and the coat his father had sent him the money for the previous Christmas, a navy wool jacket from the army-navy store.

Still, it made him feel guilty, how neat and comfortable his des-perately poor little life was. The guilt prodded him to ask the doctors the same question on the visiting days, twice a month on Wednes-days, *when will she be ready to come home,* and pricked him again when he felt relief at their lack of answers.

The visits themselves were painful at best. Sometimes she was herself, yes, the sweet woman who had protected and loved him his whole life, the only real kindness he had ever known, the only thing he could trust. Sometimes she was a stranger to him. Sometimes she cried that demons were torturing her, flaying the skin off her flesh, couldn't he see them? Sometimes she insisted that everyone, including him, was a ghost, that they had come for her but they could not have her yet, she was not ready. Sometimes she had messages to deliver to the world, vital, important information, and why was no one letting her do so? Furious and anxious, she would scream at Santiago, blaming him, sure they would listen to him if he insisted that they let her go. Santiago tried to explain that he had not put her here, in fact, she had checked herself into Bellevue after her neighbor had called the fire department, smelling smoke when Esperanza carefully burned all of his father's clothing, things Santiago Sr. had left for when his son was old enough to wear them, on their fire escape. The scent of a lambskin coat burning had scented the entire apartment building for weeks, like something roasting and dying at once.

Once his mother was gone, his life fell into patterns. School, afternoons spent bagging groceries, weekends at the nearby Jewish Boys Club, which he had been going to for the last six years, despite being Catholic, where he practiced boxing and competed in mathematical contests. He would have liked to avoid the rest of his family completely, but while they largely left him alone, allowing him, a child, to live untethered, freed by their apathy, he saw them every Sunday, for dinner at his grandmother's apartment, at which he wondered, every time, if she were trying to poison them all with terrible food. He also saw his grandmother when Esperanza's welfare check came in, usually at the beginning of every month. Although he hated her, his grandmother was the one who helped Junior cash his mother's checks, which, along with his pool hall winnings and the pittance he made at Gristedes and the little that Teofila herself, begrudgingly, contributed, grumbling that she still didn't see why Santiago couldn't come live with *her*, was enough for him to scrape by. But they both knew neither wanted that, that his grandmother was relieved that he didn't live with her and her motley crew of children, that she would have been horrified and horrible to him if he had tried to move in.

Generally speaking, the family avoided the subject of his mother and her absence completely, acting as though she were busy, or merely out of town. His uncles and aunts never brought up the subject; well, they were children themselves, for the most part, and too wrapped up in their own needs and tragedies to care much about his mother. They were a violent lot, who begrudgingly acknowledged him as one of their own, but still found him, his academic interests, his quiet, his round owlish glasses, his disinterest in violence, to be alien, troubling, unmanly, strange.

Such was the population density of the city that his aunts and uncles were in a different school zone than he was, although they lived only blocks apart. They had no interest in school, not like he did. Learning things made sense to him. Especially numbers; they curled into his brain like the birds dressed Cinderella in the morning, in the movie, naturally, comfortably, with no hesitation. Around his family, Santiago hunched low, to make himself shorter, smaller, look weaker, so they would not see him, not notice him, but not, as they thought, because he thought he was better than them. He held himself apart because they stole things from him, they hit him in the shoulder, hard, they broke his glasses. The rest he could live with, but with Esperanza's medical bills, and the cost of heat in the winter, he couldn't afford another pair.

They didn't all live with his grandmother. His oldest uncle, Rodrigo, who was only thirty, and a truck driver, had been married for a few years to Marisol, a sweet woman, or so they had thought. However, one day, off a tip from a friend who had seen Marisol out and about with a dark-skinned man the friend knew from his days running with the Mau Maus out in Brooklyn, Rodrigo ended his shift early and surprised his wife and her lover in a diner in Midtown. She barely had time to get the requisite *ay, baby, it's not what you think* out of her mouth before he shot her, twice, in the chest and throat. Known to all as a kind and gentle man, Rodrigo then hit her lover in the face with the butt end of the smoking gun, fracturing his jaw, and then quietly waited for the police to come, Marisol's dead body bleeding all over the floor of the diner. This had been the past spring, and he was currently serving his two years for manslaughter out in Rikers.

Santiago's uncle Samuel, who everyone called Rowdy, was just two years older than him, and had been caught trying to burgle a warehouse in Williamsburg that summer. Given the choice between prison and the army, he had chosen active duty, and in October he had been shipped off to Vietnam. They got letters from him every other month, and an occasional crackled phone call. Teofila was quite proud of him. He'd become a sniper, and already had three kills to his name.

Why is it, Santiago wondered as he walked to Teofila's house one Sunday night, the first winter after his mother had been institutionalized, his breath white clouds in the heartaching cold, *that one of my uncles is in jail for his excellent aim with a gun, while the other is rising through the ranks?* But then, Santiago himself was no stranger to the curving line of moral relativism.

"You're late," Teofila said, opening the door and looking him up and down with, as always, clear disappointment at his existence, before turning back and walking toward the kitchen, leaving him in the doorway, her duty to greet him done. She spoke in Spanish, as always, for she spoke almost no English.

"I was doing homework," he called out, closing the door behind him. A lie; he had simply not wanted to come, he had been reading something his English teacher recommended, *The Count of Monte*

Cristo. He loved the way that the Count remade himself from the ground up. It confirmed what Santiago already knew, that reinvention was a matter of will, and strategy.

"Always your nose in a book. Useless waste of time," Teofila called from the kitchen, her derision clear. *How would you know?* Santiago wanted to ask. His grandmother could not read. Instead, he hung up his coat, neatly tucking his scarf into the sleeve of his jacket so that it wouldn't fall or get lost. He had very few possessions, and had learned how to take care of them. As he turned, a punch to his stomach knocked the breath out of his body, his hands flying to his nose to protect his glasses. His body healed for free, but glasses cost money.

"*Maricón!* How are ya, Junior?" His uncle Roberto, who was six years older than him, asked, his mouth curved in an evil smirk. Of all his uncles, Junior couldn't understand how kind Rodrigo and cheerful Rowdy had ended up, respectively, imprisoned and in the army, while Roberto, who was a sick, smug bastard, roamed free. But he was smart, his uncle, not as smart as Santiago, but smarter than many, and Teofila's pride and joy. He worked by day as an elevator repairman, taken on by a friend of Isadoro, his father.

Santiago straightened his glasses, got his breath back, and sighed.

"I'm fine, Tío." Santiago called all his aunts and uncles by their familial title, no matter their age. Roberto hit his arm, hard, laughing again.

"I bet you are, pansy."

Santiago sighed again. Hitting him back, which was what he wanted, what Roberto would have respected, would only end in more pain. His only real option was to remain a punching bag for his uncle until he got bored and gave up. He had a cat's attention span, so it shouldn't be too long, Santiago hoped.

Small hands crept around his waist, squeezing at his bruised stomach, but he closed his eyes against the pain, not wanting to yell at the hugger, Irena, his eleven-year-old aunt. He liked her well enough, and Roberto wouldn't hit his sister, she could be a shield.

"*Sobrino* Junior!" She cackled, amused as ever that her nephew doubled as her babysitter. She called him Junior, like they all did, even though Teofila loathed his father, his namesake. "I have something to show you." She took him by the hand, past Roberto, who had slumped down in the living room, his eyes glued to the television, a beer in his hand, and down the hallway of the three-bedroom apartment.

Isadoro, who worked every day but Sundays, usually spent the day napping, so Santiago would greet him at dinnertime when he emerged from the room he shared with Teofila, a sleepy bear of a man as gentle as a butterfly. Irena shared a room with her half sister, Carmen, who was nineteen and wild, out with every bad character in the building, and the larger neighborhood, any chance she got. Recently she had been seeing a member of the Ghetto Brothers, a South Bronx gang that also played music. Teofila was sure she was going to come home pregnant, but Santiago privately thought one day she just wouldn't come home at all. Little Hermando now had a room all to himself. Roberto had his own place in the same building, something Teofila had been able to finagle through sheer intimidation, but he came over most days for meals, an act of madness, according to Santiago. Anyone who could avoid Teofila's food should do so, no matter how hungry they were.

"Come on," Irena said, leading Santiago to the dining table. Dinner that evening was a mofongo, dry as chalk and twice as tasteless, filled with stewed chicken, which was both tasteless and oversalted. Roberto, the madman, had three helpings, while Junior, hungry despite it all, cleaned his plate and asked for another chicken leg, earning him a glare from Teofila, and a smile from Isadoro, a man who loved to feed people. Their pairing was so strange that Junior wondered if Teofila had herself resorted to magic years ago, hanging love charms around her bed to render her gorgon-self a beautiful princess instead. Carmen had come home halfway through the meal, and sat, scowling at everyone, the hickeys on her neck standing out like neon signs. She and Teofila were locked in a battle of wills, silent but deadly, with each one refusing to acknowledge the other's existence.

"I think it's going to help a lot," Irena said, out of nowhere, over watery flan soaked in syrup that had burned, and was now bitter.

"What is, *mija?*" Teofila asked, her tone sugary and kind. She was making it clear that she loved Irena, to spite Carmen, but Irena, focused on her goal, did not bask in her mother's sporadic attention.

"My altar," Irena said, like they'd been talking about it the whole time. "I'm using herbs and offerings to cleanse Esperanza's *ache*. It's going to help with her illness. She's been in the hospital for a long long time, so this should help."

Irena's declaration that she was practicing black magic was met with complete unsurprised silence. Carmen's defiant pout had become a look of pity, aimed at Santiago, while Roberto's smirk had widened.

Santiago wondered when Teofila would explode. She hated magic, called it the devil's work, spat at Santeria shops and crossed the street when she passed them. Her mother had believed in the old ways, but for Teofila there was no way but Christ, and she would beat the opinion out of anyone who believed otherwise.

Everyone looked at her, waiting for the eruption. But she just looked tired, and closed her eyes, rubbing her forehead. She looked defeated. Santiago had no sympathy for her, would never remember her as anything but a horrible woman, but in that moment he looked at her face and saw his own future, the way his mother would weigh him down, the way he, like Teofila, would carry the weight of her forever.

"Can you pray for Carmen? She's like the village donkey, some ride is bound to break her," Roberto said, breaking the moment with his crude cruelty.

It was his mouth that would get him killed. By 1975 he was in prison serving a five-year sentence on a charge of manslaughter for blowing a man's face off with a shotgun. The man, a member of a rival gang, made a comment during a drug deal that Roberto was awful fat for such a little guy, and Roberto found out where he lived, followed him, knocked on his window as he was parking, and shot him, point-blank, splattering his brains all over his car, in full view of the man's wife and young child. He served three of the five years of his sentence before starting a prison riot by calling a large Dominican man who had strangled his own father to death *pussy* for liking beans more than meat. That man responded by strangling Roberto, too, stopping that mouth forever, doubling his own sentence from life to life plus life, infinity.

Teofila smacked her son on the back of his head.

"Fuck you, Robbie," Carmen said, without heat. She didn't like Roberto, few did, but she rarely let him anger her.

"I'd have to get in line," Roberto said, eager to get a response. Carmen just rolled her eyes, stood, and smashed the plate holding the rest of the flan on the ground, and then stalked off to her room, leaving it for them to clean up. Teofila sat, stone-faced, as the rest of the family cleared the table.

As dinners with his family went, Santiago reflected, this one ranked among the more positive he had experienced.

On his way out the door, Isadoro hugged him, warmly. Santiago felt tears gathering in his eyes. His own father hugged him when he came to Puerto Rico, but it was tentative, almost squeamish, as if he didn't know how. It was nothing like the way he hugged his new children, his new family. His mother, in her last visit, could not bear to be touched, she told him that her skin was paper, and he would crumple her. When was the last time he had had physical contact with anyone?

Isadoro stepped back and reached into his pocket, pulling out a wad of bills. Junior blushed, but took it, smiling gratefully.

"Bless you, son," Isadoro said, and Santiago wished he believed in God, like Isadoro did, even like Teofila did. He wished he believed in magic and Santeria, like Irena did, or in his dick, the way Roberto did, or in love, like Carmen did, or in cartoons, like Hermando did. But all he believed in was himself, his own ability to keep going, to face the cold of the night and the cold of the world, and walk on.

Sixteen

The road from Ponce, nestled into the coast, to San Sebastián, a little town in the interior of the northwest of the island, takes Elena from the dry forest, still rich with trees and dotted with cacti, to the wetter, slightly cooler mountains, jutting up in lush vine-curled little green bumps. Elena has read that this is what earned the municipality its nickname, El Pepino, that the settlers believed the hills and mountains looked like cucumbers. To her, they just look like mountains, and she wonders at the whimsy of these Spanish colonialists.

She had thought that this area would look different, that somehow it would be like going back in time, the way her aunt had talked about it. But really, it looks just like the rest of the island, peppered with branded fast-food outposts and car dealerships and strips of shops.

The island is far from overpopulated. She never remembers seeing it crowded, and she knows, from the news, that people are fleeing now, packing up their things and moving to Florida. Soon these places will have even fewer people, which doesn't seem possible, she sees no one. It is such a stark difference from New York that she cannot believe it, sometimes, how few people there are, how empty the roads seem, unless she hits traffic, how isolated the houses. She passes fields of cows and the occasional single horse, grazing placidly under the gaze of the sun. She passes chickens, molting chicks following hens in bobbing lines, showy roosters puffing their neck feathers. She passes seas of greenery and flowers, and cement houses and beauty salons and roadside restaurants and signs telling her to sign up with Claro for internet services and reminding her that Coca-Cola is *pa'todo,* the adds mimicking the Puerto Rican habit of cutting the *r* and the *a* off *para.*

If she broke down out here, what would she do? Who would help her? There is no one to call out to, no one would pass by. She might be left here, alone, lost. The thought is frightening, but not overwhelmingly so. If she got lost, disappeared from her life, she could lay down her burdens. She could consign the task of finding her father to someone, anyone, else. She could escape the world, live wild, let go of houses and jobs and wanting things she cannot have. She could stop asking for information that will never be hers, stop excavating the past, desperate for answers that may not even exist.

She pulls over to the side of the road, both sad and elated at her total isolation. She puts her hand in her pocket, to find her phone, but her hand brushes something else, her father's rosary. *Why did he keep this?* she asks herself before she can help it, and knows the wild is not for her. She could not stop asking questions if she tried. And besides, she would be found by someone eventually, taken to a nearby Church's Chicken and fed until she recuperated. It's a small island, a hard place for anyone to truly hide. *Anyone but my father,* she thinks.

She looks at her phone. There are texts from her mother, and Diego, but she doesn't want to talk to either of them. She thinks about her friends in New York, but the idea of contextualizing all of this for them, telling them all the things she hasn't told them so they will understand where she is and why, sounds exhausting. As far as any of them know, she's in Puerto Rico visiting family. She thinks of calling Daniel, but then she remembers sitting in his childhood home last Rosh Hashanah, and how calm and normal his parents were, how moderate and gloriously boring and sane. Daniel, who could never understand why her father hadn't just gone into rehab. Daniel, who had asked if an intervention would work, and never understood that a person had to care about other people, what they thought of him, for their intervening to be efficient. Daniel, who had started monitoring her wine consumption the day she told him her father was an alcoholic. No. She doesn't want to talk to any of them right now.

Instead, she pulls up a contact, and dials. He picks up after two rings.

"Where are you now?" Fernando asks her, no hello, no nice to hear from you. His directness is comforting. She doesn't have to explain her emotions to him, just her location.

"Near San Sebastián. You ever been here?"

"No," he says. She hums. "You think he's there."

"If he's not, I don't know where else to go."

"I shouldn't have left you all alone there," he says, a pinch of regret in his voice.

"We hardly know each other. You don't owe me anything," Elena says, and for some reason she can feel tears in the backs of her eyes.

"I shouldn't have told you like that. I'm sorry. I should have . . . I shouldn't have said anything at all," Fernando says.

"I know why you would want the house. It's, it's the same reason I do," Elena says, a peace offering.

"I think I just want a piece of this place. The storm, it makes me feel like the island is going to blow away. Everyone I know is jumping ship. I want to stay. I want to be rooted here. Help it grow." *He's such a botanist,* Elena thinks.

"Tell me about the ceiba tree," she demands.

There is a pause, Fernando clears his throat.

"It has thick roots that rise like walls. When I was a kid, I pretended this one in a park was my fort."

"Fort-tree. Like *fortress*."

"Fort Fernando. I wasn't very creative. I'm still not. Later, I learned it was sacred to the Mayan people. They believed it bridged the gap between the underworld, the human world, and the heavens."

"A botanical ladder."

"I suppose so. I like the idea of something natural that connects realms, something from the earth, something born, not made."

"It's a nice idea," Elena agrees.

There is silence on the line, but it is not uncomfortable. She hears him clear his throat. "If you find him, Elena, can you tell him something for me? Tell him thank you."

"I'll do my best," she says, and ends the call. Well. At least someone knows where she is now. She puts the car in drive again.

Soon, too soon, she is crossing the lines between Lares and San Sebastián, a sign welcoming her to the new area that looks just like the area she has left. She comes upon the town itself quickly. It is colorful, as all Puerto Rican towns are, and dingy, which some are, fraying at the edges, and she can see things that might be the storm or might be neglect and lack of money: an overturned postbox, a broken shop window, some abandoned buildings, a for sale sign, then a dozen more.

She parks the car near what her phone tells her is the main town square. Puerto Rican towns mimic European ones, with central market squares flanked by a large church in many of them. This church is a dull tan trimmed with white, *Parroquia San Sebastián Mártir* inscribed above the entrance of the building, echoing the words on her father's rosary. The square houses a fountain, which isn't running, and it is surrounded by bright buildings, a green mansion, a gray and pink building that looks like a movie theater from the

1920s, now vacant and for sale, a blue building that says *Alcaldía,*
the mayor's office, and a pink and burnt-sienna building that proudly
proclaims it is the Archivo Histórico, the history archives. She takes
photos of it all.

Nothing is open, she notes, walking around the perimeter of the
square. Instead, handwritten signs explain that these buildings are
closed because of the hurricane. The plaza is completely empty. It
feels like she has arrived in a ghost town, something from the Old
West. At any moment, she expects that someone will come around
a corner in chaps and spurs, guns pointed, looking for horse thieves.

This is where her family is from. She tells herself that, over and
over again, hoping that it will spark some response. Instead, she
feels nothing. She is numb. Her body is sweating, the sun high and
the day already warm, and she can feel her face burning, the skin on
her nose crisping.

What is it, exactly, that she hoped to find here? she wonders as she
walks on, making a left, then a right, walking randomly around a
town that is just a town like any other, a collection of houses and
stores and cars and *things.* What was supposed to happen when she
arrived? A group of sprightly villagers welcoming her with open arms
and leading her to her ancestral home? A banquet of spirits waiting
to cheer for her, to give her a seat at the table? Her father at the head
of it, alive and well and whole, holding the deed to the house in his
hands, all ready for her? She passes empty barbershops and empty
lots. She sees a shop with a shopkeeper dozing in his chair, and on the
other side of the street, a man chatting with a woman at a little café,
chewing on a flaky pastry. A car drives by her, and then a motorcycle.
Some signs of life. But no parade to greet her, their lost child. She is
an idiot. She keeps walking, cursing herself, cursing her stupidity, to
think that this is another kind of story, the kind where what is lost is
found, instead of what it is, a story about wasting time, a story about
wasting hope. She passes by a long white wall that abruptly becomes

something else, a plaque, an iron gate, and inside the locked doors, a cemetery.

She stops. *A cemetery.* Spirits, ghosts, her family are here. Maybe not the way she wants them to be, appearing at her side like magic birds to guide her to her destination, but they are *here,* in the cemetery. She leans into the plaque, hoping to see opening hours, but instead she sees that this is a historic cemetery, that no one has been buried here for over a hundred years. Where, then, do the more recent bodies rest?

Within ten minutes she is back in the car, on the road, driving toward the only other cemetery in the area, according to her phone. She hates the hope rising in her breast, the sense that there will be something, someone, waiting for her there, and tries to focus on the road.

How does any of this help you find your father? her brain shouts at her, and she opens the windows of the car to drown out the sound of her own mind.

The other cemetery is not far away, and it has parking. More important, it is not closed, and Elena is grateful for this, thanking her own god, and even offering a nod to Jesus, though of course she does not believe in him as a deity, but he's big on the island, so she figures it's polite. Inside its gates the cemetery is vast, and sparked with color, bright plants and fake flowers, and she realizes it is massive. How will she find anything in here?

She enters the small cemetery office, and sees a woman, middle-aged and bleach blond, curvy and comfortable-looking, squinting at a computer. Elena smiles at her, nervously.

"Hello," the woman says in Spanish, smiling up at her. Elena returns the greeting, and wonders how to begin asking for what she needs.

"Are you looking for someone?" the woman asks, and Elena blinks, suddenly close to both laughter and tears.

"I think I have a family member here. Maybe more than one," Elena says, speaking slowly, trying to enunciate her Spanish, both so she doesn't make any mistakes and to indicate to the woman in front of her that she needs the same treatment in return. The Spanish she hears in Puerto Rico is often fast, letters slurred together, softly pronounced. A Spanish teacher would call it sloppy, and it certainly neglects formalities. Elena has never heard anyone on the island use the formal *usted* to say "you." Elena likes the way islanders speak, much as it presents a puzzle to her, but now she needs to be understood, to understand, and she returns to classroom Spanish, stilted and formal but clear.

"We have a map. Maybe I can help you. What is the family name?"

Elena thinks. This is a reasonable question, but she does not know how to answer it.

"My father's family are Vegas," she offers. She has no idea about her grandmother's maiden name, does she? Inspiration strikes. It's early, the bar isn't open yet, he might not be busy. She opens up Instagram on her phone, and finds Hermando's profile page. His last name is Marin, she notes, and she quickly messages him, *Do you know what your mother's maiden name was?* He might not respond, but it is worth trying.

The woman smirks.

"Vega is fairly common." Elena nods, she isn't surprised by this. "We have a whole section, I can show you." Elena nods again.

Her phone buzzes, a message from Hermando. Elena thanks whatever god might be listening for the advent of social media, which can get her information she needs so quickly. Would that each part of her father's life revealed itself to her this easily. *I think Caneja? Her first husband was a Marin, some names in the middle, and then we are Ortiz's.*

Thanks, she writes back, and gets a smiling face in return.

"Caneja," Elena says. The woman looks at her, surprised, her well-drawn eyebrows arching up.

"Caneja. Okay. That's a little rarer. Do you know, is it a family plot?" Elena doesn't understand the vocabulary at first, but the woman is kind, and explains, using a little English. Elena shrugs.

"I'm sorry. I wish I knew more," Elena says, the words the exhausting litany of her life. The woman shrugs, and stands up.

"Let me show you the way."

They walk through the cemetery, and the clouds have gathered, now. It looks like rain, which comes and goes so fast on the island it's rarely worth worrying about. But the darkened sky, with patches of fierce blue here and there, and still-brilliant sunlight, makes the landscape otherworldly. The woman, whose name is Naomi, Elena finally gets around to asking, deftly leads her through rows and rows of graves, festooned with teddy bears and incense holders and mounds of fabric flowers and candles and sometimes nothing at all. Some are new, others older but well cared for, some completely broken apart, tipping and cracked. Birds, pigeons, rock doves, and the little black birds with long tails fly grave to grave, while their footfall disturbs tiny lizards, who scatter as she and Naomi pass by.

Elena loves cemeteries. She finds it odd that some people she knows think of them as scary or creepy. She finds them charming and strange, the way people work impossibly hard to celebrate the dead, to give them a final resting place made of marble, to glorify them with a memorial they will never see. The performance of it, the pretense, it's endearing, the way people pretend it is for the dead person, and not the living. Like an infant's birthday party, an event for a guest who neither knows or cares about it.

This one may not be as fancy as some of the famous ones she has seen in her travels, like the one she saw in Buenos Aires filled with Argentine celebrities, or as well planned as the Greenwood cemetery, in Brooklyn, whose rolling hills and colonial graves make it a tourist attraction, but she likes it, nonetheless. It reminds her of the one she played in as a child, the one connected to St. Peter's School, the elementary school she attended. When her father was late to pick her up, which was every day, she would play hide-and-seek in the cemetery, sometimes without anyone there to seek her, just hiding, hoping someone would come. He never found her there, never even looked, to her knowledge, and eventually she would emerge to find him talking with a teacher, or reading a newspaper, or not yet there at all. Yet she never stopped hiding, never stopping wondering if this day he would finally come and see her, crouched behind the grave of a Revolutionary War hero or a well-loved housewife. And here she is again, decades later, in another graveyard, waiting for him to find her all over again.

Now, she wonders if he let her play. If he knew how much she loved it, and let her be, in her happiest of places. She wonders how much time she has spent thinking the worst of him because of what he has become, rather than seeing the change in him over time. He is her father, and he has failed at that, but didn't he also succeed, sometimes? Weighed down by the deaths of people she will never meet, the many stories of his life, his past, that she will never know, and yet he did come, every day, to pick her up, and let her play in the gravestones. That isn't nothing, is it? There is so much about him she will never understand, but what she has, what good and true there is, she can't let be clouded by the pain she feels now, can she?

She thinks of what Diego said about him, that he hated himself most of all. She wonders how much of her father's life in the last decade and a half, or even longer, has been an act of escape, from everything he doesn't want to be, the things she doesn't know he is, and the things she does. She has always thought he left her, abandoned her because he preferred oblivion. Perhaps he does. But maybe it wasn't really her he is escaping, but himself, and the parts of her that remind him of himself. Elena wonders what her father sees when he looks at her. Does he see her, some version of her, or does he see pieces of him and Rosalind, and his family, and his mother, and Rosalind's family, like a mosaic? Maybe he sees in her all the history he has denied her having. Maybe she can never be a whole separate person for her father, but a sum of parts, a refracted vision of his life and past and pain.

Naomi stops, pointing at a grave that is decently cared for, with a few flowers, faded but not decayed, resting at the base of the tombstone. It reads *Teofila Caneja, 1914–1978.* There are some other Caneja graves nearby, but this is the one that Elena's eyes are glued to, for this, she knows, is the grave of her great-grandmother.

"Oh, that's lucky. Do you think they are related?" She barely hears Naomi's question, and looks up, confused. The woman is pointing to the grave next to Teofila's, and when Elena's eyes focus on it, she reads *Esperanza Caneja Marin Vega, 1930–1986.* Her grandmother's grave. And there are flowers on this one, too, the same ones that sit fading on Teofila's grave. Elena recognizes them as *azucenas,* sweet-smelling white flowers that grow in the mountains. A man walks around San Juan during the week in the mornings selling them, his loud call of *ahhhhhhh-zu-CEN-ah* audible through thick walls and closed doors.

"Yes. I do," Elena says, faintly. Naomi looks at her for a moment without speaking, and takes out her phone.

"I think there is someone you should meet," Naomi says, explaining. Elena nods, looking at the graves, barely registering Naomi's words. This is her family, lying here. She sees more Canejas around Teofila and Esperanza, the dates on the stones reaching back into the past. She does not need to look for Vegas, she decides. Her grandfather was buried in the military cemetery. But her grandmother and great-grandmother and other people whose blood has eked its way into her own veins lie before her, a family tree with bone branches. There is a Marciano Canejas who died in Vietnam, and an Ana Lopez Canejas who lived just seven years, dying in 1904, and an Aida Canejas who is mourned by her husband, Ivan, and a Jillian Gonzalez Canejas whose grave is covered with wreaths of electric-blue fake flowers, grimy with age. There are people here she will never know, stories she will never hear, a whole legacy of nothing for her to mourn. She carefully takes photos of each grave, each potential relative who is also a total stranger. She barely hears Naomi speaking on the phone next to her, and startles when she feels a hand on her shoulder.

"Are you all right?" Elena realizes that she is crying. But why? Who are these people to her? Of course, it is not them she is crying for, and she knows that. She does not mourn the dead people she will never know, never have anything of. She mourns the living. Where is her father? Where are the things he promised her, the house he said was hers, the love he owes her? He is as lost to her as all these dead bodies, rotting in the rich soil of this fertile place. *But not all of him, there are pieces that will always be yours no matter how much you are missing, aren't there?* She does not know which part of her to listen to, the pained bleeding half or the adult thinking about another adult who is her father, yes, but also so much more.

"Yes, sorry. It's been a long day," Elena answers in English, unconsciously, her defenses down. Naomi nods in sympathy.

"You want some water?" she asks, also in English, and Elena is struck by the change. In Spanish Naomi's voice is fluid, sweet. In English it is marked by the way Puerto Ricans speak English, elongated vowels and twang around consonants. "I call my friend, I think you maybe should meet her. You can wait?"

Elena nods, and allows herself to be led back to the little office, a freezing box of air-conditioning. She sits, sipping water, as Naomi works away. She wonders what Naomi does all day in this job, how many people die around here, how many graves must be allotted and coordinated day by day. She wonders why Naomi chose this job, to deal in the logistics of death, if this is what she wanted to do when she grew up. It seems a strange and soothing task, in a way, not unlike Elena's own work, former work, finding homes for people, it's just that Naomi's tenants are all dead, and probably complain less about maintenance.

The door to the office opens and a tiny woman, deeply tan and impossibly wrinkled, her face a mass of lines, her eyes two shiny black beads, stands in the doorway. She looks like a little doll. She is round and small and covered in a sack-like dress in a floral print and she looks at Elena, her eyes piercing her, her mouth opening into a little *oh*, sending her wrinkles scurrying around her face.

"Junior's daughter!" she says in Spanish, and grabs Elena, tightly, holding her in her arms, cradling Elena's larger form in her own as if Elena were a small child. Elena does not fight her, couldn't if she tried. The smell of Florida Water and muscle rub envelops her in a calm, as strange as the rain now falling outside, although the sun is still bright, as this little ancient woman she has never met before strokes her hair and tells her, over and over again, that she is home.

"She knew the second she saw you that you were your father's daughter," Naomi says, and Elena tries to keep a smile on her face while her heart drops out of her body. It should not hurt a child to feel that they are like their parent. It should not hurt her that this is the comparison; she does look like her father, and it's not as though anyone is telling her she inherited any of his other, less desirable traits. She got his dimple, and his curly hair, and his eyes. But still, she trembles at the idea of similarity to Santiago Vega Jr., even as she hopes that this woman, Tía Goli, as she has introduced herself, might be able to help her find him.

They are in Tía Goli's little house, a few miles away from the cemetery. It is made of cement, as they all are, and painted a cheerful bright green with yellow trim. Chickens pick at worms and bugs on the tiny front lawn, and Elena sits on a wooden chair in Goli's little living room, looking at a wall covered in images of the Virgin Mary and other virgins of the New World. Most of them look vaguely like Jennifer Lopez, and they are surrounded by babies that range from pale to darkly tanned. On another wall there is a wedding photo, beautiful and well aged, showing a woman who Elena can only assume is Goli herself, brimming with joy, looking up at a slim man only a few inches taller than her who looks straight into the camera, unsmiling. Goli's dress spreads across the ground in all directions, and they look like they are floating in the sea of her ruffles.

"He was short, same height as her, but he wanted to be taller for the photo, so he's standing on a little stool there, and her skirt is covering it," Naomi explains, observing how Elena is looking at the photo. Naomi's mouth quirks and Goli bustles in from the kitchen with a tray of drinks.

It turns out that Naomi knows the woman well, as Goli has come twice a month to lay flowers on the graves of the Canejas and the Vegas in the cemetery for the last forty-five years or more. Of course, she is under no obligation to lay flowers on the graves of the Canejas, Tía Goli says, with Naomi helping translate the words Elena doesn't know, the country slang the older woman merrily speaks. Goli is herself a Vega, or she was before marriage; she is Elena's grandfather's older sister. But this is a small town, and once these two families were united in marriage Goli decided it was only right. And then of course when one after another of the bodies of the Canejas who made new lives in New York found their way back to the island, it seemed like there was no one else still in San Sebastián to clean their graves and give their spirits flowers, so Goli made both families her responsibility. When Naomi realized that Elena, too, was connected to these graves, she decided that Goli might want to meet the girl who claimed to be a Caneja, just in case she was a Vega, too.

Goli offers Elena something in a glass, and Elena looks down at it, unsure. It is clear, but there is a very small amount of it in the glass, far less than anyone would give someone if it were water. Elena takes a tentative sip and coughs, immediately, as the liquid burns her throat horribly. She looks up and finds Goli smiling at her cheerfully.

"What is this?" she asks in Spanish, her voice hoarse. Naomi's smile turns wry, and she sniffs at it.

"*Pitorro.* You'd say 'moonshine,' I think. It's a liquor made from cane. She makes her own. Deadly stuff." Naomi drinks hers down in one gulp.

"You like it?" Goli asks, her hand reaching for a bottle with no label on it. Elena puts her hand over her glass, smiling in a way that she hopes is polite.

"It's very strong," she says.

"Your father, he loves this," Goli says, cheerfully. "I always bring it out when he comes." Elena's blood runs cold, and she finds herself sipping the stuff again, for courage. It still burns her, but she swallows it down.

"Have you seen my father? Recently?" Elena asks, trying not to seem desperate, trying not to get out of her seat and shake the little woman in the hopes the information will tumble out of her.

"He came by. He comes sometimes. He came by a few days ago, he brings me some things. He's a good boy," Goli says, nodding and smiling. Elena's mouth opens to ask more—he's been here recently, *where did he go, is he still here*—but she feels a pinch on her thigh. Naomi's face turns a little sad, and as Goli bustles back into the kitchen with the bottle of *pitorro,* she turns to Elena.

"Her memory is not so good now. She thinks that people come visit her, people who have died. She don't always remember what happen when."

"Oh. Because I'm actually here looking for my father," Elena says. Naomi nods.

"Okay. You should ask her, then. But just, it's not all true, what she says. She think it's true, maybe it was true, but it might not all be in the right order. I don't want you to get upset. I don't want you upset her."

"I understand," Elena says, but inside her stomach is rioting, from the stress and the drink and the futility of all this. The way hope is offered to her and then taken away. She tries to focus on the person in front of her, Goli, this new person she knew nothing about, another piece of her family, of her past. She can mourn her father, who is absent, or see the person who is here. Her task was to find him, but her task is also impossible, a quest meant for a better heroine than her. And besides, when one encounters an old woman in the woods, one must sit and listen to their tale, give them all one has, thank them for their generosity, everyone knows that. Elena cannot let this piece of history go just because it is not the thing she is looking for, just because it might offer her no answers in her task. It might offer her a host of other things instead. She has a translator, and a family member; she would be a fool to give those up.

Goli sits down on the couch, the first time she's sat since they entered the house. Her little legs stick straight out, and she smiles again, a smile so sweet and unlike Elena's grandfather's perpetual grimace that Elena wonders how they can truly be related. But they are. And so is she.

"Tell me about my father," Elena says. And Goli does not even blink at this request, at a child wanting to learn of their parent. Instead she just leans forward over her little legs, and begins to talk.

Seventeen

At night, when the air was swollen and the tiny tan frogs that sang their famous refrain were beginning their repertoire, *coqui, coQUI,* as the jungle sighed and the mountains stretched into themselves and the chickens fluttered their feathers in sleepy twitches, as the scent of sugar and earth and pig shit wafted together into a heady perfume, Junior's *Tía* Goli would raise her arm, and with a steady hand, slash into his boils with a red-hot razor blade.

At sixteen he was slim as a snake, taller than his father, but then, most men were. In the army, his father had been called a midget by his fellow soldiers. Junior's second family—his island family, people he saw once a year, children a decade younger than him who smiled shyly, his stepmother, Chavela, who was kind and soft—were all small. It was his mother's side that had been tall, still were tall, pushing out of their genetic predisposition to stay close to the ground like bolting lettuce.

Back in New York he lived with his mother, Esperanza, and her wandering mind. She would be there, in the apartment with him, and then she would be gone. She would not be back for days. Sometimes her body, too, would disappear, and he would look for her, after school and at night when he should have been doing his homework, sleeping, dreaming of movie stars touching his body, but he never had time for things like that. Worrying about his mother was the life he knew.

His father had retreated to the island years six ago, defeated by her wandering mind, the way she would appear and disappear, the way her brain invented things, stretched out her fears, accused strangers of plotting against her, certain there was poison in her coffee, certain that Jesus was speaking through her, certain that the children she had miscarried were in the room, ready to carry her to hell. There had been no question that Junior would stay with his mother. Even if she had been willing to give him up, Esperanza's mother was militant in her insistence that Junior be with his mother's family, who were all in New York. Junior wasn't sure why, as the woman seemed to hate him, although to be fair, she seemed to hate everyone. But his father, Santiago Sr., had capitulated easily. After all, he was the one doing the leaving, the one asking for the divorce. He sent money, and a plane ticket, every year, and Junior would put his clothing in a duffel bag and kiss his mother goodbye, uncertain if she was there or not, and take the A train miles and miles out to the airport, the only time he ever left Manhattan, and board a plane to the island where it was always summer.

On the island, Junior tried to forget about New York. He tried to pretend it did not exist, despite the fact that in his heart he knew it to be the center of the world. He knew many people there, but he was always alone, as isolated by his brain as his mother was in escaping hers. He had a curse, too, like she did. He was smart. Not like his uncles, who were the kind of smart that makes you a good getaway driver, a good lookout, a good man to have in a fight, men who could count and break someone's limb at the same time. No, Junior was smart like a whip, smart like a knife.

He lived in books, in his mind, in mathematical calculations and iambic pentameter. His grandmother spat at him, when he passed, her rage a familiar and a foreign thing, constant but confusing, and told him he was showing off when he sat, silently reading. Perhaps it was because she couldn't read at all. She thought he taunted her. As a small child he had asked *why,* and been slapped for his trouble. Now, he rarely spoke anymore, worried that something he knew would come out, escape his brain, and he would never get it back.

The boil on his back had grown throughout the winter. His young body was sleek and taut and lightly tanned, growing more so each day on the island as he worked in his father's garden without his shirt on, or lay in the Caribbean sun, which is the same sun as everywhere else on Earth, only it feels different. Through the year, small cysts occasionally gathered, fatty pustules, harmless but bulging, across his shoulders and cresting over his buttocks. He left them alone at home, but here, sleeping on his stomach shirtless, they were visible to the world. The one just above his tailbone had grown, and grown, becoming angry, swelling with rage at the New York cold, at the long days spent in thin coats, at the task of caring for Esperanza, finding her when her body followed her mind, when she stopped taking her pills, when the prayers to Jesus and Mary and the five great orishas and anyone else listening weren't enough. Now, Goli's aim was true, her weapon ready, and the boil, so plump and proud, found itself attacked by a force much greater than itself, its clear foul-smelling liquid mixing with Junior's blood as his uncle held him down, as he muffled his screams in the pillow.

"Good," Goli said in Spanish, satisfied. Junior looked up at her, his eyes plaintive. "Better this way." She soaked a clean piece of fabric in something that smelled like Junior's father did by 6:00 P.M. every day, and dabbed it on the incision, which sent fresh flames running along his nerves. He winced. "Baby. I did this for your father when we were growing up. He never even woke."

Junior nodded. To not agree about the superiority of his father would cause more trouble than it was worth. Next to him, his uncle Luis stretched, his bones cracking. It was late at night, but Luis worked odd hours at the Maidenform factory that had recently opened on the island and he had just gotten home from work, right in time to help Goli with her operation.

"Late for you," Goli observed, washing her hands and giving Luis a plate of rice and beans, drowning in *sofrito,* the mixture of peppers, *culantro,* and onions and garlic that Goli blended in the morning and used for most of what she cooked. Junior slept on the couch in their living room, which led into their kitchen, and he sat up, wearily, to give Luis room to sit.

"Thanks," Luis responded in Spanish, the *s* at the end of *gracias* almost inaudible. When Junior spoke Spanish in New York with non-islanders, they told him that in Puerto Rico even the Spanish was lazy, lopping off the ends of things, swallowing syllables, assigning genders at will. *But why shouldn't things be both man and woman?* Junior wondered. In New York men met in secret in the bathrooms of subway tunnels, or in the park, paying each other for affection. Who knew what women did. But on the island, things were less fixed, no matter how they were repented on Sunday. *El agua, la agua,* surely the water could be both?

"You want?" Luis asked, gesturing to the plate. Junior smiled, guiltily. He did want. He always wanted. His mother, when she cooked, was a terrible cook. Everyone said his grandmother poisoned her food, and besides, she rarely did anything for anyone, let alone some kind of labor. He was always hungry; they had always been poor. Working daily out in the sun had only made him hungrier. And Goli was a very good cook. Luis gestured to Goli, who smiled.

"Where do you put it all?" she wondered. She, like her husband, like Junior's father, had the stout bodies of most of their family, gravity sinking its way into her hips, the hint of Taino tribesman spicing their blood, drawing them down to the equator.

Those long-lost tribespeople left their mark on Puerto Ricans in square middles, blunt foreheads, black hair, brown skins, cheering on the arena where Spanish blood vied with African in the faces and bodies of each islander. In Junior's family, their skins made a spectrum of color, from the pale olive tones his mother carried, her fair beauty disguising her madness, to his aunt Marisol, who they called Mariche, who had been, they joked, baked in the womb, emerging earth brown.

He shrugged, his mouth already full.

"This is why your father has you stay with me. He knows only I can keep you fed like this. Chavela would have given up years ago." Junior looked up at Goli quickly before looking back at his food. They never discussed the fact that he spent at least a week, year after year, in her home instead of his father's. Goli and Luis didn't have children. After years of trying, they had put the image of an infant beaten out of tin next to the Virgin Mary of Guadalupe on their home altar and decided that they would accept God's will in their lives. Goli laid out bowls of food for the neighborhood cats daily, and cooed at them as they wove their way around her legs, purring with gratitude, and Luis called the birds who came in the evenings his children. When Junior came, they treated him as their son, proud of his presence, bragging about his grades in school, his many accomplishments.

Junior stood, and took his plate over to the sink. He was so used to doing everything at home that the old order of things on the island—women cooking, men sleeping, women serving, men drinking, women washing, men dirtying—never felt like it applied to him, no matter how many loving aunts or fearful uncles, sensing revolution, assured him that it did.

He could feel the boil on his back weeping, gently, mixing with his sweat, which was cooling and drying in the mountain air. Tiny San Sebastián, El Pepino, was like a postage stamp compared to the great letter of New York, but he knew New York far better, trusted it far more, than he knew this little mountain town. This place that he came from that never felt like a part of him, or if it was, it was one that he was eager to expunge, to cut out, to lance like his boils.

"Your father has off tomorrow," Goli reminded him. Junior nodded, absently. His father was a postal service worker, and tomorrow was the Fourth of July. A national holiday for an island without a nation. Puerto Ricans celebrated it, though, *any excuse not to work,* his father would joke.

"He said he wants you ready early. He's taking you to Luquillo with his children." Goli never referred to them as Junior's siblings, though of course that was what they were. He wondered if Goli knew how strange he felt about these siblings he had here, these little strangers who looked at him in awe. At home it was just him and Esperanza. They had moved out of her mother's apartment, fleeing his grandmother's crowded home, filled to the brim with the many children she had had with the many men she had defeated. Teofila, his grandmother, checked on them occasionally, treating Esperanza's growing madness as others would try to treat a common cold, with deliveries of chicken soup and advice that if she walked about more, she might feel better.

"I'll be ready," Junior assured her, and Goli smiled, sadness leaking out of the edges of her upturned lips. "Are you coming?" he asked, hoping he wasn't pleading, hoping she would ignore it if he was. While he loved his mother fiercely, he took care of her, he worried for her. His duty colored his love. Goli took care of him, and he wanted her to have the joys of life, a day at the sea, cold beers and fresh fish from one of the little shacks that littered the shores of Luquillo, time away from the backbreaking work of the farm.

Goli shook her head.

"This is time for you and your family." Junior looked away, and without a word walked back to the couch, lying on it like a heap of laundry, boneless. Luis was already asleep, having gone into his and Goli's bedroom, exhausted, his body metabolizing his food like a slumbering snake. Junior felt Goli's lips brush over his forehead as she turned out the light, and went to join her husband.

They belonged together, Goli and Luis. They fit. They were the only people he knew who did. Junior's parents had separated when he was an infant, divorced before his third birthday. His father had tried to stay in New York, but had given up on the winters, and the hardness, and had left it, and him, behind. The people he knew in New York, everyone who was with someone, clashed against each other, their romances fraught with broken hearts and bones. One of his mother's boyfriends had almost put him through a wall of another of their old apartments, on Allen Street, while his grand-mother had knocked out more than one of her husband's teeth. His uncle Samuel, only a year older than Junior, who everyone called Rowdy, because he *was,* had new girlfriends every week, and they were always either crying or screaming. Chavela, his father's second wife, was almost silent, kind to him, kind to everyone, but she was a woman with a plate of food where her voice should be.

Junior wished he knew how his father felt about him. He wished he knew how he felt about his father. Sometimes he hated him for leaving him behind. Sometimes he wanted to be like him, to do the leaving. Sometimes he admired him for the things he had done, given what he had come from. Sometimes he longed for him, wished he would be like the fathers Junior saw on television, in sweaters and asking about his day. But for that night, at least, it was enough to sleep, to wake with the dawn, to pile himself into the beaten Chevy his father drove like a visiting dignitary, his body squashed in between the sticky sweet forms of his much younger siblings, who clung to him, brown berries on a vine. To watch the never-ending sugarcane fields end, to climb through the hills and down the valleys, to span almost the entire island as the sun rose higher and higher, to pass San Juan by, and *El Yunque,* the rain forest, and panting dogs and women in printed dresses gossiping and a hundred churches and every house bright like candy, and not enough people, after New York everything felt empty, and to arrive, desperate for the ocean. To dive into the water with his father, silent, beside him. The other children splashed about in the shallows, and built sand castles, and screamed for food from Chavela, and pulled each other's hair, and made new friends, and discarded them.

Junior merely stood in the ocean with his father, a man he barely knew, a man he craved something from that he would never be able to ask for, and never get, a man who had left an infant with a woman who was outside of her own mind, locked out, no keys, no window to break. He thought about asking his father why he had done it, why he hadn't told Esperanza that he was taking his son with him. But he knew that would have been impossible. No one would have let that happen, not his grandmother, not his uncles, not even himself. Six years ago when Santiago Sr. left New York, he, Junior, already knew that without his help his mother would crumble and fall. He wouldn't have left her then, even if he had a choice, just like he wouldn't leave her now. *Someday,* a voice in his head murmured, but he ignored it. The thought made him sick, with guilt, and with longing.

The ocean was blue enough to break hearts, and he wanted to stay in it forever. Instead, he sat with his father in a small beach shack, watching him drink beer after beer. He lay beside him, as he napped, his face red with alcohol and sun, and sat beside him on the way home, as Chavela and the children, drowsy from the sun, slept. He knew his siblings so little that he had a moment of absurd worry at one point that they had forgotten one of them, that he had counted wrong, that he had one more, or less. But Chavela wouldn't forget her children, not like Esperanza sometimes forgot him. Junior was comforted by the thought that for all Chavela's silence, her mind seemed to stay firmly in her head. She always greeted him as *mi niño*, my child. She was kind like that, to count him among her blessings. Sometimes, when the children were screaming at her, he had to clench his fists not to hit them, not to scream at them, *Don't you know how lucky you are?* He had to work hard not to envy five-year-old children. He looked back at the littlest one, Juanito, who clung to Chavela even in sleep, holding on to her as if his life depended on it.

"How is your mother?" Santiago Sr. asked, his voice husky from lack of use, quiet, so as not to wake his sleeping wife, his many children.

On these trips to the island, there would always come a point when Santiago Sr. asked this. Junior knew this, and yet he never knew how to respond.

"Okay," he said, shrugging. There was too much to say, so he said nothing, really. How could he tell his father about the days when she was normal, absolutely normal, and then she would get up from the lacework that she made and sold by the piece and leave their apartment and he would find her, in Union Square, certain she could communicate with the sun? How could he tell him about the days when she was catatonic, when she refused to move, to eat, she barely breathed? How could he tell him about all the things in between, about the fact that these summers in Puerto Rico were both escape and torture, that his fear for his mother ate him up from the inside, that he knew someday, soon, he would have to leave her behind, he could not take her with him, and that knowledge made his stomach into a lead casket? How could he say anything at all, to the man who had done the same? How could he tell him, *Someday I think I will become you, without wanting to, without knowing you at all?*

Santiago Sr. nodded.

"That's good."

Junior looked out the window, watching the light fade.

"She's a good woman, your mother," Santiago Sr. said, awkwardly. He stumbled over the words. Santiago said nothing. "Terrible cook. Goli is feeding you better?" He nodded. His mother *was* a terrible cook. She barely ate, both through lack of care, and because she was desperate to maintain her slim figure. She liked dating men, liked meeting them, having them take her out on the town. Junior wondered if she liked it because she could pretend, with a new person, that her mind was whole, unsplintered. Or maybe it was just that they could afford things Esperanza couldn't.

"Has she gotten sicker?" Santiago Sr. asked, his tone tentative. Junior was confused. His father didn't usually linger over this topic like this.

"I don't know." He really didn't know. It was hard for him to tell, better, worse, about his mother. She changed so much all the time; how could he say what was sicker?

"Your grandmother thinks she has," Santiago Sr. said, his voice heavy. Junior was startled. He didn't know that his father even spoke to Teofila.

"She's a bitch, that woman," Santiago Sr. said, almost under his breath. Junior laughed, nervously, and his father joined him. They didn't look alike, but when they laughed their faces were the same. They both laughed like they were afraid.

"She's put Esperanza in the hospital," Santiago Sr. said, and Junior realized that this, like the car winding up the mountain, was what his father had wanted to say the whole time, but he had tried to sneak up on it, approach it sideways. The whole day, the whole purpose of it, was to inform him of his mother's captivity. He knew what *hospital* meant. It meant *institution.* It was a decision the family had debated and prayed over and lit candles about and pretended was an impossibility for the majority of Junior's life. And now it had been made, without him.

"Which one?" he asked, his voice hoarse.

"Bellevue," Santiago Sr. said, as the car turned a corner, rolling through sugarcane fields. They were close to Tía Goli's house, close to safety, close to a place that was like a home but it was not his home, nothing was, not really. Even his home wasn't his home anymore. Not while his mother wasn't in it, not now that Teofila had had her own daughter committed.

"Your grandmother said it is for the best. It's an expensive place. They will treat her well, help with her sickness," Santiago Sr. said, his voice as doubtful as his words were confident.

Junior just nodded, unsure if his father could see him in the fading light, unsure if he cared.

"I will give you some money, when you go back. To help," Santiago Sr. said. Junior nodded again. "She's been sick for a long time."

He wanted to ask his father when he knew, when he had seen Esperanza's mind escape her body, when it had become clear to him that the pale pretty girl he had met in church in El Pepino, the town whose dust coated the Chevy's tires even now, was a madwoman. Was it before Junior had been conceived? Was it when he had come out of her? Was it when he started to crawl? He wanted to ask his father what would happen now, and if Esperanza really could get better, and why, why, had he left his child with her, why had he left New York, why had he started a new family with a silent woman and made loud babies? Why had it taken him all day to tell him that his mother was in a mental institution? And what would happen now?

But he didn't. And the car stopped, and Junior peeled his sweaty sandy back off the car seat, and opened the door, stepping out into the night and a thousand mosquito stings.

"Hey." He looked back, and his father was looking at him. He reached for something, and Junior realized it was his own shirt, which he had taken off before they had arrived at the beach, and never bothered to put on again.

"Goli got you?" his father asked, and Junior nodded, reaching for the lanced boil. "Did you scream?" Junior shook his head, lying to his father. Santiago Sr. smiled. "Good. Reacting to pain only makes it worse, you know."

"I know."

And then Santiago was gone.

Eighteen

Elena spends the night on Goli's overstuffed little couch. By the
time the woman was tired of talking about her nephew the shadows
had begun to deepen, and Naomi was yawning. Elena wondered
idly how it was okay for this woman to just leave the cemetery for
the day and not go back for hours and hours, but that was Puerto
Rico for you, and besides, it's not like there is much to steal in a
graveyard. Goli insisted that Elena stay the night, and she cannot
really refuse. She does not know where else to go, or what to do now,
even. She texted Diego about her plans, and received a thumbs-up
in return. Funny how the older people here seem so excited to embrace images as words. She texted her mother, too, a few short sentences, and Rosalind wrote her back, *I'm glad you're meeting Goli.*
Elena's heart aches at this. Is Rosalind really glad? She hopes so. No
matter her anger, she really does hope so.

Goli talked and talked about Elena's father, Junior, never referring to him as anything else. Her memory was sharp as a tack in
some places, blurry and flawed in others, and sometimes words failed
her in Spanish, leaving Elena and Naomi shrugging. But most of it
was achingly clear. Goli thought of Junior as a young man, still,

under her care. She spoke of how smart he was, what great things life would hold for him. She told Elena of his college admittance, of the first time he brought Rosalind to the island, mixing up time, patching it together like a quilt. In one story he was still seven, in another it was his First Communion, then he was a man of twenty, then fifteen again. Elena listened to the stories like they were about a stranger—well, they were. The Junior of Goli's stories was sweet, and serious, and always reading. He was easily amused by parrots chattering and dogs playing, but he was good, too, eager to help his grandfather, Goli's father, in the fields despite it being his vacation. He loved the ocean, he would run into it screaming and stay in it for hours, and here Elena saw herself, ever ready to be in the sea. He loved San Juan, and he would go, when he was old enough, for a day, with fifty cents from his father, and wander the streets until his father could pick him up at the ferry terminal in Bayamon after he had finished his mail route. He always brought gifts for her and Luis, her deceased husband, little things they treasured, which Goli showed her, a glass figurine, a postcard from Mexico, a statue of a saint from Spain.

There is so much Goli cannot tell her, so much the woman doesn't know, or doesn't remember. His life in New York, his family there, his time at Stanford and Yale, how he met her mother, how he felt about himself, about his world—Elena knows she will never know any of this, never really know his story. So she clings to what she gets, little pieces of driftwood in the sea of his life.

She stares up at the ceiling now. It is early, ten o'clock, but past Goli's bedtime. A lizard walks across the walls of the house, Elena can see it moving fast, then stopping for long moments, then running again. An extreme way to live life, either running or standing still, but it works for lizards, she supposes.

She had asked Goli one question that had given her some kind of useful response. She asked about Santiago now, where Goli thought he might be. She wasn't really sure why she asked it, except that she wanted to know, even if it was meaningless. She wanted to ask someone else so she could stop asking herself. Goli had smiled her wrinkled little smile.

"*El Balcón Familiar,*" Goli said, winking at her. Elena looked at Naomi, who shrugged.

"It's a bar in town," Naomi said. Elena nodded.

"He loves that place," Goli said. "His father did, too, and Luis. Might as well be our family home!" Goli giggled at her own joke, and Elena joined her, weakly.

Now she thinks of that name, wondering. She shouldn't have any kind of hope, really, she knows, but she does. She tells herself that she will just leave in the morning, return to Rincón, give back her rental car, go back to San Juan, book her flight home, leave this all. Let go of the house, let go of her father, let go of expectation and need and anger and the desire for anything that comes from here, from him.

But in the morning, she knows she will be at the bar, instead.

Goli feeds her breakfast cheerfully, although Elena wonders if Goli quite knows who she is when she sees her in the morning. There is a moment of uncertainty before the smile, and Elena reminds her, *I'm Junior's daughter,* just in case. This earns her toast with guava jam and a bottle of *pitorro,* which Elena is sure will burn the lining of her stomach, as well as the command to come again soon, like they have met before, like Elena even knew she existed. Elena hugs her, and even takes a photo of her with her phone in front of her little home. Perhaps she will print this, and all the other photos, and make her own album, she thinks, start her own book of Puerto Rico memories that are really hers, not borrowed ones. Because yes, this island is her father's. But is it not hers as well, just a little bit?

No matter what Rosalind thinks or wants, isn't it Elena's choice to take what has been given to her? It is there for the taking, if she decides she can.

Elena drives into the center of the little town, following the directions on her phone. It is early, of course, but bars open early here. He won't be there, she is sure, but this is it, this is her last lead, her last piece of magic, the last spot on the map. After this there is nothing, just the knowledge that she failed, and she holds on to the chance that she might find something, might find him, for a little longer. Just a little more. There is time enough for reality later; for now, she will dream.

She knows some part of her believes in movie endings. Some part of her hopes that finding him will mean some kind of transformation. She wants to kill the parts of her that still have hope, but then what will she be left with, other than pain and anger?

She parks the car, and walks up to the door of the bar and opens it, immediately blinded by the contrast between the brilliant light outside and the shadows of the interior. When her eyes adjust, she sees that the waiters are looking at her with resentment. Clearly her presence means they have to get to work, and they are in the midst of a card game. One starts to stand, but she waves him back to his seat. He shrugs, obviously unconcerned; if she needs something, she will ask for it.

Elena looks around. There is no one here but her and the apathetic waiters. Of course there isn't anyone else. It's nine in the morning. It's a random bar in a random town. It's nothing, she has nothing, she never had anything. He's gone, or he's not gone, the house is hers, or it's not hers, it doesn't really matter anymore. Movies aren't real, life is life, and she is, as always, alone. She sits down, weary despite the night of sleep. All of this is her fault, not the chase for him, but the belief that it might lead to anything. The thought that coming here might mean something to her. The search for graves and deeds and people like they will give her what she wants, him. Answer her questions, fill up the space he's always left behind. Oh, they have given her things, and she will forever be grateful. Diego and Hermando and Irena and Goli, they've given her little bits and pieces, more than she ever had before. She is a selfish person, she knows, but she had hoped for everything, not a pittance. She had hoped to know her father, know his life. She had hoped that she would be enough for him to want to keep living it. Silly girl. She barely has a life of her own to live.

She stands up to go. She will get on the road, brave the commuter traffic, take the next step and the next and the next, unstick herself from this place and the past and make some kind of something of her future. She reaches the door, which opens without her pushing it, because it is being pulled by someone. She looks up, into a pair of eyes that are a lot like her own, dark and brown and crowned with thick eyebrows. She looks up and sees her father for the first time in years.

Nineteen

How has he become so old? Elena thinks. She thought he was old when she saw him in New York those years ago but now, now the years have worn their way into his face and an old man looks back at her. Her *grandfather* looks back at her through her father's face. The bags under his slightly bloodshot eyes are pronounced, and his jaw has softened. His hair has receded, an army retreating the battlefield of his forehead, but he still has some, and what he has is grayish brown, curly, cut short. He's clean-shaven now, although he had a beard for most of her childhood. His stomach has grown, and it strains at his belt. He wears a tropical shirt that is tight across his belly, but loose at his shoulders, which have shrunk, lack of exercise, she thinks. His eyes look surprised to see her, but only vaguely, like he was expecting her, but just in an hour or so, like she's early to meet him. He smiles at her, and she wants him to open his arms, to draw her close, so she can wrinkle her nose at his smell of metallic sweat, so she can be held. He does not do this, and she has to clench her fists to keep from reaching out to him.

"Elenita," he says, like he saw her yesterday, like he saw her ten minutes ago. "Hello."

"Hello?" she asks. But is she really surprised that this is all he says? A little, and she hates herself for being so.

"How did you get here?" he asks. She stares at him. Here? To the bar? To the island? To the world?

"I drove," she says, simply. He nods, as if it makes sense that she would drive all the way from New York. "I came to San Juan. I went to Rincón. I found a map. I rented a car. Diego helped me," she says, hoping to jolt him, remind him that he has never mentioned Diego, hoping for some reaction.

"Oh, that's good. Long trip?" he asks. She shakes her head. It is like a conversation with a stranger. Of course it is.

"Have you been here before?" he asks her. He should know she hasn't. He must. "Come, let's get a drink." He walks past her, and takes a seat at the bar. Elena walks toward him, and sits at the bar, leaving a seat between them. She feels like she is in a dream.

"What will you have?" he asks her. She has no idea what to say. She has been chasing him for days, unsure whether he was even still alive. She has hoped and despaired and now he is here and it is nothing. It is nothing, like they met after a week apart and not years and miles and storms. She wants to drink a whole bottle of rum and then vomit for hours, purging her system like the ancient Romans.

"Water, please." Elena's father gives her a long look, and orders them two rums. "Where have you been, Papi?" Elena asks, struggling to keep her voice gentle, like she is talking to a skittish deer in the forest. She isn't sure if she means recently, or ever.

"Oh, I been everywhere," he says, tapping his fingers on the bar in a drumming rhythm. "Did you read about those red pandas? I thought you would like them. So cute!" He had sent her an article on red pandas in the Bronx Zoo six months ago. "Did you go see them?"

"Yes." She had, actually. It was a special exhibit on animals of the Himalayas and her father had been delighted by the red pandas. He had never heard of the animal, and he had emailed her about

it, saying, *ALMOST SEVENTY and there are STILL things that are
new to me!*

"Cute little guys." The rum arrives, and her father sips his, deeply.

"Where have you been *recently*, Papi?" Elena asks again, trying to
be specific, trying to be patient. Trying not to cry.

"My parents grew up here," he says, happily. "It's nice to come
back sometimes. Did I ever take you here? Man, it's all built up
now. We still might have some family here. Did you know that? I
should find out."

Elena thinks about all the things he hid from her, how easily he
shares things now that he has given in to his thirst for alcohol, given
in to the ups and downs of his mind. The way he talks to her like
she knows the intimate details of his life and not the CliffsNotes. She
thinks about Goli, and how her father is like his aunt, how reality is
something that comes and goes for both of them. She takes out the
albums she has carried with her and opens the one with the oldest
photos.

"Oh, look at that," he says, looking at his parents' wedding photo.
"That's my mother. Wasn't she beautiful?" He strokes the photo
with his index finger.

"Yes." She was, but for her eyes, which are too bright and burning
to be beautiful. Her eyes give her away.

"They cut all her hair off the third time she went to Bellevue. She
wouldn't wash it. I was so sad for her, she was always so proud of her
hair," her father says, and Elena wonders if he realizes he is saying
this out loud, realizes that he is telling his daughter the things he
told her she would never, could never, know. "Did you ever meet my
mother?"

"No, Papi."

"She wasn't well."

"I know."

"She heard voices. All the time. She just wanted it to be quiet."

"That must have been hard for her."

"I loved her," he says, and he sounds like a child.

"I'm sure she loved you, too." He nods.

"She was the only person who loved me for a long time." Elena does not know what to say. Her father looks at her. "How old are you now?" he asks.

"Thirty. Thirty-one soon," she says. Her birthday is in July. He nods once.

"Yes. You came, and Neil left. I ever tell you about Neil?"

"No, Papi."

"Sad. He was my first friend, first real friend. I think I was his, too. He would have liked you."

Elena does not know what to say to this. She doesn't quite understand what he means. A thousand questions ring in her mind, but she doesn't ask a single one. She just stays sitting next to him, her body tense, hoping he will not disappear.

"How did you get here?" he asks her again.

"I drove."

"Only way to do it. You see the island that way. What do you think? You ever drive around the island? Beautiful, isn't it?"

"It is." The island has been devastated by the hurricane, it is flailing and failing, but it is still beautiful. It seems wrong that it should be so beautiful and so desperate at once.

"Paradise. Not like New York!" he says, laughing and drinking his rum. Absentmindedly, when he finishes his own, he reaches for Elena's, which is still full.

"No. Not like New York."

"You been here a long time?" he asks.

"No, Papi. Not long."

"Did I know you were coming?" he says, lightly, but she can see the furrow in his brow. He is not sure.

"No, Papi. We didn't know where you were. No one could get

ahold of you. Mom was scared, actually." He pushes at the air like a cat at this.

"Your mother worries too much. God, I love her. When's she gonna come down here? She said she would come. She never does." He looks sad. "You know, it's not her fault about us. I don't want you to blame her." Elena almost smiles. As if she would blame her mother. "I still love her so much. It's not her fault we grew apart."

Grew apart. Well, her father has had a long time to create a fiction that suits him. There is little worth saying now to contradict it. He tells himself the story of his life to survive, but who doesn't? Elena just wishes she knew more of it. And maybe she will always mourn all that she doesn't know. But mourning won't give her any more than she has.

"You didn't tell anyone where you were going or anything, Papi. I've been, I've been looking for you." He looks surprised at Elena's careful, *careful* words.

"But I was right here the whole time! You should have come here. I could have shown you everything!"

"How long have you been here?" she asks, trying so hard to sound even, to conceal her panic, her anger, her fear. He shrugs. She knows that this is like talking to an animal, a dog who sometimes looks like he understands every word you say until he starts biting at his leg halfway through your statement.

"Oh, it's good to see you, baby," he says, and he hugs her, tight, the way he always did. Elena has not been hugged by her father in years. For a moment it feels like all of this was worth it, and then he pulls back.

"How did you get here?" he asks her a third time. And she knows that there is nothing she can say to him that will mean anything, not her anger or sadness or pain. Nothing means anything now. He is as lost to her as his history is.

"I drove, Papi," she says, her voice soft and calm.

"You want to see my father's old house?" he asks. She nods. "You can leave your things here. This is heavy. Eduardo will look after it, right, young fellow?" he calls to the aged bartender, the way he does to everyone, calling them *joven*. The bartender nods, once, his eyes on the card game, which he returned to after pouring them their rums. Elena watches her father walk away for a moment, but really, it is no choice at all, she is going with him, no matter how useless the act of it is. She will cling to whatever she has until it is gone. That's who she is. She knows that now.

They walk along the road, which has no sidewalks. Elena mentions this to her father, asking if this is safe, and he snorts.

"You sound like your mother," he tells her. "Is she here?"

"No, Papi," Elena says, her voice low.

"She said she would come but she doesn't." He sounds like a child again, sad and small.

"I don't think she likes it here anymore, Papi," Elena says, trying to be nice.

"But you do, don't you?"

Elena thinks about this question.

"Papi? Did you sign the house over to me?" she asks, before she can stop herself.

"The house is yours," he says. "You like it here, don't you?"

"I do. I love it here. But what does that mean, it's mine, Papi, can you tell me?"

"I don't need it anymore. It's yours," he says, like it is so simple, and perhaps in a way it is, and he turns and continues walking, leaving Elena behind him. She does not want to follow, she wants to stand there and demand that he answer her, really answer her, but she doesn't. She walks on, catching up to him, and he takes her hand in his. They pass chickens rooting for food in the undergrowth, and Elena wonders how people know whose chicken is theirs, and where the hens lay their eggs.

Soon they are standing in front of a small dilapidated house, half
cement, half rotting wood. It is set back from the road, and a little
away from the center of the town, the more developed areas, but
close enough to be accessible. It has sunk into the forest around it.
A tree is growing through the roof. Beside the house, beyond the
overgrown trees and vines and bushes, Elena can see farmland turning back into forest, abandoned fields reclaimed by native plants.

"All sugar," her father says. "My grandfather cut cane. I would bring
him lunch, when I visited. Nice man. He cut until he went blind, and
then he died." He points to the left, but Elena can't see anything.

"So your father lived here?" Elena asks. He nods. "And your
mother?"

"Nearby. They both grew up here."

"I saw her grave," Elena offers.

Her father nods. "Your aunt Goli brings flowers. She's a good
woman, a sweet woman."

"Was your mother a good woman?" Elena asks.

"She was a sad person. I think my mother suffered from being
unloved. There was no one in her life who really loved her other than
me." In a moment like this, he sounds the way he used to sound,
whole and firm, like a real person. But soon he will ask her a question, or say something that will show her that he is gone away again,
and this will break her heart. The way he dips in and out of being a
person is worse than if he were just completely gone, she thinks. It's
a trick, and she hates being tricked.

"Did your father love her?" Elena wonders.

"I think he tried." Elena looks at her father and for a moment she
is amazed by his generosity. There is forgiveness in his voice and she
does not understand how people can do this, be kind and cruel and
good and bad all at the same time. Forgive their parents and punish
their children and hate and love and *be. But you are doing that, aren't
you? You love this man, and you hate him, and you wish he didn't exist,*

and you are so glad you found him. To be a human is to be a hypocrite in one's heart, perhaps. And Elena is no less of one than anyone else.

"Do you come here a lot?" Elena asks. He shrugs again. "Did you used to come here, when you were a kid? To the island?"

"I used to come here every summer until I was sixteen."

"What happened when you were sixteen?" she asks.

"I stopped coming."

"What *happened*, Papi?" she asks, her voice cracking with her pathetic needs, her frustration, her fear, her rage.

"What happened when?" He looks at her, his eyes wide and untroubled.

"Why did you leave? Why did you just leave San Juan and where did you go? Who is Diego, who is Neil, what happened to your parents? Who are Hermando and Irena, who else is there that I don't know? Who is Goli? Who are you? Where have you *been*?" She asks question after question wildly, desperate for something, anything, from him.

He looks around.

"Right here. What are you so upset about? Everything is wonderful. It's a beautiful day, I'm here with my daughter, we're in paradise. Why are you getting worked up? What's wrong?" He does not understand. He will never understand. He will never *see* her, never see anyone but himself. He has nothing to give her of himself, nothing more. And she is a child, a spoiled kid who cannot be content with what she has been given. *Because it has never been enough.* How can she forgive him for this? How can she forgive herself for still, after all that she knows and will never know, wanting more?

"Do you like it here?" He spreads his arms, and she does not know if he means the town, or the island, or the earth.

"Do you?" she asks. She knows the answer. He loves it, and it consumes him, and he is bleeding away into it, and happy to be doing so. He came back to the island to sink into it, to let himself go. To let it receive him as he fades away. *Like* is not the word.

"It doesn't matter if I like it. It's home." And then he turns around, and walks back in the direction of the bar.

And it is in this moment, watching him walk away from her, after all of this, that Elena knows fully and completely she will never have more of him than this. She will never get what she wants from her father. This is not, as she has always somehow secretly believed, because there is something wrong with her. Something that makes him unable to be close to her, to share with her, to love her as she should be loved. It is not because she did not try, did not come for him and find him here. It is because he does not know how. He does not know how to love people, because he can never love himself, never trust that he should be better than the worst of himself. *I think my mother suffered from being unloved.* But that was not his fate. His fate was to be loved, and not understand the value of it, the care of it, that love must be respected and maintained in order to survive. He does not understand the work of love, the work he owes it. Owes those who love him. He cannot be different than he is. His body, his condition, they created great barriers to this, chemical pathways and dependencies that made it so much harder than it was for the rest of the world. That does not mean they could not have been overcome, but the work is hard, so hard, and he has given up the task. He fought, she knows he did, but now he has laid his weapons down. She is in his Valhalla, and there is no coming back from here for him. What warrior leaves Valhalla for another round of battles?

She found her father, yes. But he will always be lost to her.

She thinks of the person Diego told her about, the person she has glimpsed through photographs and stories. The man who came from nothing, who had nothing, who clawed his way up out of poverty, yes, but also out of a family that would have drowned him, a mother who was ever descending into worlds no one could visit in her mind, relatives who didn't, wouldn't, deal with it, and so many other things that Elena will never understand, never know. This man was an astronaut, he shot out of his world and into another and he never looked back. In another person, with another, unburdened brain, with better internal chemistry, he would have stayed as great as he once was, maybe. He would have risen higher. She would have him still, the better parts of him. He wouldn't have left her behind.

But he isn't another person. He's himself, defeated by his past, betrayed by the brain that once saved him, buried in his parents' sins as badly as if he had never left New York behind. The "gifts" Esperanza and Santiago Vega Sr. gave their son are poisonous ones, eternal thirst and a brain that moves in circles, up and down forever, but he cannot part with them. Elena always thought it was a choice he was making, and perhaps some part of it is. But it is also a compulsion. Maybe her father did leave her, like she thought, but maybe he wanted to save her, stop her from watching his decay, protect her from himself, his history, his curses and his gifts. She wishes she could have seen him at his best, his most brilliant, seen him shining bright. Her childhood images of him sparkle and she knows that there was something brilliant about him back then, dulled as he has become now. What a life she might have had if he had never faded.

What a life she has, now that he did.

She looks out at the house he has shown her. Perhaps this is her grandfather's house, or perhaps it is not. Perhaps her ancestors walked these streets and lived and died and left their essence for her to find, or perhaps they would have spat at her and cast her out. The decaying house in front of her doesn't mean anything. It doesn't move her or fill her with a sense of coming home, of family, of return to self. It's just a house, falling down on itself. It's just a town, a bunch of cement boxes and wires and pipes. It's not hers, not really.

It isn't places that have meaning, really, but people. People give things meaning. Home is people. And there is no one here for her.

By the time she returns to the bar, he has started a game of pool with some other people, regulars, she supposes, men like him who arrive at the bar before noon. She retrieves her belongings from Eduardo, and stands, clutching the albums, looking at the man she has been chasing. The ghost she has sought out. He is comfortable here, with strangers who are all like him. They bear the easy sodden looks of lifelong drinkers, and they laugh at his jokes, ones he has told them a thousand times, ones they will never remember. None of them are talking to each other, not really, she can tell. For each of these men, the rest of the world is a blurry audience, not exactly real, but real enough to reassure them that they are not entirely alone. She wonders who comes and gets them when they have passed out, if they cannot stumble home. Who will come and get her father? But he does not want to be fetched, she understands now. He wants to stay where he is. Maybe he will come back to San Juan someday, or New York, or even Philadelphia. Maybe he will show up at her doorstep, maybe he will fly to Paris.

But probably not. Because home is here for him.

He makes a tricky shot, and the other men clap for him. He readies himself, surveying the angles, aiming carefully. He is so agile with the pool cue, his hands gentle and sure. She remembers the day a boy pushed her in the schoolyard when she was seven, and how her father picked her up from school that day. He had been concerned about the Band-Aids all over her knees and palms, placed by the school nurse, and that night after her bath he replaced them all, his hands careful, his aim true, to cause her as little pain as possible as he attached each one on her body, shielding her wounds from the world.

He looks up once, before he makes the shot, and smiles at her. It is the same smile he wore when he first saw her, happiness to see her, the recognition that she is dear to him, but no surprise, no sense of remorse, no relief or sadness or regret. It is love, but with nothing else attached to it. None of the work, none of the effort, no promises of more than the feeling in his heart. If she doesn't see him again for another decade, if she sees him tomorrow, she knows that this smile will be no different. There is nothing she can do to change it. Or him.

And so, after days of searching, after worrying and thinking and wondering if her father is alive or dead or in pain or happy, after thirty years of wanting more than she has gotten, Elena Vega walks out of the El Balcón Familiar bar in San Sebastián, Puerto Rico, without a backward glance. She found her father. Now she must let him go.

Twenty

By the time she has gotten on the road, the little green hills that look nothing like cucumbers in her rearview mirror, she is crying. She ignores the tears, the way she ignores the quick rain showers that douse the island with a burst and then run away. They will pass, all things do. She will cry until she does not need to cry anymore. Later, she will cry again, and again, until she finds herself crying less and less, until there are whole parts of each day in which she doesn't think about her father at all. There will be a tragedy to that, too. She will mourn that pain when she gets to it.

She realizes she has been unconsciously following the signs to San Juan, rather than to Rincón, like a horse moving back to a stable, and she wipes her tears, and reroutes herself, following the signs to Rincón, every mile a chance to compose herself, to manufacture a sense of normalcy to present to Diego. She will visit him after she returns the car, she must, she knows. She does not know how she will get to San Juan from Rincón, but she trusts that she will find a way when she arrives, perhaps she will pay a taxi service far too much money, it will not matter. Her journey, her quest, is done, and all that is left is, well, the rest of her life.

She refuels in Aguada, and has the car in Rincón by evening, returning the keys to the kind-eyed attendant and walking toward Diego's house. It's a mile at least, but the breeze is strong and cooling. She finds Diego on the beach, gazing out at the ocean. There are inky gray clouds on the horizon, and he is watching them approach, waiting for the storm to come. She takes a photo of him from behind, noting how his body and the ocean blur into each other, just the way he wants, and then she sits beside him on the sand, looking out at the sea. It has already begun to rain over the ocean, she can see it, how water from the sky meets water from the land about a mile out from them.

"Did you find him?" Diego asks as Elena tries to calculate how long it will take for the rain to come, for them to be soaked.

"In a way," she says. Diego nods. He says nothing else, asks for no details, and for this she will always be grateful. Someday soon she will recount all that has happened, this strange trip and its conclusion, both devastating and meaningless at the same time. But for now, not talking about it is a gift.

"Are you all right?" he asks, his voice kind. She shrugs.

"I guess I'll go home, now," she says. Diego turns to her.

"I thought you were home." He smiles. She looks away, unable to bear his gaze.

"It's a good thing you did," he says. "Find him. Maybe it won't be important to him. But maybe for you, it is, to know that you at least tried. Because really, I believe what we do is not really for other people, but for ourselves. And you did something for yourself that you will always know, even after he has forgotten. *You* didn't give up. He is fading away, I know that. We are all fading away, we who have lost what we loved most. We are losing ourselves, too. I've been losing myself for decades. But you aren't. Now whatever you have of him is your own."

Water hits Elena's cheeks, and she thinks for a moment that she is crying again. But she is not. The storm has found them, the sudden downpour of the Caribbean, as fierce as it is rapid. Diego makes no move to go inside, to run away from the rain, so neither does she. They merely sit on the dampening sand, letting the water soak them, letting the storm wash them clean.

Elena returns to San Juan the next day. Diego gives her a ride, and they stare silently out at the empty roads, the damaged island.

"What do you think is going to happen now?" Elena asks Diego. She means after Maria, but she also means to her. What is going to happen to her now?

"The island will recover. Slowly. Painfully, without as much help as it needs. Bastards in Washington." Elena nods along with his words. "People will leave, but people are always leaving. And coming back. And they will fix some things, and other things will be tangled up and corrupt, and in the next storm it will happen all over again. That's what I think, at least. It's nice living here. Nothing ever really changes much. It's soothing," Diego says, wryly.

"I can't believe that," Elena says. Even with everything that has happened, she can't.

"Give it time," Diego tells her, smiling sadly. "And pain." They pass a roadside snack stall that has been overturned by the storm from last night. Men have gathered around it, and are struggling to push it back into its correct place. Elena thinks again of the storm that blew away her grandfather's garden shed all those years ago. She wonders if it became a food stall, if it landed somewhere and the people who found it thought it was a wonderful gift from the gods. Oh, the cruelty and generosity of the gods of storms.

They are soon in San Juan, and Diego is pulling up to the house, without her instructions.

"What are you going to do now?" Diego asks her as she stands on the sidewalk in front of the house that may or may not be hers, may or may not be her father's. *But it's all the same, isn't it, really,* she thinks, *it is mine even if it is his, who else would own it?* There is no one else left to receive whatever her father has to leave behind, no one else will inherit anything of him. All that he is on this earth is hers to take or throw away.

"I don't know," she says, honestly. "My life is in New York." But of course it really isn't anymore. She has no job. Her mother is in Philadelphia and Elena knows she will have to deal with that eventually, deal with Rosalind, but she has saturated herself with one parent, she needs a rest. Diego nods.

"Are you happy there?" Diego asks. He barely knows her, so she can be completely honest with him.

"Not really," she says. "It just goes on and on. Nothing anchors me. Nothing weighs me down either. I almost wish something would." But does she? She's cast off every tie. A fiancé. Work. She keeps her friends at a distance, she looks at the city like she's on the outside of a snow globe. She's never tried to root herself in New York, not really.

"Are you happy *here?*" Diego asks. It is a hard question for her to answer. She hasn't been here for years. She has spent her entire time here chasing her father. The island is crippled by the storm and will be crippled by new storms, by its debt, by its corruption, by its history. She doesn't know anyone here, really. She wants so badly to belong here, but she doesn't know if she ever will. She wants to be a part of this place desperately, and worries it will never want her back. She is still separating what parts of the island are the island, and what parts are her father. She may never be able to separate the two. This house is falling down, and there is someone who would buy it from her, free her to go back to her weightless life in New York. Her mother will kill her if she stays. She struggles with her Spanish, she struggles with everything.

She thinks of the feeling of the ocean, the way it calls to her body.

The way she thinks about sinking to the bottom, but the ocean holds her up, keeping her light but anchored. Both at once.

"I am," Elena says.

"I understand what it is to lose someone. I can't imagine what it would be like to lose someone who is still alive. But this place is yours, no matter what any document says, and I know he would like you to have it. I don't know what will happen, if he will be alive tomorrow, even. If any of us will. For today, this is your home."

"It's a ruin," she says. "It could fall apart at any time." He smiles.

"These houses have been here for centuries. They've withstood floods and fires and bombs, earthquakes and even the Dutch. I wouldn't underestimate them, if I were you."

Elena smiles, too. It is true, she knows. Time has seeped into the foundations of these buildings, each one of them built to last. Diego kisses her on both cheeks, lightly, in the Latin way, and Elena blushes. He gives her a hug.

"I'm glad I met you. I always wanted to."

"So did I," Elena says, although she had not known of his existence. But she is not lying. She had always wanted to meet Diego, even before she knew of him, because she had always wanted to know her father, even just a little bit. If this is all she has of him, perhaps some of it is the best of him.

"Come by and see me sometime. You know where I live, and I always like visitors."

"I didn't say I was staying."

"You didn't say you were leaving either." And then he is gone, the car tires bumping on the uneven cobblestones. Elena watches him until the car turns the corner, then lets herself into the house. She surveys it, the mess half sorted. She hears cooing, and sees that a pigeon has made itself comfortable in a pile of clothing on the second floor. She shoos it away, noting how its newfound nest has also become its bathroom.

The place is very much still a disaster, maybe even more so now that she tried to improve it. But it is not her mess, not really. She could take her things and go, buy a ticket at the airport, lock all this up and let it rot and go to ruin. Perhaps her father will come back for it, perhaps he won't, but she does not have to take this on, does not have to accept it as hers. Because if she does, she will have to live with the knowledge that she made this decision, that this house is hers because she decided that it is, her inheritance. Because her father is alive, but gone, and this is what he has left her, and she accepts that, accepts what he has to give. Because accepting this means accepting all of it, all that he is, all that she will never know about him. Every person in the albums, every secret he keeps, all that is hidden and all that is gone and all that may come, all the madness she carries in her blood, all the pain he has lived, all the things she will never get to have. She cannot have the house and not the rest. It is an all-or-nothing deal.

Elena is a student of history. What's past is not prologue. What's past is present, future, eternal. It is no choice at all, really.

She puts down her tote bag, and gets to work.

The call comes later that day from the lawyer, Victor Padua, the one Diego had referred her father to, with the news that he had, in fact, prepared a will in Puerto Rico for her father, though of course the contents are sealed. Elena does not need to see the document to know what it contains. This house was always hers, always for her, like her father told her. He has broken many promises to her, through forgetting them entirely, but not this one.

It is almost an afterthought, hearing this. Because Elena already knows everything Santiago has left her, although there is so much about him she will never know. Because the house is hers, a piece of history, an anchor, a home, on the first Spanish colony in the Americas, the island the farthest east in the Greater Antilles, the gateway to the New World. Hers. Completely, now and always.

Twenty-One

Esperanza had hoped that they would not let her board the plane because she was pregnant, that something would stop all this, save her from having to cross the ocean and live far from the island, from everything she knew and cared about, but instead the flight attendant just congratulated her husband and wished them the best. She was only three months pregnant, barely showing, but she cradled her stomach as the plane, the first she had ever taken, prepared to fly. The terrifying speed of the great metal thing charging down the runway, the moment it lifted off the tarmac, the world falling away from her as she went up and up into the air, was horrible. Her husband, the man who had coaxed her into marrying him and was now demanding that she move to a city that everyone in her family said was cold and sad and strange, was delighted.

"Isn't this amazing?" he asked her. "In the old days people spent their lives on ships, taking months and months to get anywhere. Now we can fly!" Esperanza closed her eyes, and didn't open them again until they landed.

New York was a wonderland to Santiago, and a nightmare to Esperanza. They moved into an apartment next to her mother, who was on her fourth and final husband, Isadoro. Santiago loved the city, its millions of people, its flashing lights and constant change. Esperanza found it frightening, overwhelming, dirty, and, as the child swelled inside her, harder and harder to navigate. She prayed constantly, both at home and in the nearby church Teofila had found, where the priest, thankfully, spoke Spanish. Esperanza had learned a little English, all Puerto Rican schoolchildren had to, but she had never had to use it before. While Santiago was much better at it, having worked with the postal service, which had required him to have better English than many, she struggled constantly. She was embarrassed every time she went grocery shopping when she had to ask for something, and she often simply agreed to whatever she was asked or bought things she didn't know what to do with, which caused her husband to scream at her come dinnertime, setting off a new round of tears.

She did piecework for an embroidery factory, something she could do even from home, which was good because being with all the other workers, unable to communicate with many of them, made her feel alienated and small. In her neighborhood, at least, there were many Puerto Ricans, so many that she could divide apartments by what area of the island they were from. Old arguments and prejudices had traveled with them, and swelled through the absence of foreign blood. Her neighbors argued about whose grandmother had stolen whose chicken fifty years before back in their seaside village. Lopezes refused to speak to Riveras and Barrios, because *they knew what they had done*. Thousands of new people came every year, carrying the same things with them, grateful for the bodegas on every corner, the piraguas stands in the summers peddling shaved ice, the neighbors whose nuanced grudges and tips on where to get cheap rice, decent peppers, and good cuts of pork reminded them of home. She thanked God each Sunday for each new fellow Puerto Rican who entered the bustling city, each of them making it a little bit easier for her, a little more like home.

She and Santiago thought that the fall in New York was the coldest anything could possibly be, but when the winter came they knew the world must be ending. Teofila, by now an expert in winter, having moved to the city two years earlier, helped them with coats and sweaters but they found the whole idea of layering clothing upon clothing to be impossibly strange, and it was difficult to fit the hand-me-down clothing over Esperanza's growing stomach. They clung to each other at night, not out of affection, for that had quickly left their relationship, but to stay warm. She had always thought hell, a subject she reflected on for hours and hours, was a hot place. But it was cold, obviously, this was clear now, because the winter was torture. She did not know how she had sinned, but she apologized for it on her knees, begging God not to end the world and bring on the Day of Judgment just because of her transgressions. He did not listen, instead sending snow through the air to punish her further.

She did not think they would survive the endless days of cold, but eventually, her prayers were answered, and it became warm again, little by little, and nothing like the island's glorious sticky heat, but better and better. On the first truly warm day of spring, as Esperanza stood in front of her apartment building, her aching ankles demanding that she sit back down again, she basked in the sunshine, trying to absorb it, letting it warm her, and for a moment she could pretend she was home, her real home, not this horrible city where everyone was mean and everything was expensive and the demons of her imagination seemed all around her, waiting to eat her up. She smiled, imagining being back in San Sebastián, smelling the earth and fields and sweet sugar in the air, and as she did, her water broke.

Santiago Vega Jr. was born ten hours later, early in the morning, as his mother, exhausted, her body shaking with pain, let out one final push, while her husband slept, comfortably, in their bed, having asked the hospital to call the bar under their apartment when it was all over. Teoﬁla, her mother, sat beside her, urging her to bring her child into the world, holding the child she'd given birth to a year before, her ﬁfth, Samuel, who everyone would call Rowdy.

Esperanza's son, for her husband had been right, it was a boy, cried just enough to let the doctors know he was alive, and then quieted, tucked against his mother's breast and suckling happily. She looked down at him, his transparent nails soft on his little ﬁngers, his swirl of dark brown hair just like her own, and for the ﬁrst time since she had moved to the mainland, she knew that she was truly, really, absolutely not alone. She had her child. When all else was horrible, she would have him. When the world was confusing and painful and too much, as it so often was, more and more now, she would have him. At that moment, she was sure that nothing could ever separate them. He was the prize for all the pain, he was the gift she had been praying for, the salvation, he would free her.

His father, when he met him, felt strange at the sight of his child. How pathetic children are, he thought, how vulnerable and defenseless. He wished humans were born with protection, a shell like a turtle, instead of being all pink and soft and nothing.

"I thought we could name him after my grandfather," Esperanza said, softly, not wanting to wake the baby. "Or my father, maybe, or even yours." Santiago snorted, uncaring about disturbing the child. Being a father meant being listened to, obeyed, and accommodated, not the other way around.

"We will name him after *his* father," he said, ﬁrmly. Esperanza wanted to protest, but the baby squirmed in her arms, and she was overwhelmed with love for him all over again. "Santiago Vega Jr. Born right here in New York."

"What do you think he will be when he grows up?" Esperanza said, impulsively, her love for her son making her bright and whimsical despite her exhaustion, the blood and ﬂuids still leaking out of her.

"If he's lucky, he'll be just like me," her husband said, putting out his finger. Santiago Jr. grabbed it, prompting a begrudging smile from his father. "He'll be American. Not just a Puerto Rican. When people see him, that's what they'll know first, that he belongs here," he said. "Aren't you glad we came?" But he was already bored with this, his limp wife who couldn't fetch him anything, his pink lump of a son who ate and ate while his father went hungry, and he wandered out into the hallway for a smoke before he could hear Esperanza's whispers to the baby.

"You'll be better than both of us, my son. You'll be better than us all. Promise me that, that you'll be so much better, and that you'll never leave me, promise." He pulled hard at her breast, drinking in her words with the milk, and Esperanza was sure he understood her, sure he would keep his word.

She fell asleep smiling, secure in the knowledge that she was loved.

Twenty-Two

It takes her two weeks to sort through everything. She focuses on a room a day. She is not looking for clues anymore, and that makes the work a little faster, but it is still sweaty, dusty, exhausting labor. She finds so many dead spiders and lizards that she considers putting their little heads on sticks at the perimeter, as a warning to the others. She goes through several bottles of floor cleaner and surface spray. She buys stain and sealant and brushes and treats each piece of wood in the house, becoming light-headed with the strength of the chemicals. She throws away more and more things, finds a place in San Juan to donate some of the books and gives bags of items to the junk shop, asking for no profit in return, relieved that the owner does not want *her* to pay *him*.

Her mother is indeed furious. And then sad. And then apologetic. Elena endures it all, through many phone calls, and once she finally gets Wi-Fi in the house, more than a few video chat sessions. She forgives her mother, she always knew she would, in exchange for stories. Information is her currency. She asks about college, about graduate school, and Rosalind gives her all she is willing to give, and Elena forces herself to accept this, because that's what legacy is, what people are willing to give you. If some part of her can forgive her father, and it seems that some part of her can, and some part of her can remain on fire with rage at him, and it is very clear some part of her can, then she must afford her mother the same courtesies. Rosalind tells her she will be back in New York soon, and Elena says nothing. Whatever she does or does not do, it is hers to know. It is her turn to keep secrets.

She returns to the archives, searching out the historic information of the house, and finds that there are indeed records dating back to the 1700s, before which perhaps the city did not keep records; she doesn't know and neither does the archivist, a very kind woman from Mexico named Maria Antonia who wears a fleece vest as protection against the merciless air-conditioning and guides her through the strange systems of the institution, the way she needs to request information one day and get it the next. Elena finds blueprints from 1876 and 1905, requests for alterations, remaking the façade, moving a window. She sees the names of other owners, like Don Juan Ramon de Torres, whose handwriting is strange, with loops and dark lines in the words, like he wrote with a quill pen well into the nineteenth century. She sees how the archivist changed over the years, from Carlos Castro to Pedro Luis. She longs to dive deeper into these people's lives, their stories. She wants to know more about them, she wants to know everything. Investigating her father has reawakened her appetite for the past. If she can't have his, she wants everyone else's, she wants the island's.

She reads every entry in her cousin Jessenia's blog. They fascinate her, and she thinks a lot about them. One sticks in her mind more than the others, because it tells her something about her own family.

Puerto Ricans do not have good immigration stories because Puerto Ricans are not immigrants, we are migrants, and have been for over a century. It is an unfortunate fact that means our narrative is different than anyone else's and people do so hate being different. Luckily, many Puerto Ricans were also desperately deeply dirt poor, thank goodness, so that part of the Latinx narrative is right where it should be, but the rest, the easy plane ride instead of a desperate run for the border, really confuses people and loses us street cred.

To be born in Puerto Rico is to be born in the United States, and this has been true for over a century except that most people don't know. So what does it mean to be Puerto Rican? What does that say about your makeup, your background, really? What stains of human- ity have made their way into the mix? Pick a flavor. Spanish, yes, but what kind, even, old monarchists or immigrants from Mexico or people fleeing Santo Domingo or giving up on Cuba, moving from here to there as the 19th century becomes the twentieth, as you, a merchant, a tradesman, a con artist, follow the money from place to place. French, British, Dutch? Yes, yes to all, and perhaps even mixed with someone else, an African slave whose own country of origin is lost to history. Or maybe not mixed, the island was a haven for many slaves fleeing other islands they had been brought to by force, or had been born on as life-long prisoners. Or maybe not mixed because you became a part of the thin crust of de facto aristocrats and attended lavish balls in the white house where the captain-general governs the island on the birthdays of your distant monarchs.

Others? Of course, this is a brave new world that has such people in it. Irish and Scottish immigrants, redleg Protestants leaking off the British islands, bored of plantation condescension. German and Italian men, in droves, leaving a conflicted Europe for a conflicted Caribbean. Then, mixes of all of the above, blending together, travel- ing themselves, the wealthy ones, of course, abroad, to become educated, to become radicalized, to marry foreigners and bring them home with them, blending in again, and again, and again, until the genetic makeup of the island is a smoothie, a blended soup, everything swirl- ing together, each flavor blurring into the next.

Many of these colorful Puerto Rican people would come to New York City, the elite trickling in in the 1800's, a new onslaught after 1917, and the deluge, the great migration, a preponderance of Puerto Ricans, came in the 1950's. They took over neighborhoods, renaming them, titling the Lower East Side Loisaida, stepping into the run of laborers that previous generations of immigrants were just stepping out of, custodians, garment workers, maids, elevator operators, cleaners. The name they would give themselves, Nuyoricans, began as a taunt, a way for island natives and first generation New York dwellers to shame their assimilated relatives and friends, isn't that cute? You are not a part of our island, anymore, but this one, more loyal to your new land than your old. You are other here, and other there.

This would only layer onto itself over and over again, as the push-pull of identity encountered time. From a generation that started organizations to teach their elders and their disadvantaged English, to a generation struggling to teach its children Spanish. From fighting for equality, activism, community, on the mainland, to fighting to rid the island of corruption, violence, brain drain, economic depression.

Every immigrant's child has known the in between state of being, the futile hours and days and years and lives spent chasing enough; become enough, they tell you, and you will be something, at last; stay not-enough and what will you be? Pastel, and secondary, never bold and true, never primary colors. The multiplicity of in-betweenness is infinite, a line whose limit does not exist.

It is this entry that drives her to do the thing she knows she should have done from the beginning, and she sends her cousin a message on Instagram, asking to meet up, telling her what her words have meant to her, how they have said the things that Elena has often felt, or didn't know she felt. Elena sends her the photos of her trip, and tells Jessenia what she has done, leaving out the most painful parts, and when the response comes from her cousin, a girl she met once as a child, it is effusive and welcoming and so warm Elena could cry. Jessenia is traveling right now, with her boyfriend in Eastern Europe, of all places, learning about Jews, according to her message, which makes Elena smile. She has promised that when she returns to the island next they will meet, and talk, and she will tell Elena everything she knows, because they are cousins, they are family, and they have to share their stories so they don't die. Elena couldn't agree more.

She prints the photos at a Walgreens, and finds an album that is empty in her father's everlasting clutter, and she makes her own album, like she decided to do. She puts them all in the living room, where they should be, the photos that piece together her family's past. And its present.

She thinks again about going back to school. She looks for programs that are strong in Latin American history, Caribbean history, she reaches out to old professors, asking for advice. She buys new sheets, after finding holes in every single set that her father had in the house, some splitting the linens almost in two. She rips the old ones up and uses them as rags. She takes her time, she has nothing but time now. She fixes the kitchen, then the living room, and on the final day of her cleaning, she restores the second-story bedroom, hers now, to a livable space. She makes the bed with the lovely new sheets, and takes a shower, rubbing herself dry with a new towel, and then, finally, spent and done, she collapses on the bed, sleeping a dreamless sleep.

When she wakes up it is still dark, and her phone tells her it is midnight. She tries to sleep again, but she cannot, and so she gets dressed and walks to the one place she knows will be open, El Batey. It is crowded, of course it is, it is a Saturday night. She had no idea. She has lost all sense of time. The smoke hits her face, and she smiles. She looks to the corner, and Fernando is there. Of course he is. He looks up at her, and winces. She has not contacted him again since their last phone call, and yet it does not feel like they have missed any time. She smiles, crookedly, yes, but still a smile. He smiles back, and the string between them pulls tight. He could be her friend. He could be more, too, but she does not want to think about that now. Let it be a surprise, weeks, months later, when he kisses her suddenly, pushing her gently against the walls of the San Juan Gate, as they return from visiting the colonies of cats that live along the rocks outside the original city walls.

His smile is tentative and sheepish. She sits down beside him, and motions to the bartender, a man this time, who looks like a bodybuilder, almost bursting out of his tank top, but he doesn't see her.

"How are you?" Fernando asks, his voice calm. She smiles again.

"I survived."

"How was San Sebastián?"

"I found him." Fernando nods.

"That's something, then." The silence stretches between them, but it is calm, and almost sweet.

"You found me, too," he says, and smiles at her.

"I knew you would be here. It's late, though," Elena points out. Not his usual routine, beers over grading papers. He nods.

"Weekend," he says. "Can I buy you a drink?" She nods, and Fernando calls for the bartender, addressing him by name and asking him for a rum.

"You remembered," Elena says, smiling.

"It's an easy order." He shrugs. He looks at her, tense. "So. The house."

"The house."

"Have you thought about my offer?"

"I have." Elena smiles at him. "But unfortunately, I have to disappoint you. You aren't going to get to restore it." She continues, ignoring his sputtering. He looks at her, his brows drawn, as she smiles. "I am." She takes a sip of her drink. His mouth is open, and when she taps his chin, he closes it, with a snap. He looks at her for a long moment.

"Well. That's better than nothing, I guess."

"You'll have to help me," she says, smiling to take the sting out of the order. "I'll be all alone and I won't know how to say lots of words and who to contact for things and if I'm being cheated and if I've picked the right paint colors. Can you help me? Will you?" He shrugs, and sighs, then nods.

"As I said. Better than nothing. Alone?"

Elena nods, and Fernando's face goes pale.

"Oh, no, not like that. My father is, well, he's alive. In his way. But the house is mine now," Elena says, and color returns to Fernando's face.

"How was he?"

"He didn't realize he'd been missing," Elena says. She has nothing else to say about it. Nothing else seems worth the effort.

He looks at her for a long moment. She can tell even though she is staring straight ahead, she can feel his gaze on her, the pity in it. She steels herself against it, and looks at him, and sees that he isn't looking at her at all, he's looking at his beer bottle, peeling off the label. She finds great kindness in this.

"I'm sorry," he says, looking up at her, and she can see it in his eyes, that he really is sorry. She nods. So is she. They both take long drinks.

"Fernando? Can you do something for me?" she asks, quickly, before she loses her nerve.

"Yes," he says, no questions, no qualifications, and she forgives him, she realizes, for everything all at once, whatever little piece of resentment was still in her has dissolved.

"Can you tell me about my father? When you met him, what you thought about him, what he talked about? It's just, I don't know what it would be like if, if I didn't know him. If I could hear about him, what he's been like for the last few years, from someone who just met him—maybe it would be better, if I could see him from the outside. Maybe I could see him more clearly, or in some other way. And maybe, maybe that would be a good thing." Elena looks at him, willing him to understand her, hoping she will not have to explain. She worries she will take it back if she has to explain it. But she can see in his eyes that he does indeed understand her, and relief floods her veins. He nods, once, and closes his eyes, in thought, she realizes.

"The first time he came to the island was for his First Communion. He was amazed that any place could be so green. The most green he ever saw before, he said, was in Central Park, and this was like a whole island of that, but better, because it was so warm." Fernando's eyes are open now, but Elena closes her own, listening to him. It is like hearing about a stranger, it *is* hearing about a stranger, and she smiles as he continues, the bar noise fading away, until all she can hear is this.

Later, hours later, Elena walks into the ocean as dawn breaks over the island.

She is tired, for she never went to bed, but the ocean will revive her, she trusts it. The bar is true to its promise, it does not close until six in the morning, but Elena leaves at four, her mind buzzing, her heart weighed down heavily. She walks past the house, hers now, and past San Cristóbal fort, hulking mass that it is, and down the road, and past the capitol building, lit up despite the hour, and down the dark steps to the beach. She takes a photo of this beach, empty of people, as the light slowly creeps up the horizon. She sits on the sand, her mind humming.

Eventually she will have to go back, to figure out what comes next for the house, for herself. She will have to make plans, and plans for plans. But for now, she can just be, here on this beach, and breathe in the humid air, the fertile smell of the island mixed with the salt of the sea. She thinks of all the things she will never know about her father, and all the things she does. She thinks of the things that live inside her, the problems that may come, the gifts he has given her, good and bad. They press on her, but not the way they used to; they neither hold her down or let her float. They just are.

In the water, she leans back and lets herself float. She is wearing her clothing, but it does not matter, the sun will shine as it rises, the walk home is short. *Home.* Home is people and places at once. Home is ghosts and things and what people leave behind and what you wish they had. Home is a place that is hers, that she can own without reservation or qualifiers. The warmth of the water, the warmth of knowing that she can think of this place as home now, that it is not lost to her, that it is a part of her and she of it, floods her, lifting her up, making her body buoyant.

She thinks about her father. Maybe she will see him again. Maybe he will live in San Sebastián for the rest of his life. Maybe he will wake up one day and walk into the forest, letting the trees take his body, letting the vines strangle him, becoming a part of the earth. Maybe he will walk out into the ocean, like she has, but he will let the sea embrace him, as it embraces her, and maybe he will give up his need for oxygen and sink into the deep. Maybe he will be happy, then, his body becoming the island, sinking back into the place from which he came.

For a moment, Elena holds her own body below the waves, feeling the power of the water, the tug of the current, knowing how she could let herself go if she wanted to, let the ocean take her life, become a part of it, suffer and need and want no more.

Instead, she emerges, breathing deep, letting air fill her lungs, feeling her body float in the sea. *Ten more minutes,* she tells herself. *Ten more minutes in the water, and then home.*

But this is a lie. She already is home. She has been the whole time.

Acknowledgments

I've lived with this story for a long time, and I've tried to tell it as a movie and as a play, but now, finally, I believe it has found its best home in a novel.

This story, while fictional, comes from many real experiences in my life and in my family history. My agent, Julia Kardon, has been invaluable in helping me find the fiction in the non-fiction and craft a story out of life, which often resists well-structured narrative. I could not have asked for a better agent, and she is probably far better than what I deserve. My editor, Rachel Kahan, is certainly worlds beyond what I deserve, but the generosity of the universe is sometimes bountiful, and I am so much more than lucky to have her hand on this story and her voice speaking to my writing as a whole.

I also want to thank Ariana Sinclair and Hannah Popal, whose insights, organization, and positivity have buttressed the process of this novel. Every book that is published represents the labor of so many talented and insightful people, and for this one, some of those people include Amelia Wood, who marketed this novel, Stephanie Vallejo, my production editor, and the saintly Karen Richardson, my copy editor, who waded through my careful words and careless syntax and corrected my many mistakes.

On top of all this, Mya Alexice's thoughts and comments were deeply helpful, and I am so grateful for their sensitivity read of this novel.

My family deserves my infinite gratitude for their support, love, care, and critique. My mother, Deborah Solo, can not and will never be thanked enough for all she does, but I can try, at least. If I felt anything went without saying, I wouldn't be a novelist. Thank you, Mom. For everything.

And finally, but never last or least, thank you, Rohan. I am the writer I am, and the person I am, because of myself, but also very much because of you.

About the Author

Leah Franqui is a graduate of Yale University and holds an MFA from New York University's Tisch School of the Arts. She has two previously published novels, *America for Beginners* and *Mother Land*.

A Puerto Rican–Jewish Philadelphia native, Franqui is currently teaching and pursuing her PhD in creative writing at Georgia State University. She lives with her Kolkata-born husband and Mumbai-born cat in Atlanta, Georgia.